Treading
Water

By,

Adam Misner

To Beamer

Chapter 1

Simon

Sit down. Stow your belongings in
the netted compartment in front of
you. Pull the bar towards you until
it won't click any more. Keep your
hands and feet inside the car. Enjoy
the ride.

Simon inhaled deep, filling his lungs with the cool air of
Space mountain. The car rolled forward and he let himself be
gripped by the gentle G-force of the ride's jerky start, rocking back
into his seat with a soundless thump. The din of the line faded away
behind him as they were zoomed along to the safety check. Before
anyone could even ask, he was already presenting his yellow safety
tab for the cast member to tug on and confirm his restraint bar was
firmly in place. They wished them all a safe space-flight and slapped
a button on their console. Simon lifted his chin into the
air-conditioned breeze as the car was rushed around the bend. The
air had this very distinct scent, pure and refreshing, like wind off an
underground lake. He let his mind be swept away by that wind,
carried off to old –better– memories; memories of Disney World and
the happy kid he used to be, the kid mom still asks about every

christmas.

Secreted away by the mellow shade of the ride, the stress of errant eyes evaporated from his skin. Simon shut his eyes above a thin-lipped smile as they plunged into the black of the ascension tunnel. The staticky scifi monologue, telling them about the future of commercial space travel, vanished behind them and the rattle of the tracks beneath took its place. His head jerked back against the seat as the train halted to latch onto the chain that would drag them up to the top of the starting hill. Simon could feel every click of the chain course through his seat as they climbed the slope, and that rumble of the car being dragged up to the summit spurred excited murmurs in the first time riders behind him.

Their giggles of excitement and whispers of fear buzzed about in a white noise that let him drown out the voice in his head that kept trying to remind him to be miserable.

Simon filled his lungs with cool air, as they crested the hill, and he held that breath for the long moment they lingered in that weightless place without inertia. As the magnets in the track switched on, to give the train that first shove into the momentum of the hill, he exhaled a sigh hidden from the world within the roaring of the tracks. His knuckles went white on the bar and his smile showed teeth as he opened his eyes into a sea of stars rushing past him.

The ride was serenity. Somewhere amongst the neck jerking turns, and the gut twisting rises, Simon lost his problems. In that star-lit darkness orientation quickly became unreliable, and gravity meaningless, like he was tumbling in the surf. His head poked above the ocean of depression that had been drowning him the past few weeks. He didn't join the snake of howling cheers behind him, however. He didn't quite manage to make himself *happy* like they did. Treading water was the best he could do.

Unfortunately, like most roller coasters, the ride was rather short. Three minutes made for a meager respite.

Make sure to gather all your belongings from the netted compartment in front of you. Exit to your left. Think about your ex. Have a magical day.

By law of osmosis Simon should have been able to be happy in the happiest place on earth. Simon walked out the exit into the warm Florida sun. He heard the ambient sci-fi music of Tomorrowland and smelled the powder of astronaut ice-cream puffing into the air as people tore their packages open walking out of the gift shop. Simon squinted against the hard reflections of sun off chrome structures that towered above and let the happiness crash over him like a wave. He sucked in a shaky break of warm, humid air and Simon wished he could soak the happiness up through his skin like a frog in water.

As the chilling aura of air conditioning dissipated, he dimly looked to his forearm where he could feel the tight sensation of goosebumps fading. The sleeve of his white button down was bunched up slightly too high on his forearm, because Simon didn't have the muscle or fat to keep the sleeves at the allegedly more stylish halfway point. The sun beamed through his blonde arm hair, making it mostly transparent, and his fair skin flashed back light like a pearl. He'd heard somewhere that lighter skin tones produce vitamin D more efficiently, and that it helps with improving one's mood. He wasn't sure it was true, because as he cooked beneath that florida sun, he still felt unbelievably shitty. As that warmth crept in, so too did the thoughts he'd rather keep suspended, so he turned and walked back up the exit.

How bright would the sun have to be?

Simon sidestepped patrons, woozy from the ride, with the fakest tight-lipped smile. Some people he passed were confused to see someone walking the wrong way but he wasn't breaking any sort of rule. It was a little known trick that, as long as you were alright with sitting alone, you could go up the exit and be seated with parties of three who left an empty seat in the four-man trains. This worked out for Simon, because he was definitely alone.

**

Sit down. Stow your belongings in the netted compartment in front of you. Pull the bar towards you until it won't click any more. Keep your hands and feet inside the car. Enjoy the ride.

Make sure to gather all your belongings from the compartment in front of you. Exit to your left. Have a magical day.

For the entirety of that three minute ride, Simon's head was pulled above water, out of the ocean of thoughts that he wasn't doing himself any good by thinking. But then three minutes wasn't quite long enough. Splash Mountain was ten, he knew, but it was a long walk. You can do quite a bit of thinking on a walk like that. The walk down to the exit and back up was already of a length he could barely manage.

That day Simon found himself on a particularly long trip down the exit; his typical speed-walk stifled by a couple, whose hand holding roped off the whole corridor. This slowed the pace of traffic down to their speed. Simon didn't want to be stuck behind them. He also didn't want to squeeze around them and disrupt what they had. He'd make them conscious of how inconvenient they were. They'd be embarrassed and, staring hard at their joined hands, he decided they shouldn't be.

It is sweet. Public displays of affection are not inappropriate. They're just nice things people do when they're dating. Simon argued, finally, long after the fact.

The boyfriend pointed at one of the fake space travel agency advertisements lining the wall, for some far away planet. He said something brief and they both laughed hard, like only an inside joke could inspire. As the guy withdrew his hand, Simon noticed a bracelet on his wrist. It was a worn leather cord that matched his sandy blonde hair, with a silver puzzle piece affixed to it, which gleamed starkly against his surfer-dude tan. Around the girl's slender wrist was a matching bracelet, wrapped several more times to fit her. That cord too had a puzzle piece affixed to it that –though different– Simon was sure would fit with her boyfriend's. Simon wasn't convinced it was tacky.

The girl stopped her boy, tugging down on the hand she held, and popped up onto her toes to plant a kiss on her boyfriend's cheek. Simon jolted to a stop to keep from trampling into their personal space, and the girl noticed the movement.

"Oh my god! So super sorry!" the girl exclaimed, blinking at him from behind stylishly big round glasses, thick enough to make her eyes huge. They were an oppresssively bright green that pierced so intensely Simon's eyes naturally recoiled from eye contact.

"No, no! It looked important."

They made room for him to pass and he did so swiftly, as his anxiety around the exchange expanded to crush all other thought against the inside of his skull. Being caught off guard, his delivery had been forceful. The sentence replayed in his head, again and again, as he pondered if he'd sounded awkward, friendly, or just insane. Next he reviewed his mannerisms, attempting to recollect if he'd remembered to smile or nod as he departed. Then he analyzed the wording, wondering if he'd sounded strange.

Important. Lingered in his mind; the word choice confusing even him. *I guess it **did** look important.*

That couple behind him would take some time to get to the exit. Simon couldn't bear to walk past them, seeming strange, and he definitely couldn't sit still to wait for them to pass. So Simon power-walked across the park to Splash Mountain, trying all the while not to wonder what it was like to be kissed. Simon knew what it was like to kiss a girl; to be kissed back even, but he couldn't remember a time he'd ever really been kissed.

Sit down. Stow your belongings in the netted compartment in front of you. Debate whether you're just not someone special enough to inspire passion. Pull the bar towards you until it won't click any more. Keep your hands and feet inside the car. Enjoy the ride.

Make sure to gather all your baggage from the compartment in front of you. Exit to your left. Have a magical day.

Chapter 2

Morrigan

A cacophony of distortion heavy noise assailed Morrigan ears, sounding much more like death metal than a stock alarm tone. She extended a lethargic claw from beneath her many blankets and plucked the old Nokia brick phone from its charger, instantly extinguishing it's ancient battery, and let it fall to the carpet with a thud. She'd already been awake but lacked the will to actually get up. The bleak grayness her window let in didn't motivate her to do much but stare into space.

Morrigan groped around in an open drawer of her nightstand for her smartphone, finding it at the end of its own charger. She'd decided to separate the two phones for fear of blearily abusing the less durable modern phone.

Out of reluctant ritual she opened her text messages. With her face mushed against her pillow she puffed sigh out one nostril and flicked her thumb along the list of text threads, scrolling down the list at hyperspeed. She watched the word 'sent' hoping it might change like a flip-book. When she hit the bottom with all the automated texts from businesses she noticed a thread from a restaurant she hadn't gone to alone and deleted it. Then Morrigan scrolled back up to the top and stroked the screen several times just in case there was another, newer, thread that hadn't been seen. But there wasn't. There were no new texts and no one else she could reach out to and start a new conversation. Morrigan let the phone flop face down on the pillow, then got up and away from the thing.

She padded over to the dryer and squatted down to rummage for clothes. Before she could find a second sock Morrigan decided it was *far* too quiet. She stomped over to an old guitar amp, pausing briefly to tap the power-strip on with her toe. Laying on top of the amp was an ipod Classic with a broken display plugged into the amp by way of a fraying aux cord.

She didn't dare pick up the ipod and risk disrupting the delicate positioning of the frayed wire and end up deafening herself with feedback. Instead she delicately spammed the home button and then blindly navigated to playlist seven. The rush of noise was immediate.

Raw screaming Black Metal blasted throughout Morrigan's double-wide; a priviledge afforded to her by having no neighbors. It was one of the few benefits to living in the only non-condemned house in her complex.

Bent over the speaker, her oversized T-shirt hung in front of the onslaught and kick drums puffed against her shirt with gentle punches of bass. She straightened up and thrashed the bedhead out of her hair while harsh vocals screamed all black thoughts from her head. Happy music was too obvious a contrast to hide a poor mood, and sad music was so insistent a reminder, but she could soak in the rage of satanic scandinavians and feel free of it all.

Morrigan never got angry, not even through the worst of it. The emotion was experienced instead vicariously through her music. It was a pleasant fantasy to her, that she might be consumed by fury instead of wallowing in depression. Anger seemed so much more productive.

Clothes in hand, Morrigan sprung to her feet with a bounce,

swinging her hair back and clear of her face. She remained there, suspended with her chin to the ceiling opening her airways as wide as they could go, and filled her lungs. Her eyes were shut and her hair hung behind her swinging gently against her back as her head bobbed softly to a pleasant acoustic solo buried in the chaos of a brutal song. The instrument was some forgotten medieval thing with strings tight like a violin's and any two strings resonating harmonized like the edges of two scythes scraping together.

The solo ended with an abrupt pause and she counted two half beats and joined the song with her voice as it returned on it's warpath. At 6:57 AM Morrigan belted out a roar like a demon, rising up onto the balls of her feet before slamming down into the first strum of an air guitar.

She dropped a sock in her enthusiasm and abruptly snatched it up before continuing to the bathroom. The shower was still a disaster zone. The tub hadn't been draining completely for several days and though she'd finally gone out to Walmart and grabbed some Draino, she needed to wait for the tub to actually drain completely to use it. There was still a few inches of water in the bathtub and she *did* consider just pouring half in then, to see if it would drain by the time she was back from work.

Morrigan sighed and resigned herself to use the work showers, despite finding it impossibly weird and gross and uncomfortable to take a shower anywhere but in her own home.

She stripped and flung her balled up clothes into their proper heap by her bed, before dressing herself in a pair of not-that-ripped-up jeans and a band shirt turned inside-out in case one of her co-workers managed to decipher the hieroglylphic font concealing some obscene band name.
"Just gotta get to my locker and the shower." She told herself in the mirror. "I can change in the shower-stall."

Morrigan slapped the hot water on and let it warm up .

"Until then, I just need to be passably above a trash goblin."

While she waited on the water-heater Morrigan hefted a large container of bleach out from under the sink and spun the rattly plastic cap off. She poured a splash into the bath just in case the stagnant water attracted mosquitos. It was a minor nightmare scenario of hers to discover mosquito larva in her bath-tub.

Morrigan let out a sigh of relief when she saw the mirror fog with steam. Another day where the sun rose and her water-heater still worked.

In an effort to save herself the trouble of doing laundry for one more wash-cloth she slapped at the stream of hot water and then set about washing her face with her bare hands. She kneaded her fingertips against the bridge of her nose, and her forehead. The warm water lifted a night's greasy sweat from her face. She rubbed a layer of stress away with it and wished for the third day in a row that she could take a shower in her own bathroom.

She leaned over the sink, with her hands in the warming stream letting the hot water take the oil from her hands. Morrigan wondered if it was worth harassing her landlord to fix *anything* anymore. He couldn't charge her rent without spending money on repairs and she wasn't sure that was such a bad deal. Besides, getting her landlord to come required confrontation.

She sighed again and wet her hairline, cleansing the collected grease there, before finger-combing her hair out to a passable level. When it was done she stared at herself in the mirror. Fat cheeks, thin lips, narrow neck, and her nose was bad too. She went back and forth on exactly *why* but she didn't like it. She smiled and that just exaggerated the flaws.

Her mother's words echoed in her head. *'Prettiness is the **best** band-aid to a relationship.'*

She spat a real sharp comeback and soundly won a confrontation that didn't exist. She gripped the sink with white knuckles, to stop her hands from shaking, and looked down, unable to meet her own eyes in the mirror.

After a moment she swallowed and looked back into the mirror. She sucked in a breath through her nose and straightened her posture. "Lets kick today's ass," she concluded half-heartedly, highfiving herself in the mirror.

Chapter 3

Orbit

Sit down. Stow your belongings in
the netted compartment in front of
you. It's just a break up. Pull the
bar towards you until it won't click
any more. Keep your hands and
feet inside the car. Enjoy the ride.

Make sure to gather all your
belongings from the netted
compartment in front of you. Exit to
your left. Have a magical day.

"Oh uh, huh-hey. Hi." Said a girl that Simon walked past.

'Hey' and 'hi' did not apply to Simon. Friends said 'hey' and
'hi' and it had been three years and five months since Simon had
really had time to hang out with friends. A relationship is a big time

commitment. Mature men in relationships do not *hang out* with single friends.

> Sit down. Stow your belongings in the netted compartment in front of you. Pull the bar towards you until it won't click any more. Keep your hands and feet inside the car. Enjoy the ride.
>
> Make sure to gather all your belongings from the netted compartment in front of you. Exit to your left. Think about your ex. Have a magical day.

"H-hey. Um I just-" Said a girl who tapped Simon gingerly on the shoulder.

Her finger just barely pressed against his shirt hard enough to be felt on his skin but the sensation made Simon's spine stiffen like a gun was being pressed against his back.

Simon turned, with a startled jerk, and then he saw a girl. That girl, was looking, at *him*.

"Oh." He blinked. "Hi there."

The girl was an employee. Simon had noticed her a few times. She was a ride attendant that usually directed people to the exit when the ride was over. He recognized her by the hair. It was a big wispy thing, mostly oblivious to gravity, that looked soft and inviting, like ruffled down feathers. Most of it had been brushed over to one side, almost like an emo cut, but not quite, as she could still see with both eyes. At one point it might have been a punk side-shave cut, but it had long since been overtaken by nature, like the post-apocalyptic ruins of a city. On one side it was almost pixie short, then the rest of it spilled over her shoulder and back like an inky waterfall. The chaos of hair was hacked into many different lengths, giving it a kind of accidental layering from neglect. It was a *fantastic* disaster. Her hair swung lightly against her cheek with a cock of her head.

Oh shit, did she say something? Oh she did, definitely did.

She shrugged and looked at the floor. "I just ask because I was working yesterday and uh I think Tuesday? And I saw you go on a bunch then, sssss- so I guess you must like the ride a lot, I- I guess."

"I'm not autistic."

"What?" she asked, snapping her attention back to his face. Hair slipped loose and eclipsed one of her very big brown eyes.

"I- I mean it *is* a fair assumption. I *have* ridden this thing like eighty times today and it's only..." Simon raised his arm and shook back his sleeve to reveal a watch but, before he could read the time, a hydraulic hiss shushed him and the girl's attention jerked towards the tracks.

Simon exhaled a very small "I'll see ya then." and jerked a half-wave out of his hand before back-pedaling down to the exit ramp.

She turned and smiled,
so he wore one too.

***

Yeah that'll convince her. Nothing says "I'm not autistic" like blurting out "I'm not autistic." Totally thrown her off the scent.

The dull wonder crept into Simon's head over whether or not that girl was cute. He'd been nervous, but it took no special attributes to inflict *that* on him. Simon knew if she *was* cute, that would mean he was getting over his ex. Simon was the sort of man to make himself sick with guilt over being attracted to anyone aside from his girlfriend, and an unfortunate mental spill had left him now somewhat passionless. It was as though every girl was a song overplayed on the radio for three years and five months.

Simon stopped and looked around. She was at *least* cute enough that he daydream-walked himself out the exit and all the way out of Tomorrowland too. He found himself on the Tomorrowland bridge leading towards the center of the park.

Simon noticed his cheek was faintly burning and touched his hand to his face. He relaxed a smile he didn't know was there and flexed his jaw.

*That smile stuck around long enough to make my cheeks sore? Is my **face** out of shape? How long has it been since I've smiled like that? Christ.*

Suddenly conscious of the surging crowd surrounding him having to walk around him to cross the bridge, Simon moved to one side and leaned against the rail. The bridge was supposed to be from the future and that meant chrome, once upon a time. Simon reflected that metal might not have been the smartest material for a theme-park in Florida, as it burned him through his pants. Although *he* didn't mind. After being chilled in Space Mountain's air-conditioning for so many hours, it felt somewhat pleasant.

Simon looked left as the monorail passed over tomorrow land. It was built at a time when monorails belonged in the *realm of tomorrow.* Walt Disney was an optimist. He wanted people to feel happy and excited about the coming future instead of fearful of a nuclear holocaust. Shiny chrome buildings, frozen lemonade stands, and spaceship rides made it an easy sell.

Simon turned to the right, and from his vantage in the middle of the bridge where the arch swelled to it's apex, he could see above the heads of the crowd: the bronze gleam of the Walt and Mickey statue at the center of the park. The perfect photo-op for couples and families, with the castle just in the background. Everything was happy, and a harsh contrast.

*What the fuck is wrong with me? I can't even be happy **here**. What's going to happen when I finally ship off home? Am I going to explode like some deep sea creature being brought to the surface?*

Someone wandered past with a turkey leg and the aroma reminded Simon that he was starving. Without a second thought he shoved off and headed off towards fantasy land on a quest for food.

Chapter 4

Gravity

After standing at the concert for so long, it felt good to walk, better to feel the night wind chilling her face where sweat had cracked and smeared thin her corpse paint. She strode hard into that cool air, her silver wallet chain jingling dully as if underwater, muted by the ringing in her ears. Driven by the lingering sense of power the encore had imbued her with, her pace was so aggressive she had to stop short for the automatic doors of Walmart to rattle open for her. After the red tint and strobes of the concert, the harsh white of relentless fluorescent lights drove her eyes to a squint as she entered.

She felt like an outlaw entering a saloon, by the way the late night denizens of Walmart glanced at her. Being scary felt just as strange as being friendly at work, and just as easy. She wore a uniform to let everyone know she was nice and there to help, just like she wore a leather jacket with shiny spikes on it to let everyone know she was a spooky girl to avoid. She enjoyed a familiar kind of shelter from it. She didn't need to endure the uncertainty of a stranger's opinion about her if she firmly chose a conclusion for them.

She'd ended up down the drink aisle out of instinct, ingrained in her from years of ritual. Morrigan swept her eyes across the drinks as she made her way with slow meandering steps in big stompy boots. She wasn't really looking for anything as much as she was hoping she'd see something she wanted. More compulsion than desire had brought her here, after all. Morrigan had gone to Walmart for the same reason she'd gone to the concert alone: to prove that she could.

The independence of it provided her with a rush she hadn't felt since sneaking out to see Cradle of Filth when she was fourteen. She'd gone all out tonight. She'd spent an hour and a half putting on an intricate corpse-paint design. A white base with sharp black lines like cracking ice that led up to the eyes where she flaired the black outwards like fire. She knew it looked awesome, because some Scandinavian chick with a crazy thick accent told her so.

It felt great to rebel against her own anxieties, but that good feeling bled out of her over the course of the night. She was lacerated by feelings she tried to dismiss. Long after being drained of excitement she kept putting herself through all the motions of someone having a good time. This late night Walmart run was the last ritual she could perform before admitting she was alone, *and* it sucked.

The friends she used to haunt this Walmart with were still in her phone, but indefinitely unavailable. One turned out to be a piece of shit, while the other two went away to college and never came back. One got a job, the other got a girl. She was Swedish, from Sweden, so 'good for him' was Morrigan's official position. She really was happy for those dudes, but that didn't keep her from being sad.

Morrigan stopped. It felt natural to stop where she did, but the memory didn't come with the instinct, so she spun slowly, scanning the shelves around her. Her attention was snared on a shelf of drinks, and it felt like waking up from a long nap. The fridge door came open with a dull pop, from a two fingered yank. Her elbow popped out on muscle memory to keep the door from swinging back shut. It was the Arizona Ice-Tea fridge. A dollar for a huge can of a sugary drink was an easy sell for a couple of teenagers.

She dragged a can free from the shelf and let the train slide forward with a clank to replace it. Turning the can around Morrigan inspected the nutrition facts without any real context for what the numbers meant, but those things had been her sworn nemesis when she was younger, after she realized they were likely the source of her acne.

She jammed the can back into it's slot on the shelf, shoving the line of cans that slid down to take its place back. But, before closing the freezer she spotted her old favorite: mango strawberry. Enslaved by curiosity and nostalgia, Morrigan plucked the can from the fridge and let it slam shut.

Departing from the drink section, she held the can by the top with her nails to keep the cold metal from burning her fingers. Swinging her arm, as she walked Morrigan wandered her way in a wide loop to the register. Another muscle memory from her teenage years when there was no better place to be than out with friends.

Eventually she surrendered to the realization that there was no place else to go but home, and headed to the register. There was a line and Morrigan got trapped in it. The only escape from melancholic thoughts of the past was her classic strategy of people watching. It was how she got through work too. She'd pick a person and then imagine what their life was like. It was different, of course, at a Walmart at 2am. Instead of 'how did they pay for the vacation' it was usually 'are they high? how high? and on what?'.

The woman ahead of her either ground up chips and sprinkled them into her keyboard for fun, or was going to be huffing compressed air canisters. It seemed hazardous to make eye contact with her so Morrigan took a sweeping look around the room and spotted someone that surprised her.

It's that fucking guy. The guy who's been riding space mountain on *repeat for like two days straight. The guy who's **not** autistic.* She thought, suppressing a giggle that might make her seem insane.

She squinted at him, trying to discern any detail that would help solve her greatest mystery: the guy, on vacation alone, who rode space mountain all day for days, and *didn't* seem to be mentally deranged. Here he was at a 24-hour Walmart at 2am, which did support her 'inconspicuously insane' theory.

Part of what made it hard to believe was the fact that he was so handsome. It was weird to imagine crazy people being put together like he was. It felt more natural to assume his distant stare was deep rather than vacant.

I bet it's just a girl. I bet you're not so fucking deep. There's only one thing that makes people sad enough to ride a roller coaster for eight fucking hours a day. You didn't lose an arm, nobody died. You're just...

He picked up a bag of candy, stared at it dispassionately and then shrugged and dropped it into his basket. He did it like the candy wasn't even for him. Morrigan crept up on her tiptoes to peer into the basket, but he shifted arms and her vision was blocked.

I bet he's just buying random shit to make himself feel better. Maybe I should talk to him. We can bond over being sad sacks.

It was a pleasant fantasy but she wasn't really going to just talk to some stranger. Weirdos did that.

Chapter 5

Hiraeth

Simon walked watching his phone like a treasure map. The rideshare app he was using somehow viewed Wallmart's parking lot as an abyss of nothingness and his ride was going to be picking him up behind the parking lot in some industrial park. There were no signs that said you weren't supposed to go behind a supermarket sized store but Simon had always assumed the whole zone was 'employees only'.

He approached the corner cautiously as his imagination kept him apprised of all the things that could be around the bend; junkies, homeless people, muggers, a crocodile. When he *did* clear the corner he saw instead a scene so captivating it made him wish again he could paint.

A flickering beacon of light cut through the darkness, cast down from a streetlight with a yellowing bulb partially filled with stale rainwater. It was in that imperfect light that he saw her. A girl sitting alone on a rubber bumper of the unlit truck-dock, clad in a uniform of black jeans ripped at the knees and a ratty leather jacket glinting with sticky splattered beer-stains. She let her legs swing idly, clacking steel-plated heels of big stompy boots against the concrete beneath her seat, chipping free the occasional puff of debris. She sat back against the hard concrete platform and hung her elbows on the rough wall like it was a couch in a nice club. The bright colors of a tall can of Arizona Ice-Tea set beside her burned like a gem in the gloom of the scene.

At the time Simon didn't know what made the sight so striking that his eyes couldn't be sated with a glance. It could have been as simple as how the light struck her. It might have been her expression, deflated by a sigh, or maybe the facepaint coating it that melted off from a night's sweat and fidgetting. It might have been the Fundip stick hanging out of her mouth like a cowboy's cigarette or it could have been the way her slouching silhouette mimed his own feelings with perfect accidental mockery.

The sight of her reminded him of looking up at a leafless tree in winter, against a starry night sky, because a camera flash would entirely miss the point of both. Cameras didn't know how big the moon was, and he couldn't ask a picture what was wrong. Then again, Simon couldn't ask *her* either. He didn't know this strange girl, and he had no right to know her problems. Still, there was nothing he knew of that could make him feel better than being there for someone when they needed it. The certainty of being valuable, through value to others, held an intense allure that rooted him to the spot. But even though he'd never see this girl again, and he would never meet the friends she told, he couldn't bring himself to be a weirdo and ask after her feelings.

Then the scary girl looked in his direction, tilting her head as much as turning it to see him. She cocked an eyebrow, like a weirdo didn't phase her.

Panic froze every inch of him, even his thoughts, so his mouth went on alone.

"Are you okay?"

"No."

"Right..."

"You knew that. I look like you feel, don't I?"

He blinked "I.. I guess you're right. What's the saying? Misery loves company?"

She nodded and casually hurled her drink at a dumpster. It gonged against the side spraying frothy fluid skyward to splatter down like rain onto the asphalt. They both watched the liquid spread out under harsh fluorescent light, until his phone buzzed. His driver sent a message through the app, asking where he was. He wrote out a message explaining he'd be right there, but then he stuffed the phone back into his pocket, leaving it unsent.

"Hey listen I don't know you, but... you wanna go for a walk? Talk about it?"

She huffed a laugh out her nose and cocked her eyebrow higher. "Why do *you* give a shit?"

"I guess... it's probably because you're right. You *do* look like I feel, and something tells me you don't deserve to. I'd like to listen, because I know that can help, and maybe if I make you feel a little better, I'll feel better too."

She smiled and, even through all the scary make-up, her smile was pretty.

"And hey, no pressure to say yes. If you're too scared, you'll be the first person to ever think I'm threatening."

She tossed her head back and belted a laugh to the sky with a lock of hair stuck to her melty facepaint. She laughed like a girl who needed to, and it was enough to make Simon smile. The sound funneled into a giggle as she stifled it. "alright, alright. I'll pour my heart out to you, stranger, but there's no place good to walk from here and I'd been on my feet for a couple hours before I sat down." She gestured to the rubber dock bumper next to hers, several feet away. "Join me?"

"Sure." He swung his bag of candy aisle bullshit up onto the truck dock and climbed up with as much athleticism as he could muster.

"Used to walk here from the Banshee's Labyrinth, this edgy bar venue up the road. Super fuckin cool place, especially when you're barely a teenager and you've only ever seen sick venues in music videos. It's this big factory building, smack in the middle of an industrial park; all brick and stone and its got all these tunnels winding around with all these nooks to sit and chat in. The music sounds so fucking crazy in the tunnels, reverbs like a ghost in the shower. We'd stand in that crowd for hours then walk miles to get *here.*"

Simon waited, but when she was quiet for a minute longer, he prodded her on with a word. "We?"

"Yeahhhh, man. Used to be a 'we'. *We* would get there early and walk around those tunnels, then we'd scream our throats raw on the opener, spend our legs jumping with the crowd on the first real band of the lineup, then we'd thrash our heads until they throbbed and retreat to those tunnels for a band, and we'd shove our way into the pit for the headliner. The best nights we ended up on the front railing, windmilling. Then we'd just fucking walk because we were dumb kids without cars. We'd hydrate on sugary garbage and walk until our parents were sending texts in all caps with double question marks."

She got quiet and Simon looked over at a girl quaking gently with a longing for another night like that. The passion was so unreasonably infectious he missed it too. He stared, in spite of his instinct not to be weird. There was something fascinating about her, something compelling enough to quell anxiety in the face of curiosity. He'd never see this girl again, anyway, so he stared and wondered.

She wasn't particularly attractive. In fact, she repelled. She wore a stiff leather jacket covered in sticky beer stains and silver spikes. She was decidedly unhuggable. Her hair was matted with some combination of sweat and accumulated oil from going unwashed for days. A hand combing through her hair would be snagged and pull unpleasantly.

A tear globbed up in her make-up and she raised a sleeve to wipe but stopped short and sighed nasally, resigning herself to the fact she'd only make it worse. Her eyelids drooped with her shoulders, but her eyes were still just as striking as when they'd been on him. They quivered, staring at a horizon she couldn't see, and spoke of a quick moving mind. He watched her lips part and then purse again and her jaw clench with frustration, a tendon rising visibly in the soft skin of her neck. Something about the palpable sharpness of her mind, the fire of her frustration, and her despair that was all too familiar, made Simon wish he knew her. He wished he'd been born a thousand miles away from brunettes with long legs that don't hold hands, to grow up next door to a scary girl like her.

"Somebody's gonna fall in love with you one day."

Her eyebrow raised high enough to crack dried make-up on her forehead. It struck him with a rush of adrenaline, but he reminded himself that it didn't matter what this strange girl thought of him.

"Sorry to be weird." He exhaled, squeezing his eyes shut to steady himself. "But I really mean that. Some people kind of just *exist*. I don't... I don't really know how to explain it, but you're different." He opened his eyes and stared off at the puddle of mango strawberry tea. "The way you talk about days gone by with enough passion to make someone who's never lived them miss those days. The way your jaw clenches with discontent, ready to explode into action to change things. Some guy's gonna fall in love with that stuff one day. You'll get a prince in shining... uh, *leather* armor?"

He glanced at her and she smiled weakly at him. "Yeah, happened, actually. Didn't work out so good for me."

Her words sunk in his stomach. The crestfallen note in her voice was all too familiar.

"I'd give you an autopsy, but it's not unique or interesting. It just sucks. He cheated, a lot. So much people stopped feeling bad for me, started getting annoyed that I wasn't breaking up with him. He was good at that kind of thing. He could make me feel embarrassed to be upset when I found out. To everyone else he played it like he was my boyfriend just to placate me, like it was only serious to me, and... well I guess... I guess it was."

"Sounds like a real piece of shit."

She looked at him sharply enough to make him flinch.

"Sorry! I didn't mean to alarm you."

Her head cocked in such extreme confusion, she looked like a puppy dog.

"I shouldn't use that kind of language. I know. It's a bad hab-"

"What? Where the fuck are you from that cursing scares people? You live on fucking Seasame street?"

Simon laughed until he was out of breath. Something about her delivery made him forget his embarrassment and just laugh with her.

"That's nice of you to say by the way." she said with her first breath back. "Not a lot of people are bold enough to say something like that."

Simon shook his head. "Oh please. You really don't know me, if you think I'm bold. I just know what it's like to be there.

Nothing quite so dramatic as cheating, mind you. You thought your, uh, *autopsy* was uninteresting? *Nothing* really happened in mine. She just wasn't that nice to me and I wasn't happy but I also wasn't brave enough to break up with her. I'm too much of a..."

"Pussy?"

He shrugged. "Yeah."

"Say it."

"Pussy," Simon said in a volume far lower than his speaking voice. The girl laughed at him and he yelled it in a wavering voice that made her laugh harder.

"I hope you're not offended to hear me say: that's actually adorable."

"*Anyway,* my point is: it's not bold to say that guy's an asshole. He is. I get to be honest because I don't know you or any of your friends. I'll never meet them. I'll never even meet *you* again. You get to hear my honest unfiltered opinion. And if no one else has told you he's a piece of shit, then they're a fence sitting bitch like me. I just know what it's like to have an ex that's more likable and charismatic than me. I wish one fucking person would have told me, but I don't think I would have stuck my neck out like that for someone until it happened to *me.*"

She swore with the froggy voice of a choked up girl, and Simon felt dizzy. He couldn't piece back together what he'd said so he could obsess, but the anxiety was still well intact.

"Thanks dude."

"You want candy?"

She coughed out a laugh.

"No I mean I have a bag of candy... umm..."

"Yeah I got it."

"Sorry, that sounded... I don't know. I'm just..."

"I'm a girl. Of course I want candy."

They were momentarily blanketed in brightness as a car rounded the corner. When the lights switched off Simon saw the lit rideshare dash sign.

They found me after all. I guess I should have canceled the ride.

Simon hopped down and waved politely to the driver.

"Oops, I forgot I... uh, anyway, just take the whole bag."

A "hey," turned Simon around. "Thanks for the... uh... candy."

Simon nodded with a soft smile, before taking his exit.

"Hope you'll fly with us again soon, on your travels to the stars," she called as a final farewell.

Simon's mind was inhibited with the awkwardness of getting into a stranger's car. With his brain so focused on the appropriate application of polite smile and pleasant comment, he didn't process why those words sounded familiar until the car had begun to move.

He turned sharply to the girl, her big stompy boots still idly dangling beneath the dock bumper, watching him go. Seeing the stunned recognition she flashed a white grin in the flood of red tail lights.

Chapter 6

A bazooka in a golf bag

She's probably not even working today, he thought to himself as he ran fingers through his longish hair, meticulously shaping a subtle blow-back cut. He always wore his hair slicked back, but today it had to be slightly messed up, as though he was stylish without really trying. *Even if she **is** working today, who knows if she'd want to talk to me?*

His arguments to himself were disingenuous, but pessimism made him feel armored against the blow of disappointment. Simon bunched up the sleeves of his button down over his biceps and did his best to flex them as much as he knew how to. *God help me if she **does** want to talk to me.*

"So why do you ride this roller coaster so much?"
"Oh well my girlfriend broke up with me and I just turned five apparently."
" I'm so sorry. Were you together for a long time?"

"Yeah it was a misery that went on for precisely three years and five months."

"Oh that must be hard."

*"Not as hard as being **in** the relationship. She was constantly cruel to me and demanded control over every aspect of my life, whilst draining me financially. She also would constantly shame me for being a man, telling me that all men are ugly, me included, and that women didn't enjoy sex except in the vicarious way of pleasing their boyfriend. I probably believe her a little bit too. I'm such a pushover I'll even change my own opinions to make a girl happy because no matter how many girls I date, while I'm in the relationship they're perfect and I'll never meet anyone as good and no one else would probably date me anyway. I even laughed at all her jokes about the various gross features of male anatomy. Objectively, her breaking up with me could have only benefited me but still I feel drowned by this awful crushing nothingness that won't even let me feel something normal like sadness."*

*"Woah, so you're **really** pathetic, huh?"*

"Yup."

Simon jerked to a stop, and back-pedaled a few steps. He had nearly daydreamed his way onto the tracks. Simon held up one finger and called to a cast member with a trimmed ginger beard. "Single rider."

While he waited for an odd numbered party, to provide an empty seat, he glanced around. The girl wasn't on the exit side he was on, like yesterday. At first he felt a strange kind of relief, a comfortable disappointment. But then, he spotted her. She didn't see him, but there she was, across the tracks seating people onto the ride.

He felt a warm familiarity at the sight of her, and yet she was so jarringly different without leather or spikes. Something about the sight of her made him want to laugh, with the sharpness of a shiver in the cold, without really knowing why. She was rolled up onto the balls of her feet, her pale slender neck stretched tall and chin slightly upturned, to count the smaller numbered lines of those about to board the next train. From across the tracks he could see her mouthing the numbers, her lips barely parting for each inaudible vowel. Making herself tall enough to see above the crowd made her footing unstable and she'd teeter to one side before staggering a step like a clumsy ballerina, but while somehow retaining all the grace of a dancer. Her concentration on the task placed a blank expression on her very expressive face, and it was impossibly endearing. Had she not been so plainly oblivious to her charm, it would have been obnoxious to make a face quite so cute. It was a beauty that needed no mirror, makeup or special destination to warrant its existence. She had a kind of accidental allure, like the softness of pajama pants worn on the couch beside you, and it exerted over Simon a charming accidental seduction.

Simon's eyes had been rooted to that face when they spoke. But now, without fear of being thought some kind of degenerate, curiosity dragged his eyes down. Her uniform was designed to be very far from form fitting and yet it couldn't obfuscate her very enchanting silhouette. Every motion brought rebellion between her clothing and the riot of flesh it concealed. Each battle evoked a shameful imagination in Simon. He found himself enchanted and the longer he stared the tighter her grip over him became. She was overwhelmingly attractive, but it was not the threatening weaponized sexiness of some femme fatale super spy. Instead her allure was entirely unutilized and jarringly out of place, like a bazooka in a golf bag.

She went about her job carrying herself as though no one were watching. She maintained no deliberate posture nor resting expression. It seemed so strange but then, as Simon examined the crowd around her, he realized that no one *was* watching her. For every party she needed to fight for their attention, calling loudly and waving, to get the number of people so she could seat them. Simon alone heard her siren song.

Simon felt a gentle but urgent touch on his back. "Line three, sir."

Sit down. Stow your belongings in
the netted compartment in front of
you. That's got to be a push-up bra.
There's just no way. Pull the bar
towards you until it won't click any
more. Keep your hands and feet
inside the car. Enjoy the ride.

Make sure to gather all your
belongings from the compartment
in front of you. Don't stare. Exit to
your left. Have a magical day.

As Simon stood up he saw a familiar mop of black hair and
snapped his head back to facing forward. The instinct to not be
creepy clutched Simon's nerves tight.

Shit. How did she get on this side? Did she swap with someone?

Afraid to look directly at her and be weird, Simon stood rigid
and observed her with his periphery as he started off towards the
exit. He saw the motion of her hand half raise, and her shoulders lift,
only to sag a moment later. Her hand hovered for a second in front
of her chest, with her fingers limply curling, about to retire to her
side when some instinct in Simon forced him to turn and look
directly at her face. He braved the awkwardness and didn't look
away, he pinched his lips into the tiniest of smiles that said: 'yeah I
recognize you, and I'm happy to see you.' as best he could say it;
which is to say, not with actual words.

The lingering image of a face, consumed by the gloom of
being ignored, burned into Simon's memory then. Her very
expressive face had a way of looking so terribly sad for that instant.
Her lips were parted so very slightly in this tiny sad 'O' shape where
a tiny "hey" died. Her large brown eyes thought they were looking
at someone who didn't want to talk to her, didn't want to remember
her.

But then, in an instant, that sad face vanished. She was struck by a flattering shock of glee at his recognition. This girl popped up an inch onto her toes and flopped back down onto her heels with a bounce that jiggled down in his periphery. He strangled the temptation to glance down with the fear of what she might think of him; a fear of looking back up at those brown eyes and finding disgust in them. The hand of gently curling fingers that had just drifted down so glumly snapped back up in a wave. The jerking motion was so sudden, Simon reflexively mirrored it with his own muted wave.

Her face bloomed into a bright smile so quickly Simon was effected sharply by it. Like a squint at a flash of sun reflected off shining steel Simon smiled, reflexively, without consulting his depression. He smiled a big natural smile bubbling with little guffaws that would mortify him later, in bed, when he had time to care about things that didn't matter, like being embarrassingly happy at the sight of a pretty girl's pretty smile.

There was something so adorably goofy about her severe range of expression. She'd gone from a wet cartoon dog to a princess singing to a lovebird. Her face seemed like it must have been softer than other faces or perhaps there was extra skin stored in her puffy white cheeks, because Simon had never seen a face that looked quite *so* cheerful and so *naturally* so. He imagined in that moment, that like some people were double jointed or had photographic memory, this girl was born with a face that could express higher heights of glee than other people could.

"Hey."

Simon was so flustered he couldn't be sure which one of them had said it. Some quick thinking blurted a "Sup" out of his mouth. This way he could be responding to her or at the very least not repeating himself.

She waved enthusiastically and moved closer to him, too close in fact, and took an awkward step backwards. "Hey! You're back."

"Nope, I'm Simon," he said, extending a hand.

Oh no. What did I say? Why? Why would I do this?

The girl swung wide, slapping his hand away with an excited high-five and an eye roll. "Hey!thought you said I'd never have to see you again? What gives?" asked a girl who didn't seem unhappy to see him again.

Before an awkward Simon could get his brain to make words, the girl giggled and jerkily picked his hand back up to shake it. She shook his hand with such rapid, shallow movements that there was, again, a jiggle he forbade himself from even glancing at. He kept his eyes focused on their hands and mentally prepared himself for the treacherous journey across her chest to her face. Simon looked up sharply, –too high– missing her face, and looked back down into her big brown eyes. He decided he should repeat the movement in a sort of nod to make that motion seem logical.

Oblivious to his battle against her breasts she went on without pause, "But hi, hey. Nice to meet you- well nice to know your name, Simon. And, uh, I'm Morrigan. So... hi!" She began to release his hand then re-gripped it hard for a moment. "Oh and I'm also not back." She let go and replaced Simon's hand at his side.

They shared a short, tense, laugh before the hiss of hydraulic brakes drew Morrigan's attention back to her duties.

"Looks like you've got, uh, cadets to deal with." Simon said with a salute as he stepped backwards towards the exit.

Morrigan matched his salute with just enough enthusiasm to cause herself to flinch when her fingers hit her forehead.

Simon smiled but he saved his laughter until he was a decent ways into the tunnel.

Man she's fucking weird. And definitely cute.

His brain's job was to ridicule him for how nervous he'd been and how he struggled like a teenage boy to avoid staring at her breasts, but his brain was busy. He couldn't help running over her salute in his mind; how her smile paused for a second when she hit herself and then resumed right after; how she closed one of her eyes on impact and then opened it, bright as ever and focused on him. That look of hers energized him to go for a walk around Tomorrowland, but he soon found his way back.

> **Sit down. Don't slouch and look like you have a gut. Stow your belongings in the netted compartment in front of you. Pull the bar towards you –with confidence– until it won't click any more. Keep your biceps flexed. Keep your hands and feet inside the car. Enjoy the ride.**

> **Make sure to gather all your belongings from the compartment in front of you. Exit to your left. That's where the cute girl is. Have a magical day.**

When he got off the ride, Morrigan made the suggestion, purely in the name of common sense, of course, that he not bother going down the exit if he was just going to ride all day anyway. He accepted and they talked. They talked about her job, and they talked about his job. They talked about hometowns and Halloween costumes they wore when they were little. They talked about that cute alien at the start of the Alien Encounter ride, that gets silly spiky hair when it's electrocuted. They talked through the lunch break she forgot to take.

When the park was closing, she moaned about having nothing but cheese and bread in her apartment. He thought about all the nice restaurants in Downtown Disney that were all just one Disney bus away, which were *far* better than grilled cheese, but he didn't have the balls to ask.

Chapter 7

Kino

Morrigan had been singing along to power metal long before she started blasting it through her earbuds.

"We *journey* to A-val*on*, wanderers *of* the **sun**."

Her head bobbed and swayed in a tight 'V' that swung her bangs against her cheeks while her fingers twitched, itching to be pressed to frets. She was blissfully in another world, full of swords and sorcery, where every problem was caused by an evil emperor who could be slain (gloriously). She was no longer just walking out of work. Morrigan was on a grand quest and she planted each step like she were journeying to a new and fantastic land, full of grassy hills, misty waterfalls, and really gorgeous unicorns.

In an instant her sanctuary was shattered. One earbud popped out of her ear and instantly the epic symphony was paired with noisy hallway chatter. She sighed, immediately irritated with herself for catching the cord on something, but as she looked to see what she'd snagged it on, Morrigan realized she hadn't caught it on anything.

"Mo? *Hello?*" It was Jake, a co-worker. He stood there,

grinning like an asshole, holding an earbud by the cord. He'd yanked it out of her ear.

He looked at her like she was going to be embarrassed, and apologize for having her head in the clouds; like it was going to be this fun moment where she laughs about being a ditz. But it wasn't an accident that she'd deafened herself to the world. She didn't want to hear anything but Johan's beautiful voice. She didn't *care* what Jake had to say and it was astonishing that he still didn't seem to understand this.

Morrigan had only seen one broken nose in her life. When leaving a show, one time, she saw two Hispanic girls brawling. Alcohol and boyfriends had apparently been involved. This skinny chick, missing two fistfuls off her hair, was on top hammering punches into the other girl's face with her tiny arms. When they pulled the girl off, by her pentagram harness, the other girl's nose was sideways.

Looking at Jake's stupid smug face, she wondered how hard she'd have to punch him to break his nose that bad. That girl had been pretty small.

"You couldn't hear me again?" He asked it in this condescending way that only charming people can get away with. He wasn't charming.

Again, images of extreme violence flashed through her. She remembered another concert where communist protesters had decided to enter the mosh pit with flag poles. One of them had hit her in the back of the head as they raised it. She had never seen something quite so satisfying as watching a shirtless, hairy, fat man with a giant beard pick up that skinny communist, lift him over his head, and throw him at the ground a dozen or so times. By the way the kid started crying, she knew he'd never had his ass kicked before. She wanted to replicate the ever so satisfying expression that loser's face had made as he was peeled off the floor, sticky with spilled beer, and pelted against it again.

Morrigan had never envied a hairy fat man before that moment. If she could have picked Jake up over her head, she would have lost her job to do it in an instant. She was sure of it.

"Oh *Momo*, what are we gonna do with you?"

Morrigan, my name is Morrigan, not Morgan, not Momo, not Mo. I'm named after a badass goddess of ravens, war and doom.

"What the *fuck* do you *want*?" She exploded, exasperated and loud enough to turn passing heads.

His ego repelled all evidence of him being unwanted and he got closer, trying to listen to her music, playing it off like she was kidding or playing hard to get. He acted like it was a cute moment as she tried to pull her earbud away from him. He made teasing noises, exerting force to overpower her. Morrigan wanted to hit him badly. She wanted to punch him so hard his head would bounce off the wall.

"You know I used to listen to music like this too." He told her as though he'd just revealed his secret identity as a superhero.

The stench of his sweat burned her nostrils.

"Fucking *cool*," she snarled, yanking the earbud out of his ear and walking off.

It was slimy from his earwax.

He laughed at her, following invasively close behind. "You're so *weird*."

Morrigan stopped and turned on the spot, grinding grit loudly under her heel.

Whatever she was going to say was scorched from her brain with a flash of rage and revulsion. Her sudden stop caused him to collide with her. He stumbled, displacing her with his girth like a big wave of sweat. She staggered, and he staggered with her pressing himself against her, plowing her down the hall, pretending with oafish noises that he was losing his balance, and all the while craning his head over her to look down her shirt.

Morrigan's brain became a wet log thrown into a bonfire, splitting to shriek steam from inside.

His hands groped for her, to steady himself, and instinct took over. She reacted like she would if she were repelling a drunk idiot at a show about to fall on her. Baring her teeth she slapped a hand over his greasy face and shoved *hard*. With a desperate strength she overcame his oafish weight and threw him backward. She felt instant satisfaction, a rush from forcing her will where she'd been powerless.

Adrenaline dilated time and she watched the result of her broken patience in slow motion. Even how he fell annoyed her. His bulk transferred to the floor with loud stomping steps that slapped the floor as he stumbled. He landed on his butt looking shocked and offended, as though *she* was being unreasonable. She had to resist the urge to punt his head off.

"Now I *know* you're a fucking idiot, Jake, but you're not *this* dumb." She breathed, shaking with rage as she spoke. "You *know* I don't like you. I'd even put so much faith in you as to believe you know that I *dislike* you. Yet you keep talking to me. You keep asking me out. I get that guys need to approach. I get that you miss a hundred percent of shots you don't take, so you keep taking shots. I get it."

With a trembling fist, she stuffed her MP3 player into her pocket as one big tangled mass of wires.

"You keep taking shots because you don't think of me like a person. You don't care what someone thinks of you if they're someone who would turn you down. So you practice your shitty pick-up game on me because, in your head, there's this *one percent* chance that I'll say yes." She leaned closer and through gritted teeth she spat: "But I *am* a person Jake, and you're **bothering** me." Again she watched his ego struggle against reason. His demeanor was dismissive but his eyes were distant as he wrapped his head around the idea. "Let me make this very clear Jake. I'm not playing hard to get. You disgust me. You smell, you're pushy, rude, and the sound of you breathing makes me want to bash myself in the head with a heavy rock until I fucking die. So fuck off, Jake. **Fuck. Off.**"

She stormed off shaking, adrenaline surging into her arms. She was primed like a bomb to explode as soon as he inflicted any of his usual 'accidents' upon her. She was so ready for him to step on the back of her shoe or walk too fast and bump into her or reach over her to get something and scrape his hairy forearm across her neck, or whatever other excuse he'd conjure to touch her. She'd grab him by the face and slam his skull into the pavement. She could envision it in her head. She'd commit murder. She was positive. It was the best option. She could just see the police officer taking her report, shrug at his dead body, flattened head being scraped off the ground by the coroner. He'd let her go, of course, remarking 'yeah he looks like the kind of guy to be acting like a little bitch and get their skull smashed open. I'll let you off with a warning this time.'

He's fucking ugly too. I should have told him that. I can't fucking believe he's so god damn delusional that he would think what he has to say would be better than my music. The fucking audacity.

She opened her car door so aggressively that some lady in front of her apologized. Immediately Morrigan's rage was extinguished. She did her best not to slam the door when she closed it, so as to not alarm anyone.

Alone in her car she let out a shaky breath and a trembling hand set about the disc changer. She put on some Burzum to calm herself down. Every anxiety began to build up. Had she overreacted? Would Jake go to HR? Should *she*? What if they believed *him* because he talked to them first? Was he angry? Was he going to get revenge? Would he attack her outside of work? Follow her home? Was he stomping up to her car right now?

She locked the door and turned the key to start the car. Her hand hovered over the shifter, and balled it into a fist. She could feel a fit of hyperventilation coming on, and decided she'd rather get mad than anxious. She punched the top of the steering wheel hard and shook her head with a jaw clenched so tight she felt her head tremble.

Just as quickly as it came, it went, and Morrigan threw the car into reverse. As she backed out of the space, she wished she could call someone to talk to on the drive home. Someone that could keep her calm.

For just a moment she thought about calling Mars, a friend she'd kept from middle school through college. However, the thought of Marissa was inseparable from leaden memories that mixed with her current emotions to color them only darker. It had been 2am the night after breaking up with Sean. Morrigan couldn't sleep so she went out to a diner with her best friend to eat waffles until she had to go to work. She'd needed to ramble and she'd needed someone to listen. But, around four, she looked over at her friend and she was smiling at a text from the same ex she'd been venting a year and three months worth of complaints about. She knew he'd smiled too when he sent it. It hurt her with a sickening pain, too familiar to bear. The twist in her gut when she realized all the time she'd wasted with Sean came back while she waited for her friend to notice she'd stopped talking.

Morrigan turned up the music.

The crush of sound enveloped Morrigan in safety; the roar of an angry Norwegian, venting pure elemental emotion when she couldn't. He screamed himself raw about an ancient grudge, a problem safely far away from those in her head. The adrenaline flow slowed and left her with a warm tingle in her skin. In the wake of the previous moment's intensity, her thoughts were dull and wandering.

With her mind drifting and relaxed she said his name, where it would be secreted by a drum fill. "Simon." Even *she* couldn't hear how it sounded, but it felt good to say. "Are you a piece of shit *too*, Simon?"

At a redlight she wondered what it was like when *he* hit on a girl. She couldn't imagine him being so physically aggressive, like Jake was. She couldn't imagine him employing *any* of the normal methods inflicted on her. She had never worried about standing too close to him and inviting a heavy arm around her shoulders that would drag her into a sweaty armpit. He didn't seem like the type to track her down to a corner of a club and slap a hand on the wall to bar her from escaping a conversation with him. She couldn't even imagine him trying to guilt her into letting him buy her a drink and she definitely didn't see him as someone who would get pissy and aggressive if she didn't want one.

Those methods had always bothered her. When she really liked a guy and he made a move like that it always hurt. It was an appealing fantasy to think of a guy like Simon operating differently. She mused to herself how someone like Simon might make his move.

Couldn't be anything physical. Guy's too respectful to yawn an arm over a chick. Dude probably pulls chairs out for girls, then does that thing where he pushes it in while you scoot forward.

The thought passed a smile through her lips briefly.

Yeah... He seems like the kind of guy who'd help you put your coat on, and do a really good job too. Wouldn't surprise me if he somehow knew how to put coats on way better than most people, like he could help you put your arms through and show you you've been shitty at putting coats on your whole life.

She let out a laugh that no one heard, not even her, muted by roaring death metal that rattled her windows.

She wished then that she could have called *him*, to talk to on the ride home. The guy was an easy person to talk to. He would care about her confrontation with Jake. Simon was sweet like that.

45

Chapter 8

Sweet dreams are made of her

When he returned to his hotel room, Simon didn't bother to turn the lights on or change. Once his shoes were off, Simon flopped onto the bed without bothering to pull back the comforter. With his eyes shut, Simon stretched out and felt soreness in his abs from laughing at Morrigan's jokes. It had been a while since he'd laughed like that, and he'd gotten out of shape.

Simon lay there expecting his traitorous mind to seep down through the cracks and drip down into the spaces of his memory he'd rather not dwell. He expected a new autopsy report on the corpse of his failed relationship, or a memory of another indignity he suffered in it. But they never came. His brain was too busy. His wandering mind was consumed instead by unraveling the various elements of weirdness that made up Morrigan's bizarrely irresistible allure. He'd spent the whole day with this girl, and felt overwhelmed by her. Like a day swimming in the ocean leaves a person rolling in the surf when they close their eyes, Simon could hear her voice saying mundane things, feel the brush of her hair against his chin when she turned too fast and whipped him with it, and he could feel the weight of her eyes on him. They were dark brown eyes with a brightness beyond their hue, and they looked him over with a quickness. Her eyes had this way of darting over him in a quick twitchy motion before they were snagged on his. Simon wondered dimly what the girl might be looking at when she did that. It was a mystery to him what made a man attractive, but then he still couldn't say what made *her* attractive either.

He reasoned the attribute that allured him must be physical. After all, what right did he have to count himself among people who knew her? To be *emotionally* attached to her would make him some kind of crazy stalker. He bludgeoned himself with the logic that there must be some aspect to her that he could see with his eyes that made her so magnetic. An easy answer was to say her breasts, but Simon knew it wasn't so simple. She was very *something,* something beyond just attractive. It couldn't be sorted into pretty or cute, though she was both in spades. It was something else, something he didn't have a word for. It was something about the clumsy grace with which she moved and how her face looked, blinking at him, while she listened to him speak. She seemed to hear even the smallest comment he made at a higher volume than other people.

Simon knew that dreams were often formed from thoughts lingering before sleep because so often he'd been flayed by nightmares born from thoughts of the past, but that night was different. He dreamt instead of a girl he had no right to dream of.

Chapter 9

Grilled Cheese

With one small socked foot planted crossways atop her ratty converse Morrigan tugged her foot free and stumbled a step forward, out of her shoes. She bent over to fix one half sock that tried to escape her foot with the shoe and, as she did, Morrigan nearly tipped over. She stuck her arms out like she were walking a tight rope and teetered back to her full height, before padding off to the fridge.

"Grilled cheese, huh?" She sighed looking over at a pan soaking in her sink. There was stuff stuck to it and she looked at the sponge with her arms crossed. "You give me too much credit, Simon."

It felt strange to say his name. She didn't feel like she had the right to use it. He'd at least told her his name himself, so that was something like permission, she reasoned. Still, she didn't want to act anything like Jake. It felt so invasive when *he* said her name. She'd never introduced herself, he'd just heard her manager call her Morgan one day, and started talking to her like he knew her. He'd never once used her actual name, calling her Morgan or some other nickname he had no right to assign her.

From her sparse fridge she retrieved American cheese, whitebread and the last hunk of sodabread.

"That why you didn't offer to take me to dinner, *Simon*?" She mused aloud tossing the bags onto her table, disrupting the library of receipts on it. "Afraid of being a creep like Jake?"

She sat with a sigh and shook her head. "Why didn't I take *you* to dinner? 'Hey jerk, you made me miss lunch by being so fun to talk to. Take me to Taco Bell.' Wouldn't have even been any kind of big deal. Not a date, just... hanging out... when I'm not working."

Morrigan gave herself over to the beast and began just eating slices of cheese. She was painfully hungry after skipping breakfast and lunch.

"Aw, that's so considerate of you to ask, Simon. I actually *am* a little sick. Why? Well Simon I ate one hundred percent of my daily calories in cheese yesterday because I'm a monster." She mumbled to herself inspecting the nutrition facts on the package.

Tossing the package back on the table, she shut her eyes and imagined a world where she wasn't just eating slices of cheese but a crunch quesadilla. While she was at it she added a Simon to her fantasy. Just her and Simon alone, in an empty Taco Bell just talking at a table in the back, watching headlights go by and talking about *stuff*. Of course her fantasy Taco Bell had no crackheads or homeless people, just good company and easy conversation. Maybe she'd show him a video on her phone and sidle up next to him. She'd have an easy excuse to press up against him, maybe work up to laying her head on his shoulder. He was so agreeable she could drag him anywhere and he wouldn't tap his foot and sigh and ask to go find a bed someplace. Everything would be at her speed.

In her fantasy she didn't imagine ever going back to his hotel. She saw herself dragging him to a crowded show for an excuse to hold his hand so she could lead him through the crowd to a cozy corner. She could show him that talking low in someone's ear is easier to hear than yelling in it when it's loud enough. She could sneakily say things just a little more sultry, bring her lips a little closer. She'd brush her hair over her ear and lean into him, looking sideways at him all innocent. She loved his voice. It was warm and relaxing and only loud when she made him laugh. She was sure his voice would sound sexy if she tricked him into talking low in her ear.

She blushed so hotly the air got cool around her cheek and ears. Her eyes opened and she stared at the ceiling wondering why it was just a fantasy. She couldn't understand why she hadn't just asked him out. She'd had the perfect set up to casually ask him to dinner and she chickened out. The conflux of hot skin and cooler air sent a shiver rippling up her skin and Morrigan sat up. "What is wrong with me? Why do I give a shit if I fuck this up? He's just *some guy.*"

Simon was a good looking man, but it was such an objective fact. He was attractive, but to a *normal* girl; a girl who wore *blouses,* not a girl like Morrigan who wore shirts. She didn't look at guys like Simon. Morrigan was attracted to punks with swept over mohawks who showed off modest biceps by tearing the sleeves off all their shirts, or vikings with braided beards and Norse runes tattooed across hairy knuckles, or skinny goth boys with crow-skull rings and tight pants who wore sunglasses at night and looked like vampires. She wasn't into guys like Simon... but then she *was* into Simon. Besides, if she was being honest with herself, Morrigan assumed she could get him into a pair of black skinny jeans if they were a thing.

She groaned and rubbed her face. "*No*, stop it, you're not dating some dude on vacation."

Despite their difference, somehow their personalities and temperments fit together like puzzle pieces to make conversation. Simon listened so intently that it almost felt like eavedropping and he worked his way through the conversation with this incredible charisma that he seemed entirely unaware of. Simon was never maneuvering to get her to go someplace alone with him to take advantage of her. He made her feel so safe Morrigan felt like she could agree to go anywhere with him. If she climbed into a sleeping bag with him, she was sure there wouldn't be a wandering hand anywhere on her. He was so delicate with any amount of physical contact that she wasn't even sure he'd even hold her as she slept unless she asked. He seemed so intimidated by her, and yet she was so enamored with him she'd have stuttered to reject even the most rude of advances. The more respectful of her personal space he was, the more she wanted to surrender it to him. She was so used to uncomfortable, invasive advances that she wondered if Simon was really so respectful or if he wasn't even attracted to her. She worried that he wasn't a gentleman, just disinterested and not desperate enough to stoop for her.

She curled forward, resting her forehead on the edge of the table with a dull thunk.

"Maybe he's gay and my ex fucked *him* too."

He was so delicate, even with his eyes. They were a blazing bright gem-like blue that would have been piercing on anyone else, but instead only occasionally flashed towards her, like sunshine off turbulent water. He never stared for long, but for those few moments he let his eyes linger on her, he looked at her like no one else ever had. Those eyes brightened when they saw her excited, were always distracted by her smile, unrelentingly attentive when she hinted at some misfortune and mournfully sad when she wouldn't tell him more. But they were timid eyes, and could only meet her gaze for a short while before politely retreating. Sometimes, when he looked at her, she thought about closing her eyes and basking in his gaze. She imagined him smiling that soft smile of his and caught herself red-handed, with a stupid grin on her face.

Morrigan groaned loudly, lolling her head back and shaking out her hair with both hands. "One night stand, or a bunch of nights stands, whatever. *That* is my goal and I shouldn't be nervous about it. There's no consequence for aiming low because it could never..." Her words got sluggish as she loathed to complete the thought, to give it validity. "...be anything else."

Everytime she imagined going home with him, there was so much that was unattainable. There was this physical closeness she yearned for that existed apart from lust. She wanted to be held tightly like it was urgent, as if she'd been crying and he had license to exert an inappropriate degree of affection towards her. In her fantasy they exchanged sweet words near enough that the sound doesn't outpace their breath. Those words are spoken softly, humming just beyond a whisper, in places too private not to oblige the removal of clothing instead. If she really allowed her fantasy to succumb to naked want, her hand was always held gently in his.

"*Stop*," she whined, begging her brain to relent. "Don't hang me on disappointment."

She didn't have a right to silly fantasies like that. This man, no matter how eccentric, would eventually fly home. She couldn't ask for anything more than a one night stand.

She resigned herself to the consolation that if they slept together she would have the excuse to fall asleep in his arms. Of course for that she'd need him to like her in the first place. Where other guys would doggedly pursue her over any minor display of friendly discourse, Simon seemed willfully oblivious to her advances.

It made her wonder if this was called 'playing hard to get'. She quickly decided that technique was for psychopaths. It seemed so insane to pursue someone, not knowing how they felt. In the end he might not even like her and she'd just be spending so much time climbing higher just to fall harder. She began to feel sick thinking about it.

Morrigan wished she'd been brave enough to get his number. She could call him and even if she was too scared to ask him directly, they could talk. He could make her feel better, just by noticing that she's feeling down. He might even be able to tell that the reason she's sad is because she's lonely. He might even offer to come over and talk and she might even seduce him into cuddling.

He was so nice he might just do it out of pity.

But for that she still needed his number, and that she didn't have. What she *did* have was cheese.

Chapter 10

Days of the week

Friday was very busy, but Morrigan managed to fill every spare second with conversation. Every moment she could steal with him, she used to tell the next disjointed section of a story or fact about herself. She told him of her fondness for the particular shade of violet that white lettering on black band-shirts adopt under black-lights. She liked a great many bands too but Simon didn't know any of them. He'd never really thought about what music he liked; a fact which dumbfounded her. She vowed to make him a CD of some sort. Later Morrigan told him the story of how she got caught skipping class in highschool because her friends were too high to stop hitting the underside of the bleachers in order to make a laser sound. At one point she claimed to be 100% Irish, though Simon figured that couldn't be entirely true since she had black hair, not ginger, and he couldn't make out any obvious freckles. Still, she'd talked at length about it. She'd told him she was so Irish her birthday was December 17th, though before he could ask her to elaborate, her mind had flown to another topic. Of all the many things she told him about, a boyfriend was not mentioned.

She had such a great deal of things to say that he suspected she had very few people to talk to. To Simon's mind it made a great deal of sense that someone would have to be terribly lonely to enjoy talking to him as much as she seemed to.

***

On Saturday he watched her trying to find a spot for him on the ride, instead of searching with her. Some embers of a joke reignited a laugh, and she looked so pretty it hurt. Her skin was soft and impossibly pale for a girl living under the Florida sun. She'd left her collar open by one button and from the side he caught a glimpse inside the ill-fitting uniform. There youthful skin clung tightly to a defined collarbone, yet readily shifted with the vibrant alacrity of life. The supple flesh of her neck yielded easily to rising tendons as poorly restrained giggles burst from her.

Simon envied the kind of guy who could be a boyfriend to a girl like her, to have permission to watch her laugh and smile and not feel creepy.

It was unfair to her, he knew, to take pleasure from her company and then to inflict some obligation of affection on her. She was sweet and a touch awkward. Simon knew it would have been rude of him to force her to go through the stress and guilt of rejecting him, and yet the temptation was there. She looked so pretty, laughing at his shitty jokes, and he thought that she really ought to know.

***

On Sunday, out of nowhere, Morrigan told him that "She was an idiot for letting him get away." She read the surprise on his face and explained "like recognizes like." with a wink before stepping away to help someone with a big backpack off the ride. When she came back it didn't come up again, but he didn't stop thinking about it.

Later Morrigan admitted she was dreading Monday because she was to be assigned to Splash Mountain and she wouldn't have "a Simon" to talk to, helping her get through the day. He wondered what "a Simon" was to her. He wondered if "a Simon" could get her number to text her and keep her company that way. But he just *wondered* and didn't ask.

***

She'd mentioned having to work Splash Mountain Monday, and so that's where he showed up. He was, of course, terrified she'd be unsettled by him coming to see her. Logically Simon knew she wouldn't mind having company, and she'd even said as much. Still he was haunted by his imagining of how her expressive face would look upon a stalker. His gut twisted to imagine her usual banter that was so free and warm, becoming stiff and apprehensive. Despite this, the thought of her being alone bothered him. It was an easy emotion to act on too.

He waited on the regular line to give himself time or maybe plausible deniability. If she thought he was weird or scary she could just pretend he was a stranger, say "Enjoy the ride, sir". When he saw her, he felt nauseous from worry, but still smiled softly as he watched her. She rose up on her tippy-toes mouthing the numbers as she counted the length of the line for each row so she could distribute groups over them. Her head cocked slightly at parties of big numbers indivisible by four, and she twirled with a triumphant point when faced with the perfect number to fill up a car, like a long block in tetris. The moment she spotted him, Morrigan's pout of concentration turned to an open mouthed smile. She popped up even higher onto her toes like a ballerina and staggered a step. She almost looked like she'd just walked unwittingly into her own surprise birthday party, or had run into a good friend somewhere. All his sickening trepidation vanished that instant and the leash on his smile was cut. Morrigan nearly tripped as she flopped back down onto her heels, and her hair was thrown in front of her face. When she looked up, hooking her hair back with her ring-finger and pinning it behind her ear, she blinked wide eyes wearing a face so cute he felt nausea all over again. Hollowly he felt a pang of jealousy for the kind of man who could date a girl like her. The boyfriend's job of making her happy paid a high wage with that smile.

When Simon got to the front of the line, Morrigan *did* act like she didn't know him, but it was playful. She spoke in a musical kind of cursive, like they were both secret agents, as she asked how many were in his party. She hopped inside his personal space with her wrist clasped behind her back and her chest thrust forward with a posture that was cartoonishly perky. She cocked her ear towards him, inviting herself another two inches closer to him to hear something she already knew. Morrigan got so close her scent cut through the heavy odor of bromine treated water. She had on this perfume only *she* could like. It smelled like a dozen different dollar-store air fresheners, and despite how nervous she made him with her nearness, her silly perfume let Simon laugh along with her whimsy. When she directed him to his seat, she touched him. She pressed herself close, and laid a hand on his back. Having been starved of physical contact of an affectionate nature for so long, Simon was stunned by how sharply it could make him feel better about himself. Morrigan leaned in so close he could smell past her perfume too, to the pure scent of her skin. She brought her cheek close to his, brushing him with her soft hair. She pointed to a row and instead of telling him which number row to sit in, she told him that he was sweet. She said it in a voice only meant for him. She thanked him, told him how he'd made her whole day by stopping by.

She turned to him with a snap of her neck, asking if he saw where to go, as a curtain of hair slipped free from behind her ear and brushed against his lips. She could have kissed him then. If she'd been a song, that would have been the next note. Behind that curtain of hair she could have given him a peck on the cheek and only the two of them would have known. She didn't. She just sucked in a breath and slid her hand from his back to direct another customer.

His heart was beating so hard when he sat down that he hid his hands so she wouldn't see them pulsing with his heart. When they went down the big drop Simon didn't even flinch. In the aftershock of her warm reception nothing seemed so intense.

Simon reasoned that he'd been the collateral damage of her excitement, an unintended beneficiary, like a gay kid in the locker room. A whisper in the ear can communicate gossip, threats and secrets. It was no fault of hers that Simon's mind was inclined to imagine a connotation that she couldn't have meant to attach.

When he got off, he looked across at her and Morrigan made the effort to wink at him. Simon went up the single rider line and went on twice again before Morrigan swapped with someone to talk to him. Every time he went on the ride Simon risked getting soaked, and every time he escaped dry Morrigan gave a little fist pump of celebration. When he did get wet, she mournfully suggested Thunder Mountain next door. Morrigan didn't understand that he would have kept riding in a blizzard so long as she was happy to have him around. He rode until he was soaked and left to buy a Briar Rabbit sweatshirt and Cowboy Mickey pajama pants so he could come back dry. It made her laugh when she saw him and she told him it was sweet of him to keep her company.

At the end of the day, after the sun had gone down and cool night air began to settle over guests, few sought out the water ride. As they often did, management re-allocated staff to other areas of the park. Thus, Simon and Morrigan were left alone. Without the interruptions of guests getting on and off the ride, their conversation was given much more time and they both found it hard to fill the silence. Every thought had all the time it needed to be expressed, and it had the effect of making ideas seem somewhat exposed. Without the regular suspending of their conversation from her tending to her responsibilities, there was no natural opportunity to gather thoughts unless Simon could trigger a tangent from her. She was too polite to dominate the conversation, however. Morrigan was under the impression that what Simon was saying was important and interesting and she would patiently wait for Simon to finish his sentences, even over long pauses. This led to Simon discussing all sorts of emotions and reflections that didn't even seem real since he'd never voiced them aloud before. Simon found himself constantly wondering if he sounded stupid without the shield of careful consideration before each burst of conversation.

He was so used to editing every statement that he was plagued by a bizarre worry that his thoughts might be somehow *incorrect*. She asked for his thoughts on things he'd never spent time thinking about, and so he formulated his thoughts right in front of her, discovering them in the air between them, alongside Morrigan. He wondered if his ideas would be different if he were given time to ruminate on them alone. He wondered if those different ideas would be more true to who he was. The people who knew him back in New York would probably think so. Still, when Morrigan said '*Simon*', she said it like she knew him, and he believed her.

To make matters worse, without customers to divert their attentions they had no excuse not to look at each other. For the last few hours of her shift they ended up sitting on the floor by the start console, talking face to face. It was achingly intimate and it tortured Simon that she was just *some girl*. Morrigan's eyes were the same dark brown they'd always been but, then, somehow more piercing than the palest icy blue. She'd lamented to him once that she didn't have the faintest starburst of hazel in her eyes, that they were boring. If he'd been brave enough to be honest, he'd have admitted that *instant* that they didn't need even a hint of emerald to burn like gemstones.

It was probably in the way they watched him. Those big brown eyes had a brightness lit by this curiosity, too eager to wait for words. He couldn't remember anyone looking at him like she did. Not even on a first date had anyone been so discerning. It felt equal parts exhilarating and stressful to be seen by eyes unashamed to stare. Simon wished she saw something worthwhile in him, but he just couldn't imagine what.

At the end of that day, when she said goodbye, she reiterated in this achingly cute soft voice how happy he'd made her by coming. She said it with overwhelming sincerity, without veiling it in any kind of joke, and he could only respond by blushing. Then she went in for a bizarrely angled high-five like some rapper from the 90s. It was goofy and a perfect knife for the tension. She used it like a surgeon to make him laugh, even throwing out a matching low-five with her other hand. It was such a weird angle it almost looked like a hug.

***

On Thursday she was back to Space Mountain. Something had put Morrigan in a good mood and she was extra bubbly, even going so far as to accidentally touch Simon on several occasions. She'd gesture broadly and let her forearm gingerly bump his shoulder, or she might lay a hand on his back as she passed behind him and, to her, they would be inconsequential, innocent accidents. They were moments she was achingly oblivious to. Every time she did it, every time she touched him even lightly, his skin felt her touch like his eyes saw bright white sparks. That sensation lingered for a while, like a warm handprint on bedsheets. He could feel that phantom of her touch after every reckless graze.

Her smile was obscenely pretty when she was happy. It bewildered him that people could walk by without staring at it. One man, impossibly ignorant to this fact, yelled at her for more than a minute about how the seats on the ride were too small and too low to the ground. He asked angrily if she knew that he'd gotten a cramp in his leg, and hurt his knee, and the man demanded that they put up a sign warning people of the danger of hurt knees and cramped legs. She was immediately flustered, as if she'd tripped on her good mood. Her words came out misordered and she fished around in several pockets searching for her extra Fast-Passes. Once he realized his ability to dominate the conversation he didn't let go of it. The man repeated himself, making circular points until he was out of breath and then stormed off. He didn't want excuses, or apologies, or even free stuff. Making a twenty-something squirm was his compensation for sore knees and a cramped leg.

When he left, Morrigan sighed a shaky adrenaline shocked sigh, and Simon let out a one word impression of Donald Duck. It was so perfect, it surprised even Simon. Morrigan's good mood rushed back to her and she smiled so bright her cheeks pressed her eyes into a squint.

She was so pretty it made Simon want to be *anyone* else. A singer in a metal band, someone who went to highschool with her, a neighbor, anyone who knew her well enough to even know her last name. But he wasn't any of these things. He wasn't anyone she'd ever consider dating. He was just *some guy.*

Morrigan wasn't shy like he was. If she'd wanted him to be part of her life, her real life, and more than a pleasant distraction to help her get through the day, she would have done something about it. Whatever her conclusions from her rabid curiosity the day before, she hadn't decided to ask him to hang out when she wasn't working. She had a whole existence outside of work that he wasn't welcome to be a part of. For all he knew her good mood was born of a first date that had gone well.

The uncertainty of it made him want to run far from her, but Morrigan wasn't an easy person to give up on. Every day they spent together Simon felt this addictive sense of progress. He was either discovering the depths of his delusions or...

He paused, too embarrassed to even think it, and watched Morrigan high-five a triumphant kid; just old enough to ride and still dizzy.

Hey Morrigan? You're really the best part of this vacation. I don't wanna stop hanging out with you when the park closes. We should go to some shitty diner and just talk, until you've gotta be an adult and go sleep. Also, full disclosure, I should let you know your smile is incredibly pretty today. I hope that's not weird to say, but it just feels dishonest not to tell you that I'm hoping you'll call it a... date.

She was so welcoming he could almost say it. Even a 'no' would let him escape from the pressure of these feelings, but it wasn't fair for him to ask that of her. She was too nice not to have her day ruined by rejecting him, and she was having far too nice a day for him to do that to her.

Though he *did* want to, Simon didn't tell her how pretty that smile was. Shamefully, it didn't take an enormous force of will for Simon to choose innaction.

Simon left to get lunch early, so he could decompress. He didn't get back until she was on her own lunch break. By the time he saw her again the blazing glee in her had cooled to pleasant embers.

Later in the day there was a lull in the action after someone held something over their head on the ride and set off a safety sensor, so they needed to run several test rides with no passengers to verify it was just a false alarm. While they waited Morrigan asked, absent-mindedly, for his opinion on her posture. She mused aloud whether he imagined it contributed to her back hurting after standing for much of the day. Receiving an answer of no particular expertise she grew silent, lost in quiet ponderings. Not wishing to intrude on some emerging thought, he waited a moment before responding and while he did, he couldn't help but examine the posture in question. He'd meant to be objective when he did, but Morrigan's silhouette drew the eye to more than the straightness of her back. He couldn't deny, to even himself, the physical component of his attraction to her.

With lust came this scolding shame, but before he could look away he was trapped. She leaned her head back and stretched, vocalizing the relief in her muscles with a muted closed-mouth moan. Simon felt all the helplessness of a sailor being led into the rocks by siren song, as he watched what he was sure was nothing more than the most casual gesture take hold over him like it was Aphrodite walking out of the sea. She reached with her arms, gingerly crossing her wrists above her head and gently arched her back completing an enrapturing contortion. The backward position of her arms thrust her chest forward, straining her clothing against her. The normally formless uniform was pulled taut against her body and her breasts were given a precise outline made vulgar by her proportions. As the stretch reached it's apex, she rolled her shoulders back trembling subtly with the strain, rose up on the balls of her feet and twisted her chest towards him to crack her back, straining her shirt like she were wringing water out of it. For that second, there were no secrets kept by her shirt. Every detail burned into Simon's retinas. Her bra was scandalously undersized and visibly dug into the soft flesh of her breast causing a portion to spill free on the underside; something exaggerated by the nature of the extreme pose. Simon was hypnotized beyond fear of shame.

Morrigan snapped out of the stretch, unexpectedly quick, and looked right at Simon. His eyes snapped up to meet hers, from a place they had no right to be. Her eyes were bright and excited as if a thought had just come into her head, and she was turning to share it with him. He looked away, with such a sudden jerk that his neck cracked louder than her back. It was loud enough that he knew she could hear it too. His heart started to beat like he'd been struck in the face. It felt like he'd been caught watching porn.

In desperate pursuit of nonchalance, he looked back at her, hoping she wouldn't have seen his gaze as having any purpose but to appraise her posture. Their eyes met for a moment, and she winked at him. Simon started to drown.

It had been a trap, a prank. The kind of thing one plays on a *friend.* He was supposed to get caught, laugh, roll his eyes, and make her feel good about herself. His desperate fear of being creepy was vanquished in an instant by the abyssal dread of being thought of as a silly delusional child with a crush on their babysitter.

Her lips parted, words he dreaded to hear gathering in her lungs, but someone needed assistance getting off the ride and she rushed forward to help. Simon wouldn't be there when she turned back around.

Chapter 11

Assumptions

Simon abruptly halted his anxiety powerwalk and rubbed his eyes past the bridge of his nose. The pulsing in his head made him sway slightly and he pinched his eyes shut tighter, steadying himself with a clenched jaw. *What the fuck am I doing? Am I leaving?*

He opened his eyes and stared into the three dimensional starry night created with mirrors in the ceiling above. He stared at the gleaming holographic photo rendering of the moon and wished it would plummet screaming to the earth to obliterate him.

"The longer I'm gone the more awkward it is to go back." He breathed, alone in the corridor between flows of people coming off the ride. *I can still say 'I had to go to the bathroom',* he offered himself, not at all believing he'd ever go back to see that girl. He could die never revealing to anyone that he'd let himself fall for a ride attendant. That way he'd never have to hear himself explain these feelings sounding so pathetically lonely, sad and stupid, that no one would even mock him.

A hand clapped over his upper arm, like handcuffs, and

Simon looked down sharply from the ceiling. He levelled his eyes at Morrigan, casting a baleful glance over her shoulder as she passed him without pause. He stumbled forward, being towed down the hallway.

She dragged him into a nook at the side of the hallway, by some 'cast members only' door. Morrigan turned to face him fully and, until she did, Simon thought she was angry with him for walking away.

As it always was, Morrigan's expression was so malleable to emotion and a number of them fought across her face. Frustration, gloom, exasperation and a pleading desperation pulled at her as she sighed his name with a whine that made his chest ache.

He wanted to lie and reset it all to zero, but that sigh carrying his name had stripped her of all poise. She wore her turbulent emotions openly as she searched his face, and it beat the words out of his chest.

The staff door began to open and Morrigan did a great impression of a girl who was fine. "Right this way Sir, our lost and found is just through here."

Her hand came away from his arm and he watched it return to her side, thinking dimly that an employee probably wasn't supposed to grab a guest like that.

Morrigan's manager emerged with a bounce to her step that made a flail of her ponytail. Her face was full of glee and she beamed it at the two of them as she passed, pocketing a thick stack of free ice-cream coupons and set off down the ramp for a morning pick-me-up of making kids smile.

Morrigan held the door, with a smile dying off her face, and gestured him inside with her head without looking at him. When they were alone, she was still quiet for a long minute.

"I'm sorry I dragged you in here. I know it's fucking weird of me. I just had this awful feeling that if I didn't go after you, I'd never see you again."

Morrigan's face without any happiness was overwhelming and Simon was woefully unprepared to meet those eyes. He looked down, guilty. "I'm sorry. I should have said something. I just- I felt weird and- and I... I just wasn't thinking."

Her eyes stayed sad and her lips silent, but all the rest of her face was fraught with conflict over words he was afraid to hear. The two of them were flung out into the limbo between her and those words she wanted, and Simon flinched.

"I just thought it'd be best if I just fucked off out of your life."

Again, Simon was woefully unprepared to see her so very expressive face looking so very sad. He blinked, his eyes falling from her. She let out the kind of laugh that made Simon wince.

"Am I that fucking disgusting?"

"What? *No*, that's not at all-"

"Mhm," she cut in, talking over him for the first time. "I have this friend, *had* this friend Mars? was her name. Marissa really, but Mars is more metal. God of war etcetera. So she was vegan, probably is still. I went to a show with her and it was in a warehouse. It was like this underground show. You'd think they happen a lot, but they don't. Anyway this one band?" She leaned in and whispered with none of the intimacy of the day before. "They were named *Nunslaughter*." She straightened, not lingering for even a moment. "Very edgy, you see. So to supplement their playing they decided they'd bring along some roadkill they picked up along the way. They hacked it apart with a *zweihander* –a kind of huge german sword– during one of their songs, and **boy** you have no idea how much a dead deer can bleed. It's incredible. A *living* deer having that much blood in them would have surprised me. Anyway they tossed the head out into the crowd and it hit Mars, *vegan* Mars, and then she looked at me and asked me if we could leave."

Simon wished he could swap places with that deer.

"Yeah that face she made? That's the face *you* made too."

He'd wanted to be immune from the tyranny of physicality and safe from the embarrassment of being caught checking her out. Simon had been selfish in that pursuit. Meeting the eyes of a pretty girl that felt only as pretty as a mutilated deer carcass taught him that.

The blood that had rushed into his face abandoned him, fleeing someplace else and leaving him cold and dizzy. His field of view began to narrow, blackness encroaching on his vision, making her seem so much closer –too close– and he took a step back. He shouldn't have.

"I said yes," she snapped. "I told her she could leave. Because I don't mean to torture nobody."

With a jerk he stuck his hand out to shake. "Sorry, I never meant to upset you."

Her eyes flashed with a strange fury when she looked at his hand, as though her parents had been killed in a tragic handshake accident. It startled him and he withdrew his hand an inch. Her own hand lashed out and slapped around his wrist like a handcuff, squeezing it so hard her fist trembled. She spoke to him in a dangerously low tone, through gritted teeth. "Upset? I'm not upset. I'm sad. I'm so fucking *sad*. I don't have any god damn friends, Simon. I'm a loser. I'm a sad loser. I don't talk to anyone but *you*, and *you* ditched me. You didn't say anything. You just left. So now my only..." She blinked and when her eyes opened they were uncertain. "*friend?* Has just walked out of my life forever. Upset? fuck you, *upset*." Her anger had vented out with her words like hot air and by the time she'd said what she needed to her voice was almost pleading.

Her grip was intense. If she'd told him she didn't want him to leave –if she'd said it in words– he wouldn't have believed her. He'd have dismissed the claim as something rooted in obligation but, in her grip, he could feel a bruise forming on his forearm where the skin was being pinched between fingers.

"Morrigan... I didn't realize..." He touched his hand to hers, but he didn't know how he was supposed to touch her. The firm pat of a friend? The warm clasp of a lover? He settled for the barely grazing her knuckles with the timid fingertips of a guy who had no real idea who he was to her.

The moment his skin touched hers she shrunk. Her eyes were cast down and fluttered. Her grip loosened on his wrist, and her hand fell away to swing to her side. "I'm sorry. I'm crazy, and I'm lucky you're so patient. Forget about it dude. Just uh, Have a magical... *life?* I guess."

"Wait. Listen. I- I was. I *was* checking you out." he told her, like he was reading out a suicide note. "Obviously I wasn't disgusted or anything. That sour expression I made was for myself. I've never wanted to be the kind of weirdo who ogles their friend's boobs."

She winced at the words, nodding concession. Her mouth opened and the words weren't there right away. She needed time to find them. They were alone in the dim corridor but still she spoke softly; softer than even the quiet intensity of before. This time it was a gentle kind of quiet that seemed so much more important to hear, and so much more uncertain. "You're right. It was weird to impose on you to- I mean... I shouldn't have been fishing for compliments at the expense of your dignity. I'm sorry dude. You've been... a really cool... um, *friend* to me, and I really appreciate it."

The emphasis on *friend* hit him like a gut-punch. It was emphasized like 'this word, and not any other'.

In his silence she floundered, struggling to make it all make sense outside her head. "You came to Splash Mountain and got soaked all day and you didn't have to and it was really... *cute.*"

Cute. Like a kid with a crush on a teacher.

She could see a result she wasn't looking for on his face. Blinking, she searched for more things to say to fix it. "I'm sorry. I'm out of my mind. You enjoy your vacation. I have no right to tell you how to spend your vacation. I guess that's it. I just... thanks for being cool and stuff. And- and also thanks for showing me that people like you exist, because..."

"Thank you." Though he didn't feel much like talking he knew she needed him to say something. She'd gone out on a limb with her feelings, even if they weren't the kind he wanted to hear. It wouldn't have been right to leave her hanging. "I'm really glad you enjoy my company. I like being around you too. You make my day better, a lot better. You're really funny and uh... it's nice to laugh."

The words made him feel hollow. They were too easy to say. All of them were small confessions that were no longer meant to build up to a greater one. They felt meaningless –weightless– but her reaction showed that she needed to hear them. She smiled, happy to have a new... *friend.*

Morrigan's eyelids fluttered, shifting her gaze to the hand he'd held out for a handshake. She cast his hand away with a force that jerked his shoulder and turned him an inch. Her voice was small and vulgarly cute. "You *hug* girls, dumb ass."

"Oh." His hands were so heavy, he could hardly lift them. Accepting a hug as a friend was too much. He knew it wouldn't be good for him but he raised his arms anyway. He was at least *something,* he reminded himself.

She hugged him and he felt sick. Her arms wrapped about him too gently, her hair touched his face, and her breasts *existed.* This hug was meant to be enjoyed by someone else, someone who could make her smile brighter than he could. His imagination drowned him with the things he'd never have. A walk alone with her, lit only by starlight and her smile with her clinging to him for warmth against cool night air. The freedom to sigh soft words of unrestrained affection and have them embraced by a smile all his own, burning with excitement.

He must've been bad at hiding his discomfort because she pulled away after just a moment. She thanked him for the hug but her face was far too expressive to let her be a good liar.

He'd wanted to give up, to leave and forget he ever met her, to save himself the embarrassment and heartbreak of rejection. But sad and lonely decisions are easy to make while sad and alone. It was a different thing to be around her, inside that corona of *Morrigan* that radiated from her. It was where the first puff of breath before she laughed was, where her feet tapping to some song he'd never heard pulsed gently in the soles of his feet, where her attention would snap to a sentence he'd falter on starting. It was where she could see a frown and ask after it, where he could be heard by someone who cared. But then it was also in that aura of hers that her hand hung, unheld. It was where she'd rest her head on the wall and not his shoulder when she was tired. It was where she frowned because she'd wanted a real hug.

He acted with an instinct like catching a glass before it falls to the ground, considering no other options for fear of the lethargy of overthinking, and reached for her. In that moment he did exactly what he dreaded doing. He grabbed hold of Morrigan and pulled her into an embrace, a real one. He held her like the girlfriend that she was not. His body was too honest, giving Morrigan every bit of the warm affection pent up within him. The same affection his ex had always been overwhelmed by. But this girl felt so different in his arms. Morrigan didn't lurch from his grip.

Morrigan softened against him. She went limp in his arms, her cheek laying heavily against his breast, and let out a wavering sigh into his shirt with her limited breath. He had to hold her tightly to keep her from slipping to the floor and she didn't seem concerned at all. Her trust was absolute. She curled, bringing her hands in front of her chest, within his embrace. She was still, save for the gentle trembling of waning adrenaline.

He felt like a weasel. A guy who's been rejected, who tries to force his way forward, offering hugs that a real friend wouldn't. Enjoying them like a friend doesn't. He'd taken advantage of their friendship. He'd taken advantage of *her,* but she didn't seem to see it that way.

"Where was this hug earlier? you *fuck.*" she whimpered with a sniffle.

He couldn't speak, not without exposing his tumultuous emotions. Morrigan animated her arms, sliding them out from between them and wrapping them around him. She squeezed him, pressing herself against his chest for a moment before letting go. She pulled away not even an arm's length, and looked up at him.

He looked down at a girl who was just a friend. She was made short by their proximity. The sight of her was inseparable now from the feeling of her body sweetening to his touch. "Thank you, Simon."

She said his name in a voice as tender as she'd been in his arms. It was the kind of sound that was more like an explosion. One felt it before they heard it. Simon knew it wouldn't be healthy to try to be friends with a girl who could make a sound like that, but the truth wasn't very persuasive.

She grinned up at him and touched his face. "You're so red you look like you've got a fever."

He recoiled, flinching at the comment, trying to muster an explanation that didn't involve explaining that she was the prettiest girl he'd ever seen.

"You're such an awkward duck, Simon," she sighed. "And you'd put all that blood in your face just to make me feel better. It makes that hug extra sweet."

Her smile was small and weak, her eyes distant and half

lidded. No girl, not even a friend, wanted their body to feel like a burden in someone's arms. He knew he should come clean and tell her how much he enjoyed the hug. He knew he should apologize for taking advantage and politely reject her thanks, but the way she'd said his name kept his mouth shut. She had said his name like he was this very particular person. She said this word, *his* word with an intoxicating fondness, like it had been a part of thoughts he was not a party to. When she said *Simon,* that was who he wanted to be and not the creep the truth would make him.

It was too hard to tell her the extent of how he felt, and risk not belonging to that very particular word. She wouldn't stand nearly so near and she would assign him to a new word, spelled like Simon, but spoken terribly different.

She realized she'd been holding her hand to his cheek for too long and withdrew it like his face had burned her. She coughed an apology and got far away from him.

Morrigan left him in the hallway listening to ambient space music for a minute or so before returning with a beige baseball cap. "Here," she said, slapping the thing against his stomach, averting her eyes. "You lost that. No one's coming back for it."

The hat had some kind of electric bird, a caterpillar made out of rocks, and a purple butterfly on it. In the back it was tightened not by plastic snaps or velcro but this odd brass clasp and cloth strip. It was a bizarre thing and he couldn't imagine anyone believing it was his.

"Come on. We'd better get going before my manager thinks we're off fucking in the back or something."

She walked off, mercifully turning her back to him as his face flushed red. She sighed, grumbling something unintelligible to herself, two steps out of earshot. Even without meaning to the words, she always spoke with a certain rhythm, and Simon had gotten very acquainted with it. He'd come to know her lexicon well and whenever something loud would eclipse her words, he found it very easy to patch the sentence. So when Morrigan shoved the slam-bar, opening the door, and grunted the end of her mumbled sentence with a "shhh", the whole sentence constructed itself in Simon's head.

"I   fucking   *wish.*"

The dent in his heart popped back out. The word *'friend'* suddenly lost all finality.

He realized in that moment that it was unreasonably greedy to expect to know a person's feelings, and be safe from the uncertainty of *not* knowing. How could *she* even know her own feelings? He himself had struggled for several days to come around to admitting it to even himself. Simon surrendered himself to the peaceful resolution to not know. She'd said they were friends, and they were. She never said they could never be anything more. So long as there was no one else, he could wait to see if feelings developed naturally. Morrigan was so confident, he had no doubt she would tell him the moment she felt anything, and she didn't seem the type to hide a secret boyfriend. In the end, if he was going to be rejected, he could handle getting hit unawares by it like a speeding train. Morrigan was worth it.

***

As the day carried on Morrigan became increasingly contemplative over some thought she didn't share. Simon watched it's shadow cause her to grow silent for long stretches as she grappled with it. He was reminded of the reality of the space between them. He was just a guest at an amusement park and she was an employee. She had a whole life that existed without Simon. She neglected to answer him directly when he asked Morrigan what was on her mind and it felt intrusive to pry into her personal life. She didn't need to humor him to *that* extreme.

"Looks like the park is closing soon." He remarked late that day. "I guess you're gonna finish this line and shut her down?"

"Yeah," she said with a shrug that made him glance down.

"I, uh, should let you do your job. Probably a good idea to get out of here before the parade starts."

"Oh um, I mean..." She swallowed and then cleared her throat. "Well actually I have the golf-cart today if you wanted to grab a ride back. You know, if you didn't wanna walk and don't mind waiting up for me. I just need to finish up the line and do a quick sweep for lost stuff and whatever."

Simon was lonely enough to recognize like. "Sure, I'd love to keep you company if you'll have me. We probably won't see too much of each other with Memorial day weekend starting tomorrow."

Chapter 12

Utilidors

It all starts with hey. You can say anything after hey.

The guy sat beside her in silence, the perfect silence into which a 'hey' could be inserted. And yet, the tunnels were quiet, save for the gentle hum of the golf-cart's electric motor. Wasting time with him on silence killed her. She knew she'd miss it later, in bed, when she didn't have a Simon to listen.

Talking was so easy with him. With other people she had to pick and choose only the most interesting things, to hold their ever decaying attention. But Simon? Simon was inexhaustible. He afforded her this freedom where she could just tell him anything that she thought of. It never felt like she was bothering him with a story, no matter how longwinded. He'd even keep track of where she left off when Morrigan departed on a tangent. There was always something to talk about with him, and that was exactly why she couldn't talk to him. She knew if she started talking it would be too easy for her to escape from the question again.

Ten miles an hour never felt so fast.

There was never enough time for her to bring it up. She'd had hours with Simon but no amount of time would make her any braver. There was this chasm in their conversation. No matter how close she brought the conversation to the edge, it always seemed impossible to take that last leap. She'd moaned about living alone, about being hungry after work, about having nothing to do on her day off, but it was so hard to just ask the question. She wished Simon would do the guy thing and ask instead. But that just would have been so unlike the Simon she'd come to know.

He was gentle, even with his words. Whenever he added anything to a discussion he always circled back to her last words so as to be sure he didn't steer the conversation. It was wonderful, and so different, but part of her knew it'd be easier for her if he'd just take control. He could have asked her out days ago and she would have agreed but he couldn't know that, and it seemed like such a bold assumption for the guy. Asking out an employee while they're working was an aggressive move and of the many qualities she enjoyed about him, aggression was not one of them. No, she had to approach.

She sighed, and she knew he noticed, but he didn't ask. He paid attention to her like no one else. Conversations with him felt strange, like there was this extra person in them that mattered. She knew he wanted to know what was on her mind because he'd asked earlier, but she'd already dodged the question and he was too polite – too *gentle*– to pry. It was frustrating that a trait she admired in him made this whole process impossible. Despite being degrading, a confident approach would at least bring her to the precipice where all she had to brave was one word: 'sure'.

Besides, there was no topic of conversation that could provide an easy lead in. She had to come out and put herself on the edge of the cliff with her first words, or she'd chicken out and steer the conversation someplace else like she had every other time she'd approached the runway. Half measures wouldn't do either. When she'd gone for a non-committal one armed hug, Simon had seen it as some kind of weird Nu Metal high-five.

Of course, the question itself was terrifying. So, as she drove them down the long empty tunnel, the only sound piercing the silence was the soft hum of the Golf cart's electric battery. She didn't even look at him in case it would invite conversation for her to neglect her mission with.

Even without actually looking at him, her third eye reminded Morrigan how far out of her league he was. Longish soft blonde hair, always swept back. Bright and attentive blue eyes, soft lips that yielded easily to a smile, a strong action hero jaw that was so woefully out of place on such a delicate looking face.

He's too handsome. He acts all sweet but he knows it. He laughed when I went in for that one armed hug that night on Splash Mountain. He fucking high fived me. Maybe he's not an idiot. Maybe it was actually hilarious that I would think someone like him would want to hold me.

Like doubts had needled into her thoughts, so did the memory of their last hug. The first had been a joke, the second he'd stiffened like she'd wet her pants, but the third had been so... *confusing*. Simon hugged her like she wished a boyfriend would. He held her like he wouldn't ever stop, like he didn't want to. He wasn't in a rush to do anything else to her. He just wrapped her in this stillness that quieted the screaming panic in her brain like he'd grabbed a tuning fork.

So I have no fucking idea whether he's got a thing for me or not. Who gives a shit? That's what words are for, dammit. I'll just fucking ask.

Preparing for battle Morrigan reached up to give her cheeks a smack but stopped herself before she could appear to be convincingly mentally disabled. Like the very avatar of smooth she re-routed her left hand to steer from the top of the wheel like a cool dude out cruisin' and transitioned her other hand into fixing her already fixed hair and then followed up with a small composed scratch/shake-out of her hair just in case he noticed that her hair didn't need fixing. She felt like a super spy.

"Are we making a stop in fantasy land?"

Fuck!

Morrigan's eyes opened wide and her mouth hung open as her mind ran through dozens of excuses while simultaneously debating vigorously whether she should just tell the truth and seem like a ditz or lie to him.

Simon began to giggle and he put a ginger hand on her shoulder. Like a blind man's other senses became more acute Morrigan's body ignored every nerve but those where his hand touched her. "It's okay. I've been there too. You just zone out while driving and you end up wherever."

Was I making a funny face? Was it cute? She bit her lip with a little smile to show she was a good sport and started the loud beeping K-turn that would alert anyone in nearby tunnels to her screw-up.

He removed his hand from her shoulder and she was immediately cast into a pit of wondering why. She'd raised her shoulder ever so slightly into his hand. Had he thought she was shrugging him off? Was he simply moving it so she could focus on the turn? Did she wipe her nose on her shoulder and now his hand is covered in mucous? Is her shoulder 'weird', somehow, and he can feel it through the shirt?

Where logic could provide her no answer, emotion stepped in. The answer was obvious. He took his hand away because guys like him don't want to be seen with girls like her. People might assume he'd gotten her pregnant and was stuck with her.

Morrigan stopped at yet another intersection and honked the horn twice for safety, according to protocol. However, this time, Morrigan honked by punching the steering wheel. Hard.

"Hey, are you okay?"

His tone was calm and full of genuine concern but Morrigan jolted with alarm all the same. She'd been so deep in her brooding she'd forgotten there was another human sitting next to her. She adjusted her posture and demeanor as casually as she could. She needed to be composed.

If I'm going to be lost in thought, I should look like I'm elegantly squinting at some distant horizon, not hunched over the steering wheel like a brooding troll.

"I'm sorry I laughed at you before." Simon shoved into the silence.

She felt a hesitant hand graze her back, unsure whether it could touch her.

"Oh! no! It's totally fine! It was funny. Really!"

"Oh I didn't mean to say you don't have a sense of humor or anything."

"No, I know! I just..."

Morrigan took another wrong turn. She needed more time.

Simon's hand finally landed for a stiff pat on her back. It landed high on her back, sexual harassment training video high, with stiff fingers so afraid to rest on her they curved back slightly.

"Hey, I know it's not really my place to ask, but I think I might know you enough to know something must be bothering you. You're really quiet and you're holding the steering wheel like you're trying to choke it to death. If you want to talk about whatever it is, then I'd be really honored to listen."

"*Simon...*"

"I'm sorry to pry. I just wanted to make the offer. I know I'm just like some dude or whatever but... y'know."

"That's really sweet," she heard herself say. *You're really sweet*, she wished she'd say.

"Also if I'm causing you problems by hanging out while you work I can go to another ride. I don't want to get you-"

"No! I-it's not that."

Say something. You're never gonna have a better excuse to. If you don't, you'll be telling him to fuck off about your feelings and mind his own business. Just tell him. He asked, didn't he?-Just put yourself on the edge of the cliff and let momentum say it. Just start the sentence. Hey so. Hey so. Hey so. Hey so. Hey so.

She held her breath chanting it until finally she exhaled: "Hey so...;"

She inhaled, swallowed, and then ran out of reasons not to finish the sentence. "About my whole stretching thing..."

She'd fallen off the edge of the cliff, onto another cliff. Her mind was blank of all things, but she was determined to think furiously until she could force the thoughts to come back.

"Like uh..." She stubbornly reserved her place as the speaker in the conversation in case she could figure a way of fixing it because she couldn't answer *how* but she knew she *had* messed everything up by opening her mouth.

Simon was concerned. She couldn't look at him but she could feel undeserved sympathy radiating from him. *Sean was right. I **am** needy.*

When she spoke again she did it forcefully, to banish anything he might be about to say. "I mean before when I stretched, and you said uh... what you said, well I was just wondering if you..." *wanna go out with me. If you liked what you saw, enough to go out with me. If you...*

Morrigan stopped the golf cart, squeezed her eyes shut, remembered to breathe, and ignored the many things she should say, echoing in her head. "I'm sorry. I shouldn't ever talk."

She couldn't look at him, but in that quiet tunnel she heard his mouth open, and his throat choke on silence. Morrigan flinched inwardly for that excruciatingly long second before he spoke. "I... I never meant to... make you uncomfortable. What I was saying before... I just meant that sometimes being around you can be kind of... overwhelming."

The air got lighter as Morrigan breathed it in. *Overwhelming.* that cool wind of pride swelled her breast. *All this time I've been so nervous and he's been just as-*

"Just objectively, you know? You really are just a *very* attractive girl."

That same air sunk in her. *Objectively.*

"I guess I haven't known you long enough for it to fade into the background. I only meant to explain the effect your appearance had on me, because I thought I'd adversely affected your self esteem by avoiding discussing it. I didn't mean to imply any kind of... uh, *weird* intentions."

Morrigan's lips pursed, sealing against the threat of releasing any of her own *weird* intentions.

"Obviously physicality is not all I care about. I really value the time I get to spend with you and that has nothing to do with appearance. I've been really lucky to have been able to get to know you like I have."

*No amount of hotness, not even an **overwhelming** amount, can compensate for the very core of my personality. He's gotten to know me, and he even thinks I'm attractive. Still he couldn't imagine, in*

his wildest dreams, going places with me on his arm. He couldn't
trust me to say the right thing to cheer him up on a shitty day.
Maybe he thinks I'm a slut that'd cheat.

"Morrigan? Am I making any sense?"

She glanced sideways at him, and started driving again.
"Yeah, so basically you're just like every guy trying to fuck me who
wouldn't date me, you're just too nice to fuck me."

It left her lips more aggressive than passive, and when she
heard it sound so sharp she wished she could take it back, trade it for
another set of words that would make him like her and go out on a
date with her.

"Morrigan, I don't think of you like..."

He didn't finish, not for the entire length of the tunnels.
Whether it was because he was hurt or angry, he saw no salvation in
saying anything more and whatever Simon had *not* said stirred black
thoughts in him. He got lost in a head full of them, and a sweltering
silence spread between them. Morrigan instinctively wanted to ask:
'What's wrong?' but she was *so* sure he would answer her: 'You.'

It might have alleviated some tension for Morrigan to say
anything, to steer the conversation someplace simpler but she'd
planned out such a rigid path to the question, each word leading into
the next that, having been stopped dead by his answer, she felt lost
in the forest. Her mind was robbed of all paths but 'Sorry for making
it weird' and 'You sure you don't wanna go on a date? just to see?'
But those wouldn't do. Morrigan wanted so badly to remove the
crushing certainty and go back to being harmlessly hopeful. So
instead of just asking the question, any question, she adopted an
enhanced silence. She threw on an air as though driving took every
ounce of her concentration; leaning over to look at signs and reading
the dashboard dials as though this golf-cart was some advanced
space-ship. It made her feel fortified against marauding 'no' and 'ew'
adjacent words.

Where conversation had once been so hard to restrain, there was a palpable nothing.

Morrigan had listened to the end of the tape, past the afterword and the acknowledgements and the comments from the reader, and now she was alone with nothing to keep her company but the speaker-static a girl hears when she's not invited to the ever after.

When they got to the parking-lot, it was time to get off the cart and walk.

"I'm pretty tired." Morrigan lied to explain her slumped shoulders and drooping eyelids. "I think I'm gonna head straight to bed tonight and uh... sleep."

Morrigan didn't look at him as she spoke because she'd noticed that Simon was the kind of guy to look at her face like it was a window into her head. He was always looking *so intently* through it. Like what he saw on the other side mattered. *He's nice enough that he might feel bad, but he shouldn't. It's not **his** fault that **I'm** delusional.*

"Oh uhhh, yeah, sounds like a good idea." *(A much better idea than embarrassing yourself by asking me out)* "And hey, I hope you feel better, about whatever... Also um- if you, uh, get a day off soon... um... just, I mean..." *(You could spend some time away from customers so you can find a man someplace else and stop creeping on guests like me, because your flirtatious advances are highly inappropriate and creepy.)*

After the weighty silence that had already passed, every sound he made felt so hazardously close to one that'd make her cry. The few seconds of silence that followed his words were agony to endure. Some part of her *knew* a polite rejection was coming and she could feel blood rushing towards a pre-emptive blush. Some *other* part of her thought he might be about to say something unrelated, but there was no space in her mind for the possibility that he might be grappling with the same manner of fear. And while optimism and pessimism wrestled in her head, anxiety had a sword.

If Simon was ever going to finish that sentence, he would have done so with words too meek to resist being trampled by Morrigan's groaning sigh. "Yeahhhhh, anyway I'm gonna get myself gone. Bye."

"Oh al-kay." He said quicker than he meant to, "I'll-goodnight- you... later."

The pair both nodded as though Simon's Franken-sentence had made sense. They parted then, paying no mind to where they needed to go but instead focused solely on escaping the suffocating fumes of burning awkwardness that billowed between them.

Chapter 13

Serendipity

"God *dammit,*" Morrigan groaned, throwing her phone at the passenger seat. "*Everyone* fucking looks like him tonight."

Morrigan punctuated by slamming her head into the top off the steering wheel, but missed and honked the horn. Immediately, she went into a scramble to keep herself from seeming like an aggressive jack-ass in this line of cars. She was too frazzled to do the classic 'look up into the mirror' and instead turned all the way around, almost like she was backing up, in order to pin the honk on some imaginary rude driver behind her. To her dismay there *wasn't* anyone behind her.

"Morrigan?" asked a stranger from outside the passenger side window.

A profound sense of relief washed over her in that moment. She'd been rescued. The honk was easily explained by her signaling the Uber rider she was picking up.

Morrigan inhaled through her nose so sharply it was like she was being reanimated, and declared: "Yes, yes I am."

The man opened the door while she leaned over to snatch up her phone and began fiddling with the GPS. It felt awkward to look the man in the face so she busied herself with the phone for far longer than it really took to set up the navigation. She checked the route on the map and nodded thoughtfully at the list of turns she'd make and then attached the phone to her dashboard mount.

Morrigan pulled out of the pick-up que and went through the normal lines to try and earn herself a tip. "You're staying at the Continental? I hear it's very nice over there. You enjoying your stay?"

"Y-yeah."

His tone was odd, almost amused. Morrigan didn't know what she might have accidentally said to evoke the odd manner of the man's response, but a car ride conversation with a stranger is a curious kind of kung-fu, and she fell back on her most reliable technique for avoiding the crush of awkwardness: keep talking.

"Have you been going to Magic Kingdom a lot? I know you have the monorail that goes right there."

"Yeah... I've been to Magic Kingdom a *couple* times." Along with his answer Morrigan heard stifled laughter coming from the man, as though this line of questioning was somehow hilarious.

Is this motherfucker high? It's called small talk, bitch. Fuck you. I'm not saying anything dumb.

"Oh sorry, dumb question, I guess." Morrigan said with a polite laugh that was one degree away from speaking 'haha' as a word.

As Morrigan navigated a few lane changes and exits, a tense

silence choked the air.

As they slowed to a stop at a long light, there was no distraction to keep her from her head, and so she sought refuge in conversation. "I actually *work* in Magic Kingdom," Morrigan offered, desperate to shrug off thoughts of a boy gone by.

"I didn't want it to be like this, you know."

A chill coursed up her spine, goosebumps pinched at her forearms. His words were saturated with remorse, an emotion wholly out of place between strangers. Did he regret something that hadn't happened yet? Was he going to *do* something?

"Hmmm?" She knew what she'd heard, but she needed to stall. Psychopaths like to talk and if she could keep him talking long enough she could subtly reach under her seat and get to her taser.

He escalated, his voice agitated and exasperated. "Come *on* Morrigan."

He said her name so much like Simon did. It was like he was wearing his skin. Was he a park guest? Had this guy been stalking her for a long time? How many times had he passed them stealing snippets of conversation to sound like him? His impression was flawless save for that venomous irritation born of his irrational entitlement to her attention.

"You mind if I take this road? It's got a few lights but the road is well paved. The highway has a few potholes, believe it or not."

Distract him with a question. Give him the illusion of power by deferring to his opinion, she coached herself. *Keep your tone neutral, and calm. Go for it casually like you're scratching an itch.*

"Could you stop?"

"I see the light, *slowin* down. Don't worry."

He sighed, more frustrated than forelorn. Her feigned obliviousness couldn't cool his growing aggression.

"Look, I'm sorry. Would you please stop pretending like you don't know me? It really..."

Transitioning casually from scratching her calf she reached beneath the seat. Her fingers curled around her Thor's Wrath MK IV knuckle taser

"I guess I should've cancelled the ride, but I didn't realize it was you. You look really different with eyeliner on."

Her mind raced, wondering how long this man had been stalking her to have seen her wearing eyeliner. Had he seen her when she was going to a show? Was he a fan of her old band?

His voice was distorted by emotion when he spoke "Look I'll just add a stop and change the time of-"

He shoved his hand aggressively into his pocket, grasping at some weapon there; a chloroform rag, or dagger, she didn't know. She didn't have time to decipher the machinations of this violent stalker/rapist.

Stomping on the brake, Morrigan swung her fist across her chest, pivoting in the seat, putting her shoulders and abdominals into the strike. Surprising even Morrigan, her fist landed square in the rapist's jugular with a crunch followed by a rasping whimper. There was so much force behind the blow that the man fell back, rebounding off the seat. As he came forward Morrigan pinned him back with her forearm and twisted against the insisting of her seatbelt, raising a left fist crackling with the wrath of a thunder god.

Then, she froze. Not for lack of conviction but now, that she actually *looked* at the man in her car, she saw it was no rapist. In the crackling blue light was a *very* surprised and hurt-

"Simon!?" Morrigan gasped with such a sharp intake that the word came out as a loud squeak, like a reverse whistle. "Oh my god!"

A car, oblivious to the aggravated assault going on ahead of them, honked for Morrigan to go with the green light.

"Are you okay?!" She squeaked like an embaressed wind-chime, clapping both her hands over her mouth.

Clutching his throat, Simon's look of shock and horror melted as he looked at his attacker's face. He started to laugh, an endeavor which is not recommended to those who have just been hammer-fisted in the throat.

"Oh my *god* Simon, I'm so-" a long honk cut her off and she snapped her attention ahead and then back to Simon.

He wheezed in a breath and Morrigan put the car into park running her fingers through her hair. "Oh *Simon*, I'm so sorry I-I'm-"

Another honk and a pick-up a few cars back swerved out of line and drove past with a rumbling engine.

"Are you okay!?" she asked again, her voice locked into a cartoon-barbie-like tone.

"No." he croaked with something of a grin.

"It was an accident! I'm so sorry! I thought you were gonna rape me or something!" Morrigan was clutching her head so tightly the tazer-knuckles began to crackle again and the proximity to her ear frightened her. She swung her hands away from her head and smacked them down into her lap. She delivered a shock to the sensitive skin of her thigh and swore so severely her voice stopped being so high-pitched.

Simon reached forward and hit the hazard light, wheezing a

laugh past his injured throat. Angry cars roared past, each one glaring down at an apologetic Morrigan, clutching her inner-thigh.

The light turned red again and Morrigan pulled the knuckles off of her hand before thumping her forehead on the steering wheel. Her hair falling over her face, forming a protective curtain.

A hand, embolden by an ice-breaking throat punch, reached over and swepted Morrigan's hair past her ear in just such an imperfect manner that when she cast a sideways glance at the intruder upon her bubble of self-hate a lock of soft black hair swung itself down, eclipsing her sight. She fixed it with an instinctive jerk and grazed his hand as he withdrew it. She met his eyes then, for longer than she'd ever braved. They were overwhelming; *so* blue and full of a compassion she was uncomfortable receiving, as though she were impersonating someone who deserved it. With his other hand he still clutched his throat and yet somehow he found it in himself to give her a sympathetic wince, empathizing with her embarrassment.

She wanted to ask him how he could still care. But she couldn't. What if that was the tap that shattered him, made him realize he shouldn't, made him realize he *didn't.*

His eyes were glassy with the wetness that came with being hit and they trapped light in them. The ruby of taillights streaked across, while the amber of turn signals flashed, and the emerald LEDs of her aftermarket disk changer oscillated, but the sapphire – the blue of his eyes– was never so distracted. His attention was locked on her.

Headlights from a turning car flooded her vision and Morrigan turned her attention back to the road.

"Are *you* okay?" He rasped.

She nodded, pursing her lips.

The light turned green and Simon silently turned off the hazards. She drove forward with some extra speed to make up for the last light and nearly T-boned someone sneaking in one last left. Morrigan swore enough, in one breath, to get fired from Disney.

Her heart pounded an unpleasant rhythm against her ribs that made her chest sore. She wanted to wake from this horrible dream and curl up in her bed, in the morning before today and do it all again better. She didn't want to have hit Simon like a psycho, or be heard swearing like she was classless. She didn't even want to be driving. She wanted to pull over and cry in private.

Simon was trying to talk, but he was making this awful noise with his throat that made her scared to look at him again, as if it'd suddenly be caved in or crumpled or something."I'm sorry." She repeated without crying.

Simon's hand landed lightly on her shoulder. His touch was gentle and full of hesitation, like a kid going over a friend's house for the first time. She felt no presumption of a right to touch her, just an urgency of concern that couldn't wait for his throat. She felt like a cool breeze coursing through the torn knees of black jeans sat up high on a hilltop while fourth of july explodes overhead.

She wanted to reassure him of his touch being welcome by pressing against it like a cat, but instead she just shrugged him off. She missed its weight the instant it was gone.

"Are you alright?" He asked again, with more concern for her than she had a right to receive from anyone who'd been punched in the neck by her a few minutes prior.

"Fuck *that*." She said with a start. "Are *you* okay?" She asked snapping a few glances at him from the road.

She tried to pull the same move: put a hand on *his* shoulder to comfort *him*, but she'd been clutching the steering wheel so tight her hands were fused there.

"Hey I'd rather get punched in the throat than go through the embarrassment of assaulting someone and then pulling out some bat-girl electric knuckles on them."

He's fucking indestructable. I couldn't fuck this up if I tried.

She smiled a tiny sort of smile and attempted to blink back the wetness of her eyes.

"So are those tears for me or for your zap?"

It was enough to get some teeth out of her smile and she began wiping her eyes, now that he'd already noticed.

"They're all for *you*," she declared softly, wiping the tears off and drying her hands on Simon's shirt, like a towel, secretly enjoying the excuse to finally put her hands on the man.

When Morrigan began rounding the drop-off circle, she did so far more slowly than she needed to. It was completely empty at this hour. There was nothing to avoid but the end of the drive. She felt like she was pulling into station after a roller coaster she'd been waiting on line for and hour to ride, but she'd fallen asleep for the whole thing. She wanted to talk to Simon. She wanted to spend time with him until their last conversation stopped haunting her, like writing over a CD.

"Hey don't tip me," Morrigan said suddenly, as she eased onto the brakes. "You're really nice and I bet you would, but don't. I know you and it'd be weird to, like, have you be pressured to give me a tip."

They rocked forward gently, coming to a stop, and Morrigan looked at him as she shifted into park. Simon bit his lip. Guilty.

"Besides, I punched you in the throat. I should, like, tip *you*." Morrigan smothered her face with her hands again. "Not like that. I didn't mean to make you sound like a gimp."

"A what?"

"Like a guy with the zipper for his mouth and the leather and-" She dropped her hands away and looked at Simon with a tired smirk. "Nevermind."

"You know, I *was* wondering how people got 'thumbs down' ratings."

Morrigan rolled her eyes with the faintest shadow of a smile. "Yeah, they all punch their rider in the throat."

Simon's hand was on Morrigan's shoulder again and he pinched the muscle there, kneading exactly the spot she held her tension. Her eyes shot open and she blinked at him.

"Morrigan, you *have* to stop feeling bad about it." He said gently. "You've given me a gift. For as long as I know you, I get to give you shit about punching me in the throat."

"I hope that's a long time," Were the words that escaped from Morrigan, snitching on her. She let them escape with far more emotion than she wanted to release and it came wth such a sharp shock of embarrassment that she flinched. Things like that were all best kept deep inside where they couldn't humiliate her.

"Me too." He said it quickly, like it was the only time in the world he'd ever be able to.

His words made *it* a thing, and that thing felt so terribly fragile. A fear paralyzed Morrigan that if she thought too hard and conceptualized the thing, she would realize it was broken like shattered glass, that it had never really been a thing but shards of a thing.

"I'm really glad you weren't pretending not to know me. You're worth getting hit in the throat."

Why does he wanna know a psycho girl like me?

Morrigan needed a hug, and she knew Simon would have

given her one despite the painful center console that was destined to dig into their guts. But Morrigan also needed to become invisible or disappear, or time travel back in time and punch *herself* in the throat.

"Hey," Simon leaned down to peek under her swoop of hair which she immediately brushed back. "I've heard from a very reliable source that rapists are all over the place tonight and as I've already proven: I can be easily throat-punched by a girl. If I'm going to make it to my room, un-raped, I *will* need a bodyguard."

It made her smile and *her* smile made *him* smile.

"You wanna walk me to my room?" *(a walk might help you feel better)*

Chapter 14

The walk

Sharing pace with her was undeniably intimate, in this small but measurable way. They were, after all, together by a force beyond convenience. She should have been picking up more rides or sleeping, but she chose Simon's company over all more sensible options.

Though it was meant to be a walk to Simon's room, Morrigan lead them. She stepped with no urgency and no destination. She was also not interested in the scenery. She strode past vibrant flowers and shrubs trimmed to be shaped like popular characters, completely oblivious. Her eyes were distant and her mind focused inward.

He knew well that it would do her no good to quietly marinate in black thoughts.

"So an accident you said?"

"Mmm."

"Could you walk me through that one?"

He leaned forward into her periphery and she blinked away whatever distant contemplations she'd focused on.

"How *does* one *accidentally* punch someone in the throat?"

She groaned, a smile twitching onto her face. "Well, you start by being a retard."

He gave her a nudge on the arm with his fist, and she flashed a hint of a grin at him. Her prettiness crashed into him like a shove.

She went on explaining to a pebble in the path that she worked at kicking back to its place on the side. "I just don't really look at the passengers... It's kinda..."

"Awkward."

"Yeah..."

She glanced at him with just one curious brown eye, as though he'd revealed something interesting about himself, but then the wind parted them, casting hair in front of her face.

Her chin picked up into a gentle night breeze. Her hair was blast back behind her, billowing like a banner, and the pale white light of LEDs and moonlight lit her fair skin. She shut her eyes to the night, her head listing weightlessly as soft lips parted to take in the wind.

When Simon had invited Morrigan to go on a walk with him, he had done it altruistically. Simon hadn't thought about how much he wanted to spend time with her or that she'd help stave off loneliness for a while longer. He really *had* only been thinking about how much good it would do Morrigan. He knew the value of a late night walk. Conversation was easier spoken with words made from breath taken of the cool night air and she seemed like she needed a long conversation. Still, he was enjoying her company and that fact corroded any sense of altruism. It felt wrong —or rather less than selfless— to enjoy this walk. He couldn't deny, to himself, the intense longing he felt for Morrigan as he stole long indulgent staring spells at the girl. He watched her chest gently shift to inhale and brown eyes stare dimly into space with a head awash with bleak introspection. Simon was wholly unprepared for her to be beautiful.

Out of her cast member uniform she was so impossibly real that it made Simon dizzy to look at her. He felt like some kind of creep who had no right to see her like this. She wore a hoodie that was too big for her everywhere but her chest. It was black with thready fraying sleeves and holes worn for her thumbs but against she wind she'd tucked her thumbs away in her long sleeves. She operated the world with just the pale tips that barely peeked out of the ends of her sleeves. Her hair was *made* to be tussled by wind. And she squinted into the breeze, off the water, seemingly unaware of that graceful chaos lashing behind her. It was overwhelming.

Morrigan stared off into the night, ponderous and full of serenity, with a distant mind swimming in a midnight arena of thought. He wanted to know those thoughts, to share his own, to shatter the silence with companionship, but between them spanned a chasm of this overwhelming infinity of what they didn't know about each other.

He couldn't imagine a world where he had any right to know this girl. She wore a band-sweatshirt with "GoatWhore" written across her chest, the letters distorted by intimidating proportions. The notion they belonged together was made all the more ridiculous now. He'd known her as Morrigan in a shapeless employee costume, where her figure and bust were concealed by Disney magic, and he'd still been intimidated by the potency of her eyes, seldom cast his way. Now here she was, dressed so casually cool, and ignorant to her lethal looks. Beneath the surface lurked the secret history of a life lived in absence of him and the idea of it choked bravery from Simon. He imagined a Mad Max world filled with sensitive childhood friends and cool tattooed ex-boyfriends with big penises who probably knew her way better and who she probably still had feelings for and who could just call her and she'd...

With all the considerable power of his insecurities he tried to imagine her picking up the phone with a smile and leaving to go see some metal hunk, but he couldn't. She was in no rush to go anywhere. She was with *him.* She was *very* with him, in fact. Morrigan didn't anxiously check her phone. She wasn't even walking anymore. She was standing, together with him, enjoying the night air.

The image of her muted smile, when he'd asked her on the walk, flashed through his mind.

The longer this silence stretched, the more fragile it seemed; threatened by an energy of potential. The wind slowed to a low whistle in their ears and Simon's lips parted to speak, but she beat him to it.

"Hey," She began with a distant whisper, still squinting hard at the night.

Her gentle voice startled his heart to a thumping, as though she'd shrieked in his ear. That one word yanked him from his heavy thoughts with a flare of shame. He'd been so self absorbed with inapropriately timed affections, rather than contemplating how he might cheer her up. He underwent a frantic mental scramble for his notes, like a student caught sleeping in class.

"Can I ask you a weird question?" She looked at him and it felt like a shove. "What's your dream girl look like?"

A whole lot like you.

She stopped and Simon sauntered a few more steps, as though he could walk away from the question.

"Like, what's hot to you? We're in Simon land, and we're looking at the front cover of Sports illustrated. What's the bikini model look like? What's she got that..."

Don't say big boobs. Say anything else. Skinny? No that's shallow too. Everything physical is shallow.

"Oh well I'm not really sure. Bikini models aren't really... well they're really thin so the bathing suits just look really good on them, so it's kind of more about just how they-"

"Coat hangers. Yeah." Morrigan hurled, turning away from him, dejected.

Simon didn't understand her reaction and panic refused to let him think for any length of time. "Their backs."

Morrigan slowly turned, her eyebrows contorted with abject confusion.

"No I mean, the string. So you know, how like... well it's small. The thing that ties in the back? The string. It's narrow so you see more of the back, and so they need to have really nice backs."

"Their backs."

"Yeah."

She blinked. "You think, on a super model, their most attractive feature is their *back*?"

"S-sure."

Her look of amusement radiated an oppressive aura of disbelief.

"I don't know!" He shot, before she could speak. "Who cares about a girl in a bathing suit anyway? A really pretty girl looks incredible in a sweatshirt."

Simon realized with dread that *she* had a sweatshirt on, a

zip-up *hoodie* really, and he *had* been imagining a pullover sweatshirt, but he had also been envisioning her in it. He wanted to snatch those words back, but she'd heard them and they made her smile. He wasn't being inappropriately bold.

Suddenly the shrub beside Morrigan, trimmed to look like Donald, became very interesting to her. When she returned to walking along the path she stood a whole lot straighter.

A blanket of pleasant silence fell on the pair then, broken only by laughter carried across the pool from a group of drunks in the hot-tub, the last hold-outs on sleep besides the two of them. The pair instinctively wandered, together, to solitude without a word. They ended up at the river that ran along the hotel grounds, forearms slung over the railing.

It was Morrigan, again, who broke the silence. She did it with a weak "hey." Evidently the thought had come suddenly to her, catching her in the middle of an exhale. She paused for a long breath and finished her thought more forcefully. "Hey, I think I *did* need this walk. So thanks."

He nodded, a soft affirmation that didn't overly disrupt the soothing silence between them. He stole a glance at the girl, soon after, and saw brown eyes lost in bleakness. "You know you shouldn't worry about that stuff."

The moment her eyes turned from gloomy thoughts and focused on him, he realized he couldn't get away with throwing out a comment like that with her.

"You were asking about what was *hot,* and I think... I think you're underestimating what it feels like..." Her eyes were potent, as they always were, but this time he didn't look away. "You don't know what it feels like to hear a *cute* girl laugh, or to be smiled at by a *pretty* girl."

Morrigan broke eye contact first, casting her gaze back out at the water. "Christ, you really know how to make an ugly girl wish she wasn't. Here I was thinking the scale went the other way. Pretty, cute, then hot, but god damn you make being pretty or cute sound a whole lot better."

"Morrigan-"

"What's hot feel like? Just a hard-on? Or is that magical too?" She spat forcefully.

Her bitterness withered his bravery, but the words still echoed unsaid in his head. *You **are** pretty Morrigan. You're cute and pretty and beautiful.*

"Sorry. I didn't mean for that to sound bitchy. It's a good thing that you're like that. I've just got sour grapes. It's just- I mean that's the kind of shit a boyfriend says to earn points, but you're actually for real. You make it really hard not to want..."

Simon blinked. "Sour grapes? What does-"

"You know you're real fashionable too." She cut in, flashing a fake smile at him. "Kinda surprising you're not into girls who wear tight dresses and heels. Sweat-shirts for you, huh?"

He looked down at the same combination of a button-up and jeans that he wore every day. "I'm fashionable?"

"Are all guys just hopelessly clueless? I'm used to gross pushy assholes who have no idea they're not charming, and now I've met this gorgeous man who acts like he should be apologizing to everyone who sees him."

Morrigan leaned an elbow on the railing turning her chest towards him but Simon felt safer perpendicular to her face, and it's power, so he kept his neck stiff. He was already dizzy with her words alone.

"Oh! Uh, thanks," he said, hurrying to remedy his silence.

"I guess you're a good person to ask. I was thinking about switching up the hair. Nothing too crazy because of work, but I thought maybe like a real long ponytail with one of those, like, metal vikingy pony-tail things, or maybe shave the side again and hairpin it for work. I don't know, I just think I really need a change."

She was moving the conversation along, but his mind still lingered on her compliment. To stay silent felt like a lie. So he spoke without having any words ready in his head. He just trusted his mouth. "Hey, wait, thank you. It um... You just caught me off guard, but- but I really want you to know that uhh... well it means a lot coming from you, that you think I'm uh... 'gorgeous' and all. That was really nice of you to say. Really does mean a lot, especially coming from you. I have really bad- Just as a guy you hear a lot of jokes about like- Like everyone always says how guys are gross and it can just really like... *grind* on you."

Simon had forgotten how big Morrigan's eyes could get until she looked at him in that moment as his words got heavy and clunky and his throat got too tight for them. Simon blinked and took in an emergency composing breath. A wave of embarrassment flushed through Simon's head for letting his damage spill out of him. And, while his eyes were closed and he pinched the bridge of his nose, it hit him; or rather, *she* hit him.

Simon had never felt like a man with a particularly impressive mass to him and in that moment Morrigan's enthusiasm, and perhaps her robust chest, added fourty pounds to her. She slammed into him with a hug that nearly knocked him off his feet and she squeezed him with an enthusiasm which shocked him even more than her compliment. As fast as the embrace had come, it ended. Morrigan pushed him to arm's length and held him there. "You're gonna make me fuckin *cry* dude. You're really handsome man. Who the fuck is telling you otherwise? Cuz they're *dumb*. You're cute. Don't let some slut tell you otherwise."

He watched familiar alarm bells ring in her head, and the fire in her eyes was hastily snuffed out. She let go of his arms and Simon felt an urge to grab her by her ratty sweatshirt and yank her back over, into a hug. But Simon couldn't picture a world where she'd hold him back, so he let her step out of reach.

She looked back out over the water and he followed her eyes out past the railing too. "Your hair is *fine* by the way."

He thieved a sideways glance at her, and got to see the profile of her smile and the small lines of strain that preceded a brighter one that showed teeth, before she reined it all in with a pout.

"*Fine*, just what every girl dreams of hearing." Morrigan said, sticking out the very tip of her tongue. "Maybe I'll just buzz this weedwhacker hack-job short and give up on trying to be attractive."

His fingers curled slightly with a twitch, like she'd flicked his puppet strings, but he resisted the instinct to look at her.

Tell her. 'You're very pretty'. Say it.

Simon opened his mouth to tell her, and he really did want to, but he couldn't say it. He knew it wasn't just a word. It was inexorably bound to a club of rejection raised over his head, ready to strike him down.

If he said pretty, he'd need to explain what it meant. He'd need to explain his feelings and if he did it poorly they'd be lost very easily in translation and he was too much a coward to bring them up once, let alone twice. All of this choked his brain with indecision but he knew he had to say *something*. So he did.

"Your hair is this fantastic kind of mistake." His tongue explained ahead of most of his brain. "It exists in this weird kind of twilight along with wild flowers and water-glasses left in sunny windows that filter sunsets into rainbows on the wall.."

She looked confused, he probably did too.

"It's just made of all these ingredients that you can only add by accident. Like one day you'll go to a stylist that doesn't see it and they'll make your hair into what *they* like and it'll be gone until some other fantastic accident brings it back or doesn't. But for right now, there's this amazing thing crafted by a mix of a girl cool enough to get a crazy haircut and lazy enough to let it grow in for so long but still self conscious enough to try and fix it like..." Simon touched her hair. He *touched* her. He could feel his soul drift out the tight spot in his chest and yank viciously on the reins to his body. "*Three* times? and never do it like the stylist did, but every time add these perfect imperfections that just make it more wild and more *you*. And you're just this girl walking around with this hair that you don't know is just *so*... Morrigan. It's so fucking tragic that one day this awesome disaster will be gone, and nobody will get how-"

She reached out and covered his mouth. Her hand was gentle but the physical contact stunned him silent. "You're upsetting my self loathing Simon. Be merciful. I can only take so much flattery before I faint like a little southern belle."

She smiled an uneasy smile and her hand trembled on his lips. Her fingers curled –making the smallest accidental caresses with the very tips of her fingers– as she drew them back.

Simon saw an uncomfortable girl in front of him so he breathed an apology with what breath he had on hand before realizing his hand was still in her hair. His middle finger was hooked, very slightly, around the back of Morrigan's head. A flash of temptation shot through Simon, to draw her closer. His heart punched his ribs and Simon sharply inhaled through his nose, withdrawing his hand with a jerk.

Her head had a tilt to it and she cast her eyes down, off and away from any chance meeting with his, so he looked away too. She pivoted towards the railing, without shuffling over out of his personal space, and looked out at the water. He did too, with his mind's eye occupying his attention entirely with the shoulder only an inch, or maybe two, from his.

A loud wind blew between them, enforcing the silence, but

Morrigan called over it. "Got me curious. This whole pretty, cute, hot thing. I never knew there was a difference. Thought people just used whichever they liked the sound of. Tell me about it. What's cute, and what's pretty?"

"Oh, I suppose that depends on the person. It's a fairly subjective thing. But I think most guys think of them as meaning different things."

"Fuck what every other guy in the universe thinks. I'm asking *you.*"

Feelings were plasma cutting through his blast door of anxiety and Simon pulled the pin on the grenade in his throat and let it all explode out his mouth.

"Pretty feels like the tightness of a laugh in your chest, or- or that edge the wind has in fall. Pretty is that first flash of a smile. It's when hair slips from behind a girl's ear. Then *cute* is the look that a girl gives past that lock of hair. It's a cocked head, fluttering eyelids and parted lips. Cute feels like a painless ache in your chest, a longing for those eyes to look at you, even while they are.

He said it all in one breath, then gasped, like he'd exorcized a demon. Instantly pacified, she blinked at him with eyes that made him ache. He forced words out the moment he had the air, but by then his senses were restored and his mind was flooded by a desperate conviction that he keep his explanation impersonal.

"Does that make sense? Pretty is bright and cute is soft. Neither is better than the other. A pretty girl you dream of seeing every day, of hearing too. Her singing, laughter –especially that you've inspired– but then cute? A cute girl you want to touch, to hold. It's not lust, but it's easier to pretend it is. Hot, you'd lust for, and it's easier to not have hot."

She tried to speak, but he couldn't let her. He wanted to bury everything he'd said in a lecture's worth of more.

"Beautiful though, that doesn't have to do with anyone. Beautiful is a girl staring off into the night with her hair blowing in the wind. You don't feel beautiful in your chest."

"I get it." came from her so softly that, for the first time, Simon spoke over her. He continued on explaining on autopilot, but he'd heard it, and his tongue slowly rolled to a stop, after voicing more of an explanation neither of them heard.

She kicked at the pavement with the toe of her fucked-up shoe and Simon could feel the bad news approaching. He'd been sufficiently creepy and she was going to tell him about the wall that had been there the whole time. He couldn't take himself off the tracks, however. It might have been merciful for the both of them if he'd changed the subject with a joke or an insult against her hair and then they could move on and he would just *know* that there was no hope. But he knew himself. He was desperate and alone and he wanted her to hit him hard enough that he'd stop getting up, stop hoping, and just lay flat and *alone*.

Morrigan was conscious of the awkward silence and she intruded upon it before it could drown Simon for too long. "Listen, Simon, I consider you a friend."

He tried to swallow, and his throat was too tight. *Friend.*

Morrigan was struggling to continue but Simon didn't need her to. He'd been released from his sisyphean pursuit of this girl. He hoped a fresh misery might heal quicker and cover up the pile behind it.

"I need to ask you a favor, as a friend," she said finally, with eyes only for the floor. "I know it's awkward, but it'll really help me to just *hear* it."

Simon transitioned very quickly from self pity to concern and confusion towards Morrigan.

"It was really nice, what you said about my hair, and I

appreciate it. You're a nice guy and I know you're just being nice *you,* but... But I'm a little... like..." another breath and finally eye contact. "I think what I really need is just a clean slice. Simon, you..."

Suddenly Morrigan's brow furrowed and she leaned in closer to examine Simon's face. "Are you *nervous*?" She accused, incredulous.

Simon just blinked.

"**You**." She breathed hotly like she had just found the killer in a murder mystery. "You're *blushing,* you- you mother*fucker.*" Morigan grabbed his face and misery fled from it, to be replaced by utter confusion.

"I'm sorry?"

"I can *feel* it, you fuck! You're blushing. Your cheeks are hot as shit!"

Likewise he could feel her hands. They were soft.

His courage failed him and he was helplessly silent in the face of her volatile frustration. He blinked through overwhelming nausea, to look pleadingly at this girl who he very *subjectively* thought was wonderful.

Morrigan cocked her hand back, positioned for a haymaker of a slap, but she stopped herself. Her shoulders slumped and she shook her head at him. "You motherfucker." She said again, weakly, this time on the verge of tears. "What the fuck was this all about? You shut my ass down *hard* on the golf-cart. Then you took me on the 'easy let down pity walk' and gave me the 'get back out there' confidence booster speech. You're standing there giving me a bullshit essay, ready to die on a quicksand hill, about how my shitty hair isn't so bad and this whole time..."

Simon's legs took a step and Morrigan retreated a step half

the length of his, like he was waving a burning poker.

"This whole time you coulda just *said* it. You can read my face so good you know when I'm hungry, which co-workers I hate..." Her eyes flared, wide enough for a pair of tears to cut down her cheeks, and she jabbed a finger at his face like she was about to shoot him with it. "*You... You* fucking knew that Jake had flirted with me in the past and that I wasn't attracted to him and that I thought he was an asshole. You fucking *knew*. You looked at my face like a *window* into my fucking *head!*" Her rage cracked her voice but she went on. "What the fuck did you see when I looked at *you?*"

Again he took a step and again she stepped back, so much quicker than before but with such a shallow step.

"Fuck!" She swung her arms down and her sleeves flew forward, covering them like a sulky wizard.

Simon stepped forward and grabbed a hold of her shoulders as gingerly as he could and when she looked up, her cheeks glistened. They were wet with running tears. She sniffled and reached up with her big sleeves to begin wiping them away with the clumsy things. Simon grabbed them, without knowing why, and held them. Through the ends of the sleeves it wasn't quite holding hands.

Morrigan's wet eyes darted around Simon's face. She wrinkled her nose along with her mouth and then lightly pursed her lips and looked right into Simon's eyes. "You know I gave up hope. It was super easy. I'm really good at being hopeless. Having hope is way stressful dude."

Simon smiled and borrowed one of her sleeves to wipe his own eye and Morrigan let out a short giggle.

"Morrigan?"

"Mhm?" She squeaked in a tiny voice.

"I think we might *both* be retarded."

His words were all he could muster to keep ahead of the white wave of thought threatening to tumble and drown him. His thoughts were unwieldy, and his head was unsuited to hold them. He could see, in her softening eyes, that she could recognize a struggle to bring emotions to order. In their mutual turmoil of the heart, they were a pair.

The idea that a girl had affections for Simon was so alien to him that he felt embarrassed to believe it. The assertion that those affections could be so significant as to cause some kind of stress made him wonder if she was talking to the right Simon. He didn't *feel* like a person who someone would go through this kind of trouble over.

The top of his chest felt tight.

All of this came before the doubts over his own affections could hook their claws into Simon's brain. Simon didn't trust himself to judge whether he was truly attracted or just desperate. Was it even *fair* to pursue a girl so far from a home he planned to return to?

The constriction of his chest spread to his throat and choked him there.

All those questions seemed so unimportant and as deafening as they were in his head, they formed nothing more than white noise. One thing felt real and important then, as Morrigan stared up at him. Her eyes were wide and they carried their own burden of questions. For hers and his, he knew one thing well. He was a boy standing in front of a girl, and they were standing *so* **very** close together.

His grip loosened on her frayed sleeves and the slightest nudge of an emerging hand began to sneak from her sleeve.

There was but one question that mattered then, and Simon swallowed the lump in his throat to ask it.

That gulp was like a lever to a trap-door. The muscles in his upper chest and throat relaxed and for the smallest fraction of a second Simon realized he'd made a critical error. In that same fraction of a second Morrigan's nostrils flared with the intake of a breath that would fuel a question of her own.

Simon didn't recognize the signs, because it hadn't happened since he was very young, and so he was just as surprised as Morrigan was when he began to projectile vomit. Simon puked all over Morrigan and their questions were forgotten. Obliterated by caustic stomach acid.

They had drifted so intimately near each other that Morrigan had to look up at Simon. He held a few inches on her. This made Simon's mouth, functionally, a shower-head and –pressurized by anxiety– Simon's mouth became a puke *hose*. She had faced Simon so earnestly that the distribution was perfect. The vile stomach slurry washed over her entire face like the flume hitting the water at the bottom of Splash Mountain. Her tender expression, full of a shy curiosity about Simon and the inner-workings of his heart, was instantly extinguished.

She recoiled, raising her hands in an unheeded surrender, and Simon too attempted to back up away from her. He couldn't move his torso or neck against the powerful instinct that demanded stiffness but his legs were not part of that coup. It would prove irrelevant, however, as the pressure built up within him was enough for the throw-up beam to still reach her from several steps away.

Finally after several full seconds Simon's insides had been emptied onto the cute girl he was about to ask out and he wanted nothing more than to puke again. He keeled over, dry heaving and spitting, shaking from the exertion. Morrigan too he heard spitting with a revilled emphasis and again Simon dry heaved as he realized he must have vomited into her mouth.

He looked over at Morrigan and saw her keeled over too, heaving, getting ready to throw-up. Simon had heard of girls holding each other's hair while they puked and in that moment he felt like it was important to do, so Simon wiped his mouth on his forearm and rushed over to help.

It was wet. He couldn't back down and let it flop onto her head, but it had a *texture* to it. Morrigan hurled like she was tossing out a glass of water. It hit the path and splattered against Simon's shoes and shins. After she'd coughed and spit out the remnants Morrigan slapped his hands away and croaked: "Don't you dare fucking look. Look out at the water. Don't turn around."

Simon only dimly realized what she was doing, once he'd heard the squelch of her puke soaked hoodie hit the hard concrete. She was going to wash off in the pool.

Simon did as he was told and looked out at the water. He spat again, over the railing, and rubbed his temples against the throbbing stress. He squeezed his eyes shut, feeling the burn in his throat, and worried about hotel employees coming by and being very upset about the vomit or guests seeing Morrigan in some stage of nakedness.

There was a quiet splash behind him, like a diver on a mission.

"This doesn't make us *even* by the way" Morrigan called before dunking her head underwater.

Simon groaned as he imagined all the filth that would come away from her hair in the water, like a drop of food coloring the shade of his dinner.

She burst to the surface and he could hear the slap of hair being swung against the back of her neck. "If I *had* tazed you: *maybe.* If I'd got you right in the nipple-" She spat. "-*and* couldn't figure out how to turn it off right away."

"I'm- I'm sorry." He projected over his shoulder.

Chapter 15

Bodily fluids in the pool

His apology was frustratingly heartbreaking. He was *too* god damn sweet, and she wasn't interested in *not* being mad. Of course, after she thought for a moment, Morrigan realized she wasn't mad at *him*. She was frustrated, so much so that she could grit her teeth, turn red, and cry like a kid who'd waited in the sun on achey legs for two hours only to be too short to ride.

She wanted that moment back. That place in time where she'd been promised a sweet word or a gentle touch paired with meaning. They'd known, even if they were both too timid to admit it, that they shared this certain kind of feeling between them. Her faith in the existence of that feeling was woefully fragile and to *ask* for confirmation felt indulgent. But it had been there, hadn't it? They'd been *so* very close to *something*, something she wanted badly. An acknowledgement, a question, a next step. Progress beyond this suffocatingly delicate stage, the existence of which, was questionable.

Her whole body felt tight, including her mind, squeezed by anxiety. If either of them could just admit it she could relax, but those words were inaccessable now. It had been on his lips, she *knew*, just like it had been on hers. But now she was afraid that moment was gone. It would fade into never-ever and the two of them were so awkward that she thought they'd both slide down one side of the mountain. They'd either pretend it *had* been said and she would miss out on the moment she wanted so badly, or they would pretend like it had never happened and she wouldn't have the strength to climb back up to the top.

"I *know*." She called back, more annoyed than she meant to sound. She hissed a curse quietly and loudly dunked herself underwater, slapping a pause on the conversation, to buy time to come up with a less bitchy amendment to that answer.

She opened her eyes underwater to try and wash some of the stomach acid out of them, and she saw a plume of *gross* spreading from her hair. She swam away from the cloud of filth washing off of her and emerged with a gasp further away.

"I wasn't assuming you did it out of spite." She looked over at him, slumped glumly over the railing. "You're not a vulture, are you? They puke in self defense."

She saw him soften a bit, and her scowl softened with him.

"You know I still feel bad for punching you in the throat? It's really unfair." She called. "I guess now we *both* have fuel to mock each other over." Again he softened and she sighed wistfully, safely out of earshot. "I thought *you* were a rapist and you thought *I* was a coyote and employed your secret vulture powers to defend yourself."

From afar, she spied his shoulders quake with some laughter. She watched him for a long moment, with a tiny satisfied smile, before bobbing down to wrestle with the filth embedded in her hair.

She surfaced again and swung her *mostly* clean hair out of her face, slapping it into the back of her neck. "You know you managed to puke down my shirt?"

"You think you could just taze me in the nipple?" Simon asked tiredly. "It might not make us even, but I could go for splitting the difference."

It was *her* turn to laugh now. Simon's voice was quiet from where he was, so she knew he couldn't hear her laughing, but she wanted him to. Morrigan called back, "A tempting proposal," with words flavored by laughter. She watched him perk up and went on, making sure to speak with a smile he could hear. "but If I taze you for too long and imbalance the guilt, then will I have to play baby bird again?"

Morrigan smiled at Simon's inaudible laughter and glanced around the pool for any wanderers from the hot-tub. She'd had to strip down to her bra and now that she'd begun to cool on the situation, room was made for the fear of being seen to creep in.

She flinched at the clumsy laugh of some drunk from the hot-tub. Though they were far away and out of sight, the bark-like nature of his voice made him sound alarmingly close.

Feeling exposed, Morrigan rushed to the side of the pool in order to extract her mostly un-puked on T-shirt from her hoodie.

As she submerged the shirt to clean it, Morrigan murmured a joke she wasn't brave enough to let Simon hear. "This isn't quite how I imagined taking my shirt off for you." Immediately she felt the rush of catharsis. It was somehow so much more satisfying than just *thinking* her thoughts. She could whisper anything and he wouldn't hear her. "This isn't how I imagined you getting your bodily fluids all over me."

It was exciting, and made her feel like she was a confident sexy chick who calls themselves a bitch without hushing their voice and glancing around for children. Then a floating mass of "do not look" bumped into her arm and she hopped away to cleaner waters with an empty retch. All she could do was remind herself that chlorine sterilizes and to be thankful she could only smell the pool and not *anything else.*

Morrigan fiddled with her bra under her shirt, desperate to be free of the unspeakable filth she could feel trapped there, without actually taking it off. She felt like a nervous teenage boy trying to unhook a bra. To her defence, Morrigan had never been wild enough to have any experience robing or disrobing in a pool.

The loud cackle of a hyena-woman made Morrigan jump, and suddenly question the wisdom of washing off in the pool. It had seemed so necessary a minute ago, when she'd been dowsed in puke, but now it felt childish to *need* to wash off immediately instead of just driving home and taking a shower.

Morrigan gauged her ability to withstand a thirty-ish minute drive in her current condition. She tried to visualize the shower and how worth the wait it would be. She saw the shower in her mind, then she saw the ankle deep water still in the tub that wouldn't drain.

Every emotion on the spectrum between humiliation and frustration coursed through that soggy girl, setting her to a tremble. She was covered in someone else's vomit. She could feel the texture of it shifting in her bra when she moved. If it was available that instant She would have stepped into a hazmat decontamination shower with water pressure strong enough to leave a bruise.

If she were alone she might have screamed or cried. She would have let the universe know exactly how unfair and upsetting the situation was. But Simon was there, so she told him instead.

"This is *really* disgusting."

She declared it with an honest bleed of emotion, and Simon responded with an alarmingly appropriate degree of concern.

"Do you wanna use my shower?"

Morrigan hadn't expected a solution. She'd been seeking sympathy alone.

"Do you want my shirt? Like did it get inside your sweatshirt?"

Morrigan could hear the familiar note of self consciousness in that boy's song. *It's really not fair that I have to feel bad for the idiot who just puked all over me, but he's just such a poor injured bird. He sounds so fucking scared to be shirtless.*

"God fucking dammit Simon, I'm not done being pissed. You're relentless. Could ya hold off on being a sweet-heart until I've washed your puke off?"

"I'm-"

"Simon! Shut-up. I *know* you're sorry." Morrigan navigated to the edge of the pool. "Take me to your fucking room."

Suspecting she'd given him cause to turn around, Morrigan tried to get out of the pool like a bond girl, sexy and cool. He didn't know the horrors going on inside her shirt and if he did she could still be gross and *cool* at least. It was a move she'd always wanted to do, to get out of the pool backward by pushing herself up into a sitting position and then swinging her legs around, but it turned out she was too weak. It always looked so effortless, but now Morrigan was convinced they used CGI or a scuba diver to shove them up from off camera. she ended up facing the edge using every muscle in her body and kicking with her legs, thrashing in the water, to propel her to the point she could get her knee under her and roll herself across the concrete onto her back, then gingerly onto her side and then finally get her hands underneath her to start the last scramble to her feet with a sloppy spattering of water. She was panting by the time she finished but fortunately Simon was still loyally back-turned and too far away to hear the heavy breathing.

While she caught her breath, Morrigan picked up her

sweatshirt. She wrapped the cloth around the soiled portion, turning it into a safe-to-touch bundle.

"You can look at me." She called to his back. "I'm obviously not naked dude."

Simon turned around and something about his demeanor made her feel like she'd driven through a red-light. She was going to his room. She would take a shower there. Showers are taken without clothes on.

Shut up, he just puked on me. He's not thinking about that. I'm not thinking about that. No one's thinking about that.

She was woefully unequipped to be sexy. She smelled like chlorine and vomit. They didn't make candles with that fragrance combination.

Chapter 16

A shower

He inserted the keycard full speed, without hitting the edges of the slot. He was supposed to fumble with the room key, and she was supposed to giggle, but Simon wasn't nervous. He opened the door like a samurai.

Morrigan wished her rage hadn't cooled. Then she would have at least known how to act when she was led inside. Simon was acting like a surgeon, as if she had been wounded and required triage. He showed her briskly through an exceptionally expensive-looking room, or rather a suite. It was nicer than her house, possibly bigger. The bathroom was huge too, and obnoxiously nice. The walls were a shining stainless steel and the floor was green granite. Her mother dated a contractor once. He re-did the kitchen with fake granite.

She stepped into the bathroom behind him and he showed her the marble shower, equipped with enough water jets that it looked like it could be a teleporter. Simon explained the nuances of the shower's mechanics, somewhat hesitantly, to an observer standing clear of him across the room. She didn't need him associating her with the smell of chlorine and vomit.

"Oh and there's towels. This rack is heated so uhh... yeah. The bottom towel is the big one and the top one is for hair, or I mean you could just use the other big towel for your hair too. Whatever."

Hair towel?

Curtly Simon showed her the drawer he'd stashed the extra bodywash and conditioners before getting out of her way. Morrigan watched him dimly as he passed to leave and mumbled a thanks.

Sean acted like hair towels were a fucking conspiracy to waste towels. Morrigan reflected, getting the hot water started.

She sat, not on the toilet, but a buttoned white leather changing bench to take off her soggy shoes and socks.

"Hey Simon?"

There was no response and she called again but the shower was too loud. She sighed and set her bare feet down on the floor. It wasn't cold, as she'd expected, and when she reached the door she found controls for a floor heater beneath the light switch.

Morrigan raised her eyebrow at the opulence of a heated bathroom floor and opened the door. "Hey Simon?"

His response came from far away to the left, behind the open door, as a stuttering mess of a "Yes?"

Her eyebrows shot up and she hooked her chin around the door. "You okay?"

Unmuffled by the door her words struck his back with a sharpness. She watched him straighten up and give a much more convincing "Yeah, I'm fine. You just... uh, surprised me."

He was standing there, doing nothing but looking nervous with his back turned. She ducked back into the bathroom, brow furrowed, and noticed the mirror was fogged over.

This isn't your shitty double-wide Morrigan. You don't need to heat up the water first. He thinks you're already naked.

"You know my voice still has clothes on. Keep it together." Her brain slammed it into reverse and self deprecation burst from her before he could respond. "You don't have to sound *that* revolted."

She bit her lip and hissed a curse under her breath. She was fishing really deep for a compliment and she knew resting her self esteem on Simon's bravery was a recipe for capsizing. Impatient, she peeked around the door and spied Simon, his back still courteously turned, gesturing emphatically to himself. He was so visibly flustered and irritated with her self image, and maybe his own bravery too. It was enough for a little smile to creep onto her lips but she couldn't help but be greedy for something more concrete.

She rolled back around the door, squeezing her eyes shut. *Just gimme something. Come **on**, man. Say it so it's real. Not objectively, **subjectively**.*

"I'm just teasing you!" she called, conceding.

She bit her lip and thumped her head against the wall, listening to Simon's deafening nothing.

"You ever have long hair? Simon?" she asked, picking at the conversation like a scab.

"N-no? Why?"

"You knew about hair towels is all. I'm impressed."

"Oh... yeah I..."

'Dated a girl with really nice hair. She was hotter than you. More confident. She was worth doing nice things for like getting an extra towel.'

"I used to work as a PA on pool shoots. One of the things I had to do was get two towels for each girl."

"A physician's assistant?"

"Photographer's assistant. Listen uh... sorry about leaving you hanging before. I know you were just teasing but-"

She hissed like he'd just talked a papercut into her skin and threw words out the door to bump into his. "I'm sorry dude, I know I shouldn't fish for compliments. I'm just an insecure cunt. Don't mind me."

"Don't be. Insecure I mean."

He paused and she held her breath, straining her ears to hear him.

"I should've learned this lesson after I hurt your feelings when you went for that stretch stunt. You wanna hear it, so I'll come clean and say it. I was nervous –not repulsed– because I... *I think* you're very attractive... and you were mentioning being... uh, like naked or whatever. I just... yeah..."

Morrigan wasn't stupid. She could have connected the dots, but it wasn't as real as a theory. Suspicions and *objective* opinions, didn't make her heart beat like it did. His new confession was far from poetry, but he owned those words and they echoed in her ears until they were burning.

Her throat was tight and her eyelids fluttered over searching eyes that could find nothing sexy, clever nor profound to say. "That's really sweet."

He was quiet around the corner. Morrigan shook her head and corrected: "Flattering. Coming from you, that's really flattering."

With a surge of confidence and a devilish temptation to make the man sweat further, Morrigan undid the buckle of her pyramid stud belt. He couldn't see her from where he was. The bathroom was opposite a closet in an alcove off the main room of the suite. The door opening out obscured her further and she could tell from his voice he was turned away from her but *still* somehow the idea of being naked in the same air as him gave her a head-rush.

"Oops, the water's already hot." She called. "I didn't realize the hotel water heater was so good. The mirror is already all uh, steamed up and stuff."

She wanted him to *know* she was disrobing. Making Simon nervous was exciting and felt refreshingly innocent rather than slutty. He would need to be able to hear her clothes coming off above the shower so she tried to let her pants drop to the ground and let the belt buckle fall with a metallic clink against the granite floor but her pants were stuck. Moisture had adhered them to her thighs. She had to peel the things off of herself, hopping on one foot to yank the other free. Then, once they were entirely off, she raised them above her head and hurled the pants at the ground. They impacted with a clang that was *far* from natural. She clapped hands over her mouth, stifling a sharp giggle with trembling hands.

A few dozen feet away was a cute boy who *knew* she didn't have pants on. She'd never been such a 'dare-devil' in her life. Morrigan's hands were so enfeebled by quiet laughter that, at first, she couldn't grip her shirt firmly enough to lift it.

"Hey before I get-" *naked? Just say it. Casual like. As if you're just a quirky girl who's comfortable just dropping that mention and being like 'yeah by the way I'm hot'. Fuck I paused too long. It'll be weird. Abort.* "-into the shower, um... tell me about being a photographer?"

Why'd you say it with that weird inflection? Fuck! It's not a question. I'm just telling him to do it.

"Oh uhhh..." Simon's voice was drunk with nervous stupor as he collected himself. "I wasn't a photographer. I was a PA. I just set up the lighting and carried some of the props for backgrounds and stuff. That's like the real job they pay you for. You gotta know how all the stuff works, like the mirrors and whatever. Then once it's set up they have you do busy work, since they pay you for the whole session.

Shivering, Morrigan pulled her wet shirt off and painstakingly inspected it for vomit before balling it up. With her hand cocked back, she sighed as though she were gracefully disrobing and prodded him to say more. "Why kind of busy work did they have you doing?"

"Oh just like fetching stuff or shifting stuff in the background. Whenever the photographer says something like 'can *someone* do... blank.' then I'd be that someone. I guess sometimes I would have to-"

Morrigan threw her wet shirt against the wall opposite the bathroom door. It hit with a wet slap and flopped to the ground. Simon's thought was banished from his head and she had to smother another giggle in her hands.

"I uh, I would have to go on a coffee run sometimes. I guess."

Her heart was pounding now, hard enough she felt it pulsing in her cheeks. She'd been robbed of whatever word they would have exchanged by the water and she fervently clung to her consolation prize. His nervousness was a promise that those words would still come to her. It legitimized her hope and she couldn't help but squeeze more nervous words from the man. She sternly held her tone to one of curiosity and prodded boldly. "You ever have to spritz those models with mist or rub on some baby oil?"

Simon responded reflexively, too nervous to pick up on her

teasing. "Oh no that was make-up's job."

Her instinct was to retreat back into the bathroom before disrobing further. She had complete concealment from Simon's eyes but that wasn't quite enough to make her feel comfortable. Granted she didn't really *want* to be comfortable. She wanted the rush of flying in the face of her awkwardness. Simon had admitted she was attractive, enough to make him nervous. That was a metric she could get behind. She might have felt guilty exploiting him so, but she could tease any amount of ego padding out of a man who'd recently projectile vomited the length of her body.

She took a steadying breath. "Must be hard working around such beautiful women all day. You said you did photo-shoots with swimsuit models? You ever get nervous?"

Say no. Say I'm prettier. You can lie. It'll still be sweet.

Compliments had a way of feeling predatory, like an announcement of vulgar intent. But Simon's wavering voice felt so innocent and sweet she knew it wouldn't feel bad to hear one from him.

Morrigan's hands fumbled about her bra. Her fingers pulsed with each beat of her heart and she couldn't grip the hook. Instead she just pulled the thing over her head like a nervous virgin. She got her hands under it and tucked her elbows before heaving it off with the jerk of a shiver.

Her bra was an old beige thing. It had been bought a full size ago and was worn from strain and time. There were tears wherever seams could be found and Morrigan was surprised every time it survived another wash. This minor violence she inflicted on the thing was more than enough to destroy it. The wire snapped like a guitar string and whipped her viciously. It cut Morrigan in an arc from her sternum up through the underside of her breast and into the tender skin beneath her armpit.

The pain was nauseatingly intense. She found herself

lowering into a squat, biting her forearm to suppress a sob.

"Nervous? Not *really*," Simon blundered on, oblivious. "Like I was saying before: swimsuit models tend to look really good in bikinis because they're all super skinny and pretty flat, and for whatever reason it just looks very aesthetic, but that's not really the same thing as *attractive* necessarily. And models usually are very striking, either piercing eyes or exotic features, or sometimes they're just kinda weird looking. They make you look at the poster and they make the clothing look good but they're never really cute or pretty looking."

His statement was puzzling. It seemed honest but delusional, and Simon had always seemed to be rather grounded. Regardless, the screaming pain Morrigan was in disrupted any thoughtful analysis.

Being unable to respond without emotion flooding into her voice she fled into the shower wordlessly. Under the water she shut her eyes, and hunched over her injured chest. She didn't want to see exactly how bad it looked, and she was tired of being covered in filth. She wanted to just stand there under the water for a while until everything was okay again. When she finally *did* straighten up, it had been long enough that her back cracked though not so long that her fingers had pruned.

Though a few moments before she might have imagined the bra wire must have cut all the way to her ribs, when she craned her head around to examine the damage she found nothing but a raised welt. It was redder even than her skin, after standing under such hot water for so long. She ran her fingers gingerly along the mark, marveling at just how far the wire travelled. She'd worn more than one bra to death, and this wasn't the first wire that had snapped, but it had never been quite so devastating.

The girl snapped out of her daze and busied herself washing away any trace of the smell Simon had retched onto her. She squeezed every ounce of bodywash she could out of the cute miniature Micky-shaped bottle left in the shower. Even smacking the thing like a ketchup container, she couldn't seem to extract more than half of its contents.

As she crept from the shower to forage from the pile Simon had left her on the counter she mulled over what he'd said about the models. Her instinct was to be upset. If those models weren't pretty than how could *she* be? But then he'd been very clear that she made him *nervous*. So logically she was prettier than a model. But was she? After all, he treated his attraction to her like some kind of sick fetish.

What's so wrong with thinking I'm hot? Does he think I'm taken? a tranny? A literal horse?

The chill of air conditioning jerked her from her thoughts and reminded her she was naked in air shared with the suite. There was no physical barrier between her and Simon. The open door was no longer a giddy invitation to lackluster voyeurism. That temporary madness had been extinguished and Morrigan tip-toed nimbly back to the shower. When she realized her underwear was still on she removed them and tossed the soggy panties outside the shower unceremoniously.

Her earlier antics had been fueled by a self confidence that now felt delusional, and yet Morrigan's mind was restless on that point. Not even the serenity of a hot shower could blank her mind of the puzzle. Simon *had* said she could make him nervous. He could have been lying to get in her pants, but that seemed too generous an estimation of his seduction skills. More likely to her, he was just an idiot.

A stupid person isn't attracted to models. They're the most attractive people. That's the common definition of the word. If he isn't nervous around models but he's nervous around me he's a dumb person. He's so self unaware that he can be around naked models, look at them, get a boner, and then not notice his boner.

She began to pour bottle after bottle of shampoo into her hair, dreading actually having to use her fingers to work the product in and risk touching anything that had been inside Simon's stomach.

*He **could** be gay. A gay idiot. Maybe he likes dudes and is in denial. When I wear my uniform I look more like a man, and he **did** say backs were the hottest feature on a bikini model. Kinda sounds like a gay guy who doesn't know what's attractive on a woman. Besides, backs are muscular. What guy is into muscles on a girl? Maybe they make him excited because men have muscles and he likes men.* She mused, laughing softly through her nose. *God I wish he was within earshot, so I could tease him more; put a blush on those fair cheeks of his. Why you like sweatshirts simon? You like sweat? Know who sweats? Men.*

She found a grin on her face, imagining him flustered as she went from teasing to fishing for compliments.

After three containers the shampoo began to run off onto her back in a cold stream and she was forced to actually wash her hair or risk wasting all the shampoo and having to go out of the shower to get more.

Maybe he has a back fetish. Models probably have shitty backs. No one likes backs... except Simon. Simon the back fetishist.

Her hair had turned into a mass of suds that ran over her like a fountain. She ended up working the excessive shampoo out of her hair for so long her hands got tired and she took a break. She let her burning forearms hang at her sides and stuck her head under the water. With her eyes closed, her mind called up the image of Simon shamefully jerking his bright blue eyes off of her breasts, clad in nothing more spectacular than a sweatshirt.

She sighed and let a nagging thought run it's course through her mind. *Maybe I'm just his type. He might just be picky and only like girls that are...*

Morrigan lolled her head back, letting the water wash over her eyelids, in an attempt to free her face from the cascade of caustic suds flowing down it from her hair.

Whatever I am. She opened eyes that burned with chlorine, but mercifully not shampoo. She stared at the marble wall of the shower expecting to find some epiphany of self reflection there. *A girl who wears black? A pair of tits? A big fucking dairy cow.*

"What a shitty consolation prize." She mumbled with her lips pressed to the stream. "Instead of getting to know how he feels about me I get 'you make me nervous because you're hot'.

*Attractive, she corrected. Hot isn't the same as pretty. Cute is its own thing. Sexy, beautiful, pretty, cute, and hot. They're all different. Why? who knows. Which ones are good? It's a mystery. I'm **attractive**. The most lukewarm of all compliments. Is that a polite way of saying **objectively** attractive, meaning 'I understand why someone (not me) might find you attractive' or is it a way of not commiting to a more serious compliment?*

She turned so the shower would bombard her hair and raised her hands to assess how much more shampoo was embedded there.

Who the fuck am I when I get out of the shower? Sexy girl who got out of his shower? Platonic friend who happened to be naked nearby? Oblivious girl who might be interested AND REQUIRES HIS CLARIFICATION ON HOW HE FEELS? 'Hey Simon, gotta go. I have to return home to stargaze. If I see a shooting star I'll wish I had a skinny blonde pretty-boy for a boyfriend. Also I'm a G cup. Kay bye!'

Morrigan groaned in solitude and slapped on the 'massage' setting. She held up her hands in surrender as a firing squad of water jets hit her from all angles.

*If that piece of shit thinks he's off the hook because he admitted I make him nervous and **almost** said more, he's out of his mind. He needs to tell me, with words, that he likes me. He needs to ask me out. I'm not going to be the dude and ask **him**. It's **his** job. I don't know anything more than that I make him nervous. Open flames and chainsaws do that. What do I know? I'm **objectively** attractive, but* *not to him, as far as I have any right to know. If I'm sexy it's an accident.*

The thought made her smile and strike a confident pose.

And that's fine. I'll just keep being accidentally sexy and if he wants anything to do with it, then he should do something. If he wants me then he's gotta ask for me.

She grinned a big toothy smile and smacked the water off. "Alright lets accidentally seduce this fucker."

Stepping out of the steamy shower she was greeted by air that was lighter and cool by comparison. The open door had let the cold air-conditioning of the room blend into a soothing mixture. She could see steam wafting from her arms and she rolled her shoulders, now loosened by the hot shower. She stretched a big luxurious stretch and it eased her muscles like a massage.

Morrigan peeked at the fogged over mirror and was pleasantly surprised by her silhouette. The distortion served to make all her usual nitpicking impossible and without that to distract her she found herself calmly content with her physicality. She gave all the credit to this particular pose she'd discovered.

I bet those dumb models never tried stretching for a photo-shoot. The secret weapon of every accidental seductress.

Morrigan padded over to the rack and grabbed a towel, with another for her hair.

'Thanks for coming in, Morrigan. I received your application to be my girlfriend. What exactly makes you qualified for the position?'
    *Well you see sir, I can lay this towel on my boobs after I get out of the shower, see? And it doesn't fall down. Now this **could** be because they're wet, but fuck you that's not why it's because they're super big.*
    That's great to hear, but you also wrote here that your boobs are actually so big they look kinda gross and bloated. It also says

*the left one is a little smaller and your nipples point slightly
different directions like a pair of googly eyes.*

*That's correct sir, but with a shirt on no one can tell. I make
the perfect accessory to show-off in public. Even though I'm
uncomfortable with low-cut shirts I can easily be pressured into
wearing them so that your ego will be boosted.*

Morrigan pointed a warning finger at herself in the mirror.
*Hey cut that shit out. You make this guy nervous. Stop being a
depressed loser and start being accidentally sexy.*

The play was obvious. She needed to walk out of the
bathroom with a towel on and ask to borrow his clothes. It gave her
the opportunity to be cute with plausible deniability.

She wrapped the hair towel tight around her head, then
rewrapped it tighter, then looser. She started with a standard conical
shape and then decided she should mix it up and tie it like a
medieval chaperon. Morrigan let a lone lock of hair escape the towel
and dangle down past her nose like a librarian, then she decided it
looked weird on it's own and added one longer lock to hang past her
ear, framing her face. Then she realized she might look bald and
gross from behind and let a bit of hair escape there.

She struggled for a bit tying the towel around herself. It
wasn't something she really did. She usually just put her clothes on
immediately and if she didn't, she still lived alone. This towel tying
technique was unique to movies, she concluded, but in order to
'accidentally' seduce, she had to jury-rig something.

While she struggled, Morrigan realized she had to do
something to explain the time it was taking her to get out of the
bathroom. For this, she began to hum. It made more sense in her
head but once she started she couldn't just stop. Insane people did
that. She began humming extra loud so he could hear it over the
shower, but of course she then realized the shower was off and she
sounded crazy. Quickly she switched to soft singing so she would
seem less insane. She hoped some bathroom reverb might make her
voice sound princess-like. Eventually she managed to tie the towel

around near the front where she could quickly grab in an emergency.

She stood at the threshold and took a breath before losing her nerve to step out. She took another breath and again failed to leave the bathroom. After a minute of this she counted a tempo and stepped out on the four count like she were beginning the vocals to a song.

"Hey Simon? I need to..." She took another few steps into the larger room, finding him nowhere. "...borrow some clothes. I hope you don't mind."

She searched for a minute and found him outside, hunched over the railing. She peered at him through the window and sighed. He seemed glum, disappointed. A soft smile touched her lips.

Maybe that moment isn't gone. Maybe he's stewing about how he can get back to it.

She resolved to hug him. It would be an accidentally cute hug. He looked like he could use one.

Morrigan crept away from the window and set about searching for some clothes to borrow. He had an alarming number of empty bags from the hotel laundry service and yet in his apparently extensive stay here Simon hadn't moved his clothes into the drawers. She found his hoard of clothes stuffed into a carry-on duffle sticking halfway out of a closet. Nothing but different button-downs and jeans. She tugged a pair free and the leather label on the back marked them as Levi's. The button downs heaped alongside them were all from a Hanes multipack.

Not exactly the wardrobe of the super rich now is it? Morrigan mused, feeling very much like a super spy.

She leaned further into the closet, righting her hair towel as it leaned even further. Inside she discovered a few other garments on hangers. She found Armani Button downs and Hugo Boss jeans. Once she read the labels she avoided touching them like they were gems in the cave of wonders. Instead she grabbed a white button-down from the duffel and a pair of cheap jeans and scurried back to her bathroom lair. Being seen getting dressed seemed weird. What if she got dressed in an accidentally *gross* way?

She set her towel aside and hastily threw the shirt around her shoulders, stuffing her arms through the sleeves. Before she even finished the buttons she was shaking her head at herself in the mirror.

That's not cute. That's whory. She remarked to herself looking at how the ill-fitting shirt displayed vulgar spaces of flesh between each button. *I look fat too. It's not even sexy. I've managed to make my boobs look fat. It's like a slutty cow with fat udders that's about to...* She raised her eyebrow with a touch of mischief. *Explode, out of this shirt.*

Morrigan thrust her chest out experimentally. The shirt tightened. *I'm sorry Simon, I guess I just didn't realize how... biiiig they were.* She bounced her eyebrows at herself and rolled her shoulders back.

Guilt began to seep in as her attempts to ruin the shirt's buttons failed but she was determined. *It's okay he's rich and this is one of the cheap ones.* She stifled a flash of doubt that urged her to re-check the label and gripped both sides of the shirt. *I'm sorry Simon I'm not confident enough to just **say** it.* With a minor application of force several buttons popped from the shirt and clattered into the sink. She nodded with satisfaction seeing one button hanging by a stretched out thread and unbuttoned the rest of the shirt. She delicately lay the garment down on the counter, chest up, and rewrapped her towel to go on another scavenging mission for clothes.

Her search turned manic. She really did need clothes to leave in, and getting back into her soggy clothes was far from appealing, or attractive. She really wanted to find an oversized T-shirt of his to wear and then have to bring back to him. It would look cute and he'd have to see her at least one more time to get the shirt back.

Behind the expensive clothes Morrigan found the sweatshirt and pajama pants he'd bought when she was working Splash Mountain. It had made her laugh then but, without Simon to see, they made her smile. She grabbed them immediately and scurried back to the bathroom to put them on. The sweatshirt was big and terrifically soft with no shirt underneath. She hugged herself experimentally to test if he could tell she wasn't wearing a bra. She wasn't sure where exactly the line was between whorish and her new trademarked 'accidentally sexy'. Morrigan noticed her face and looked back at an expression of such unease and terror it made her laugh. It was an ugly, anxious sound that made her gulp.

You're cute you pussy. Just hug him from behind so he doesn't know you're a wreck.

With some haste Morrigan gathered up her clothes and put them into one of the empty laundry service bags. She stuffed her feet into her shoes and ground her heel in so she wouldn't have to waste time tying them. It was a determined march she took to the door, but she paused before opening that door. It felt to her like the chance to hug Simon while he leaned over that railing was vital to her efforts. He looked to her to be slumped over with the weight of tumultuous emotions and she was sure it was something she should capitalize on.

Her hand hovered over the door-handle, shaking. *Don't hug him like 'yeah I like you too' just hug him like 'friendzone? whats that? oh by the way I'm **lonely** –not lonely in a desperate way– and uhh... I could use a...*
She shook her head. *Simple message. I'm soft and I give surprise hugs.*

She threw the door open with force and rushed the last few paces to Simon's back like he were about to turn around swinging a goddamn sword. Her hug was like a tackle. It winded him on the railing and some part of his skeleton clanged against the metal.

She slid half sleeved hands over his chest and gave him a

gentle squeeze. She was pressing her boobs into the back of a man shy enough to puke at a cute smile. He squeezed a "Hey, there." out of his winded lungs. He was trying to play it cool but her ear was too close to his heart and it called him a liar.

Morrigan breathed a "Hey," back to him, without thinking about what sort of words came next, but they came anyway. "just wanted to make sure you believed me when I said I wasn't mad at you." She spoke softly, puffing each word into the back of his shirt with a gentle breath. "I just hate forgetting what I was going to say, and you interrupted me. Now I can't even remember what we were talking about by the pool. I don't suppose *you* remember?"

If Simon had had enough breath to answer, he still might not have.

She sighed hot enough for him to feel it. "I didn't think so."

She withdrew and her hand grazed his where it hovered over her sleeve, not holding her. A finger twitched as if to grab her hand, but then it didn't.

Her withdrawal from him exerted an unseen force that turned Simon to face her. He wore a nervous expression and she was trapped sharing hers too, like a deer in the headlights. His jaw clenched. A tendon rose and fell in his neck. He chewed his lip. But Simon didn't speak.

A line popped into Morrigan's head, in that moment, that she thought was the smoothest thing anyone had ever said. "If you *do* remember, gimme a call. I've got tomorrow free." She said it walking backwards and had to stop herself from snapping and shooting him with finger-guns.

"Wait, I don't have your..." Simon blinked, noticing what she was wearing. "...number."

"Oh I don't have my phone on me. You can just hit 'add comment' when you rate me on the app. That's how every creep sends me their number. Not that you're a creep. You're not." She made a dismissing gesture so emphatic it bordered on casting a spell. "Also, hope you don't mind me stealing your clothes."

Morrigan learned incidentally then that walking backwards was a skill, by walking into someone else's door with a thud. Somehow she'd walked not straight down the walkway but in a curve.

If someone answers the door I'll fucking throw myself off the side.

Simon's face softened with a chuckle and Morrigan stuck her tongue out at him.

Shit. When's the last time I brushed my tongue?

"Yeah sorry about that. I forgot to find you clothes. I'm glad you found something that fits though."

"Oh no, don't worry about it."

She shrugged and it was like flicking his puppet strings.

Oops.

"Yeah um uh, also uh, I have your- I put your sweatshirt in- into the uh..."

"Ah, shit I forgot the *rest* of my clothes in your room too," she said, taking a step back towards him.

"Oh, I stuck it in the laundry service bag. I thought I'd have it washed for you. If you're okay with that, I mean." He said with a much less distracting shrug. "I can have the rest of your clothes washed too."

"Aw that's sweet."

The pair of them nodded to each other, while they waited for words to come along through their heads. Her wandering backwards had created a space that Simon leaned into, tempted to close. Maybe he might offer to walk her to the car, she thought. She waited, but a second can be a very long time.

Her heart beat heavy. It pumped another thought through her head each time. *The air is cold. The sweatshirt is thick. Don't worry.*

The towel she'd forgotten about on her head decided to unravel and fall over her face. When she could see, she saw Simon. He was very close.

He's smiling. It was cute. A real accident.

Gently Simon took the towel from where it collapsed over her shoulder and chest. "Here, you were so curious about me giving towels to all the bikini models..." He positioned her head gingerly, only *suggesting* movement with delicate fingertips. "This is a half lean, and that's about a thirty five degree angle. It's like a standard thing they would know. So I just tell them half lean and..." His voice was soft and hushed by concentration.

He was standing close. A whisper could get closer.

He combed his fingers through her hair gently, somehow not catching a single knot on their way through, with the precision of a hair stylist. His nails grazed her scalp like a massage on their way through and while she would never have rushed him, Simon was done gathering her hair in a second. As if he had three hands for the task, Simon wrapped her hair in the towel, softly describing each step along the way. He straightened her neck and then his hands left her face.

She swallowed. His eyes were busy examining his work, while hers were left hanging.

"Oh and if you wanna tighten, you just pull this part." Like a wife fixing her husband's tie he tightened it a very exact amount, adjusting the towel to fit her snugly without pulling at a single hair.

"There, how's that?"

When he said those words, he had wanted to say different ones. Perhaps words related to the ones lost earlier. Morrigan heard that. Importantly though, he hadn't.

A quiet panic rose like smoke in her that their moment had been lost forever.

It wouldn't have been enough even if she *knew* what Simon would have said. It was not the same thing as being told. She yearned to hear Simon tell her she was the prettiest and she was the only. She wanted a concrete *something*, and she wanted license to cry over it shattering into splinters.

She'd always allowed it to be skipped, pretended to be too cool for flowers, but she wasn't. It was a thing a teenager had the privilege of wanting and expecting, but she was old enough to feel obligated not to care. She felt like she was supposed to skip the intro track, to start several steps in at sex and assume all prequisite feelings were accounted for.

They couldn't stand outside talking forever. She would have to leave or go back inside his room.

Standing before Simon, her gut was heavy with dread that he would let the almost something he almost said substitute for an 'I like you'; or worse, he could invite her back inside, asking her to skip that step she clung to.

It would circumvent those words drowned in vomit earlier. Morrigan could no longer pretend she would be satisfied with anything simple that might help her move on. She hoped she would say no, if he asked. But, even if she did, it would be such an adamantine thing to say. If she left to go home *then*, she'd be telling him 'No' to everything else that accompanied it. Whatever the nothing that existed between them was, it would end.

"I gotta go." Morrigan couldn't remember what he'd said last, but it was her turn to say a thing, and that was what she *needed* to say. She needed to go home. She *had* to. Her brain was on fire and she needed to get away.

She stepped back and Simon stiffly pretended not to be reaching towards her. "Are you okay?"

"Yeah I'm good."

She wasn't convincing.

"Hey again I'm sorry about-"

"No it's cool."

"Listen, it was really nice to run into you tonight." Simon spoke firmly and coming from someone so gentle the words felt rougher than the man could possibly have intended. "I'd really love to do it on purpose. If you're free tomorrow I- I wanna see you."

Morrigan's eyebrows raised in surprise. She blinked and her lips parted but her throat was tight and she wanted him to keep talking anyway.

"If it's weird I can fuck off. I just-"

She nodded at him and might have even croaked out a "Yeah me too." but she wasn't sure.

"I just really enjoyed our conversation and uh... I'm-"

"Yeah I did too." She squeaked unnaturally high.

"Awesome, yeah I'm sorry about y'know..."

"No it's cool. Just buy me some food tomorrow and I'll just chuck it up all over you and we'll be even."

Simon tried laughing. It came out like a stiff whistle.

"Hey thanks for taking me on a walk too. It was... really sweet of you to make me feel better after hitting you. And I really needed a walk anyway, so... thank you."

"Next walk I take you on, I'll try not to puke all over you."

She flashed a smile and nodded. "Next time."

"So food and a walk? Tomorrow?"

"Yeah, yeah. *Also* uhhh shopping. I gotta take you shopping. See I fucked up one of your shirts, so lemme buy you a replacement. It just- it didn't fit, right? so I tried to force it and um the buttons popped off. I'm just fat and I shouldn't have-."

"Oh don't worry about it, really."

"Or I mean I could sew it."

Simon rolled his eyes with a good spirited sigh and extended a hand to shake. "Okay fine. You buy me a shirt. I buy you dinner, or lunch or whatever. Then you vomit that meal on *me* and then we go for a walk and then we'll be all evened up."

"Yeah! it's a-"
Date
        "-Plan."
Fuck.

She shook his hand with a hard jerk like a 1920s railroad tycoon and watched his eyes with vigilance. He looked again. She marked another point on a mental score-board.

Morrigan took a long meandering step backwards, and then another. Simon swung his hand up in a wave that mimicked nonchalance.

Her words were long and lingering, hanging on vowels as

she tugged herself apart from his company. "Alright *Simon*, I guess I'll *see you when I see you.*"

"Have a good night Morrigan," Simon exhaled. "And drive safe."

She turned, with no particular haste, making a somewhat obvious effort to keep her eyes lingering in his.

She tried to walk away cool and sexy but Morrigan had never been the kind of person who had any idea what to do with her hands, much less her ass.

"Hey," He called after her. "I know you said not to tip you, but that was before I puked on you *so...*"

"No tip." She yelled back with a smile she made sure Simon could hear.

Chapter 17

Envy

Morrigan checked her bank account for the third time and *again* checked her text messages. Still no message from Simon. She could only stall so much, as the air-conditioning was quickly being cooked from the car and Morrigan couldn't keep it running until her anxiety went away. She didn't have that kind of money.

She was parked outside the mall, specifically near 'Whole', a plus sized woman's clothing store. It was in an awkward spot and no one used it as an entrance unless it was Christmas and the parking lot was swamped. That is, no one that was Morrigan's size.

She locked eyes with the smug model on the huge poster above the entrance. It was overweight model in underwear shoving a science classroom skeleton out of frame. A reminder that she was an invader.

She had all the bounty for none of the hunt. Morrigan had large breasts but she hadn't paid for them like they had, and they *hated* her for it. They hated her worse than they hated a regular skinny person and that animosity had lingered in her psyche. Morrigan remembered what it felt like to be glared at, to make eye contact and break away and know they're still watching; analyzing all the faults in her appearance with magnitudes of hate.

She was sure they'd turn away with satisfaction once they spotted her flat ass, giraffe neck, and thighs that blend in an almost straight line into her calves. They probably laughed to themselves, thinking 'lollipop' like her mom, or maybe 'dairy cow'. She was sure, that if anyone could hate her more than she hated herself, it was them.

Morrigan put the key back into the ignition and turned on the car again. She pressed her nose against the air-conditioning vent and promised herself, "Just one more round of AC and I go in."

She wished she could just drive home and buy online, but last night had made her optimistic, and very wary of the neglected condition of her bras. If things *did* happen with Simon, she couldn't let him see the raggedy quality of her bras, or worse have a wire snap on him. She'd seen someone get their hand whipped by a snapped guitar string, and she imagined it would kill the mood about as effectively as puking all over him. She knew this was her only option for a really nice bra. She could buy a pack of plain bras at a department store, that would at least not explode on her, but she wanted something that looked nice. Anywhere else she got a nice looking bra, it wouldn't fit. It had to be here.

She wished she could get in and out like a strike team, but employees in boutique places like that got paid on commission and she knew they'd snag her. She'd always window shopped, because their bras were so cute, but the one time she'd been brave and gone in she ended up trapped in a conversation with a sales associate who rounded the holy trinity: The importance of safe sex, the negative impact on society of breast implants, and the health risks of not getting a breast reduction.

When it came time to check out, the cashier let two people

cut in front of her, and then went on break, walking right past her. Morrigan still had fantasies about clothes-lining her.

She felt a familiar dull lurch in her gut and her mind wandered into unsafe waters to find the memory attached to it. Her ex's face lit up by a phone, the clack of his long finger-picking thumbnail against the screen as he scrolled through stuff that bored him as much as her story, and his shrug. Those memories were a tar pit she wished she hadn't fallen into. Before she could get trapped in them, however, she thought of Simon's clear blue eyes. It was hard to imagine them uninterested. He was always looking away, his head caught in some innocent anxiety, but those eyes always snapped back to her with a kind of energy. She couldn't imagine him apathetic to a tale of passive aggressive store employees.

Morrigan ripped the key out of the ignition like she was pulling the pin on a grenade.

*If I **ever** get that far with Simon he's not going to see me in some worn, threading piece of shit bra with an exposed wire digging into my ribs. I don't know what he's going to think of me without a shirt, but he's not going to think I'm poor, a slob, or some bimbo-idiot spilling out of a miss-sized bra. I'm gonna get something cute enough to give me the confidence to take my own damn shirt off. And I'm gonna make him fucking nervous too.*

She punched the steering wheel and busted out of the car like a cop on a 911 call.

Chapter 18

Weighty silence

Alone on the raft Simon was held to no pretense of happiness, and he disturbed no one with a great mournful sigh. He stared up at a bleak, cloudy sky eclipsed by tattered cloth hangings strung on criss-crossing clothes-lines overhead. Their colors were sun-bleached by days brighter than this one to a bleak shade that matched the ocean of grey beyond them. His view was briefly eclipsed by the water sprinkling down from an elephant statue that marked the end of the ride. Simon unbuckled the raft ride's strange seatbelt with the ease of someone exiting their car, but otherwise didn't shift his gaze from those hangings. A weak wind battered them, setting a dull tempo for them to dance to. He didn't move, didn't open the water-proof container in the center of the raft and retrieve his phone, not until he had to.

Please keep your hands, arms and feet inside the raft, and remain seated until a cast member comes to assist you. It's her day off. She's probably sleeping in. We hope you enjoy the rest of your day, in Disney's Animal Kingdom.

He waited for the jolt of the raft, gently knocking against the dock, to rock himself forward and out of his seat. Simon took his phone, quickly like tearing off a band-aid, and then spent a measured smile on the cast member helping him out of the raft. That expression melted from his face once he was a step beyond them.

The grey gloom that consumed the sky made so few interested in a water ride that the rest of the cast were loitering about the barren entrance line talking. One noticed him, with a jolt, and broke away from her conversation to direct him to the exit with a grand gesture. She noted his shirt –wet from a drenching several rides ago– with some concern. Simon put on a big fake smile and remarked, not for the first time, "no line!"

They all smiled back. It was their job.

Sending her his number was easier than he'd anticipated. He'd done it just after hanging the laundry request bag, with her puke clothes in it, on his door-knob. Normally it would have taken him a few days deliberation but her insistence had freed him of his normal trepidation. He checked to make sure it was the right number –only seven times– and then sent it.

The much harder task was turning his cell service back on. He'd shut it off because he'd needed a break. Functionally it was the same as having his service turned on, as no one ever texted or called him, but so long as it was on, every day was a new rejection. It was a circumstance of his own doing. He'd turned down every invite he had received while he was dating a girl who would disapprove of him spending time with friends and those invitations didn't persist for three years and five months. He'd neglected his friends for so long that it felt selfish to even tell them about the breakup. He couldn't come up with a reason why they should be there for him.

He used his phone soley for Uber or Lyft. Only with the promise of a text from Morrigan had he braved re-enabling his texting app and it hadn't taken him long to abandon ship. After shutting his phone off to restart it and apply changes, his will to turn it back on failed him.

If he was going to turn his phone back on he wanted to be *sure* there would be a text from Morrigan waiting for him, but it was hard to convince himself. If she really wanted to text him she'd have given him her number to begin with, not played this game with the app, he reasoned. When he turned his phone back on he might confirm his fears that she wasn't really interested. That alone might have been liberating, even if it was upsetting. To be bombarded with a salvo of texts from his ex at the same time, however, was *far* more daunting.

Evidently no one else had similar concerns. No one else had a live grenade in their pocket. No one had pulled the pin he had. They worried instead about whether it was going to rain. Simon didn't need to walk up the single riders line because there *were* no riders. It was cold. He alone rushed from the exit back to the start of the non-existent line to get on again, and again, stepping quickly past lethargic guests squinting at a bright grey sky.

He was soaked, by now, and with it came the memory of that day on Splash Mountain. His idle mind forced to the forefront the smile she gave him when he returned with those ridiculous Cowboy Mickey pajama pants from Adventure Land. Her smile had been so bright it had embarrassed her. He remembered the bad pokerface that followed. In his memory it was so clearly burning with excitement. He remembered last night too, and the air that whirled around a girl in no rush to be anywhere but with him.

Simon stopped walking through the empty maze of a line and leaned against a Chinese guardian lion statue. The stone had been baked in the Florida sun and it was still warm. He could feel it cook his shoulder through his damp shirt. He lingered in the privacy of the deserted line, his hand on his phone and inhaled as deeply as he could. Holding that breath he squeezed the power-button blindly to restart it, and waited for the buzz to signify start-up finishing. He'd already changed the setting to let his texting app receive messages. A restart was all he needed to do to let the floodgates open.

Simon knocked his head against the stone once and pulled his phone out of his pocket. A quick breath and he thumbed the button on the side. The screen came on and he winced. 43 unread messages from his ex, that he panic swiped into the oblivion of archived message threads, and a meme from his friend. It was from a month ago but still marked as unread. He opened it, finally. It was a sad looking sloth, a reminder that there were people that missed having him around. It was more than Simon felt he deserved. He'd let his ex alienate him from his friends and he deserved to be lonely for that. He ignored them when they wanted to hang out and Simon was not ignorant of the fact that often the easiest way to talk about problems is under false pretenses. Being a friend meant being around, just in case something was up. He'd ignored them to earn points with his ex. He'd even joined in on her mocking of his friends behind their backs. Worst of all, he'd let himself believe some of it. He'd stopped being Simon because someone told him to. If someone could convince him to not be himself then to respond to the meme felt like impersonating himself. He couldn't really just go and pretend to be a person, could he?

Simon laid a fist against the hot stone and shoved himself upright. "Yeah I wouldn't text *me* either."

Chapter 19

Advanced Texting

Morrigan watched her phone restart for the fourth time. The phone was set on the carpet and she stared down at it with her stomach on a partially deflated exercise ball and her hands occupied by 4lb yoga weights while she did her daily reverse flies.

I really only have myself to blame. I woke up way too early to buy the bra. Now the day is longer and I can fit more disappointment in.

"Come on *man*, you have my number. You could at least say-"

Morrigan dropped the weights and snatched up the phone. She opened up the text history between them and saw it was completely empty. Morrigan hit herself in the forehead with the phone.

"I never texted him." She whispered, eyes squeezed shut, knocking the corner of her phone against her forehead. "He *doesn't* have my number. He's been waiting on me. He probably thinks I'm a jackass."

Morrigan got up off the exercise ball in a demonstration of questionable core strength and coordination. She began by falling as slowly as she could off of the ball and then Morrigan scrambled from her hands and knees to get her legs under her before springing to her feet.

She began to pace. The first text was something she should have been thinking about all last night and this morning. Now it was nearly eleven and she should have already texted him *something*. She knew it had to be casual, and the kind of nonchalant that made her seem cute and available, without seeming too desperate or giving him the impression she was a slut, while also conveying – very subtly– that she was also somewhat nervous. Relatable and attainable without being a mess, but not so put together that it was intimidating.

"Hello? No! That's so formal it sounds *angry.* I could add extra 'O's, and make it a casual '*hellooo*'. No. He could be annoyed I forgot to text him. I could use an exclamation mark to show I'm excited to talk to him. '*Hellooo!'* No, no, now I sound like I'm fucking Barney the dinosaur. Good morning? It *is* technically still morning. Maybe lie and tell him I just woke up? No I can't have him thinking I'm a fucking bum. He probably wakes up early to like jog or have business calls and *brunch* and shit."

Morrigan was thrown into a minor panic at the thought she'd missed her chance for a casual lunch. Her thoughts ran away from her and she dreaded the idea that Simon might be too fancy for lunch or breakfast and instead only have brunch. The stress of sharing a much more serious meal: dinner, or being the only one eating began to weigh on her, but then she remembered he ate lunch at the same time as her one day. (Regular lunch and not brunch).

She'd had to eat separately because she wasn't allowed in the park with a uniform on if she wasn't on the clock. He got her a purple slurpie because she mentioned that she liked mixing blue raspberry and cherry but never got it when she couldn't do it herself because she felt weird asking the attendant to do stuff that wasn't on the menu. She thought of awkward Simon asking for a purple slurpee and she smiled and hugged the phone like a teddy bear.

With another minor panic she checked the phone to make sure she hadn't typed anything and saw that she'd typed '**P**' and sent it.

"*Fucker*!"

Immediately she played an intense game of scrabble in her head and sent along "***Sup**"

Something had to follow that. She couldn't just hang a 'Sup' out there. She thought for barely a moment before following it up with the '*perfect*' thing. "**Sorry, forgot to text you.**"

This was when she made her fatal mistake. She added: "**It's Morrigan.**"

She had then entered the realm of the triple text, and she'd done it without throwing out a question to ensure a response. To make matters worse, she was technically a quad texter if she was counting the 'P'. She couldn't text anything ever again, and certainly not again today. This was her only day off for a while and Simon would likely be leaving soon.

She threw her phone at her bed. "Fuck!"

Can I text him in an hour and say that I'm getting lunch? I could ask him if he wanted anything.

She groaned, tipping forward and flopping face down onto the bed. "No, he's in the parks. What can I offer him that would even make sense? *Cheaper* food? He's too rich to care that a personal pizza at Pizza-Planet is twelve dollars. *Fuck!*"

Somewhere on the bed her phone buzzed, and she scrambled for it.

"Oh hey, I was just thinking about grabbing lunch. I don't suppose I could interest you in joining me?"

She kicked her legs with giddiness, slapping her shins against the bed. "That's too casual and the grammar is too perfect. I fucking know that game. You pasted that from your notes app, you adorable, anxious, little loser."

She wrote back: **"Oh sick, I'm starved. Should I pick you up?"**

Morrigan rolled off the bed and yanked her new bra off the hanger in the doorway like it was a superhero costume and knee slid to the dryer to grab some even cleaner socks. She recoiled from the conflux of dollar store air fresheners as she opened it and was pleasantly surprised to find, not only dry, but slightly warm socks inside. They didn't smell mildewy at all. It was a good omen.

Another text came in: **"Oh sure, that'd be great. Where did you wanna eat?"**

Morrigan dropped the phone and stood yelling like a super villain in mock despair. "Simon! you little bitch. I wouldn't need a man in my life if I could fucking decide where I wanted to eat you fucking-"

Another text came in and she dropped down to a squat. **"You wanna just walk around Downtown Disney and see what looks good?"**

Genuine relief *did* wash over Morrigan and she laughed softly, musing to herself: "What a fucking *man*."

Chapter 20

Radiance

As Simon made his way out of Animal Kingdom to be picked up by Morrigan his head was a vortex of incredible possibility. The surge of confidence from asking Morrigan to a casual lunch was unreasonably immense and it made saying *anything* to her seem possible.

There's so much about you that's captivating in ways that're unreplicatable. Your walk, it's so mesmerizing like you're moving to this inaudible cool rythm from a lazy cello that plays for you alone. And the way you give a quickness to how you turn to share a smile, like it's important, and I guess it is. Your smiles are great, from the coy ones you restrain to the ones that are explosively happy. Your soft skin yields so honestly to every emotion. Oh and your lips too. They're so cute and thin. The way you purse, pucker and twist them when you're thinking. and how they make your eyes look so big. You have no idea what it feels like for someone to look at you the way you look at me. The way my name sounds when you say it. In fact the way you say everything is nice. Your voice is this symphonic thing, deep but unmistakably feminine. You know, even when you're quiet and I'm not looking at you there's this powerful magnetism to you and it makes it impossible to feel alone.

"Too much. Don't ever say that." Inner Simon had played near the edge and had fallen over the cliff. He wrapped his knuckle against his forehead and groaned. "You'll sound like a god damn maniac. Way too clingy. *Jesus.*"

There was a buzz in his pocket. Simon flinched. Morrigan had obviously sent him a text message telling him that she couldn't go out to lunch because he was a creep.

Simon looked up at the canopy above, squeezing his eyes shut and sliding a ginger hand into his pocket. He felt another buzz. Obviously that was a followup text telling him his penis was small too. There was just no other explanation.

Holding the phone above him, he peeked with one eye and read: "**I'm here by the way ;)**"

Simon opened both eyes and scrolled down.

"Not to rush you or anything."

A double text? His strength was restored to him. *Is that a WINKING smile? Is it a joke? Like a dude joking about being gay for their friend? No. It's an inappropriate emoticon. She didn't know what to put so she threw that in. She didn't want to sound passive aggressive or impatient so she couldn't use a regular smiley because it might seem sarcastic. She must be overthinking her texts.*

"Oops I meant: :)"

Simon almost dropped his phone.

*It **did** mean something. She wouldn't have corrected the wink if she wasn't thinking about what it **could** mean. She also could only have noticed if she was reading over her own text. People do that when they're overthinking things. Then she wrote so much to correct it and not just and asterisk. She's anxious enough to ponder the meaning of a winky smiley emoticon.*

"She's just as much of a disaster as me." he breathed, locking his phone to keep from sending any accidental texts.

With his analysis came a pang of empathy. He cursed under his breath and rushed towards the entrance of the park with big strides. If Morrigan's head afflicted her with the kind of chaos *his* did, Simon needed to hurry and distract her from it.

As he made his way, Simon let out a long groaning sigh, tapping the corner of his phone against his forehead. "I can't just leave her hanging, can I?"

Simon wrote out: **"Awesome! Be there in a"** and watched that blinking text cursor for several seconds before taking in a breath and inserting a fake mistake into the text. **"Awesome! Be there in a sex."** Then he deleted the period to be more casual and sent it. Then he immediately corrected: **"SEC!"** adding caps to seem extra frazzled. Lying felt wrong but it felt worse to let her stew while he came up with a more honest life-line.

Simon thought for a moment about sending a *third* text but, while he was compasionate enough to not leave her hanging with a cold *single* text (without any mistakes), he couldn't *also* climb out on the triple text limb.

When Simon exited the park he felt as though he were taking his first step outside. He hadn't noticed under the tree cover on his walk to the exit, but that endless blanket of clouds that had persisted all day had just been shattered by sun. Without the strategic shade of a Disney park above him, the full weight of the sun came down onto his shoulders. The sensation was invigorating, given how wet he was from his revolving-door rides on Kali River Rafting. It also gave him a plausible story for why he'd been riding the water attraction so obsessively.

Simon looked out into a world of just *bright*. His eyes were driven into a squint as he attempted to perceive a landscape assailed by a very persistent sun. Every surface, even the pavement, seemed to reflect hot light directly at Simon's chest and face. By some miracle he spotted black jeans, ripped at the knees. Even blinded by the sun he could recognize her eager wave; the motion indisputably belonged to Morrigan. At the familiar sight his smile came as immediately and naturally as his squint came to a bright light. She reached her arm straight up and with it she rolled up onto the balls of her feet before bouncing back down. Her hand itself waved with a quick spasm like a jingling a bell. It was striking how pleasantly familiar a mannerism and a silhouette could be after just a week. It almost felt like he knew her.

Simon swung a hand up in a wave and then shaded his eyes with it. There she was. Even in this heat she hid every bit of herself save for the tips of her fingers escaping out the ends of her sleeves, her knees peeking through the torn holes at her knees, and the half of her face not hidden behind her mess of hair. There was a smile there, lightly concealed by blinding glare. It was a bright excited thing betraying her normal composure. It was a wordless admission of excitement for his company.

That flash confession surged excitement through Simon. His smile intensified so sharply that a giggle burst out past it before he composed himself. It felt safe to be so excited while shrouded by the squinty brightness of the sun with a modicum of distance between them.

"Sorry I'm wet," Simon called once he was close enough.

Morrigan shrugged and swung her arms to either side. "Don't worry about it. You never get tired of the smell of the water rides."

"It's bromine, right?" Simon stopped before her, then sidestepped to put the glare of the sun at his back, then sidestepped once more to cast his shadow over her.

Sheltered from the sun, Morrigan blinked her brown eyes up at him and he realized he was impolitely close. He shuffled back a step and she lurched at the movement, jerking her thumb behind her and half twirling. She said something then that was meant to explain where she'd parked and about how it was kind of far away, but she tripped over her words and her meaning tumbled into nonsense.

Simon felt a pang of comradery. He could feel the twist in his gut like it'd been *him* who blundered their words. His first instinct was to pretend he'd understood her impeccably but he knew if it was him, that blunder would keep bleeding hours later if it wasn't cauterized now.

"You just have a stroke?"

It wasn't funny but that didn't mean anything to a nervous girl choked by awkwardness. She laughed and turned to give him a playful shove. Mirth turned her might feeble and she fell gently against him. Simon hooked a hand around to keep her from falling. It was almost like a hug, or perhaps a *half*-hug but so long as he didn't let his arm linger around her too long it wouldn't be. It was just a free touch that they could both enjoy and pretend –for the sake of their nerves– didn't happen.

She staggered a few steps away, recovering from her laughing fit, and shot him a look that put *him* off balance. With one eye squinting away the sun's glare the other was aimed right at him. She snuffed her smile with a pout but her face still looked *so* happy. He looked away, sharply, like he was afraid of walking into a pole. Her face was so oppresively pretty it was like seeing something lewd, and eye contact felt as forward as grabbing her butt.

Keeping composure he chuckled softly, shaking his head like she'd done. "We'd better get some food in you soon."

The pair walked a long way to reach her car and they carried conversation with them. Morrigan had a certain zephirousness to her as they walked. Her pace carried her ahead but she'd whirl –sending her hair into chaos– now and again to make eye contact as they spoke, back-pedalling while she listened to him. She was so attentive to his words and Simon was again struck by the distinct flattery of being listened to intently, as if the things he had to say were important, even in as mundane a conversation as theirs. All they talked about was the sun. Morrigan complained about the plight of being so pale in a place so sunny. And indeed it *was* sunny, nearly enough to dry Simon's clothes by the time they reached the car.

"Hey sorry if I get your seat wet. I'm mostly dry, but I got unlucky on Khali River. I was tempted by the no-line, but..." He lied with a shrug.

"Don't worry about it man," she shrugged, before swinging down into her seat like it was a cockpit.

He got into his seat like it was a cockpit too, but less like an ace fighter pilot, and more like a reporter terrified to break anything.

"Hey so how come you don't have a beard? Mr. Viking Dude."

Simon cocked his head and blinked. Before he could answer he heard the airy sound of poorly stifled laughter and looked over to see her keeled over in hysterics.

"You've been asked that before, I take it?"

"Couple times."

She clapped a hand on his shoulder briefly. "Well you look plenty pretty without a beard."

"Thanks."

Just what every viking aspires to be: **pretty***.*

She started the car and quickly slapped the music off before it could play a note.

"You ever get the red hair question?"

"Oh, yeah a bit. Not as much as the freckles one, though. I swear I really do have them. They're just light. They come out more in the sun, but I stay out of the sun if I can." She explained, sticking her phone in the car-mount. "And apparently the red hair is from a certain place and black hair is more common in others. What's really rare is the brown eyes with the black hair instead of blue. My mom has blue eyes and black hair. My dad is a bright, fiery ginger with green eyes and his parents both had hazel eyes. You know what I mean by that? Like half brown with a starburst of green. Anyway he got nice bright eyes and then it went backwards for me. Not the end of the world to get my grandma's genes I guess. She's so Irish she referred to her hometown as 'the shire', not sure if that makes her Irish or a hobbit though..." She droned slowly into mumbles as she fiddled with her GPS and the air conditioning.

Simon was the type of driver who only ever idled out of a parking spot, but Morrigan was not. She accelerated backwards, swinging the car out into the lane without a single tap on the brake.

Wary of the pacifying effect of being driven, and the awkward silence it might bring, he nudged her on.-"Does your grandma cook any traditional Irish food?

"Nope she's dead."

"Oh god, I'm so sorry."

"What? Did you kill her?"

"No!" punched it's way out of Simon's mouth, and his ears started burning immediately.

"You answered *way* too quick. I knew it!" Morrigan jabbed him lightly in the arm.

He let out a good natured groan and Morrigan's exaggerated snickering left him with something of a grin once he was done mushing his face in his hands. "I've been found out."

"I'm sorry. I shouldn't tease you so much. I'll ruin you. You're too sweet."

She was occupied with merging and he stole a glance, wondering if 'sweet' was an adjective in her vocabulary that had a future.

"Cottage pie." Morrigan said before silence could set in between them. "She used to cook that for holidays. It's like shepherd's pie but with beef instead of sheep. It was really good."

Simon nodded, having nothing insightful to add. Upon realizing she couldn't see his nod he added the vocal equivalent, as gracefully as he could.

"Sorry. It *was* sweet of you to ask. I'm just a cunt."

He winced at how she referred to herself.

The sharpness of it spurred him on to defend her honor, even if it was from herself, but as he looked at her to speak he was struck by how casual she was. She didn't curse at work but now she swore with such strong language so easily. It was so unladylike, and yet there was something alluringly cool about a tongue so unrestrained by society.

Hearing her talk like that made him feel included in a kind of exclusive club, like he was a highschooler hanging out with the cool kids. It lead him to wonder if this was what she was like around her friends, and then it was a quick leap for him to wonder again what exactly *he* was.

White noise made of wind and engine did its best to lay silence over the two of them. The question, still unasked, had no natural lead in. There was no topic of conversation that lent a legitimate segway to the asking. For this reason the chasm of conversation between them lured him to the edge, a pivotal question tempting his lips to part.

He started the sentence in his head and it echoed there into a deafening cacophony. The words rolled over again and again in his head until they lost all meaning but none of their urgency. Still, instinct treated bringing up the topic like he was trying to touch his own eyeball. So he flinched.

"Hey Morrigan, can I ask you something?"

Simon winced. His inflexion had come out strangely like an actor on a 'learn to speak english' DVD.

After a pause in which she did *not* comment on his strange manner of speech she answered with an abrupt. "Oh, uh... sure."

"I'm kind of- I might have mentioned, or I guess alluded to the fact... uhh." Simon's mind went blank and the world didn't end. Morrigan just waited for him to collect his thoughts. "I'm sorry. I'm nervous. Last night I think I mentioned that I uh... get nervous?"

"I can't really remember. Why did you get nervous again?"

"Doesn't take much," he groaned.

Morrigan aggressively passed someone.

"Anyway, I feel like I've been selfish. I'm always so focused on trying not to feel bad or uncomfortable or whatever and it distracts me from what really matters and that's..."

He could feel her stiffen, braced for some uncomfortable advance from a weirdo which she was trapped in a car with.

"Right, well, I just wanted to say that you're... I mean, objectively, you're a really great person to be around. I think anyone would-"

"Fucking *cool* dude," Morrigan sighed venomously.

Immediately panic rattled him. Simon's brain began cross referencing every word he'd said against anything that could sound similar but be deeply offensive to her.

Morrigan slowed down at one of the booths for the parking lot and talked to the guy like she was arresting him for pooping on her lawn every day for the past six months and her parking pass was the warrant.

She hissed a swear as she navigated the parking lot. "Sorry, it's not you. I missed a turn."

He didn't understand how. They were *in* the parking lot. She *couldn't* have gone the wrong way.

He didn't know what he'd said to upset her. He wasn't even sure what he'd said. All thought melted from the man and his head dripped with it into his hands.

Suddenly self conscious of allowing someone to see the depths of his sulking Simon straightened with a jerk and a hand grazed against his back as it was hastily withdrawn.

Suddenly Morrigan turned stiffly into a parking space so sharply her back tires drifted an inch and let out a short squeak. She didn't have to rush to snag that spot. She'd parked in a vast empty section of the parking lot. The shops were so far they were obscured by a heat-haze on the horizon like a mirage in the desert.

"Don't wanna get door dinged." Morrigan explained briskly before turning the key, popping the door, and climbing out of the car in one fluid motion. She slammed the door quickly behind her, trapping conversation inside.

A parked car has a certain tranquility to it. The noise dampening meant for the highway can leave a void of peaceful silence once the engine has been turned off. Morrigan must have imagined this silence to be *impenetrable*, because she swore to herself outside as though Simon couldn't hear her.

"Yeah I'm sure he's gonna remember what we were talking about *now* you psycho cunt."

166

Chapter 21

Orpheus

Why do you have to be like this? You can't just shut your fucking mouth. You have to be bitter and cunty to the only guy willing to even tolerate you. You've fucking ruined everything, or you're going to. That's for fucking sure.

She power-walked because she couldn't run and still claim to be sane.

She was sure that if Simon was about to say anything that might officiate the transition from friends to... *something*, then Morrigan had shut that down. And she wanted him to say that anything. She wanted her moment on a grassy hill at fourth of july fireworks where a boy tells her that he likes her. She wanted to blush and giggle and be a girl –the girl– before exes and age stole her entitlement to silly cute things.

With vision blurred by hot blinks Morrigan scanned left and right for cars, without stopping, as she crossed the parking lot.

She felt greedy and childish. She could emulate the opinions of her mother and her ex and they would certainly think so. She wanted Simon to tell her that he likes her and be taken on a date and go through the many things she missed because she allowed herself to believe those things were only for girls in movies. She wanted the steps before having her bra taken off by someone who was far too good at it.

Morrigan realized she was walking fast, faster than Simon, but she couldn't stop and wait because she was too preoccupied by breathing and not looking back at that adorable creature trying to keep pace with her. Because if she *did* look, with her glassy eyes, then he'd see a dumb girl coming apart at the seams over *nothing*.

She was twenty-four. Old enough that hickies were for whores and flowers were for apologies. It wasn't Simon's problem that Morrigan had never gotten to be late for class waiting at her locker, books held against her breast, for a boy to muster the courage to come out and ask her to the prom.

She wanted to turn and ask, for all of it. While it was still the last thing that they'd not talked about, it felt possible. Still, it wasn't really a thing that could be asked for. Even if he was willing to court her, he'd just be humoring her. It wouldn't be real. She knew it wasn't fair to ask for a boyfriend out of a man who lived a plane-ride away. She needed a rebound to purge her brain of silly wants and melancholic memories. It was immature and selfish to ask for more.

So Morrigan walked with Eurydice in tow, unwilling to turn and ask a question only to see him whisked away to Tartarus before her eyes. She strode fiercely onwards and the stone in her throat began to dissolve.

Hopping down from the curb, she moved quickly between two cars parked wide enough that she didn't have to break stride. Just as she walked out from between them, she felt strong hands grasp her by the biceps and yank her backwards. There was so much force behind those arms that one of her untied converse was left on the pavement.

Her legs flailed instinctively and her right foot, clad in a faded Invader Zim halfsock, hit the side mirror of a van meteoring past.

The massive thing shoved air aside blasting a gust through the valley between cars, fierce enough to force her eyes into a squint. A black ring narrowed her vision and her heart beat frantically inside her like it was the last tic-tac being violently rattled around the container. Across from them was a 50ish mid-west woman with her hand on her heart and eyes wide.

Morrigan only processed it was Simon who'd saved her from the speeding van when she heard his very polite "Excuse me." Before he squeezed past her. She watched him with new eyes, squinting at his arms as if she'd now notice they were suddenly twenty inches across with barbwire tattoos on them.

That cute little twink lifted me off my feet?

Simon was walking over to the van, now stopped waiting for someone to back out of a spot, and she now noticed it was a "Minnie" Van themed after Minnie Mouse. They were a line of cars employed by Disney. She didn't realize what Simon was doing as her brain was dull from adrenaline and 'aggressive' was not a word she'd have used to describe Simon.

Then she saw a move she'd never seen before, used by a man that she could never have imagined using it. Simon shook his watch down past his wrist, onto the heel of his palm, and slammed the back window of the car **hard**. The resounding crack made every figure across her periphery flinch and even the car backing out of the spot stopped. Morrigan's mouth opened in disbelief as she watched Simon march over to the driver side door. Simon pulled on the handle and the door came open.

Morrigan could see the driver, his head shrinking below his shoulders, look back at her and hold his hands up at Simon. Simon stood dangerously still. The only motion he made was with his lips and the veins in his neck that bulged as he spoke softly to the driver. Unease crept in as she could sense the nearness of violence. Just as Morrigan began to fear the confronation escalate, Simon punctuated with a sharp barked shout of "You, have a magical day, buddy!" in his face. He slammed the car door on the guy, so hard she saw the van rock slightly.

Morrigan didn't know if she should be afraid of this hidden angry Simon, laugh at the unusual behavior, or clap for her savior. He returned to her, meekly, waving and saying "hi" and "hey" to everyone staring. Simon stooped to retrieve her shoe and stumbled as he stood.

"Sorry about that." He mumbled, kneeling to help her get her shoe back on.

Morrigan's chest felt suddenly very heavy as images of cinderella filled her head. She could have shoved her foot in the shoe and twisted into it against the asphalt, but she postured her foot like a princess and, after several palpable moments of hesitation, Simon too was tempted towards a silent re-enactment. He slipped the ratty converse onto her small delicate foot like this was a normal way of returning a shoe and stood abruptly.

She had been a mess *before* almost dying, and Morrigan hadn't had time to compose herself. Her face confessed that she was, in fact, an artillery salvo of emotion next to a gasoline fire. Simon wrapped his arms around the mess, without hesitation, then those arms immediately stiffened with trepidation. When she released an involuntary sniffle and followed it with a snotty "Fuck" Simon squeezed like a man who was permitted to hug her.

"I'm sorry."

Morrigan pressed into his embrace like she could burrow into his button-down.

"I know the money from getting hit by a Disney van would have been an awesome vacation, but I just really wanted to have lunch."

Morrigan traded sniffles for giggles and she could feel the laughter in her chest buffet against Simon's body.

"I'm *hungryyy* and I have *companyyy* and I'll need a ride *back...*"

Sensing the hug was coming to an end, Morrigan gave him a squeeze, squishing her chest against him like she'd done the night before, hoping it would ameliorate any discouragement she'd inflicted in the car. She pulled away afterward, and opened her eyes to find the adrenaline crash had made her eyes water more than she'd realized. Morrigan swung her hood over her face and wiped her tears on it in private.

Out of her mucousy throat her voice came small and crackly. "I was almost rich, you slut."

Simon laughed so hard, she knew he'd never had one of his guy friends call him that before. The word had time traveled out her mouth, from a time when she had friends. For her, that joke had gotten overtold back in middle school, but Simon had no resistance to it at all. Just like every one of her knuckle-head dude friends, he found the misuse of the insult hilarious and the fact eased a tiny nostalgic smile onto her face.

After a long moment, he lifted her hood to peek at her face. "I promise I'll shove you in front of an Epcot bus after we eat."

He looked at her with eyes that undermined his banter with naked compassion. The sun was caught within the facets of those crystalline blue eyes, and he pursed his lips to hold back the kind of words that soft tone was really meant for.

Morrigan punched him playfully, letting one fist linger on the softness of his chest for a long moment while she drank in the sight of him. His fair skin was bright like snow in the sun and his eyes caught that same light like ice. She pushed him an inch and knew he'd let her knock him flat on his back before pushing back against her. She blinked, looking down, and turned him around.

"You lead." She cleared a mucousy throat. "I'll..."

Do it. Make him feel good. You get one shot.

"I'll be *your* prince, if *you* walk in front of a van too."

Simon's grin was so wide she could see it while standing behind him.

Chapter 22

Magnets

Simon was not a man to whom fury was familiar. The emotion scorched the veins it had just coursed through. His forearms were faintly sore from clenched fists, and he could still feel the wake of that yell in his throat. He felt like he needed a nap.

Morrigan on the other side, seemed energized by her near-death experience and somehow unperturbed by his outburst. He followed her around Downtown Disney as she bounced from curiosity to curiosity on a whim, like a bubbly sprite zipping about a glade. He followed her, grateful to be spared the pressure of entertaining by her zephyrousness.

For a starving girl, Morrigan gave food little priority. She pointed out a shop, oblivious to the adrenaline shakes in her finger, before plucking at the hem of his shirt, ushering him along with her to explore. The store only sold magnets. Simon followed, blinking at rows upon rows of black sheet-metal panels covered in magnets; flat magnets with clever sayings, frames for photos to stick to the fridge, and various characters in different outfits.

"Hey, this one was made for you." Morrigan teased,

presenting him with a magnet that said: 'Have a magical day!'

He was slow to get it, and slower to show he was a good sport with a smile.

Simon struggled to understand why or even *how* he'd been overtaken by that sudden flash of anger. The Simon he knew in his head would have complained about how much of a jerk the driver was, and stayed by her side to comfort her. It shamed him how roughly he'd grabbed her to pull her away from the van. He'd scared her, and he could still feel in his hands a phantom of it; how she had jerked in frantic resistance. It made his heroics feel like a violation. Her instinctive physical rejection of his touch delivered an irrational blow to his ego that he couldn't shake off alone. If he asked for her absolution, he knew she'd feel obligated to tell him it was alright. It was *alright,* after all he'd saved her life, but he was sure she'd imagined a hero saving her in a manner that was far more... *princely.*

She didn't let him escape with that fake smile. She was waiting, her head cocked slightly, in question.

"Hey uhh... Sorry for grabbing your shoulders so roughly."

Morrigan raised her eyebrow so high it took her cheek with it and tugged her mouth up in half a smirk too. "I simply can never forgive you. Next time you save my life, do it gentler or you'll be hearing from my legal team." She punctuated with a gentle slap to his cheek with the magnet and when his smile broke free from the gloom, her face cracked into mischief. "God, you're such a..."

Simon cocked his head, *What? pussy?* his eyebrow twitching in protest before she could even finish.

A giggle squeaked from behind Morrigan's firmly pursed lips when she saw it.

Simon's mouth opened and hands gestured and somehow it was funnier than any vocal retort.

Morrigan bowed her face out of sight for a long second and swung her head back up, whipping Simon's chin with her hair.

We're standing kinda close.

Her face was freshly composed, and doing it's best not to mock him. "Sorry," she said with a soft smile at her lips. "You alright? I feel like I know you pretty well by now and I can't imagine you getting that angry, even after *seeing* you get that angry. Is anything up?"

Simon's first instinct was to recoil, away from the question, but he fought it. A flash of something like embarrassment, at provoking her question, passed through him but it faded quickly. He knew she wasn't asking out of obligation because he'd made her feel uncomfortable by moping. She cared, and didn't resent that fact. As it turned out he knew her pretty well too.

"I... uh... I dunno."

Her eyes were earnest and patient and he was looking into them without any urge to look away. She wanted a real answer and she wouldn't let him escape it with a shrug.

"I'm embarrassed I guess." Simon swallowed. "I don't really *do* that and I- I *did*... do that... and in front of you... and I don't even know what to think of myself anymore and..."

"Simon." She put an open palm on his chest. "Don't take this the wrong way, okay? But I'm never going to be afraid of you being a violent psycho. You defending my honor was really sweet. I'm flattered that me almost getting killed by a Minnie Van moves you enough to make you act *so* out of character, but I'm still looking at Simon in front of me."

Simon looked at her looking at *Simon* and wondered who exactly that person was, according to her.

They lingered there for a long moment, facing each other,

before he thanked her softly. His cheeks still cooked with blush but, with the slight weight of her splayed fingers against his chest, he was anchored to her. No instinct to turn away nagged at him. He belonged there, with her.

Abruptly, Morrigan withdrew her hand from him, and hastily swept hair over her ear, letting most of it fall right back into disarray. With a sharp motion she slapped the magnet she'd been holding onto one of the metal display walls. "Hey we should check out the Lego store. I haven't been there in a while and I bet they have new statues."

*Is she nervous too? Because of **me**?*

Her sudden movement spurred Simon to step with quickness in her wake but just as his foot caught her shadow she halted, whirling to face him again. "Unless you're hungry?"

Simon stopped short with the urgency of a train conductor who has realized the bridge is out. He leaned backwards and sucked in his chest as though if he were to accidentally come into contact with her breasts he would be sparking together the ignition wires to a bomb.

"Oops," she said with a laugh, clearly not recognizing the 'severity' of the situation. "Anyway sorry to get carried away. I don't wanna starve you if you wanna eat, I'm just enjoying having a shopping buddy. Not that I like shopping or whatever anyway. If you wanna eat that's cool. I could eat."

Simon blinked. There was something familiar about the chaos behind her rambling. He wanted to say something akin to 'yeah, me too,' but he had a question to answer, so he did. He told her he wasn't hungry. It was strange that he wasn't, given how hungry he'd been before she picked him up, but then anxiety was an odd ingredient to a meal. It made the food seem so much less important.

Chapter 23

Lunch

"Hey, what do you think about this place?" Morrigan asked, about yet another restaurant.

"Oh sure, I'm good with whatever." Simon answered again, about yet another restaurant.

Morrigan stalked about another family crowding the menu holder and reached over the short son to snatch one.

She didn't bother looking at the whole menu. She just skimmed the prices of the appetizers and passed it off to Simon. "Think you could find something you'll like here?"

"Oh, sure." Simon said with a shrug as though 50% of the responsibility of choosing a restaurant to finally eat at didn't rest on his shoulders. "I'm fine with whatever."

Mother fucker.

Morrigan shrugged and, before she could stop herself, offered –yet again– "Well we can just keep walking."

I'm going to starve. This is how I die. I deserve it too, because I'm attracted to the only other loser in the universe that's too anxious to choose where to eat.

Somewhere in her ponderings she must have sighed, because Simon looked to her. His eyes full of concern and curiosity. It was almost *intrusive*. She was used to the angst in her head going unnoticed regardless of the volume of any sigh or depth of any shoulder sag.

"Oh! I'm sorry. I should have been more decisive. I just didn't want to be pushy since you drove and all."

"Ah! Sorry. Whatever my face did, I'm sorry. I'm not used to people caring how I'm feeling. I would have bottled it up better."

Simon toned a note of sympathy but Morrigan muzzled any elaboration with a palm pressed against his face. She mushed his mouth but he buzzed an "*awww*" through it.

"Oh you shush. Get those nosey, blue, mind-reading, eyes off my face." She bit her lip with a grin.

His eyebrow slowly climbed, but he was otherwise still with uncanny patience, as she retracted her hand. "Mind reading? You have the most expressive face I've ever seen."

"Oh yeah? Well your lips are softer than mine."

His eyes went to her lips and swept up over her face as the thought of a kiss went through her. His gaze was suddenly overwhelming. She could feel her whole head getting hot with blush so she took him by the shoulders and turned him around for privacy. His body moved so easily she was startled that she might have been too rough with him, but he didn't seem jarred. She was used to men with a certain guard, a balance that kept them from being knocked over from a surge of the mosh pit spilling over into the crowd. Simon didn't feel like that at all. He was so agreeable to her jostling

179

it made her worry that she might knock him to the ground if she wasn't careful. She liked it. She wasn't sure exactly why, but it made her want to drag him backwards into a tight hug.

"Pick- pick a uh... place. A restaurant. I'm hungry."

With his back still turned she touched the back of a hand to her cheek to feel for heat. Whenever her cheeks got red from crying or exercise these ugly freckles showed themselves and she wanted to make sure they were hidden before he saw them.

"Alright, alright. Lets go to..." Simon stabbed his finger out at a restaurant. "This one."

Her stomach dropped. He'd pointed to the kind of restaurant that you didn't have lunch at when you were in Morrigan's tax bracket. They didn't use dollar signs or cents. They just put numbers on the menu; numbers like 16 and 20.

"Come on, my treat." He said with a decidedly intrusive empathy. "Call it gas money."

Her lips parted but no protest came to her. She watched a cute dork who thought he was smooth, and couldn't argue. He beckoned her along, taking a few steps backward, only to back into a wheelchair going by. He erupted into an explosion of hasty apologies and Morrigan's smile showed teeth as she watched him. He was sincere and embarrassed but the lady was having none of it. It was adorable in a 'I should squeeze his butt just to make him blush' kind of way.

Morrigan swooped in and hooked his elbow to drag him away from the woman who seemed to believe she was a great pioneer in philosophy presenting a groundbreaking thesis that people "ought to look where they're going."

Once inside Simon handled talking to the hostess and it was like watching a totally different person. He had a 'phone voice' as her mother used to say. He talked differently and there was no honest stumbling to his words. He was efficient with his words and exuded this confident charisma she didn't know he had, or could even fake.

What was more astonishing was his level of self control. The hostess was, in Morrigan's opinion, '*a fucking smoke show*'. Morrigan couldn't keep from raking her eyes up and down the blonde's curve-squeezing red bandage dress, abusing herself with comparison. Everywhere she held insecurities about her own body she found nothing but toned improvements. To make matters worse she had nice breasts too. They were smaller but she employed a wicked craft of presentation. She had contouring makeup on and squeezed them together, shamelessly tight, creating cleavage so deep you could lose a boyfriend in it.

Morrigan remembered sitting alone with a receipt that had a heart drawn on it while Sean was hopefully going to the bathroom and not talking to the waitress. She remembered being hungry and looking at her meal which she had wrapped up because they'd gotten her order wrong and she didn't want to have to tell them to fix it. She'd told him, and he told *her* to tell *Victoria* about it if she wanted them to fix it. Sean didn't want to bother *Victoria* with it because he-

"Morrigan?"

She snapped her focus to Simon, praying she hadn't been zoned out angrily staring at the Hostess's breasts. "Huh? Yeah? Whadja say?"

"Can we sit by the window or will you burn?" He asked with wide attentive eyes. "We've been walking around a lot and I don't want you to get sunburn if we sit by the window. The view is really nice though, so it's up to you if you wanna take the risk."

She blinked at Simon then and it struck her that he was in fact *not* her ex boyfriend. The fact kicked her in the stomach. She was looking at some dork who remembered her rambling about getting sunburnt when she couldn't even remember telling him. It was so jarringly sweet it almost felt as though it should have been sarcastic.

"Yeah, a window-seat sounds nice." She answered passively, at first, then cleared her throat and added more inflection. "I'll be fine. I can always move the part in my hair or whatever."

The hostess led them to their table and Morrigan dimly wondered if she belonged. She was at a restaurant which she really couldn't afford following some guy she didn't really know: Confident Simon.

If he's confident enough to talk to a blonde smokeshow of a hostess, is he confident enough to fuck her in the bathroom?

As they took their seats the hostess pulled out Simon's chair for him. As he sat she pushed it in for him too. He smiled at the hostess.

Has he already fucked her?

Morrigan sat in her chair –without assistance– and the hostess feigned a step towards her, as if to say 'Oh sorry you sat too quickly I was just about to help'. Before she left the hostess smiled at Morrigan as if to say 'I'm gonna steal your man you ugly bitch.'

"Do you know her?" Simon asked, with staggeringly genuine innocence, extending a menu to her.

She looked at the menu, then at him.

Meeting his innocent doe eyes embarrassed her to harbor such irrational thoughts. But still her heart was poisoned with animosity by the past and she snapped. "Probably just another whore my ex fucked behind my back." She punctuated by snatching the menu from him and slapping the page down in front of her.

As soon as she said it Morrigan knew she'd be replaying that in her head for hours in bed, cringing at her severe tone. She couldn't look up and face him. That snap wasn't meant for him but she couldn't apologize and dwell any more on it. She stared at the wine menu upside down, hoping that the last few seconds would melt away if she pretended hard enough that she hadn't said anything.

He said her name. He said it with a whole breath. It was a mournful exhale full of such intense pity. Her ears were hot and she swore like she'd cracked her phone. She closed her eyes and entered a dizzy dimension filled with adrenaline fueled thumping and some dim hunger pangs.

She was so consumed in it that when she noticed Simon beside her, it nearly made her jolt. He was on one knee to lower himself to her in her seat and was awkwardly extending his arms around her in a hug. She noticed his indecision over whether to try and get over or under her boobs and when his hand came into contact with her back it was so light and tentative he could have been disarming a landmine. Morrigan smiled with a quivering lip as he slowly enclosed his arms around her. It was sweet. *Simon* was sweet.

In his game of operation, Simon decided to go above her breasts and he overshot it by an adorably prude margin, making the embrace more of a headlock than a hug. When she felt his forearm graze her chin. she grabbed that arm and pressed it against her, just below her collarbone, silently accepting his hug. She could immediately feel a great deal of tension leave the man. Still he craned his head back, afraid to lay it over her shoulder in a more intimate embrace.

Still worried about overstepping boundaries? Dude, you should be stepping out the fucking door, far away from this psycho.

She wanted to wrap her other arm around him but it was trapped and she feared freeing it would shatter this *very* delicate hug that she'd just acquired.

"I'm sorry. You're not supposed to know I'm crazy."

Simon squeezed her and her chest got tight. As he began to

receed, Morrigan's fingers tightened slightly, over the arm wraped around her, to keep him there a moment longer.

Lunch seemed to be a dead time for the restaurant, as their section was entirely empty, save for them. So when a waitress approached, they heard it. The fear of an awkward interaction coursed through Simon and into Morrigan like electricity.

Simon returned to his seat and Morrigan straightened her posture with a flurry of blinks and coughs between them.

"Hello my name is Jess, and I'll be taking care of you today. Is there anything I can get you to start off with?"

Morrigan who had just oriented and flipped her menu answered quickly, as though it were a gameshow question. "I'll take a Mountain Dew if you have it."

Fuck! Is that a trashy thing to order? Is that immature? Shoulda gotten black coffee. French black coffee.

"Uh, a water is fine, thanks."

Fuck. He's health conscious?

"Actually could I get a water too?" Morrigan amended, looking up at the waitress.

"As part of our service we'll bring you both purified water with a pitcher. So you'll be just fine. Don't worry, we're gonna take good care of you both."

*Fuck you cunt. Don't you fucking condescend to me. I **know** you always bring out water. I want the big normal cup. I'm not scared I'll fucking starve... water starve. Whatever that's called.*

"There's also an award winning alcohol menu right on the back there." She explained reaching down to flip Morrigan's menu. "If you just flip that over there, it's right on the back."

Morrigan held the menu in an iron grip. "Mmm, thanks."

"Our drink specials today are on the chalkboard over there. My personal recommendation is the *Second Girlfriend*."

Whore.

Morrigan was derailed from the eye contact shelter of her menu and caught Simon's eye. Clearly he was unsure of what he'd just heard her call the drink and his expression made Morrigan giggle.

"You folks just flag me down any time and we'll get you set up with something awesome or just go talk to our bartender Sven, he's the *best*."

Does this chick get commissions for drinks?

"So you folks want me to get any starters going for you while I'm here?"

"Nothing for me."

"Yeah I think we're good. Thanks."

Morrigan who'd been staring at the appetizer page this entire time, more as a place to put her eyes than in an attempt to actually read any, noticed bottomless crab cakes for '9' a moment too late. The waitress had already taken a step away from the table –which might as well have been another dimension– so Morrigan resigned herself to ordering an entree.

With the secret-agent hush of a man who did not often gossip, Simon let out a single scandalous "*jeez*". as the waitress left to talk to some co-workers on the other side of the bar.

Morrigan stifled her laugh just long enough for the waitress to get out of immediate earshot.

"I guess she gets paid on commission?"

Morrigan cocked an eyebrow. "I don't think she had any ulterior motive for flirting with you."

Comprehension was delayed by his filter of self hate, but when he processed her compliment Simon looked down at his menu with an odd kind of stiff quickness. His head moved with his eyes when he looked at the other page. His mouth came open to give a delayed response, but still his mind was tardy with delivering it words.

He's like an innocent little squeaky toy. I just wanna give him a squeeze. Morrigan thought, biting her lip and dipping her eyes back below her menu.

"So, what are you gonna get?" She asked, rescuing him.

"Oh well I'm treating you, so I have to get the steak or the lobster."

She cocked her head ahead of her question and Simon hurried to answer it.

"That's the rule. If you're treating someone you've got to get something expensive so they don't worry about price. Cuz like, you know, if someone's treating you and you get something more expensive than *they* get..." He shrugged.

Morrigan looked at him and he retreated to his menu, but she didn't. Without customers to tend to there was no obligation to look away. She knew his face from stolen glances in the dark of Space Mountain, but here she saw him so much more clearly. The blue of his eyes was so much brighter, lit by the mid-day sun rather than LED safety lights. He finally looked up at her. Those eyes were incredibly striking, and felt so out of place on the warm expression of such a timid man. Looking into them filled her with this anxious energy but, for a beautiful moment, that energy between them was excitement, not anxiety.

"Where the fuck do they make all the sweet boys like you?"

Simon blinked at '*boy*'.

"I mean you're a *man*. I didn't mean to like demean you. You're a sweet man."

Simon opened his mouth and Morrigan held up a hand to pause his reply.

"No that makes you sound like Mr. Rodgers. You're a man, not a boy, but not like a sweet old man. I guess '*guy*' Would have been better? But you know what I mean. That was extremely sweet of you and I don't meet people like that so I wanted to thank you... on behalf of the world I guess? Just because you should keep treating people like that, me especially. I like it."

Simon nodded.

"Don't you nod at me like that made any sense. You fucking liar. I'm a crazy person."

"Um... if I may be so bold as to make an observation with my '*nosey eyes*'..."

"What? Did you notice I'm a spaz?"

"Morrigan, I can't help but notice you seem a lot more nervous today than usual. I really appreciate your company but... I just... Morrigan? Are you worried about someone seeing us together?"

"What? Why?"

"I mean we're not... There's not a lot of good excuses to be hanging around with... I just... People will draw conclusions about a guy and a girl walking together and I know I'm not the most um...

Listen if all of this is weird now that you're actually here, I don't want you to feel like you can't just ditch me."

"Simon it is some great crime that no female friend nor past girlfriend has ever told you. I think you're someone who really needs to be told this kind of thing or you'll never believe it. Simon you're hot. You're 'fuck a girl's boyfriend' hot. And that's me saying that, not the universe. It's not objective, it's *subjective*. It's true because *I* think so." She watched his face brighten with a smile she'd caused, and it was wonderful, but when he opened his mouth she flinched. "You know who should watch out is your grandmother. I mean someone might think she's hired some young himbo to be her date, but that's just because you look like a slut."

He laughed hard, and it forced that familiar expression onto his face. Whenever she made him laugh especially hard he'd make that face and then hide it behind a hand. She'd always seen it from the side, but it was cute from this angle.

After the waitress had come and went, leaving them their drinks, Simon was composed enough to speak without a chuckle disrupting his words. "So... I take it you don't like me prefacing compliments with-"

"It's *objectively* Fucking annoying."

That wasn't fair. I'm nervous too.

"Right."

"I'm sorry. I'm insane, It's just like... It's like you want plausible deniability. As if it's not *you* who thinks this or that. You're just reporting facts. I don't want to know what the universe thinks of me, Simon. I want to know what *you* think of me."

What the hell am I doing? Bullying him into confessing his feelings?

"Well... *I* think..."

I have to shut him up. I can't force him like this. It's not right. It's not how it's supposed to be.

"Do you have to say it like you're on a kid's show teaching the ABCs?"

She squeezed her eyes shut, wishing all the world would just go black too. *What am I doing? Extorting compliments out of him and then snapping at him? I'm a real fucking psyhco bitch, aren't I?. What the hell is wrong with me?*

"I'm sorry. That was mean." Morrigan hissed, thunking her head down on the table and folding her arms over her. "I'm a bitch. Ignore me."

"No, you're not. You're a nervous duck like me."

"Ducks are ugly, not nervous." Morrigan said to the table beneath a protective tent of arms.

"*No*, you *know* I don't-"

"Please don't give me any compliments Simon. Give 'em to somebody else. I wouldn't know what to do with them."

I don't deserve them.

"Oh..."

His voice sounded with a crestfallen note that opened her eyes with alarm. His face was only worse. She could see it stung like she didn't mean, confused like it oughtn't have, and inflicted the same feeling of the floor falling away that she felt. She wanted to blurt her feelings out, as a bandaid, but it just felt like she'd be throwing them hastily into the trash. She couldn't imagine he'd want them now.
She ran away, to another topic, any other topic.

"Oh you know what it probably is? You don't get sexually

harassed enough. That's why you don't think you're hot. Here lemme help, ummm... what's a good one? Oh! Uh, hey you've got a really pretty face. It's too bad you don't smile more. You should smile."

Simon blinked. "Wait, I'm confused. What's wrong with smiling?"

"No! Nothing. You're sweet. Tell anyone you want to smile. It's just sometimes guys will like compliment you and insult you, at the same time, to like throw you off balance. Then you get into this weird game of a conversation with them, where you like wanna be witty and *win* the exchange and- You know what? Never mind. That was a bad one. Here: is your dad a baker?"

"What?"

"Because those are some nice buns."

He cocked his head like a confused puppy.

"Buns, like butt."

"But how are cinnamon buns-"

"No not *cinnamon* buns!"

"I don't really know any other kind of bun. Is there one that looks like a butt?"

"Yeah I mean like... well you know like dinner rolls? The free bread at fancy restaurants? Two of those makes a butt. Nice buns. Get it?"

"Hey Morrigan, is *your* dad a baker? Because he's got some nice *rolls*."

Bubbly giggles inhibited her retort. "*Simon*, it's not a pick up line for somebody's dad. You're *so*..."

"Morrigan, I hate to tell you this, but even in jest I couldn't compliment your rolls. They simply lack all the required *girth* to be considered properly attractive rolls."

"*Ewww!*" she laughed, grimacing. "You're not allowed to say that word. You say it *so...*"

"*Girth?*" Simon asked innocently.

Again giggles bubbled to the surface to silence her protest for a long while so she had to settle for a light kick beneath the table. Simon's smile returned, and she smiled back at it and took a breath of relief. It was easy, like it always was, to fall into discussion with him about everything else in the world.

Soon the waitress returned and he ordered his expensive steak while she ordered her appetizer. Her meal cost a third of his and that guilt umbrella he provided gave her the courage to order a dessert. It was some preposterous volcano of chocolate that she would never normally order but its picture was on the cover of the dessert menu and spontaneity felt exciting. Simon ordered something too, though she suspected it was more so she wouldn't be the only one getting a dessert.

As is inevitable with things that are chocolate and melty, a drop of chocolate came off her spoon and onto her jeans. She was quick with her stain triage, dipping the corner of her napkin in her water and going to work. The downside of having jeans blacker than the darkest scandinavian midnight was that milk chocolate shows up as a vibrant brown. While she scrubbed, Morrigan noticed a second stain and then another. She felt like the most grotesque slob that Simon had ever eaten dinner with. Dread welled in her sinking stomach and she scrubbed harder, only to then realize she'd already used that corner of the napkin and was hastily applying caramel stickiness to her pants.

Simon probably noticed. He's so easily embarrassed and I'm forcing him to sit with a pig who can't remember to put her napkin in her lap.

That was enough. Morrigan's brain needed no more complex an invitation to sink.

The clink of her spoon being stolen made her looked up at him. Simon winked at her and said very simply: "We're in this together." and slapped the chocolatey spoon against his shirt.

For an instant she saw a chivalrous Prince, confident and brave, saving her from embarrassment. Then the gravity of how much chocolate he'd splattered himself with sunk in and he began to recoil into himself like a slow flinch. Then Morrigan saw a sweet loser doing his best.

She let out a mew of adoration. The kind reserved for baby animals and cute boys that are *not* friends.

Simon smiled at the sound –if somewhat weakly– and excused himself to wash up.

She giggled as he went but it was not from the humor of the situation. She was simply filled to the brim with this very unwieldy sort of happiness that formed giggles as it spilled over the top.

Relief and endearment overwhelmed her in the privacy of Simon's bathroom retreat and Morrigan leaned back in her chair, squeezed her eyes shut, and sighed. With that breath she vented the embarrassment of being so gripped by emotion in response to such a corny gesture. Simon had noticed the anxiety that Morrigan hated herself for but *he* didn't hate her for it. He didn't even seem annoyed by it.

Simon returned with a sizable wet splotch on the front of his shirt, so large it crossed over the buttons to the other side. Morrigan thanked him mildly like it wasn't that big of a deal and just *hoped* Simon understood the depth of how much she appreciated the gesture.

They swapped desserts and Morrigan filed the exchange into

a mental folder she'd pull out later when she debated in bed whether their lunch counted as a date.

The whole meal had been flavored by good conversation and it didn't end when they ran out of food. They sat there with empty plates pushed towards the center talking while the check came and went. Their conversation was expansive, but there were still things they didn't discuss. Morrigan didn't ask him where his money came from or about the girl who broke his heart. She didn't ask him what his *type* was or ask him if he thought she was pretty, cute, or at least sexy. She also didn't bring up how much she liked him and whether they were on a date.

More than that, she wanted to compliment him again. She enjoyed the weight he gave her words, almost as though she was a pretty girl and her opinion mattered.

His hair was nice, his eyes were striking, and he was her hero for splattering chocolate on his shirt. If she could just say anything of the sort, she knew his face would brighten with a smile and his fair skin would tattle on his embarrassment easily. But after how she'd hurt him running from the conversation earlier, she didn't have the confidence to go back there. Though Morrigan felt braver today, and she thought maybe some tomorrow soon she'd bring it up again. She could apologize for snapping at him and embrace his feelings with a warm hug.

But all that was for some tomorrow.

A lull in conversation coincided with a table washer pointedly interposing themselves between them, conveying the message that their meal was over, and the pair begrudgingly got up and contemplated excuses to extend their time together.

Chapter 24

Throw

He doesn't have to do much to look good. She thought, watching Simon coming out of the changing room with another outfit, looking like he was walking out to a firing squad.

"How do they feel?" She called with an upward nod.

He moved his arms experimentally, testing his range of motion in the navy blue button-down. He raised his arms and the shirt, that fit him so precisely, was lifted to his navel. At his waist she saw he hadn't transferred his belt to the pants he was trying on. The only belt holding them up was his adonis girdle, the hard 'V' shape made by his pelvic bones, that dipped beneath his waistband. There was no hint of a doughy paunch there. He had such a low body-fat percentage that when he inhaled for a sigh his tight stomach was drawn back over the subtle hinting of abs. Then, as he dropped his shoulders in a shrug, her preview was gone.

"Good, I guess. They fit okay."

"Well they look good on you. It's an attractive fit," Morrigan told him professionally, as though her thoughts had not been pointed south by that 'V'.

She had to restrain herself from rolling her eyes at the smile her comment put on his face.

"Hey thanks for doing this."

"Hm? Oh! No it's cool, man. Girls like shopping. *I'm* a girl. I like shopping. Don't worry about it, dude. Besides, I owe you. I broke the buttons on that one shirt."

"No really, I appreciate it. Most of my clothes..." Morrigan watched him pause, look away and then lie, "are from work." He looked at her. "I like the stuff you've picked out much better."

She didn't want to ask him if his ex had bought him all his clothes and told him what to wear. She just wanted him to trust her enough to let her into that club.

"What about you?"

She nodded in passive solidarity, her head in the particular lala-land of heartbreak.

"Morrigan? Are you going to get anything?"

She stiffened, as though caught daydreaming in class. Morrigan glanced around. She knew if she *did* get something she'd have to try on whatever she grabbed. She'd have to try it on *for Simon*.

She wanted to giggle at *his* masked compliments. Morrigan wanted to dress up for him like she were a princess getting ready for a ball. She wanted to throw on a low slinging racerback and stand real close, where he could see her new bra. She wanted to twirl in a dress and look at Simon looking at *her*, because he looked at her like he saw something other people didn't. Even if she didn't believe that *something* was really there, in his eyes it was there. That made it real, at least a little bit.

She wanted it bad enough to feel ashamed, like she were some dirty affection pervert. She was entertaining vivid fantasies in which a boy would smile at her, instead of shrug and look past her at the next girl walking out of the dressing room, wearing less. It was too indulgent. After being treated to a nice meal and invited along for shopping, it felt greedy to let the day be any better.

"Morrigan?"

God damn my name sounds good when you say it.

She released a tightly bit lip."Nah, you know what? I don't wanna make you wait, and I'm kinda weird about changing rooms, and I don't know how much money I have on my debit card, and..."

Her shoulders twitched upwards in a shrug that prompted a mild nod and the subject was dropped. She needed air and to be far away from any situation that she could mess up.

Chapter 25

Twilight Town

When Morrigan had said she'd wait outside Simon didn't know if she'd really be there. She'd been upset and it was easy for Simon –being who he was– to assume it was somehow his fault. At the very least she didn't feel they were close enough to share her feelings with him. That was fair enough, he thought, but it was a long line and Simon had plenty of time to wonder if she trusted someone else with whatever problem she had, and if that someone had veiny biceps and hairy forearms.

When he did see her, she was waiting alone, phone nowhere in sight. She sat on a bench across from the store, stretched out and staring at the sky. A stress headache, he hadn't even noticed, vented all of its pressure as though a valve had been turned.

It wasn't quite dark but as it crept on towards dinner the sun was no longer blaring overhead, and it had cooled enough for some souvenir sweatshirts to come out. People were leaving the shelter of air conditioned shops and forming a stream of humanity drifting towards dinner reservations, obstructing his path to her.

Simon entered the river of people a little upstream as his politeness would cause him to be carried some distance. Once he squeezed through the crowd Simon found himself sheltered from the stream beside the bench on which sat a spaced out Morrigan. He was sure she hadn't noticed him. She let her mood drip out of her in a way that she would never knowingly permit herself around Simon. The faceless crowd gave her privacy, and it felt wrong that he should take advantage to see her emotions so unconcealed by composure.

"Morrigan?" came out at a volume so embarrassingly timid he was glad only *he* heard it.

He was reticent to get within arm's reach of her, as the situation had a striking simularity to the time she'd hit him in the jugular.

Morrigan looked up with some degree of suddenness and scanned the exit to the shop he'd just left. She didn't see Simon and groaned. It was too quiet to be heard from several paces away, muted by the din of the downtown foot-traffic, but he could see it in her chest and sunken shoulders. She rubbed her eyes and the bridge of her nose with two big stretched out sweatshirt-sleeve flippers. With the bright white of her face eclipsed, Morrigan rose up to crack her back against the bench.

As she arched her back the unzipped hoodie parted like curtains. The shirt beneath was black with scribbly lettering like angry lightning. Normally it burned a stark white against the black, but now glowed with faint purple from the black-light of some nearby sign. Without the obfuscation of her hoodie he saw clearly how ill-fitting it was on her unique proportions. It was too tight for her chest, to the point that the shoulders were loose and the threads at seam between her sleeve and the front of the shirt were beginning to come loose because of it. Like a man's pot-belly, her size made her shirt creep up an inch and his eye was drawn to the revealed streak of pearlescent flesh like a live wire. He realized she'd kept these awkward proportions somewhat hidden, always maintaining a kind of casual hunched posture and she kept her shoulders rolled forward to slack the shirt in the front. He didn't know if she did it out of self consciousness or modesty, but looking at her then, without any posturing or posing, she was the cutest girl he'd ever seen sitting bored on a bench.

"Morrigan?" He called again, with a hand raised in a little wave. She didn't see him with her periphery obstructed by her hood. Oblivious, she stretched. Her skinny legs, wrapped in torn-up skinny jeans, straightened like a board and obliviously stuck her ratty Converse out into the walkway for polite tourists to dance around. Her body trembled with strain for a moment as the stretch reached its crescendo and she relaxed like a snapped rubber-band. Simon's eyes traced back up her body to her long neck and along her sharp jaw to which soft skin clung tightly. Most of her face was eclipsed by rebellious hair and a fraying hood but he could see her lips cocked in an expression that he felt like he knew.

There was something captivating about the expression on those lips and the sigh they parted for. They spoke silently of a depth in her, the depth of a life lived beyond the week he'd known her. She had insights and worries and dark storms of thought that no sigh can blow east. It had intimidated Simon before, to imagine that life filled with people –men– who knew her far better over a far longer time but it didn't bother him now. Morrigan was alone, with no bodybuilders or rockstars in sight. If she'd called anyone they hadn't cared enough to answer and spend the time to help. In the privacy of a crowd of hundreds she let heavy thoughts crush her into a slump like he expected she did alone. It was a self centered sort of moping, and not one that begged any attention or demanded sympathy. Simon saw a girl who'd stopped sharing, a girl who forgot anyone would ask about a frown.

Simon pushed into the crowd passing in front of the bench and sat beside her, well within throat punching range. "Morrigan? Are you alright?"

His volume was still timid and barely crested above the crowd's din but it was plenty loud enough to make Morrigan jump.

She recoiled in every straightened joint, jerking her shoulders forward to swing her hoodie together in front, folding her arms around her chest, and exploding into a standing position. She responded quickly and spoke fast with a tone that was too intensely casual. "I'm good. What's up? You got your clothes? Cool. I guess the line was pretty long?"

"Sorry I kept you waiting," was said passively while his eyes searched her face for more.

She shifted, grappling with words, for a long moment. Simon set his bag down on the bench and stood opposite her. "Hey so... I don't wanna like... crowd your vacation or anything. I should let you enjoy yourself. I'm tired anyway so I was just gonna like... go home."

She went on, chewing rationalizations flavored bitter with self hate, but Simon's thoughts were rooted and the words went on past him. His words were heavy and to hold on to them he slipped, unintentionally, from listening to waiting for her to stop speaking. She must have sensed this in some small way as Morrigan carried on talking, reiterating points with long sentences of little substance.

Simon let out a gentle "Hey," and her rambling tide slowly subsided. She watched him, unblinking, with eyes widened with a quiet anxiety. "You don't have to tell me what's wrong, but can I at least give you a hug? You seem like you could use one."

Morrigan swallowed and nodded with a sharp, quick motion that barely moved her head at all. It made Simon think of a bunny and so he smiled when he stepped closer.

Simon's hug was well intentioned, perhaps too much so. He was immediately conscious of her breasts and the bra-strap that must be there perceptible only to a hand on her back. In a flash panic Simon recoiled his chest apart from hers and hovered hands a breath from her back. His feet were rooted, as he was worried about stepping on her toes and terrified his groin might make inappropriate contact with hers.

Morrigan couldn't help but start giggling. When she stepped backwards out of the almost-a-hug, her face bore something less than humor. "What was *that*? 'fraid yer gonna break me? Can't even pretend to hold me because I'm so-" a sniffle surfaced from an emotion Simon didn't know was so near.

He flung her body against him, her light frame colliding with a thump against his chest. He hugged her like she wanted him to. He wrapped his arms as far around as he could. His body was honest with how eager he was to hold Morrigan. Fingers that braved little more than grazing against her back, now really held her. His hands pressed tightly enough that he could feel through her clothes the pyramid studs of her belt and the curve of a shoulderblade.

His boldness sparked a flash of panic in him and he tried to recoil, but she held on to him. She hugged Simon back warmly, and her grip was too firm to resist without violence.

He felt her shoulders sag at his hesitation and he clutched her against his chest with renewed vigor. "I- I like hugging you. It's just..."

He was suddenly very conscious of her breasts being mushed between them. They were even bigger now. Being compressed they'd spread out over a larger area, and his anxiety spiked with them. Simon was sure he was a creep, taking advantage of her emotions to get closer to those breasts.

Two words puffed against his collar. "Me too."

He relaxed, and began to passively rub her back. His hand slid up underneath her hood and lingered in a pocket of warmth there. He let his cheek rest on her temple, and looking down past her hood he noticed she was standing on her tiptoes.

It was cute. Her legs were so scrawny her skinny jeans were loose around her calves, falling like boot-cut jeans over her converse. She silently struggled to keep balanced on the very tip of her toes, and he saw one leg twitch with strain.

Spurred on by the madness of optimism Simon picked her up and swung her around. She squealed a note of excitement that made Simon's heart punch his ribs and his grip tighten. She reeled back to look at him as her shoes scraped to the ground at the end of the spin.

Her hair blanketed one eye, but the other was wide beneath a raised eyebrow. Morrigan's jaw dropped just far enough to part her lips in a pouty expression of shock, where a grin was beginning to flash through. It was a face that was gut wrenchingly adorable and *not* one of abject horror. Still a panicked urgency lashed at Simon to say every combination of words that might justify what he'd just done.

"I'm so sorry. Oh my god. I- uh- I shouldn't have done that. I should have asked."

Her head cocked to the side, swinging her hair clear of her other eye as her eyebrows came together inquisitively.

"No I mean- like I... it's not fair for me to hug you when you need a hug."

She cocked her head to the other side. "But-"

"Not that I don't want you to feel better! I just- I like hugging you and it's not fair to-"

"Simon? I *like* being hugged by you." she said as slowly and condescendingly as she could. "Please hug me more. Do it."

"No but- I can't- I mean I don't want to take advantage of you. You're upset and you need a hug and I shouldn't be the person that hugs you because I..."

Simon pinched the bridge of his nose, feeling a relief akin to shade from the small shelter his hand could provide from her earnest eyes.

"Hey..." She prompted gently, leaning around his hand. "What's up? Talk to me dude." She eased herself closer, gently laying her hands over his forearms.

"No! It's not a big deal or anything. Sorry, nevermind. You wanna get a smoothie?"

"Talk, or I'll choke you 'til you're dead."

"What?"

"Better yet, I'll shove my whole arm down my throat and puke directly into your mouth."

They laughed together and like magic his anxiety was quelled again. However, as Simon turned to leave the soft fingers grazing his sleeve curled gripping his forearms tight. The pressure continued to build, like a blood pressure cuff.

"Simon, you're leaking. You should just spill."

She was breathing hard, throwing out one breath and grasping at another with urgency.

"I like you," broke free from his lips. "More- no *differently* than a friend. Romantic. I..."

Her grip loosened. She blinked.

Unable to meet her gaze he continued, staring at the ground with great concentration. "I don't just find you physically attractive. I- I'm interested in you romantically. You're really just *great*. I can't hug you because I get feelings from those hugs that aren't *for me*. I don't want to be that creepy guy going for hugs with their female friend that isn't interested in them, hoping that they'll weasel their way into their friend's heart by comforting them when they're sad. It's not who I want to be."

"Christ dude, I had no idea. I'm sorry. I shoulda said something last night. I shouldn't have let you fry for so long. I'm sorry. I just wanted... I don't know. I'm a loser."

A pit opened under him.

I'm delusional. She's been thinking about it since yesterday, wondering how to let me down easy. I'm this big uncomfortable thing that's been looming over her. I should have just let it go.

"We should have just talked yesterday. I didn't mean to not consider your feelings, dude. I was just so focused on getting my-"

"No!" His eyes pinched shut and he began pouring out words hastily. "It's fine. It's not your responsibility to accommodate my weird feelings. I'm flattered you wanted to be my friend. Really. I'm sorry I-"

She sniffled and he looked up to meet glassy eyes.

The silver twinkle of a streetlight gleamed in a droplet running down her cheek, and the setting sun was caught in its wake, painting her pale cheek with an amber hue. He reached out for her cheek and she didn't pull away. Simon wiped her tears away with a stroke of his thumb and she rolled her eyes shut, pressing her cheek against his touch.

He pulled his hand away like it was about to be crushed. "Sorry, I really shouldn't."

"No it's fine. It's *great*, actually."

She tried to grab hold of his arms again but he recoiled. He could see it stung. Her face was far too expressive.

"No... it's- it's not. I just can't be doing this kind of thing. It's not healthy or dignified. I just..."

"Listen, you're cute, dude. I'm super flattered."

"Can we please just talk about something else? I'm fine. Seriously. I just I think I just need-"

"Simon, are you retarded? Listen to what I'm saying."

"I'm sorry to bother you with all this I just need to walk." He breathed, backpedalling with slow unsteady steps. He slammed into something as apologetic as him and with a few more steps he was submerged into the stream of humanity rushing about their vacations.

Simon managed to get a fair distance before she caught up to him. He walked the path running between the river and a row of restaurants with seating overlooking the water. Tepid conversation blew over him and the rhythmic slapping of tide smacking gently against rocks just out of sight gave his heart a slower tempo to match. Both were cut by the jingling of a wallet chain and the rapid scrape of small feet. Through the fog flooding his head they felt unrelated to him, right up until he felt the stinging impact of a slap to his ass.

"Simon you boney piece of shit! *You* have no ass either. You're just a pelvis. What's wrong with you?"

Dazed, he turned to see Morrigan clutching her hand. At her feet was his shopping bag. Dimly he realized she must have stopped to grab it after he forgot it on the bench.

"My fingers are *numb.* I bet I severed all the blood-flow on your hip bone you fucking skeleton."

"Oh, s-sorry?"

"You should be! How do you even sit? I bet your ass is just permanently bruised from being so flat. The skin there is just beaten between your ass-bones and the chair. You sit and your pelvis just goes clack."

He couldn't help but smile. "You really *are* funny Morrigan." He sighed. "And you always know how to cheer me up. I'm lucky to have a friend like you, and I'm sorry for being-"

"Simon! Shut up!"

She closed the distance and when he glanced away she slapped his attention back at her. "You're not lucky, Simon. You get all the credit dude." She said with a soft rasp that hinted at a voice crack. "You wake up every day and decide to be you, and I'm glad too, because I'm a big fan. I really like you Simon."

A statue of Mushu on the roof of a nearby Chinese restaurant chose that moment to breathe fire, washing them both in warm light. Her jaw was clenched and shadow cast by the flame emphasized the tendons in her neck rising with emotion. She watched his face for a reaction, her eyes quivering with a desperate curiosity. "...More than a friend."

Flooding into Simon came a breath like icy mountain air, banishing all humid fog from his thoughts. He felt like a contestant on a game show he'd only ever seen on TV, and he knew the answer.

Too full of passion for second thoughts, he took the girl by her waist and lifted her up with strength he didn't have. Simon twirled with her in his grip, spinning her faster and higher. She squeaked and clutched his shirt in tiny tight fists.

Her wide eyes and pursed lips melted quickly into a beaming grin to match his. She was caught up in the same fervor as he, and wrapped her legs around his back. Her ankles crossed and tugged his waist against hers, the cool steel of her studded belt pressing against bare skin, where his button-down had shifted. Morrigan looked down at him enough of an angle that her hair slid easily from behind her ear. A hand came loose from its panic grip on his shirt to sweep the hair back behind her ear and he watched a thought strike her. Her grin softened to a warm smile and her hand came slowly from her hair to rest on his shoulder. The other hand came free from its death grip on his collar and mirrored it. Trusting his strength alone to keep her aloft she slid her forearms gingerly forward over his shoulders. He felt a girl's small elbows resting beside his neck, with wrists crossed behind him, and his chest was full of thunder.

He'd never been with someone prone to passions enough to even be held in public. He was holding a girl that looked at him like he'd always wanted to be looked at. Those brown eyes were all for him, no mind paid to any staring passerby, and they were beautiful. The starry white light of a passing dining boat was caught in them, and they quivered as her attention darted across his face before pausing on his lips, then rested firmly in his eyes again.

Her face was too expressive to lie, and it told him she'd never quite been here with anyone else. He wanted to tell her they were together in that, but it was already on his face and she knew him well enough to notice.

Morrigan kept replacing one breath with another, never quite able to settle on one, while he couldn't quite convince himself to breathe at all.

Still the moment didn't end. Neither spoke, no one pulled away. They both let themselves be drawn by an obvious current. He slid a hand up her back, nestling it in the warmth beneath her hood, the small weight of his touch carrying the gentlest suggestion. She was made malleable by eagerness, her eyelids drooping as she leaned in towards him. Morrigan's arms straightened and began to slide gingerly over his shoulders. Her hood fell forward and grazed his forehead, just before.

Her eyes shut, and she stilled the heaving of her chest as she brought quivering lips together and ever nearer.

Just as Simon's eyes began to close, a final breath left Morrigan through her nose, and with it a thick bubbling lava-flow of mucous erupted onto her face. She yanked herself away with a severe curse and Simon's weak arms could not hold her. She flung herself from him like an ejector seat and he only barely managed to cup a hand behind her head before it collided with the railing beside the canal, bashing his knuckles against ringing steel.

She slid down the barrier, her shoulder-blades running across each beam musically like it was a xylophone. Morrigan clutched her hands to her face and scrambled away from him, mortified.

"Even!" He dived towards his bag of clothes "Totally even. Don't worry about it. Remember how I puked on you? Don't feel bad. *Please* Morrigan."

She felt bad.

He thrust a shirt towards her. "Here. Please. Take it."

She snatched it, in lieu of shrinking or disintegrating. She had to get the snot off her face or she'd never feel okay. She couldn't joke, grumble, or even sigh. She retreated into herself and clearly wished she could retreat into somebody else.

"I'm sorry."

"It's not your fault, you fucking idiot." She grumbled, from within a cave of hood and shirt.

"You can use my shower."

She lowered the shirt enough to raise an eyebrow at him.

"Just- y'know, in general. You can use it." A nervous laugh crept in. "Whenever you have to blow your nose, it's open to you."

Muffled laughter emanated from her shame cave.

He knew why she was upset. Just like last night they'd been robbed of a moment. His heart ached for that kiss, like his arms throbbed for having supported her weight for a few moments.

"It's not gone you know." He said quietly, squatting to her level.

She wrapped up her nose sludge in the shirt and balled it up tight, before rocking back and knocking her head gently against the railing.

He moved to sit beside her, and she set the shirt down, on the side furthest from him.

"I feel like swinging you around all the time."

Morrigan leaned against Simon, her cheek resting on his shoulder, soft hair spilling out of her hood and over his chest. The intimacy sent a maelstrom of thoughts through his head.

She's leaning on me. Is that a thing now? Are we a thing? Is she going to lean on me more? Are we a couple? Is she just tired?

"How'd anyone ever let you go?" Morrigan asked with a sigh.

Simon stiffened and his mind was plunged into a pool of oily memory that seeped into him. His shoulders grew heavy with it.

"Sorry." She straightened and her fingers emerged from her sleeves to rake through her hair, knocking back her hood. "You know I came out here because I was worried I'd mess things up. Then I go and mess them up twice."

She got to her feet and he followed assuming, for the first time, that he belonged with her.

Seeing her from behind he was reminded of the night before, and he embraced her like she'd done to him. It was sudden and full of warmth. She sucked in a breath, leaning back against him for a moment before going rigid with a familiar panic.

"I just remembered what we were talking about last night, by the pool."

He let his arms loosen and she turned, rubbing against him as she did.

"I was about to tell you that I had feelings for you."

It was weak and tired but, the smile she wore, he'd put there.

"Think you could forget what just- What almost just happened? I'd kinda like to have- for *us* to have a first..."

"Sure. Firsts sound nice. Everything was cliche before I ever got to do it. All the girls I've dated and... Now I'm twenty five and I get to have my first crush on a girl. You know, you're the first girl I've ever told? You're the first girl I've ever said 'I like you' to."

Mushu flared up again. He couldn't tell if she was blushing or if her pale skin just made a perfect canvas for firelight.

"Actually I guess I haven't, exactly. And if we're mulliganing on firsts, then I'd like to say: "I like you Morrigan Melanaphy." He let his arms slide off her to his sides. Still she didn't so much as sway apart from him. She lingered very close, and looked up at him in the way that a girl does to make a man feel tall. "Nothing is lost or forgotten, and you haven't messed anything up. We'll still have every one of our firsts."

The clinking of plates and silverware, from a restaurant on the water, filled their silence like little far off bells.

"Go out with me," burst from her so quickly it might have been one syllable. "For dinner."

Chapter 26

England

From Downtown Disney, Morrigan drove them to epcot to look for dinner. The park's main feature was the World Showcase Lagoon, a crescent-shaped collection of miniature representations of countries, stocked with bilingual natives, reconstructed landmark buildings, and, of course, food from their homeland.

After walking the length of the world showcase, perusing menus, they'd ended up in a secluded spot hidden from the path. Once it was a cleverly hidden smoking section, concealed by hedges and terrain. Now it was just a secret spot, a short trot down some stone steps, apart from the hustle of the main path.

A gale of cool wind from off the lake at the center of the park crashed against the pair, peacefully extinguishing their conversation. Morrigan was leaned with her back against the stone bulwark while, beside her, Simon faced the other direction, resting folded arms on top. Watching his blue eyes lose track of the conversation as they wandered over the water, she forgot what she was going to say too. When the wind died down, she nudged him. "Hey where are we eating?"

"You said, according to your grandmother, the British have terrible food and needed to conquer Ireland to steal their recipes. I figure Irish food must be pretty good then."

"Oh come on. I can't make you eat Irish food."

"You say that like I'm sick of you already."

Simon straightened and turned back towards the steps out, gently urging her along with a hand at her back. Mocking his delicate touch, she slumped her weight against him, staggering him a step.

"Wow, so *forward* Simon. You didn't hover your hand over my back for even a second. I'm starting to think-"

He hooked his arm around her, rolling his eyes, and she let him pull her along. She sweetened to his touch, wrapping an arm around his waist and resting her hand in his front pocket. He couldn't help but reflexively stiffen and she did her best not to be too outwardly obnoxious with her amusement. Their arms slipped from each other soon after, to climb the stone steps, and they reached the restaurant before either of them thought to reinitiate. They hadn't gone far. She'd taken him into the park through the back entrance by the boardwalk, so when they completed their loop of the countries it left them back by England.

Simon held up two fingers as they approached and while the hostess wandered a ways away to check on the status of any free tables, Simon leaned back to whisper over his shoulder at Morrigan. "So we only get the Irish food?"

"If it doesn't have potatoes it's trash. (Old Gaelic saying)."

The hostess returned to catch their hushed jesting and she smiled at the pair of them. She smiled like people smile at a cute couple. Simon didn't turn back soon enough to see it, but Morrigan did, and it made her return the smile twice as bright. Morrigan didn't know whether they really were together or not, but she could get used to people thinking that they were, smiling at them like they were.

They were seated with a view of the water, since it was early. Epcot's finale show was in no danger of eclipsing their dinner. For seats like that, they would need reservations.

The hostess left them with menus and Morrigan began to search the thing for cheap dishes and great examples of good Irish food. In this pursuit she found a conflict. Shepherd's pie was, of course, her favorite but beside that particular item was a very distressing '27'. It was such an uncomfortable number. It wasn't '30' but it might as well have been. If it'd been '24' it could have been '20', which is high, but not '30' high.

Why don't they just sack up and put a dollar sign next to the number? it's such bullshit. She thought, staring hard at that '27'.

Morrigan hissed at a '38' like it'd bit her. She slapped her small paper menu down with a nearly inaudible sound, in an unsuccessful dramatic gesture. Simon looked at the menu then back at Morrigan with an expression of amusement she'd earned.

"Alright, I know you said you were paying but –fuck you– *I'm* paying."

"Why don't we play for it? We play a little game and the winner gets to pay."

"Shouldn't the loser have to pay?"

"Good point. I forfeit."

Morrigan rolled her eyes and suppressed what she could of a smile.

"Fine. What's the game?"

Clearly he hadn't thought of one. Simon stared off for a

moment, making a face that she giggled at. It was a high pitched girly sound but she didn't blush a shade to make it. She watched the sound make his thoughts go blank and felt cute, like she was supposed to.

"Uhhhh... the question game." Simon concluded hastily, shrugging off the blush. "So we ask each other questions, like truth or dare, but just the truth and uhh, I guess you lose if-"

"You're on."

Their waitress came then. Her name was Molly, and she was more Irish than Morrigan. Her ginger ringlets bounced with her step, had some cute freckles, she even had the hot accent, prettier too, but Simon didn't seem to think so. He barely looked at her. It made Morrigan's smile bubble over into a single note of a giggle.

She cleared her throat and sat up straight. "Shirley temples for the both of us, and we're gonna start off with potato-leek-soup."

Simon was confused, but nestled easily into the safety of having someone else handle ordering and after a short round of tight, thin smiles, the waitress left to put those orders in. The moment she was more than a step from their table, Morrigan leaned in. "I'm gonna win."

"Please," Simon invited with a broad gesture. "You can go first."

Morrigan leaned back in her chair and crossed her arms over her chest. She narrowed her eyes at him like he was a card shark sitting in an old western saloon.

"What do you do? Like for money. What's your job or whatever."

He thought for a moment, either to consider why she wanted to know or how to word his response, because when he did speak, it was cautiously. "Well... I'm unemployed *now* but I mostly worked as a graphic designer in the city."

Can you get rich being a graphic designer?

"Alright my turn," Simon drummed his fingers on the table and in his deep concentration she saw his self control lapse. For just a moment his eyes dropped to her chest and a horn of victory sounded in her head. He looked away sharply and closed his eyes to concentrate on thinking of his question.

God dammit. You can look. I want you to look. Look. Enjoy looking too. I deserve extra points for these. The whole rest of the world can hate me and think I'm a whore but I am owed extra points from just one dude and that's you. Do you not like boobs? Oh you better. That'd be such bullshit. God I hope you're not an assman. That just wouldn't be fair.

"What's your type? Like *physically*, what are you attracted to?" Morrigan blurted out. "I'll answer two after this. Just tell me. And you better not say 'backs' again."

Simon's eyes shot open like she were flashing him. He floundered, mumbling diplomatic things that might keep him from giving a real answer and Morrigan rolled her eyes so hard it felt like they might tear her head off.

"Alright, let me rephrase." Morrigan said with a long steady breath, as though she were an elite sniper about to take a shot. In the interim, Simon opened his mouth but Morrigan shushed him sharply. "Okay, Okay, here it is..." She took another breath. "If you don't answer, you lose. Right?"

He nodded, unsure if he was permitted to speak.

"And, if you leave me hanging, I'll bash myself in the head until I die, okay?"

"What?"

"Do you like my boobs?"

Simon choked on air and his eyes burst wide with confusion and pity. He forced a response out, with urgency. "Yes, of *course*."

Morrigan fist pumped with the violent enthusiasm of a gladiator standing on the body of their slain opponent.

Whirling incredulity and bewilderment seemed to overwhelm Simon then, a groan being the only complaint he could vocalize before the waitress returned with their shirley temples.

Normally, when a waitress came to set anything down on their table, Simon tensed so much Morrigan could see him visibly rise up on his butt muscles alone. Something in her question had set his brain adrift. He wasn't even ready when the girl turned to him for his order. Morrigan ordered him a shepherd's pie too, that way they'd be even no matter who won their game.

"Simon?" Morrigan prompted gently, unsure of what held his thoughts so firmly in those depths. "You okay?"

He looked at her hard and words came pouring out of him. "It's just... *weird,* I guess. Maybe a little frustrating too. With guys it's this nebulous bullshit, y'know? Girls can have these specific features and when they have them, they know they're attractive because it's *fact*. Experts write in magazines about it. They sell you makeup and clothes that can make you look better and..." Simon stopped and rubbed his temples. "Sorry. I'm sorry. I don't know what's wrong with me today."

"Say it dude. You sound like you gotta get it out there, so say it. I wanna listen." Simon shook his head but she didn't relent. She gave his knee a playful shove with her foot. "Don't worry. You aren't scaring me."

Her inflexion was diminutive but she could see the recognition in his face. He knew her too well not to recognize compassion, no matter how wrapped in sarcasm. He met her eyes warmly for a while before blinking and staring off, his thoughts turned black.

"You gonna make me burn a question on it? Come on dude. I'm here listening. Talk to me."

"It's just frustrating, you know?" He blinked several times as if expecting a smack. "I would... I would give so much to have that... *certainty.*" His pace picked up and he rushed the rest out. "...To know that because I have this feature that at least there's *one* thing I know isn't wrong with me."

When he was done he looked like he wanted to smack himself. It was indulgently self pitying but Morrigan wasn't irritated or uncomfortable. Her playful cheer had been shorn in two and underneath was more sympathy than Simon could bear to receive.

He mumbled something about using the bathroom as he started to get up but Morrigan hooked her foot under his chair and pulled it back in towards the table, tripping him and causing Simon to fall back into his seat.

"Did you see that? I'm like a fucking secret agent dude."

Simon laughed, but not enough to satisfy Morrigan. She pushed his drink towards him and he looked down at the glass of pink syrup and soda. "No one's ever frowned while drinking a shirley temple."

Humoring her, he sipped away and didn't attempt another escape.

He needed to talk, now he needs to chill. Guy's an ever exploding ball of angst isn't he?

"I didn't mean to invalidate your own insecurities, by the way." Burst from him as soon as his lips parted from the straw.

"What is this insecurity highlander?" She reached over and

lifted the straw back to his lips. "I think you need some more."

He acts like if he's anything but agreeable he's gotta flee to the bathroom to drown himself in the toilet.

"I guess I shoulda let you talk more, before now. It's nice hearing what's going on a little deeper in that pretty head of yours. I'd never really thought about that stuff before. I always assumed without celebrities telling you how to be pretty, guys just assumed they were."

He shrugged, but was content to stay within the safety of silence.

She let a while pass between them, before gesturing at him with her head. "Hey, waiting on you, you're up two questions."

She immediately talked over whatever question he started to ask, demanding: "Ask me if I think you're attractive."

The gloom was quickly draining from him. "Alright..."

She gestured for him to continue, and actually speak the question. Once he began she cut him off with a chipper: "yup."

She said it with a smile and eyes hungry enough to put a blush on his fair skin.

"Hey don't you ever get confused about that, alright? You want certainty that you're attractive? You've got it. I can't break it down scientifically, but I'll think on it for you."

"Thanks."

"No, don't lie. You don't believe me. That's fine. I get it. But I'm gonna make you believe. I'll keep saying it until you do... even then I'll probably still tell you, so I get to see that dorky smile of yours." Morrigan stuck out her tongue only to retract it mere moments later, *certain* that her tongue was gross looking and Simon would rather dive through the window into the lake rather than spend a moment on a date with some filthy tongued loser.

"I saw that."

Panic seared her mind as she searched her memory desperately for the last time she brushed her tongue.

"You just zoned out to the god damn shadow realm for a second."

"I did?"

Simon folded his arms, and narrowed his eyes at her. "If you *have* to steal my turn like that then fine. What made you so sad a second ago?"

"*No.*" She whined.

"Well, I *did* really want to learn more about you, but I guess I'll settle for paying for the meal," he teased.

She chewed her lip for a moment. "Does it count as an answer if I just say I was feeling self conscious?"

He rolled his eyes. "That's so stupid."

"Man you really get mad about that, huh? You don't like anyone talking shit about your chick? Gonna fight me to shut me up?"

Simon groaned. "Morrigan, didn't I just explain how I thought you were..."

"I could hear it again."

"Morrigan you're... so..." he shook his head, disappointed in his lexicon, and then sighed: "*pretty...*" like it didn't encompass half of what was swimming in his head.

Chapter 27

Dinner

Fatigued from the intensity of their conversation, Simon withdrew from the emotion with his second question. He asked which Disney princess she would want to be and Morrigan let the conversation shift easily.

"What about Merida?" Simon asked, throwing another princess into Morrigan's fire.

"That the chick from Brave? The 3-D movies are trash, but I'd take that hair for sure."

"What about the archery? That was pretty cool."

"It was cool in the trailer dude; in the *movie* her ***mom*** saves her from the villain. Dude just maul me at that point. That's like exactly as bad as your mom taking you to the prom. Like, not only can you not be as cool as Mulan and back up your dude then finish the bad guy, you can't even get a man to save you and happily ever after your ass. You're single *and* your *mom* has to come save you?

Fuck that. Maul me to death."

Simon cocked his head squinted at the ceiling. "Oh *yeah*, there was no Prince in that one."

"Yeah compared to like Mulan who, A: genocides an entire army by being smart, B: kills the villain with a rocket launcher, then C: gets a good prince who her whole family is impressed by? Remember that scene? where like Big-General-dude-boyfriend comes to her house and everyone is all blown away and the guy's all cute and shy and gives her some bullshit she forgot or whatever? Then her grandma's like 'yo this guys a hunk dude, congrats'."

Simon watched her with a soft smile growing. The words *'cute and shy'* were loud in his ears. "Then Mulan? You're giving up musical animal taming and a pet tiger?"

She blew out a long wistful breath. "I think I'd be an Aurora, if I could choose. *That's* a princess. *So* pretty, and always effortlessly happy. But, if I'm being honest, I'm probably more of a Meg."

"*Megara*? What makes you like her? You sold your soul to Hades?"

"Mind your own business, shithead." Morrigan's eyes shot wide with alarm. She whisper yelled an apology and reached out towards him, as if she could physically peel that last word off of him.

Her tone was sharp, but her voice just didn't have an edge to cut with. He just grinned at the wide eyes she made at the sound of her own runaway tongue and mimed a dagger in his heart.

God damn, she's adorable.

"No you're right," he avowed, bowing and gesturing grandly towards her. "It's *your* turn to ask a question."

Her eyes brightened with an energy inappropriate for looking

222

at a friend. He couldn't be sure how long her eyes had seen him like that. But he was sure that, in that moment he shared with her, Morrigan's very expressive face blazed a smile brighter than he'd ever put on a girl's face before. It was unbelievably pretty, and it was his alone.

The waitress came with their soup and her lips pursed, muting the expression, but some essence of it stayed in her eyes. She was excited to sit across from him and she wasn't ashamed to be.

Potato leek soup interceded on their conversation, but the silence they shared was no less pleasant. It was a fragile silence, broken easily by the ring of a spoon set to rest in an empty bowl.

"Alright, I know what I wanna ask."

"Oh? Shoot."

"How can you spend money like you do?"

The question sunk in him like a stone.

"Is graphic design money really that good? or are you just kinda old money? Like rich dad or whatever, I mean."

Every muscle that had loosened during this discussion tensed and Simon was compressed ever so slightly into a smaller Simon who wanted nothing as much as he wanted a waitress to come bring them their meal, or soup again, or just break a glass.

"I didn't mean it like... however I said it. I- I can ask another question. Just wait, lemme..."

Simon waved the suggestion away, then wondered why he did and let his mouth respond to both of them. "No, I want to answer you. It's just that this question asks a lot of questions and it's a little overwhelming."

Morrigan put on her best impression of a sly grin and nodded at him like some cool girl from a movie. "Put em on my tab."

"What? the questions?"

"I'm making a big order, you see. Just tally up the questions as you answer them and you can just ask me a whole bunch in a row. I trust your judgement."

Her words hit Simon's ear like a song, and he took in a breath of lighter air. "Alright, I guess I'll start with your question and then work backwards. I have a lot of money from investing in a friend's business when it was starting up."

Simon stopped. He'd spent so long avoiding even thinking about what had happened that it was difficult to collect his thoughts.

"Right... so I guess the next obvious question is: 'what's his business called', but that's not the right question. If you asked *that* I might steer us off course and let me weasel out of telling you what you ought to know. What you *should* ask is: 'how much did you invest', and I guess the best way to answer that is not actually the amount in dollars."

Again, Simon had begun to stare off at the table but he caught himself and looked back at her, straightening his posture.

"Percentile, that's the unit that would tell it best. And the answer is one hundred percent. I gave him every cent I had in the bank, and I mean that literally."

Morrigan's eyes twinkled with admiration and sympathy, but he was sure that made him a liar of omission. If she wasn't alarmed at his insanity, then she didn't fully understand.

"Then the third question you should ask is: 'why?', because that's important. I didn't do it out of some kind of keen sense for business. I was shocked when it succeeded. I probably did it for three reasons, that I can figure. One is the obvious, I wanted to make my friend happy. I wanted someone to have hope for their future and take a shot at their dreams. I wanted *someone* to enjoy the money where I couldn't. Secondly, I wanted them to be grateful. I wanted to experience someone caring that I did something nice for them."

Simon stopped himself short of elaborating. *I'm bleeding baggage. I'm spilling it everywhere and it's more than anyone wants to know about.*

"Aw *dude*," Simon tried to continue on but Morrigan talked over him, rising up in her chair as if to avoid being engulfed by a wave while wading in the ocean. "You know, it just shows how sweet you are, man. You were going through some shit *clearly.* Y'know no one just drains their bank account if they're doing great with life and when you were feeling shitty you thought of your friend. It shows character."

He shook his head sharply, shrugging off unearned sympathy. "He thinks of me like a really good friend but I'm a liar. He thinks I invested in him because we're great friends but the real truth is I just wanted to throw the money in the trash. That's the third reason. I wanted to hurt myself. It was unbelievable how good it felt, the release of just... bankrupting myself. I guess I'm too much of a pussy to just open up my wrists." He watched his words hit her. They were heavy and she flinched.

Morrigan got up and had to wait for a waiter and waitress to pass with trays for a family's entree. Simon squeezed his eyes shut and sighed, silently waiting for her to leave. *Could have just pretended not to be fucking crazy.*

He felt the arms of the awkward kind of hug someone gives to a sitting person while standing. He felt like a grandma but the sweetness of the gesture was enough to thaw any dread clutching his insides.

She shuffled back to her chair. "Alright sorry, continue."

"Oh well... I don't know If there's anything left to say. I own 49% of a rideshare slash vallet app exclusive to New York and I avoid my friend and CEO because I feel guilty receiving any gratitude from him because I invested in his hopes and dreams like I was setting that money on fire."

Morrigan folded her arms across her chest and nodded thoughtfully but had a notable lack of concern for Simon's self destructive tendency.

"I had rent to pay and everything." Simon added.

She shrugged. "I mean... girls go on shopping sprees."

Suddenly Simon didn't feel like his baggage was quite so heavy.

Her face brightened with his, and she uncrossed her arms with a muted stretch, setting her arms down on the table well past the invisible halfway border. Chest welling with emotion Simon reached for the invading hand.

"Oops!" chimed a waitress that appeared from nowhere who nearly burned his arm beneath a descending shepherd's pie.

Both of them retracted their arms, sharing a look as their food was set down. By some strange instinct to avenge that hand-hold, Simon's legs went forward and wrapped around one of hers.

Her face flashed surprise that melted into a smile. Simon hadn't expected her to reciprocate the embrace but suddenly there was a tangle of legs and shoes interlocking beneath the table, hidden from the waitress. Simon thought he hid his reaction but something on his face made Morrigan burst out a giggle.

"Can I get you guys anything else?"

Simon felt a sneaky hand grab his, and he sucked in a breath.

She ordered the two of them another round of shirley

temples, never breaking eye contact with Simon. He caught a glint of something playful and mischievious twinkling in her eye, as if holding Simon's hand was something to be cocky about. Simon almost laughed at the idea that he might be something to brag about, but there she was looking at him like she enjoyed seeing him.

Morrigan didn't let go of his hand, even after the waitress left them to their food. She squeezed it like she was in danger of being swept away and Simon was holding her above water.

Chapter 28

L'Artisan des Glaces

From England, the two of them had wandered onwards through the World Showcase. Simon had followed an excited Morrigan, giddy from her victory in their question game, one country over to L'Artisan des Glaces in France. It was a very busy ice-cream shop, considering how hidden it was, and Morrigan had left Simon on a bench to brave the packed shop alone. She was determined to get Simon French ice-cream insisting that since she won their game and so was entitled to also get dessert.

"Molly..." Simon blew into the muting wind that came coursing past his lips. Like water flowing through a tributary the quick wind off the lake filled the perpendicular street. He could feel a blush Morrigan had left on his cheeks burn against the cool wind.

"How the hell would I know the waitress's name?" Simon stretched his legs out in front of the bench, like he'd seen Morrigan do earlier. His heels caught between two big grey cobblestones, worn down and polished by the rubber of countless soles. "And how did you know I wouldn't notice she was attractive?"

Warm light from the ice cream shop spilled out as a couple of teenagers filed in. The light stretched up the height of the dimly lit building, lapping each time the door fell against another forearm and was shoved wide for the next one behind.

"I'm good at two things. If I'm good at nothing else, I'm at least very good at getting stuck on girls and ignoring all reason and logic *and* cute waitresses too."

Morrigan appeared in front of the glass door of the crowded ice-cream shop, flashing bright brown eyes at him from across the way, and backed into the door to push it open with both hands occupied by ice-cream. She moved with a glib nimbleness, stepping backwards on the balls of her feet until it was just wide enough for her to shuffle-skip sideways and clear the door as it swung back shut. Morrigan twirled to face him turning into the wind sweeping up the stony street. Her hair was cast across her face in a manner just slightly too gracelessly to look like a runway model. Squinting one eye shut she held the other –less assailed– eye on him. She tossed her hair behind her with a jerk of her neck, but all the while her gaze stayed affixed.

The way she stepped quickly towards him made Simon spring to his feet so he could move to meet her halfway and hear all the random things she'd have to tell him about that'd built up while she was waiting on line.

And I'm also great at finding reasons to be upset. When I'm sad for no reason but the chemicals swimming in my head, I can find endless rationalizations for why I really should feel bad.

As they neared enough for words to pass between them, Morrigan tossed her hair over one shoulder and opened her mouth only to have the wind rebel. It picked up in a vicious gust and blast her hair across her face. All of her face was hidden by that inky frayed banner of hair, save for just the white flash of her indomidable smile. Her shoulders bobbed as she laughed freely at herself.

Simon was sure that she was very unobjectively cute. Cute enough to outshine any waitress.

Simon stepped in close and he didn't take the ice creams so she could tie back her hair. Instead he combed his his fingers through her hair, sweeping it back. It was soft and didn't snag, but the sweat left from nervously clenched fists created just enough resistance to turn her soft cheek against his forearm. Like wind felt more intense after being sheltered from it indoors, her gaze was given more weight by its absence. By how she blinked up at him with a sort of clumsy curiosity, he knew she must have forgotten how striking those very brown eyes were.

If she's another mistake, then she's a mistake I want to make.

A lock of hair from the other side slipped free and lashed about her face, forcing her eyes to flutter shut, until Simon's other hand came up to pin it back over her ear. Morrigan's expression shifted from wild mirth to something softer. Her eyes darted over him like a light glittering on water. It was as if there was a whole lot of him she liked looking at.

Simon thought he ought to kiss her then, but it wasn't quite right. Her hands were occupied, and she didn't have her arms slung over his shoulders, forearms crossed behind his neck. He also didn't feel like himself because, for once, he wasn't nervous.

He rotated around her, to block the wind with the width of his back, and took the ice-cream cups from her. She stepped in even closer, to be better shielded, and her chest grazed his as she cocked her hips forward to claw a hair-tie out of a tight pocket. Morrigan's lips curled with a hint of mischief and Simon braced his eyes. She tied her hair back like a contortionist, rolling her shoulders as far back as she could to stick her chest out against him, fishing for a blush again.

"Hey so..."

"Mmm?" She batted her eyelids at him, tucking her chin down to give him a selfie angle.

"What uh... flavor did you get?"

Morrigan answered, but her voice cracked so hard it came out more like a bird chirping than human language.

They both laughed hard. Morrigan dipped her head, head-butting his chest feebly. Hands occupied, Simon hooked an elbow over one of her heaving shoulders.

"Shut *up!*" She whined at a man who wasn't teasing her. "You were more nervous."

She tied a ponytail over one shoulder. Then, with a mock pout, she took her ice-cream and walked on ahead.

He followed her along a winding cobblestone street, framed by quaint French architecture. In a few strides he'd matched her easy pace and walked beside her. Morrigan slumped her weight gently against him, throwing him a warm side-eye.

Wind filtered noisily through rose bushes carried the fragrance of French pastries, and Simon looked to see a line blobbing over half the road. Just as he began to take a wide path around he saw Morrigan step right into it, unafraid of the confrontation of someone accusing her of cutting in line. Morrigan wove her way lithely through the crowd, with such proficiency she made the crowd seem so much less dense, slipping between people all while eating her ice-cream. Meanwhile Simon scurried along behind, apologizing to nearly everyone in the crowd on his way through it.

She waited for him on the other side, glancing over her shoulder at him. Once beside her, their paces quickly fell into harmony. They walked for a while, mouths occupied by ice cream, and soon Morrigan began to drift ahead of him. She looked across the path at the lake and began to drift across his path suddenly. Instinctively Simon reached out and touched her back. He figured he was allowed.

It was like a shark to blood. The moment he made contact, she jerked backwards. Morrigan used some advanced form of Samurai girl Jiu-jitsu and slumped her body against him, causing his hand to slide over to her shoulder. She winked up at him like she had when she'd caught him ogling her stretching, but this time she left no room for doubt by the way she pulled his arm firmly around her like a scarf.

He rolled his eyes and grinned at her giggles, but someone monitoring his heartbeat might have thought he was about to attempt defusing a bomb. Walking synchronized with another person felt daunting. He was sure he'd cause her to stumble, but walking together turned out to be shockingly easy. Morrigan had a good sense of rhythm and matched her steps to his. Of course, Simon was terrified to attempt eating his ice-cream. He figured he'd have to put Morrigan in a headlock to scoop so, with his left arm around her, Simon held his melting ice-cream in his right hand until he found a trashcan to discreetely toss it into.

Their path wound its way towards Japan and they found themselves repelled by the bright lights of the gift shop and teahouse, drawn instead towards the shade on the many steps of the replica castle. The steps were lit by LEDs to prevent tripping but they were darkened by the brighter lights surrounding them. Despite the many people flowing in and out of the various shops, the restaurant inside the Japanese castle only took reservations and they seated groups at a time so there was no foot-traffic heading up the steps. Across those grand steps, several dozen feet wide, they were the only ones who decided to find a seat there. In the gloom no wayward glances came their way. Being so shaded from attention, Morrigan and Simon found sanctuary.

There was no *leaning* going on, but they *did* happen to be touching shoulders as a matter of suspicious coincidence.

Chapter 29

Japan

"Alright, double or nothing. Let's play for the *next* time we eat out."

"You want to have dinner with me again?" Simon asked, as if he didn't know the answer.

Morrigan rolled her eyes and gave him a shove with her shoulder. "No, I wanna have breakfast with you."

A siren began to blare in Morrigan's head, before she consciously recognized the connotation. She looked at Simon, he looked back at her and suddenly they were two people pretending that breakfast was just a random meal, and not something that is occasionally had between two sweaty people at an Ihop around 4am after a busy night building an appetite through enthusiastic participation in a very particular variety of exercise.

A chasm of silence spread between them, and Morrigan lurched to jump it. "Yeah! So... question game?"

"Yep, yeah... so-"

"We up the stakes this time."

"We do?"

"We can only ask questions we don't want to know the answer to."

Simon looked out at the pagoda tower across the way and blew out a slow exhale. "Jesus, thats a brutal game."

Morrigan followed Simon's eyes to the tower, letting her gaze run off and down each up-sloping roof like rain, all the way to its base where a shirtless, bulky, Japanese man with a high ponytail was preparing for his drum show.

"I mean like questions you're afraid to ask but are super curious to know."

"Can't help yourself, huh?" Simon sat back, propping an elbow on the step behind him.

"Now you know why I've got that phobia about messing everything up. I can't stop myself. It's like a scab I can't stop picking. I don't know what's worse: asking and getting an answer that ruins everything or asking and ruining everything because I asked. I'll just call you bluebeard I guess, because I can't stand not to know, and once I know it'll be something else. I don't know if I'll ever believe-"

"I'm not gay"

She assailed him with a barrage of catlike pawings, slapping at his forearm. He flinched and giggled but didn't recoil from her.

"Lies. You are *such* a *fag.*"

He made a pouty puppy-dog face in mock injury, while She

shook her head, her face doing everything short of laughing.

Simon beamed back at her, biting his lip and giggling before he said anything, spoiling his straight face. "It's not a toupée."

Again Morrigan feebly attacked. She grabbed his head, holding his hair in a delicate fist, and jostled him, lolling his head back and forth. He was so malleable to her influence, she balked at her own roughness. Simon gave no resistance, and his eyes were whimsical and amused, without a hint of irritation. Her fingers unfurled, stretching through his blonde locks. It was soft and moved aside for her fingers easily. She played with his hair and slowly tugged him to-and-fro in awe of his patience and complete lack of ego. She imagined he might tolerate any violence she inflicted upon him and still not hate her. His instinct was so good natured she felt ashamed for handling him roughly.

Morrigan had to force herself to retract her hand. "Sorry. I got carried away." She cleared her throat and stuffed her hands between her knees. "You've got really nice hair."

She watched his face brighten far too much and felt her stomach drop. Her question was clearly senseless. How could she be jealous of a girl who'd never told him that before?

"Hey, what was your question?" he asked, shaking out his hair. "I don't want it to eat you up. Better if you just get it off your chest so you're not thinking about it."

"Hey you said chest. Is that a freudian slip?"

"What am I a goldfish? You're not gonna distract me that easily. Just ask. I don't mind."

She shook her head. "Nah, it was stupid. It'll just ruin your good mood. I was just gonna ask something insecure about your ex."

His lips, so accustomed to resting in the mirthful curve of a slight smile, now tightened and his eyes squinted in a grimace as if she'd just clawed out his intestines.

Morrigan winced like she'd knocked over a vase. *I've murdered that cute smile right off your face.*

"Just, *y'know*, what every girl wonders..." Her words didn't have nearly enough breath behind them, as though her lungs didn't trust the rest of her to make good decisions on what to say anymore. "What's she look like? Is she... pretty?"

"N... no. She wasn't really *pretty*. She was very... *put together*, I guess. Which, I think, some people like. So I guess... in a way, she was."

Sounds like a bitch. Morrigan presumed with a quiet glee.

"But I guess you want to know specifics, so you can tell whether I have a 'type' or whatever."

*I sure do **now**, you idiot.*

Simon was quiet for a long moment, and when Morrigan looked over at him she saw his eyes staring far past the pagoda tower, his mind swimming with black thoughts.

Morrigan's hand jerked toward him and stopped just as suddenly. Her nerves throbbed with a fear that it was weird and overly affectionate to comfort him. She was sure he'd shrug her hand off, and look at her like the clingy girl she was. She pushed past this vertigo, like prying a rusty nail from her skin, and reached out to touch him.

When her fingers made contact with his shoulder, it was like splashing in a still pond. Simon reacted sharply, but he wasn't annoyed. The ripples of her touch reached his face and a smile formed there, weak from leaden memories, but still a smile, and one he aimed at her.

"I'm *sorry*. Girls are insecure. We need to know."

He raised an eyebrow at that, and the bleakness was gone from his face then.

"Just girls. You wouldn't know what that's like."

He huffed a laugh, inhaled deep, and answered her question with a light sigh. "Brunette."

Simon stuck his hands in his pockets and ran down a list dispassionately. "Five-eight, all legs. She wore heels, make-up, and she put the stuff in her hair that makes it shiny like shampoo commercials. She's also not smiling, and that's either because smiling causes wrinkles or because it's demeaning *because...*" Simon rolled his eyes as he shut them and recited: "Because smiling is a signalling of appeasement, like a dog licking a master's hand."

Morrigan suddenly felt her stomach twist, like she was hearing something far too personal. Information she didn't earn.

"Her eyebrows are well shaped, because she tweezes them everyday. A very light mustache she pretends doesn't exist. B-cups, shiny legs from waxing, unshaved armpits, and uncomfortably piercing green eyes."

"Simon, I'm sorry. This was a stupid game."

A loud party left the hibachi restaurant in a mass then, and the pair stood. The large group split around them, talking in such thick eastern european accents that it even seeped into their sound effects when imitating the chopping sounds from the chef cooking on their table. Wordlessly, the pair shuffled to a spot further out of the way of any future traffic.

Before Morrigan could change the subject, Simon faced her, his hands raised in a defusing gesture.

"You look freaked out. I'm sorry. I got mad twice now. I swear it's not normal for me. I'm not like some crazy person with rage just beneath the surface. I feel exhausted, like all my muscles are sore from the adrenaline."

She placed a hand on his chest. "Simon? Please. Of my many fears and insecurities, none of them are that you would become some rage monster that would start punching holes in the drywall and throw me through a window."

For a second, Simon puffed his chest and an indignant word hovered on his tongue but in the next his shoulders slumped and his mouth shut. Morrigan shined a soft smile at him for a long moment and Simon delicately pulled her in for a stiff embrace.

The hug was loose enough that she could fold her arms on his chest like it were a school desk and look up at him. "Hey lemme make you a deal. It's your turn. You suffered for it fair and square, *but* this is my day off and I don't want to spend it being miserable playing this awful game. But how about this: the next time you can't sleep because stupid thoughts have seeped into your head, you call me."

"At 1:00 AM?"

Morrigan pinched a cheek gently. "Aw well that'd just be too darn late for little old *me*. I am in bed promptly at-"

His smile came back. Simon mushed her hair over her face as if to pull the curtains on her mocking.

"Rude." She said with a puff that failed to free her face.

"Hey you do the same, okay?" Simon aserted, combing her hair back to look her in the eyes.

She softened against his influence, letting him loll her head to one side easily. The lack of resistance made him timid, tapering his force steeply. Amusement snuck onto her face as she looked up at him. Quickly, she smothered it by slipping from his hand and giving him a squeeze.

238

"It's a deal." She concluded, her cheek flat against his chest. "If you're ever lying in bed with your brain poisoned by a dreadful curiosity over whether or not I like Insane Clown Posse, you call me. You can't feel bad about it either, because I'll be too scared to call you with my crazy at fuck-o-clock until *you* call me one night. Then I'll get to feel good about myself and everything. Alright?"

She pulled back from him to get a better look at his face and he nodded, smiling softly. "It's a deal."

Chapter 30

Viking

They wandered together through a fresh fallen night where, after a hot day, darkness still felt like shade. The cool breeze off the lake buffeted their ears, but had calmed enough to let Morrigan take down her hair. The crowds had receded to rides with no lines and spots to watch the coming fireworks. With nowhere to be but together, they walked slowly along the empty cobblestone roads, soaking in the grand architecture of replica european streets.They strode beneath grim gargoyles mounted on gothic stone arches, passed quaint Tudor beams, and rounded towering Corinthian columns. The pair lingered before dominating Gothic lancet windows, tracing their fingers along the criss-crossing mullions dividing panes of hand blown glass, each uneven like an ocean, with the occasional tiny bubble beneath the surface.

A comfortable silence fell between them and it was filled by a variety of ambient acoustic music, rising and falling as they crossed to each new country, all played live by musicians without audiences, too carried away experimenting to pack up and leave before the finale show.

The wind was chilly enough to justify zipping up her sweatshirt, but Morrigan had a warm body she could rock against that even came with warm arms. They were fickle things, always unsure of overstaying their welcome, and had a tendency to slither away. By the time they reached China she'd lost her worries over being too controlling and learned how to snatch these arms before they could escape. Morrigan wore one arm over her shoulder and adjusted it like a scarf whenever she felt a chill.

She stopped her heater before they passed a stave church lit up by flood lights, eclipsing a viking longship.

"Hey didn't you say you were Scandinavian?"

"Oh uh, yeah, Norwegian I think? Norse?"

"Perfect." Morrigan ducked his arm to trade for a wrist and pulled her man along on a short adventure.

She brought him to heavy wooden double-doors that demanded more force to pull open than she could deliver one-handed. As she reached back to re-grab his forearm, she found it above her head, propping the heavy door open for her. He tentatively leaned around her, unsure of whether they were allowed to enter. Before he could voice his concern, she rolled her eyes, grabbed his elbow, and dragged him inside.

Simon blinked, looking about the room. It was small enough to be cozy, with a soaring ceiling, two or three stories high; towering walls of carved pine, depicting the gods of his ancestors posed in heroic affect. The men were grim, long-bearded and muscular, wielding axes, swords and spears. On their shields were intricate knotting designs that framed Fearsome bears or dragons. The women were stoic, leaning on spears or shields, staring far away with their long braided hair cast about behind them by fierce unseen wind. Those intricate braids wound themselves to frame carvings of majestic wolves and longships beaten by swirling waves. As simon slowly spun to take it all in, Morrigan begrudgingly let his arm slip from her.

"...Wow."

"Yeah, all carved by some Norwegian carpenter. The guy's name is on the plaque outside."

Simon nodded and slowly his attention dripped down to the display cases surrounding them that lined the walls. "I guess I must have inherited some of my artistic leanings from my ancestors."

Morrigan followed him to a display case lining one wall. There were several artifacts there, but Simon's attention was drawn to the mural used as a backdrop. Morrigan recognized the scene. It was a depiction of Thor fighting his arch nemesis Jörmungandr, the world serpent, during Ragnarok, the end of the world. It was old art, but Christian, so Thor was drawn without armor and was dressed instead in what she could only describe as a slutty toga. This Thor was more of a bearded Hercules than a Norse god. The artist was clearly very interested in male anatomy and made as much of it visible as he could. This Thor was hugely muscular, in every area. Every lump of flesh was shaded expertly to highlight his godly physique. He was showing far more thigh than Morrigan would ever dare and, despite his bulging muscle and massive size, his clothes seemed to be about to slip off of him.

"Shame I didn't inherit the *physique* of my ancestors."

A fire alarm was sounding in her head. She restrained an 'awww' from escaping but she needed to respond with *something*. If she was silent, she'd be agreeing.

"My dad though, he sure lucked out. He did –still does– modelling for this makeup stuff. It's like the stuff girls use on their chest to make their cleavage look better. What is that called? *Contour?* Anyway, you're supposed to use this stuff to make your abs look more defined and my dad is very uh *cut* so he makes the stuff look really-"

Morrigan slapped him silent with a titanic smack to his ass that echoed in the small cavernous room. Her panic had made her stronger than she'd intended, and Simon had to steady himself against the glass. "Physique feels fine to me. Feels *great*. That's- that's a good butt you've got. You should feel good- no *proud* of it."

Simon pushed off the glass while pain, confusion, and –she hoped– amusement all fought for control of his face."Thats... uh... thanks."

Did I talk about his butt too much? He doesn't think I'm into... No! Butts are the muscle for thrusting. It's inappropriate in a totally different way. Should I say that I'm not going to put anything- no! Just don't say anything.

"I just wish I had stronger arms." He shrugged. "It was fun swinging you around earlier. I'd never done that kind of thing before. Frustratingly tiring though."

Words failed her, but she mewed a sound that summarized, making Simon blush.

He shuffled sideways down the display case, busying himself with looking over the exhibit.

"Hey you don't know about this stuff, do you?"

"Oh, uh not- not *really*? I know like: Odin and Thor and Loki, but..."

Morrigan passed behind him, hooking an arm around his elbow and towing him over to a display case in the corner. Inside was a picture of a slender man with a trimmed beard and short wavy blonde hair. "This pretty boy is Baldr. Looks just like you."

"Huh... I'm surprised there's a god that isn't all jacked. Still got the beard though."

She watched him stand up a little straighter and kept her grin to herself. *He just melts at any little compliment.*

"So is he an archer god?"

"No he..." She pulled him away from the display. "Don't worry about that picture. That's a dumb story anyway. Check out this guy. Odin, god of ravens. They fly around looking for good warriors for him and report back. Remember: good posture if a raven's watching you. He's also the god of the afterlife –well the best afterlife anyway– so you want to impress him. You know I'm named after a god*dess* of ravens? Different religion, but still. Cool bird."

"Right... Hey, Morrigan? You said I could ask a question, if there was one that was bothering me..."

"Yeah favorite bird is a raven. I know, unpatriotic."

Swimming through a thick sludge of thought, Simon's polite smile was delayed.

"Alright boss, shoot."

It took Simon some time to say it, but Morrigan was patient.

"Okay, so..." Another breath, another swallow. "You claimed to find me attractive, but I have no boobs, or butt. I don't have big muscles or abs. I guess my hair is... fine, but... What *exactly*- what traits, physical traits, do I have that make me attractive."

Morrigan couldn't help but groan. "You been listening to a bunch of Good Charlotte? Christ."

"What?"

"It's uhhh, oh what's the hook again? *Girls aren't into boy's bodies, they're into their toys and Ferraris.* It's like the great emo boy conspiracy. It's so fucking dumb. *You* totally buy into that shit too. There's hella horny sluts out there dude. You don't gotta go to the olympics to find a bitch ready to do a split on you."

"I- I know, I'm sorry. I know all this. it's just hard to like..."

"Don't-" Morrigan groaned and rubbed her face, as if there'd be another one underneath that would know what to say. "Damn man, am *I* this fucking annoying? I thought this was a girl thing to be all insecure."

Her words didn't snap Simon out of his relentless insecurity, but rather bludgeoned him. Her heart sank with his shoulders.

With a frustrated groan bordering on a screech, as her war-cry, Morrigan charged the man at full sprint like a Nordic Shield Maiden of old.

Simon braced himself for the most violent hug of his life and, to his credit, he managed to avoid a concussion against the wall. He fell hard into a seat on the replica great-hall dining bench. And the moment he looked at her, he began to crack up.

"Oh my god. I didn't mean to slam into you that hard. I'm sorry."

"You- you look like you just murdered me. I'm *fine*."

Morrigan looked him up and down, unsure if he was lying, and Simon cocked his head. "Checking for internal bleeding with your X-ray vision?"

"Shut *up*. You're such a- a-"

He made puppy-dog eyes, in mock dread of her oncoming insult, and her words turned to giggles. Morrigan plopped herself beside him and leaned out in front of him to meet his eyes. "I really *do* think you're cute."

He motioned to stand. "Oh no I'm sorry. I'm fine. I just get weird sometimes. You don't have to..."

Morrigan wrapped her arms around his neck in a WWE style headlock –a technique mastered against a Barbie junior hairstylist mannequin at age 11– and jumped into his lap. "Bitch, I bet you're fine. You think you can lie to a chick as crazy as me?

Her grip and tone softened. "You know I'm into you... you mopey bitch."

He squirmed, boiling in an embarrassment she didn't know how to save him from.

She placed one hand spread against his cheek, keeping him from turning away. With the other she combed his hair gently away from his ear. She tried bringing her lips close, to whisper in his ear, but she cursed her giraffe neck for protesting the contortion. Again Simon demonstrated his patience, allowing her to manipulate him into a comfortable position, without an ounce of irritation.

When she was settled, she combed his hair away again, and grazed her nose up from his temple past his ear, pausing with her lips hovering just apart from his ear. There she whispered an extensive answer to his question.

She began with obvious things, at least to her, such as the width of his shoulders and his long torso and his soft hair that moved when he turned. She told him how the wind blowing his shirt tight against his collarbone helped her undress him with her eyes. She explained how she admired the way his defined eyebrows, and angular chin contrasted with such a soft looking face. She liked his blue eyes, and she couldn't help but mention how it felt to have those eyes looking at her, how attentive they were.

She told him she adored how gentle he was, and how it made his body a thing she liked being close to. She explained all the things she liked about him that she couldn't explain too, like how his palms were wider than her shoulders and how he started every sentence in response gingerly, at a lower volume, wary of talking over her. She told him how it felt to be held by tentative, polite, gentle, uncertain hands, and how it felt to have them tighten and crush her softly against his chest when she needed to be held.

She went on and on, until her words were a bubbly stream of manic giggles, and even then there was so much more to say. Simon's cheek burned a blush against her hand and she felt an urge to turn his lips toward her.

Morrigan pulled herself apart and scrambled to her feet, plucking her shirt to vent some steamy air there.

"You're so incredibly overwhelming," Simon breathed.

Morrigan turned sharply around. "S... sorry... I got..."

He shook his head. "Morrigan, thank you. That was the sweetest thing anyone's ever done for me."

She rolled her eyes but blushed all the same.

"No, I mean that. I've never met a girl like you. No one's ever let me put my arm around them. My first girlfriend, when I was fourteen, said putting my arm around her was cliche. I dated a foreign exchange student senior year who said my arm was too heavy and made her shoulders tired. The girl I dated freshman year said it made her neck sweaty. My last girlfriend said it was demeaning and treated her like property."

Fuck dude, you sure have a type.

She straddled the bench beside him, wearing silent sympathy on her face.

"And listen, I *know* that's my fault. I'm like this baby seal in a shark tank. I'm so nervous about going after girls, I just convince myself that whatever girl that goes for me will make me happy. That sounds bad. I'm not saying that isn't true with *you*, I'm just saying I've just kind of..."

She found his hand and squeezed it.

"I've never felt what it's like to have a girl lean on me before. I'm sorry I almost convinced myself not to go after you."

"Better be, you fucking moron," she said with a sweetness unbefitting her words.

He laughed and she nuzzled against him, and her fingers found their way to interlace with his.

"I'm sorry to bring up old..."

"No it's cool, man. Sounded like it needed to get said."

He gave her hand a squeeze back. Her fingers felt small entwined with his.

"Hey Morrigan? You said this was your day off? Does that mean I have to go back to being a weird stalker to spend time with you tomorrow?"

She groaned. Her mind flashing with images of Jake, her least favorite co-worker, becoming progressively more disgruntled with the skewed balance of her interest in him and Simon. *It's only a matter of time before that creeper pulls a Jafar and snitches on me to keep Simon away.*

"Let's make the most of tonight then. It's your day off. What do you wanna do? I'm game for anything. It's A Small World, the Little Mermaid ride, Disney trivia at Ice Station Cool where we take a shot of that awful Italian soda if we get a question wrong. We can even chug wonderland icees and ride the Barnstormer until we puke rainbows. Anything, just name it."

Thoughts whirled in Morrigan. She thought about his question, over where they should end their night, but other things were kicked up into that storm. What happened at the end of the night? She wouldn't turn into a pumpkin. Would they kiss? more?

What was *he* expecting? Is he nervous too? Did all the talk about his ex make him think about calling her up? Does he miss those long legs? Can Morrigan be prettier than a memory? Does her baggy sweatshirt obfuscate her bust too much? Should she take her sweatshirt off? Is that whorey?

She wondered too if Simon might wake up tomorrow with his head fixed and forget her. He might fly home to put his life –his *real* life– back together and send her a melancholic text. She'd go to work alone, come home alone, and never have to charge her phone again.

Through that vortex of thought, a sentiment cut through the wind, galvanized by the fires of her personal hell. *If I'm going to be sad about a boy getting away, it'll be this one. I feel so stupid for how naive I was last time I fell for someone, but Sean won't be a reason I don't get my happily ever after. I'll go galloping full force into that fucking sunset and if it's just a mural painted on a brick wall, I'll find that out after I crack my skull on it.*

Morrigan dug her phone out of her pocket like it was buried treasure, checked the time, and what she said was drowned by the PA system blaring a reminder that Illuminations, the epcot finale would begin in ten minutes. She yelled but she could see in Simon's inquisitive expression that he'd missed it in its entirety.

"Come on! We're going to Magic Kingdom." Was all the explanation she could spare him before grabbing his hand and yanking him along after her.

Chapter 31

Quick draw

Simon didn't ask where in Magic Kingdom they were headed, but they apparently had to get there quickly. Morrigan was so eager she abandoned her car in favor of a Disney bus, as *they* were allowed to drive right up to the entrance of Magic Kingdom where as civilian cars had to park and take the monorail in.

Before the bus had even rocked back on its brakes, Morrigan had sprung up from her seat with a little hop. She reached the exit, far ahead of him, at a speed that slapping the pole by the stairs helped her round the corner. When he made it off the bus he grabbed him by the arm and groaned with impatience. Being pulled along to match her eager pace, he suddenly felt like an important part of an adventure.

Morrigan picked a line into the park that moved miraculously quickly, as though eager to be out of her way. She led Simon down Mainstreet USA like she were trying to lose a tail. She pulled him into a candy shop that connected to another shop which let out further down the way, subverting a swell in the crowd. In her haste, she nearly collided with the balloon man and had to pirouette to dodge him. Simon's wrist slipped from her grasp, at some point, and Morrigan continuously turned back to check his progress navigating the crowd.

They veered right at the Walt Disney statue plaza, straight toward Tomorrowland. Simon's curiosity was piqued. He felt like Jane being led through the jungle by Tarzan. With all the towering chrome structures in Tomorrowland, one couldn't even see the castle from the street.

She can't want to watch the fireworks from there. Maybe she's going to show me Space Mountain with the lights on as the janitors go through.

Morrigan pulled him past the crush of the crowd and navigated him between the oncoming traffic merging with the stream. It thinned and melted away until there were no heads or shoulders to obstruct the giant chrome sign welcoming visitors to Tommorowland. As they stepped up the incline of the arched bridge, a gust blowing above the crowd buffetted their ears and swept away any remnants of noise. When the brief wind died down, all they heard were wisps of mellow synth growing louder with every step.

The bridge was nearly deserted, save for a small French family, made of parents and a little boy. The mother was busy employing the ginger touch of lilly-white fingers to keep a small plucked flower –no doubt a gift from the young one– from falling out of her very short brown hair. The father held two lightsabers in one hand and, beneath a sunburnt nose, smiled a warm mustache-lifting smile at the boy who pranced between them. The boy beamed with his mother's bright blue eyes, swinging a Buzz Lightyear toy, while loudly extolling the virtues of the space ranger in a bubbly French, seeming to trip carelessly over words until his sentences were giddy avalanches.

Where Simon would have expected Morrigan's pace to

translate into a sprint he found her speed-walking instead. He understood the feeling ephemerally. Something about the presence of this happy family made him want to pretend to be a mature adult who did not break into a run in a themepark.

Simon and Morrigan split to either side of the French family, giving them room. The mother, finally securing the flower in her hair, softly reminded safety to her boy who seized all wild flailings for the moment. He chimed a polite response to his mother before breaking into an explanation to his father which involved explosion noises.

As they passed, the French couple looked between the two of them and their faces brightened sharply. The mother's expression bled excitement, and her attention jumped between them several times in those few seconds. The father smiled at Simon knowingly and gave him a nod.

Simon looked down at his shirt, and then back at the family as he passed. *Why were they smiling at us like that? What did they see?* The woman glanced obviously over her shoulder and then whispered something –a lot of something– to her husband. He hooked her closer with his arm, hanging his lightsaber burdened hand over her shoulder. She reached up and lay her thin white fingers over his hairy knuckles and he managed to spare a thumb to reciprocate.

Do they think we're a cute couple? We weren't even walking on the same side of the bridge. How could that woman-

"It's French."

He whipped around. "What?"

"They were speaking French, as in from France. We get a lot of European tourists." Morrigan explained.

"...Right."

The still wind about them was intruded upon by a breeze cast down from above and Simon looked up to see an empty monorail tour car pass overhead. His eyes followed it snaking its way through the sci-fi cityscape of Tomorrowland. In the daytime every surface was just another sun blaring it's blinding radiance into Simon's eyes. But now, at night with relaxed eyes unhindered by a squint, he surveyed a very different tomorrowland. Gleaming chrome was washed with the soft glow of LEDs mounted on high. Apparently light split through a futurist's optimism created a rainbow of neon-oranges, argon-purples, and xenon-blues. The ground too was brilliant with little fiber optic pinpricks that bled starlight. All of this color pulsed lazily through that alien rainbow, conducted by the gentle theremin music that hummed around them.

This whole Sci-Fi landscape was vacant for the moment and it charged the air. Simon's legs surged with the instinct to run, long before Morrigan dared him to race her. Uncharacteristically giddy, Simon bolted like a hare at her challenge and she ran after him. He heard the same scrape of her converse, and jingle of her wallet chain that he'd heard when she'd hug-tackled him.

The manic energy that had filled them for that instant left them quickly, leaving laughter in it's wake. Once they fell back into an easy pace beside each other, it was easy for them so slide into a comfortable silence.

They passed swiftly into the Wonderland section of Fantasyland, walking between families in no rush to get a good spot for the fireworks. Dads with soft smiles carrying sleeping kids, Mothers acting as shepherds for sugar-charged children with boundless energy, and he even spotted a big sister taking her little sister on the spinning tea-cup ride for what was most certainly not the first time.

Despite the blazing trail Morrigan cut through the park, the world seemed pleasantly oblivious to this boiling urgency in her. The night air was cool and calm enough that it never blew harder than they strode into it. Whatever magic of engineering Disney employed to dampen the din of huge crowds, rendered this relatively small crowd virtually mute.

As they journeyed deeper into Fantasyland, it became so empty that Simon felt a small rush of adrenaline wondering if they weren't supposed to be in this section of the park. They'd passed the last of the attractions behind, where a few people reveled in the opportunity to go on rides again and again, but now they were surrounded by medieval architecture and ambient music that Simon had never noticed before.

"Feels like we've wandered into that scene from Sleeping Beauty where the whole city was put to sleep," Simon mused.

He looked to her, but she wasn't beside him. He turned until he'd turned around, and saw her standing several steps back.

They were in some fantasyland square, hemmed in by tall white stone castle walls with a towering fountain in the center. The only sound between them was the faint instrumental of a Snow White song bludgeoned by the slapping of cascading water against the rocky base of the fountain's statue. This area of the park was deserted and the lights were turned down to direct everyone to the more lit area from which they intended the fireworks to be watched, but he could see her face. Her fair skin snared the dim glow of the street-lamps overhead, the harsh shine of the LEDs underfoot and the lapping glare of the floodlights beneath the fountain's pool. She stared at him lips parted and silent, with a face shining like pale moonlight. Light cut by rippling fountain water was cast up Morrigan's black sweatshirt and lapped at her throat as it swallowed.

"Is this a date?"

Simon recoiled as if she were a cowboy who'd just drawn on him.

"What?"

"What?"

"Sorry what did you ask?"

"I don't know." She answered in a tone that was an octave higher than normal. "I forgot."

They lingered in a silence so severe it choked. Simon glanced at Morrigan and saw an emotion he'd never seen in her before. He wasn't entirely *sure* it was rage but he tensed in preparation for being hit.

"Hey Simon?" Morrigan asked like a threat.

"Yup? Yes?"

"Is-" Morrigan took a deep breath, like she were about to perform a kung-fu move. "Is *this* a date?"

"What?"

Simon held up hands in surrender as Morrigan slowly looked up from her shoes like a mean samurai. "I just mean: isn't that a question for *you*?"

Morrigan blinked "I'm not asking *me*."

"But I mean... I guess *I* am?"

"Too bad." Morrigan exclaimed with stifled exasperation. "You shoulda asked first, pussy."

The insult was too unexpected not to yank out a laugh and even Morrigan's lip began to quiver.

Simon had no time to contemplate the question, to analyze and over analyze his feelings and hers, because this *girl* was standing there demanding an answer. She was holding him firmly in the present. Simon knew how hard it was to ask the question, otherwise he'd have asked it himself. He had to answer, lest he let her boil in the anxiety of it.

"Isn't that up to *you*?"

"*I'm* asking *you*." She shot back.

"I mean... do you *want* it to be."

"Do *you*?"

"Of course."

His eyelids fluttered, stunned at how easy it was to say. He felt lightheaded. There was no crush of embarrassment to match his anxiety. Morrigan didn't roll her eyes at him, sigh, and explain that he was inflicting an obligation of emotional labor on her. She just smiled, a tiny smile, and rocked once on her heels.

"Morrigan, of course I want this to be a date. You're cute and fun and I really like you."

Simon said it with a firm gaze and a strong tone. He spent every whisper of breath in his lungs on those words, and his chest was left so light he swayed for an instant. His eyes rested easily on her then, without the anxious clock that warned him of staring, and she looked back at *him*.

Morrigan was the brave one again and sucked in a triumphant breath. "Well, it's official." she declared, extending a hand. "It's a date. You want it to be one. I want it to be one. So, it is. Now hold my hand."

Simon opened his mouth and stared at her outstretched right hand but didn't take it. His joints were filled with cement.

"It's a rule. You have to." She added with mock authority.

Simon took her hand, but he did it with his right hand, like a handshake. He realized his mistake but Morrigan wouldn't release his hand. Her smile just grew wider. "Wrong hand numb-nuts."

Laughter burst from Simon immediately, like pressure released from a valve. He was nervous, eager to vent some of the joy he was restraining. Her insult was so stupid, so harmless and cute.

Simon swung her around in a mock square dance and her body committed to it, in an instant. She laughed too. It wasn't *that* funny but she had raw emotion to vent and laughter was an easy form for it to take. They acted silly and dumb, laughed and were merry. Thoughts left their heads and breath left their chests. Everything was simple. The pair collided, bounced apart, and leaned on one another while they caught their breath. They lingered on the precipice of an embrace but as their panting laughter slowed they straightened and began to shuffle off, *apart*.

Just as their fingers began to slip past each other, an elemental instinct took hold in Simon. He grasped just her fingertips and raised her hand above her head. Taken too, by some strange instinct, Morrigan twirled like a dancer. Her whole body moved with an overwhelming grace, stealing the air from his chest, like a painting come to life.

Morrigan finished her pirouette before her hair, and it swung around over her face, leaving just one brown eye to watch Simon with. She halted in a perfect stillness, as graceful as her twirl, and with that eye alone, struck Simon with all the momentum of her suspended dance.

No shame or shyness could tear his attention from the girl before him and, though her cheeks bloomed a gentle pink, her eyes didn't leave him either. He did nothing to mask his expression of stunned admiration, and Simon watched her bask in it. She beamed a wide grin at him, which shone through the hair that half eclipsed it, like starlight.

In that burning moment he wanted to kiss Morrigan, her thinking head be damned, but disrupting that smile was no easy decision to make. Her one brown eye had the barest glimmer of mischief, as their fingertips slipped past each other.

The air was light in Simon's lungs as he watched Morrigan take another step and turn from him, with a twirl. She stepped gracefully out of her loose-laced converse, dropping down another inch below Simon, on tiny feet. She took measured gentle steps, twirled and moved her arms about her in simple deliberate motions. Simon realized, only when he was immersed in it, that he was watching Morrigan dance. Her arms and legs moved with a syncronicity, one never impeding the other but pairing in captivating concert. She quickened and slowed with a tidal pace, waxing and waning speed but never letting her movements part from their enchanting flow. Morrigan's arms swam gracefully about her as if underwater, framing her hips and chest which moved with a beauty that rebelled against baggy clothes. These stark movements announced every muscle, joint and curve. Raised arms lifted the hem of her thick sweatshirt and flashed a crescent of pearlescent flesh. A reaching step tightened black jeans revealing a bold silhoutte for just one lingering stride. She was a clumsy, goofy creature that had no right to such serenity of motion.

After a long moment of awe, Simon noticed the movements repeat, and then he noticed the instrumental music had changed. He was watching a girl who was once a *little* girl dancing along to Princess Aurora, in her pajamas, on saturday, in the living room, watching a Disney princess she hoped to one day become.

Softly Simon began to sing the prince's lines and she whirled to face him, while her momentum carried her onward oblivious. Without the next step placed in her path, the surprised and excited Morrigan tilted sideways until she stumbled, catching her fall against the fountain, with one hand plunging into the water, soaking herself to the elbow.

Simon's wide-eyed apology was drowned out by a loudspeaker blaring in the empty square. "Our *Happily Ever After* fireworks celebration is going to begin in just ten minutes. We hope you've had a magical time in Walt Disney World's Magic Kingdom..."

She ran to her shoes, barely stopping to slip into them, and yanked down the zipper on her hoodie so hard it broke, clinking across the courtyard into darkness. As she ground her heels into her shoes, she crossed her arms to lift the sweatshirt off over her head. Her shirt got caught, stuck to her outer layer, and a blush scorched his face as she innocently flashed a swath of bare flesh. He'd known she was attractive and he'd known –of course– that she had a torso and yet the sight stunned him like a tazer to the neck. It lasted only a fraction of a second, but every detail was drunk in by his eyes, like he were a super-spy absorbing vital documents.

Hip bones crept above a scratched-to-shit pyramid-stud belt. Naked skin as fair as snow caught the meager light, shining a stark white in the dark. Supple ribs pressed gently against her soft skin amidst the crumpled tangle of some band shirt with lettering like angry lightning.

Her stomach was doughy-soft and disproportionally thin by a cheat of birth rather than any product of actual fitness. She had scant muscle to hold back what doughy pockets of fat she did have at her lower belly and sides. He knew from how she sucked her stomach in, that Morrigan must have had some harsh opinions about these areas but Simon's mind was loud with a very different kind of opinion. His face felt feverishly hot with blush, thinking of how a hug would press those sharp hip bones and supple ribs against him. He thought of how thin a barrier her shirt would be, between that soft pale flesh and the hands that would hold her against him.

Simon's fingers pulsed as his hand shot forward to help, plucking her shirt down to unstick it from the sweatshirt. But, while he pulled down one side of her shirt, the other rose just a hair higher and Simon caught a glimpse of something lacy and red that made his heart punch his ribs.

Simon wasn't breathing. He wasn't sure if he was supposed to exhale or inhale next. It seemed that even the part of his brain that handled involuntary functions was wondering what the rest of her bra looked like. Every function except his heart, of course. That one was positive that more blood needed to go to his everything.

Free of the hoodie, Morrigan puffed messy hair from her face and locked one eye with his.

Simon didn't look away, didn't pretend to have had his eyes anywhere but on her. This time, he let his face tell the truth.

Her eyes had the gleam of a girl who didn't mind at all. She threw the balled up hoodie at his chest with a wink and rushed past him.

Simon didn't move and his jarring lack of motion turned Morrigan on her heel, scraping grit loudly beneath it. She looked down at his outstretched hand, expression blank.

"It's a date isn't it?"

Her lips bloomed into a smile so bright it made her squint. Morrigan first placed her hand daintily into his like a princess, but then gripped him tightly and dragged him into a sprint.

Chapter 32

Kayaking

Morrigan might've felt worse for Simon than herself if they were caught. He didn't strike her as a guy who'd grown up as one of the bad kids. Trespassing seemed as likely a part of his teenage years as being a member of the X-Men.

Still, she never needed more urging than a gentle tug at the wrist for Simon to quicken his step behind her. She could feel a wordless excitement radiating from him. He trusted her. Simon trusted her enough to ignore all voices of anxiety, *and* reason as she led him onto the roof of a cottage. She walked swiftly up the thatch roof to the wall bordering it. She leapt and he followed without question. They landed between raised planters meant to lift flower bushes high enough to spill over the fence in FantasyLand.

Cameras watched the places a civilian might wander backstage and the doors where they might *intentionally* trespass. But here, where only landscapers and the occasional utility worker ever went, there was no electric eye to spy them.

Morrigan's sweatshirt bundle had broken loose and she had

to reform the balled up thing so the wet sleeve would be protected from stinging her with cold. Simon looked around with wonder at this secret passage of hers, hidden behind the Fantasyland backdrop. He snapped his attention to her, with a smile charged by the energy crackling between them. He looked at her with such wonder, his eyes expectant, and full of anticipation. In an instant, she felt like Pocahontas guiding Jon Smith.

The lights went out then, and the five minute warning for the fireworks echoed through the park.

By a miracle of no minor magnitude, their hands found each other in one fluid motion, coming together with a smack. The sound could have been a pistol shot to start a race. All the giddiness welling within them, which had been tentatively restrained until then, was unleashed.

The two of them raced through down this secret avenue and through a false wall into a hidden courtyard where she stopped Simon briefly, so she could see his face, and watched his reaction as she pointed up at a building towering over them. "The haunted mansion."

Very few people got to see the building from the back and Simon's eyelashes fluttered with surprise and he breathed a simple sanitary "Wow!" barren any profanity. Morrigan had to bite her lip and yank him onward to resist the urge to plant a less-than-perfect first kiss on the man.

She took him through a door, propped open by a pack of cigarettes rendered labeless by rain and the crumpling weight of a steel door. They entered into a room flooded with the aggressive red light of an exit sign. Morrigan stepped in past the glare, looked back, and waited for his reaction as Simon turned from shutting the door quietly behind him.

This was an animatronics repair workshop, and it was lit by just that single source of harsh red light which cast long shadows and darkened eye-sockets, lighting a sinister twinkle on the smiles of a dozen or so half assembled automatons. Simon stiffened and looked surprised but he didn't look scared, not like he was of a pretty girl.

She couldn't help but giggle and his eyes were drawn to her easily.

Wow, look at me, he thinks I'm more important than a small army of evil animatronics that might come to life and harvest his organs.

It made her want to skip, and so she did.

Perhaps out of some unwillingness to be left alone with spooky robot skeletons awash in crimson, or maybe because her glib grin had plucked a chord of mischief, Simon caught her from behind. He wrapped his arms around her waist and she tossed her head back against his chest.

Simon swung her in a small circle and a shock of surprise at his strength arced through her. Morrigan flashed a white smile in the dark and she playfully feigned a struggle. Her soles scraped gently across the floor as she was lowered back down and a palpable nothing of movement set in.

His arms were wrapped around her waist, and she could feel how he bowed his elbows respectfully away from her breasts. She could feel the frozen reluctance in the fingertips lingering at the hem of her shirt, resting on the silvery studs beneath. He was evidently afflicted by a standstill hesitation to relinquish this soft body in his arms and all urgency to move forward vanished from her.

If she broke from these warm arms around her *now* she didn't know if she could return to them later, because they would be different arms if she had to invite them around her. It was a special sort of embrace that came uninvited.

What's more, there was something there in his head, holding him still. Some action he feared to take. Some manner of acting upon her that was tempting enough to stall his sense of self preservation in a tug of war. She wanted him to do it. Whatever it was would come along with the special warmth of being acted upon by nervous hands that held her like some sacred thing.

She didn't move for a second of forever, afraid of frightening away his advance, like a skittish fawn. Morrigan wrung out her impatience in the sweatshirt she carried. Then, with a boldness unbecoming her, she pressed herself against him with a breath's worth of force. She felt her butt make contact with him and she was taken by a sudden fear that he would declare her a harlot and storm out.

He didn't, of course. He stood there. His fingers curled slightly, pressing another breath of force against her belt. Her heart thumped another beat between each beat and she crushed the sweatshirt in her hands.

After seven seconds of forever, Simon retrieved his hands. Faster than Morrigan's voice could come to her lips, a hand slid past the back of her knee and the arm that followed pressed against it. Her legs were stolen from her and Morrigan was swung sideways with a chirp.

Simon held her aloft with palm splayed firmly against her back and her knees folded over his forearm. It came with the clumsiness that accompanied a lack of practice. His hand pressed her bra-hook against her spine and he held her legs too high, keeping her at an angle of constant vertigo. Still, there was no world in which she would ask to be set down. He was holding her like a princess and, for at least a little while, it made her one. Some untouchable logic beyond all self doubt declared it so.

"Is this okay?" he whispered, to a face he couldn't make out so far from the exit sign.

She rolled her eyes and groped around for his neck to wrap her arms around. "Don't ask stupid questions, idiot. This is *perfect.*"

She couldn't quite see his face by the light of

glow-in-the-dark decorations, but she thought she heard his lips part in a smile. He navigated by the neon green paint of spider legs and tombstones all about the room, stepping carefully around skeletal limbs outstretched from the shadows clad in ghostly translucent sleeves

In his focus towards avoiding tripping or colliding with walls, he slowly began to lift her legs even higher than her chest, which felt startlingly close to dropping her on her head. To counterbalance, Morrigan began to hoist herself higher using his neck as leverage.

"Oh, sorry. I'm not super used to this kind of thing and the weight distribution is a bit weird."

"Oh yeah? Where's the fattest part of me?"

"Oh no! I didn't mean-"

"Hm? Trying to call me top heavy?

Flustered, he carried her through the door to an access stairwell bathed in the horror movie red of another exit sign. He swung her legs clear of the door with a certain grace, befitting one bearing the title 'Prince'. Then Simon, his focus narrowed to her legs and squinting himself nearly blind, with eyes that had adjusted to see on only glow-in-the-dark paint, swung her other half through the door like a kayak paddle. His measurements were somewhat less precise than they should have been. While her legs stuck out a great distance in his hold, her head still stuck out past his shoulder, an inch or so, and so he bashed her head into the metal door-frame with reckless enthusiasm. In the dead silence of the storage room the ring of the steel frame was cartoonishly loud. Her head bounced off the metal and the world went double as her eyes crossed briefly.

She might have been mad, or argued against being set down, but he'd just hit her head too damn hard. She mumbled something convincing enough to stem the tide of blurry apologies and clutched him with a pinching grip to keep herself on her feet. The bicep she held herself steady with was trembling. The muscle itself had clearly strained to hold her, and now that he'd set her down she doubted he could carry her again without shaking. The gesture was suddenly so much sweeter and also more adorable in a way that Simon probably wouldn't find flattering.

She captured the flow of frantic apologies by netting him with her hoodie, tossing it over his head. "Alright, I went fishing at the wrong time, but I feel I'm owed now. Compliment please."

His shoulders bobbed with laughter and she raised her ratty hoodie like a wedding veil. "Sorry what was that?"

"Uh, they're nice?"

"You can do better."

"Fat?"

She gave him a push against the wall, being careful not to bash *his* head too. She shook her head at him as he dragged the hoodie down and balled it up. His hair was frustratingly more gorgeous, disheveled as it was.

"I don't know what there is to say about them. They're soft and they come with hugs. They get in the way, so they make you squeeze me tighter to get closer. Talking about them makes me nervous?"

"I'll take it," she said, grabbing his arm and dragging him along in a mostly straight line up the stairs.

Chapter 33

Red as blood

A possibly concussed Morrigan led Simon swiftly through some abandoned leg of the walking tour that involved an exhausting amount of stairs that could never be made handicap accessible. She stopped before a set of double doors, only partially illuminated by the light of her phone screen. She aimed the blindingly bright display at him before pocketing the phone.

As he blinked away a purple 8:59 from his vision he heard the brass knob of the door turn and a shard of moonlight was cast inside. It lit her face and she beckoned him after her, before disappearing through the breach.

He followed her out onto a balcony high above the Magic Kingdom. Before him was a view that very few ever saw. He couldn't believe how high up the mansion was. He could see the top of Splash Mountain to the left, and off to the right was a clear view of the castle.

"This balcony can't be seen from the path. It was supposed to be part of a show. They were originally going to have a picnic lunch on the lawn down there, where characters from the ride come out and say stuff or whatever. The Balcony was going to have some woman who yelled down funny contradictions to some other character on the lawn talking to guests."

He leaned over the precariously low railing to look and indeed the lawn they'd crossed was arranged like theater seats, a semi circle formed around a flat section the actors could stand at. Subtle and effective.

"Civil engineers advised against it since foot traffic would be too obstructed and there wouldn't be room for a line for the ride and a que to be seated for picnic lunch and whatever. Then they built up behind it so there wasn't really room to fix the problem, so now it's a secret balcony with a secret lawn."

Simon backed away from the vertigo inducing ledge as quickly as he could, while remaining as stoic as possible.

"And the railing is obviously super low because, from below, it would be easier to see the performer and the perspective makes it seem normal sized."

Her words made him wonder briefly if a fear of falling to his death kept him from being eligible for a position as her boyfriend, but a flash of her eyes dissolved the thought. A strong streak of moonlight cut from between clouds, and her face was bright in it.

"So how do you know all this anyway? Spooky girls newsletter?"

It wasn't funny, but she smiled anyway.

"Spooky girl?"

He could hear in her voice that she liked the sound of that title so he prodded there. "Oh I'm sorry. Have I mislabeled you? Do you identify as a mildly frightening dame? A disconcerting gal? An edgy chick perhaps?"

She stepped closer to him. Suddenly he felt really tall. "I guess I'd call myself a goth *chick* if I were to be identified by my latin classification," he felt small fingers slide into his pockets. "...but I'll be your *spooky girl*."

His heart punched his ribs.

She said it in a voice he'd never heard her use before; the kind a girl reserved for her man. The words were spoken with warm breath, cresting gingerly above a whisper on each vowel with a tender chirp.

The lips that said it were nibbled gently beneath smoldering eyes, which carried an irresistable momentum. Mesmerized and stunned, Simon was gripped by a stillness Morrigan seemed immune to. The only sensation in Simon's universe was a girl's small hands in his pockets, tugging him towards her.

He staggered forward against her, with too much weight, but his hands came up and wrapped around her on instinct so she wouldn't be pushed away. Suddenly he was holding Morrigan against him. With a sharp vigorous breath she took on a shape in his arms. Her back arched and chest came forward as her shoulders shrugged downwards. Her body fit warmly against his in a way that made his hands belong on her.

Morrigan slipped her hands from his pockets, her fingertips grazing his chest as she brought them to his collar. Her eyelids fluttered a moment and she lay her forearms over his shoulders again. She slid them further, resting her elbows on him and crossing limp wrists gingerly behind his head, hugging his neck gently.

She swallowed, looking up at him with brown eyes now gleaming with a glare of moonlight cast down from between fast clouds. Those eyes darted about his face, taking in many details with a manic kind of attentiveness that mirrored his own anxiety. Suddenly Simon wasn't alone.

His hand slid over her back and felt her heart thumping frantically against his palm. He pulled her towards him, to press a like heart to his, and show her she wasn't alone. Along with her chest came lips, drawn to his.

But then she stopped short. He felt her tremble for an instant and her arms retracted back over his shoulders. Morrigan lay her hands spread over his chest, and she breathed with sharp squeaky breaths. She didn't push him away, and Simon knew he wasn't meant to lean back. She hadn't recoiled because she didn't want to continue. She just couldn't. She needed those lips for breathing... and then for cursing at herself.

Simon slid a hand over her shoulderblade, through her hair, along her neck, and up to her warm cheek where he lay his palm. Instinctively she leaned against it, her eyes closing. It lasted just an instant before she jarred apart from the hand, her head lost in some anxiety that only made sense to her.

The moon was eclipsed by cloud and darkness swept over them.

"Sorry."

"No," broke from his lips without consulting his brain. Seeing her so distressed upset him and it just made some sort of instinctive sense to be argumentative. Before his mouth had even closed, his brain connected that star into a constellation and he continued the blind sentiment. "I can't forgive you. I've never ever been nervous before. You're weird. Breathe normal weird girl."

He felt her giggle against his chest with what scarce breath she had and her lungs suddenly remembered how to breathe somewhat normally. Glassy eyes blinked open, glinting with a faint shard of moonlight, and by it he found her cheek again. "Sorry, I meant *spooky girl*."

A hand came off his chest and clasped over his, pinning it to her face, showing him it belonged there. Simon's thumb passively stroked her cheek and it burned beneath his hand.

A rocket came screaming past them and, though the pair blinked, Simon would have rather been hit in the side of the head by the rocket than let the girl go.

The firework exploded with an ear kicking pop and the reflection of white sparks dazzled for a moment in Morrigan's eye. More fireworks blazed past and the rolling flashes of searing white fireworks lit her face differently. The moon had been subtle and let her pale skin glow while this light flared harshly and revealed the red blush he felt rising there. Curiosity moved his hand down below the swell of her cheek and he observed her blushing cheeks as they bloomed hot.

Morrigan had claimed to be Irish, despite her black hair and only a rumor of freckles, but now Simon saw evidence he took to be iron-clad proof of her heritage. The blood rushing into her cheeks, bloomed a searing blush that highlighted all her many, many freckles. They looked mesmerizingly like lava with a warmth to match.

Her eyes fluttered as he stroked his thumb along her cheek. "You really *are* Irish," he breathed, with absent minded wonder. The words stilled her quickened breath like a fingertip against a ringing bell. Wide eyes blinked above pouting lips. Her fingers curled slightly about his collar and, in that stillness, she squeaked an inquisitive note.

The eyes she stared up at him with made his words feel heavier than he was used to, and he needed more breath to lift them. "I never knew you had such pretty freckles hiding there all along."

She rises against him on an inhale, up on tip-toes, towards his face. Her arms slide over each other, crossing behind his head. One hand slides past her cheek, combing through her hair while the other crushes her soft form against his.

They used their noses as bumpers, mashed between their passions, before their heads had a chance to cock and let their lips meet. There was no masterful form to the kiss, and Simon could barely feel her lips from how hotly nervous blood burned in both of them. Still, there was a palpable emotion in their bodies, an energy that made them squirm and tighten grip. He'd never been held with such a frantic attachment and never had he been so free to reciprocate with passionate abandon.

She parted from him once to gasp air before plunging again into his lips, melting a smile between the two of them. Soon after she broke again to breathe. The pair panted foggy clouds into the chilly night air for a moment before the inevitable magnetism brought their lips together again. This pattern repeated until she barely pecked him before turning her chin up, straightening her windpipe, to desperately gasp at the sky. Above, there was a relative stillness. Embers of white phosphorus drifted to the earth, illuminating serpentine smoke trails that crossed the heavens.

On a deficit of air, she wheezed "Sorry," skyward, but was muted by a new salvo of rolling explosions.

Simon leaned in and kissed her cheek. His lips skipped up her cheek with three pecks, all the way over to her ear and there he spoke with the lightest puff of air he could. "That was a really great kiss. It felt like I got a second chance at a first kiss, *my* first kiss, with someone really special."

One word took a loan on oxygen to escape her with urgency. *"Simon!"* It was a whiny passionate word that came along with a renewed embrace that threatened to squeeze the air from both their lungs.

His name had never sounded so wonderful. She said his name like she knew him, and it dawned on him dimly that she *did.* She knew 'Simon' and 'Simon' was this wonderful thing in her world that she was crushing against her chest.

Morrigan had incredible strength for someone who ought to

have been on the brink of passing out from hyperventilation. She released the pressure from her squeezing and hooked her arms under his armpits, gripping his shoulders from beneath. Morrigan did a chin-up to hoist herself higher and wrapped her legs around him. The intimacy overwhelmed him, stole the air from his chest. Simon had never experienced a girl wrapping her legs around him in an embrace, even in far more carnal engagements.

She held his face in her hands gently, waited for a breath to come back to him, then planted a soft kiss on his lips. With her fingers interlaced behind his neck Morrigan leaned back with a slight tilt to her head and looked him over with a wistful sigh. "Watch the fireworks with me?"

She asked it in a voice she could have asked for anything with, and he'd have agreed, so of course he did.

She slid to the ground slowly against him, her physicality made impossible to ignore. There was mischief in her smirk as she turned, snug in his embrace. With her back pressed to his chest, they watched rockets whizz past their vantage point to explode high above the castle. He had to strain slightly to keep his arms wrapped around her low, as to avoid touching her breasts, and even with her back turned she read his body language instantly.

"If you accidentally graze my boob with your forearm, I'll call my pastor. I'll call your mom too, *and* your grandmom."

He groaned and tossed his head, but it took no more than the graze of her finger to turn his chin back to her. Simon endured, looking off at the fireworks, while she craned her neck, laying her cheek against his collarbone, inspecting him. "*You,*" she began, palming over his cheek. "*don't* reveal *any* freckles when you blush. You're just a cute little tomato."

More fireworks blazing past erased his retort and Morrigan stuck her tongue out. The giggle that bounced her against his chest was muted as the concussion of explosions popping against their ears.

Some of the fireworks burst out of sight, due to the overhang. So Morrigan sat, pulling him down with her, to give them both a better vantage point.

Morrigan sat in front of him, between his stretched out legs, and leaned back into his chest. Her soft hair rested against his jaw and he could smell her shampoo. Simon held her, his arms finding a much less awkward angle with them sitting.

Morrigan's teasing, perhaps by design, lingered on his mind. His own prudishness frustrated him. He bludgeoned himself with the thought that he was acting like a child.

"You know you could hurt yourself sitting on the ground with an ass so flat."

Simon's stomach lurched. *Why do I ever say anything without overthinking it for half an hour?*

She looked over her shoulder so sharply she cracked her neck. He watched her expression go from surprised to a surprised cartoon character at the sound of her neck. Simon tried to stifle his laughter but Morrigan pounced on him all the same, flashing a smile as she playfully beat her fists gently against his chest.

Once she'd conquered Simon, she positioned him like she was fluffing a pillow and he soon found himself half laying with a pretty girl curled up, half in his lap, and one hand interlaced with hers. The two watched fireworks from their secret spot, hidden away from the world, using her sweatshirt for a picnic blanket and their hot blood for warmth.

From their distant vantage point, the accompanying music was politely faint and unintrusive. On this side of the castle they couldn't see the projection displayed on the far side but the castle lit by the cascading flashes of fireworks was pretty enough to entrance them both.

The action rose and fell at random, according to some unseen conductor, and whatever storyline that was attached to the fireworks display was drowned out by the hiss of rocket jets and explosions.

It was a long show and the length gave them time to melt closer together, with a pace quick as tree-sap. Morrigan ended up turned from the fireworks, breath spilling over the nape of his neck, and feather-soft hair splayed over his lips. Simon dared not shift, even slightly, for fear of disrupting something that he couldn't recreate.

In their stillness, they heard the narrator's voice echoing around the park and Simon made out "Happily ever after." Her cheek was pressed to his in their embrace, and he felt her smile against his skin when she heard those words with him.

Morrigan swept her hair over her ear and turned back towards the display, laying her cheek against his. They watched the finale together like that.

Simon was under no illusion of being a big strong man, but somehow Morrigan could make him feel like one by the way she nestled into him. She curled up small against his chest with her legs entwined between his.

The sparks from the final cascade of explosions fizzled into smoke, leaving them in the dark. Morrigan's fingers curled around his collar and, though she could not have known this, planted the first real kiss he'd ever received on his cheek. She didn't peck, but kissed with enough force to tilt his head and enough passion to close his eyes.

The words to explain how much it meant, failed him. To give affection and have it welcomed was one thing, but he found himself suddenly overwhelmed by receiving it unsolicited. His throat was tight with emotion and he was embarrassed to be so happy for something so simple. Simon held her tighter and, by the sound she exhaled with hot breath against his neck, he thought she probably understood on some level.

Simon didn't just kiss anymore. Simon got kissed.

Chapter 34

Embers

Everything burned softly, from her muscles to her soul. It felt good to smolder in the cool night air.

She walked with him, swaying apart several steps and drifting again to his side. Morrigan wasn't afraid he'd wander off without her, like a stranger at a party. There was an invisible tether that would yank them back together if they stepped too far afield from one another. It would drive them to bump shoulders and smile small unseen smiles.

They'd held a quick pace in fleeing the scene of their trespassing, but it had grown lazy once they began passing other couples reluctant to face the surge of patrons leaving the park. The two of them were once again in fantasyland and found themselves facing a dead-end overlooking the center of the park.

Morrigan set her forearms onto the top of the cool stone wall and sighed. Across a small duck pond, rife with lazily drifting water lilies, they could see a mass of people lit by the brilliance of light-up toys. Waving laser swords, twirling LED spinners, whipping fiberoptic rainbows, and the alacritous twinkle of souvenir ice cubes all served to outshine the lighting of the park itself and illuminate the extent of the mass that slowly shifted down mainstreet USA.

"*Fuck.*" Morrigan sighed long and emphatically.

Wordlessly Simon perched himself beside her, a body's length away.

"*That* is gonna take like..." Morrigan's head lolled from side to side, "twenty? minutes to clear up. Then we gotta wait through another huge crowd for the monorail, and then I need to get an uber over to the boardwalk to grab my car."

"We can't take a bus?"

"Nah Epcot closed, no one should be going there until the *morning*. Gonna have to Uber home, then Uber to work, Disney bus to Epcot when I get off and pray I didn't get a ticket. *And* I'm going to basicaly just not sleep because it's gonna be like midnight when I get home and then I'll have to get up like an hour early for work because my fucking..." She bit her lip against her loathing for the coming day that she'd let bleed into their night. "Hey, totally worth it, by the way," she added, snapping a hand out to his shoulder.

A glum look vanished from Simon's face with a start. "Oh- uh- thanks. I..."

"I shouldn't complain to you. Tonight's wonderful –thanks to you– but that's why tomorrow bites. And you know, it just sucks because I have to go home and sleep and then in the morning I'll have to get up super early and walk a bit before I can even get picked up by an Uber because they don't pick up where I live. My whole neighborhood is a void on their navigation map, like the friggin Walmart parking lot."

Simon nodded uncertainly. "So then couldn't you get the car *now*? That way you'd save time in the morning."

Morrigan pinched the bridge of her nose and rubbed, squeezing her eyes shut. It was late and she couldn't discern if he was right, wrong, or if both options had about the same degree of strain on her schedule. Logic and reasoning were lethargic to be called upon. Her mind had recently been used for such intense passion and emotion that the circuits felt fried.

"You know..." Simon began with a strange kind of hesitation. With her head frozen in position, Morrigan's eyes opened and flicked sideways at Simon. "You *could* just take the monorail."

Morrigan raised an eyebrow and thought the simple thoughts of an exhausted brain. " You know I don't have a monorail leading from my house to the park, right? That's just your hotel."

She didn't understand his offer until she felt an errant fingertip graze her back as he made a stealthy withdrawal.

"*Oh!*"

Simon shifted and searched for *any* other topic with a long "uhhh," looking as if he might have rather jump over the railing into the duck pond than belabor the point.

She returned an "uhhh," of her own, but her's was a frantic 'uhhh', like that of a game show contestant stalling to extend their time.

Watching him bleed self esteem, she knew she couldn't spend her usual time thinking and overthinking her decision.

"Just-" he blurted like a cough. "Just figured it made sense, because... y'know-"

"Y-yeah."

They both nodded and shrugged and didn't say anything made of words for several seconds.

I fucked it up. He meant it to be smooth and charming. I should have been excited, enthusiastic. I waited too long. Now I've ruined it. He's going to be afraid to ever make a move again. I have to fix it, make it sexy again.

"Well, uhh, where will I sleep?" The sentence came out like she was reading a sloppily handwritten note.

Sorry, Simon. You've just been cast in the world's worst porno.

He blinked. "I have a couch in the-"

"I can't sleep on couches." She shot back, her voice cracking.

Smooth

"No I mean *I* would sleep on the-"

"No!" Morrigan cleared her throat quickly. "No, I mean I can't enjoy a bed if I'm stealing it from you."

"Oh, uhhh..."

"Can we share the bed?"

Simon glanced at her chest, for the briefest of seconds, and trumpets of victory sounded in Morrigan's head as she tallied another win.

"Sure, yeah. We can... do that."

"Is it a big bed?"

Fuck! Why did I ask that? I shouldn't have touched it. It was fine. Seduction complete. Where the fuck do I go from here!?

"Oh, uh, I *guess* it's a big bed. There should be plenty of room for both of us."

"Well what side of the bed do you sleep on?"

Simon blinked. "I mean, I guess the middle? I have the room alone, but it'd be easy enough to just-"

"I sleep in the middle too."

*Is that sexy? Does he get that I want to sleep like in the same place as him? Maybe not **on top** of him or like **spooning** necessarily but maybe just **touching** in some way?*

A small smile crept into the corners of Simon's mouth. "I kinda figured. But I can always sleep on one side or-"

"Well what side?"

His eyebrow twitched as he raised it. "The right?"

Morrigan shook her head firmly. "No I sleep on the right side."

"Okay then I can sleep on the left side."

"I really can't steal the right side from you. I wouldn't enjoy it anymore."

An amused and exacerbated groan broke through any nervousness that held Simon. "Morrigan, what the fuck are you-"

"We'll just both have to sleep on the same side then." Morrigan suggested in a voice three octaves too high.

Simon's blank stare and raised eyebrow sunk Morrigan's heart, but her determination shoved her onwards.

"I also can't sleep without air conditioning and get cold easily and hate blankets."

The words gave Morrigan a rush like she'd just unbuckled his pants but the feeling faded as she watched Simon's face contort as he tried to consider what kind of person could live with such a contradictory affliction.

"Morrigan? what the fuck are you talking about? You're like a bankrobber stalling for time by making eccentric demands. What the hell do you want?"

"Snuggles!" Morrigan blurted, wincing at how stupid it sounded. "I- Just- Simon?"

"...Yes?"

"Simon, can you hold me while we sleep? I wanna snuggle up with you all night. Also I'm terrified to have sex with you. Not that you're terrifying, or that I'm terrified of sex. I like sex. I mean I like it the normal amount."

Morrigan whirled and slapped a hand over Simon's mouth. "No wait. I really fucked that up. Give me a second."

"Okay." Morrigan began again. "Simon, please hold me tonight. I like your hugs and I'd like one that lasts several hours. I promise to do my best to be a good snuggle buddy. Not like a platonic buddy though. Like a date buddy. Who is also female, which is relevant. Also don't seduce me tonight, but don't be discouraged from doing so in the future. You're hot 'n' stuff. I just- there's like a lot of steps and I want them all to be kind of there and not become silly or redundant right away because I kind of haven't gotten to do all the-"

Morrigan blinked away spots, and sucked in a breath that she'd been negligent in taking.

When her eyelids fluttered her vision back into focus, Simon was laughing and slipping his arms around her. "A non-platonic, relevantly female, buddy whom I take on dates?"

Morrigan swore and blushed, her eyes rolling closed.

"I *think* there might be a word for that."

With Morrigan's flushed silence, he pulled her gently towards him, into his soft hug. Talking had exhausted her. It was so much easier to just touch him. "But, for now, I'll cherish being your non-platonic, relevantly male, buddy that you take on dates."

Morrigan chewed her lip and looked up at him, pulling away just enough to see his face fully. The word was too heavy for her to lift to her lips.

"Also, Morrigan? Thank you. I really like holding you, so I'm glad you like being held. I'll happily hold you all night long."

"Also fair to warn that I get sweaty when I sleep."

"Don't care."

"Also sometimes roll over and stretch like a cat. I often wake up early for work by falling out of bed."

"I think I can handle it. Also can we both sleep in the *middle* of the bed? Or are you set on the *right* side?"

Morrigan started to laugh, harder than was warranted, and punched simon. It was a playful slug, straight to the meat of his thigh, missing his ass. "How *dare* you make me laugh at your shitty jokes?"

Simon staggered back half a step and then crashed over her like a wave, wrapping her in warm arms she could nestle into. She turned in his embrace, leaning back against him and pulled his arms about her like a shawl.

Together they stood in the night breeze and watched the crowd thin.

Chapter 35

Main Street USA

Simon spun slowly as he walked, pacing backwards a step or two before completing the rotation and returning to his stride at an even step. Main Street USA was peaceful at this hour; made tranquil by the calm shade of night that blanketed the few stragglers moving towards the exit. Children slept in arms or strollers and parents carried a soft satisfied smile at a successful day. Light up toys hung limply now and the last deaththroes of excitement were waning in sugar fueled children a few minutes from crashing happily on the bus back to their hotel.

It was such a pretty stretch of the park, and it felt obvious that the place ought to feel wonderfully peaceful, but he'd never gone through at such a slow pace before. He'd always darted around people, speed-walking towards Tomorrowland, but tonight this stretch of 1950's America made him glad to linger.

The buildings all had rounded edges and they were painted in pale colors that would be easy to see on a sunny day. It was clean and well paved, adorned with all the fixings of an idealized American street. A barber and a candy shop, a tall man in a white suit with a bow-tie holding a huge bundle of balloons smiling at everyone. It was condensed America, Walt's condensed America.

With Main Street USA so open and empty that they could saunter slowly down the dead middle unaccosted, it was hard not to appreciate the vision that had made this place. Simon had never really known a street like this one, but it was easy to feel the love that radiated from the design.

You could go to the future, a land of adventure, or even one of fairy tale, but everyone had to go down main street first. Simon imagined he wanted to remind everyone how special their home was, before they escaped off into fantasy, and –he supposed– after they returned from their escapism as well.

As they neared the flag-pole, waving the American flag boldly in a crossing of floodlight beams, Simon could hear a speaker in the bushes playing a chipper tune. He stopped a moment and stared up at that flag. Simon remarked that pessimism felt so far away and irrational.

"Something on your mind?" Came the voice of a girl who'd wandered several steps beyond him.

He trotted a few steps to catch up with her and gave half a reply in the form of a flustered "Oh, uhh..."

Morrigan leaned forward as they walked, sticking her face into his downcast vision.

Simon blinked at her, straightened and shedded his gloom with a shrug. "I just noticed it feels kinda *weird* to be just like... happy? I guess just not being all depressed feels sort of like I'm pretending to be someone else."

Morrigan blew out a breath with the force of a chuckle.

"I'm sorry." Simon rubbed his eyes. "That sounds really... uh..."

Morrigan jabbed him gently in the side. "Sounds really depressing and insane." Her hand, seemingly of its own volition, began to rub his lower back. "I had a similar thought."

Simon looked at her and received a playful push. "Don't you know how to bundle all your uncomfortable emotions inside and ignore them like a good Christian?"

Morrigan concealed her smile slightly by taking a pace beyond him and Simon was struck by a flash of giddiness for their shared emotion. Mischief overtook him *very* briefly and he skipped up with a hand cocked to slap her butt. Of course, his brain got hold of the reins at the last moment and pulled the plug.

Morrigan caught sight of the motion with an over the shoulder glance. She held onto a little smirk with pursed lips, until the laughter quaking in her chest broke her composure. She staggered backwards against the brick wall beside the exit tunnel doubled over laughing, her bright smile blazing amidst the hair that swung forward and thrashed gently with her bobbing shoulders.

The Magic Kingdom was normally a hard place to leave, but Simon left it with a giggling girl. It was *very* easy to leave with *her*.

She teased and mocked and giggled and provoked him incessantly. She would walk swiftly ahead only to stop short and stick her butt out at an immodest angle and then cackle when Simon would spin out of the way in alarm, as if his groin had a deadly electrical current surging through it. If Simon raised his hand to itch his nose, she would gasp like a southern belle and cover her butt with the hand she wasn't holding an imaginary handkerchief with.

Somewhere in the dark of the entrance tunnel, he finally relented and landed a smack on her butt. Though it could hardly be called a smack. He robbed the swing of all violence and it landed with such little force that it felt uncomfortably like a grope and he withdrew his hand like her butt had burned it.

Morrigan laughed so hard she fell backwards into a poster for Splash Mountain and leaned against the wall there. Her eyes were shut and he had to steady her against sliding to the floor.

She was wearing her sweatshirt again, but she'd rolled up the wet sleeve, and his fingers felt bare skin. Even immobilized with laughter, her body's natural instinct was to magnetize to his contact. Her arm nestled into his hand and he felt a gentle pinch at his elbow of a thumb and forefinger. That very feeble grip which she held him with was embarrassingly meaningful to him. He lifted her chin and she relegated her laughter to her nose momentarily.

"Would you just *shut-*"

She kissed him. Her grin was too hard to restrain and he felt his lips pinched briefly by teeth. Then the kiss was all lips and a hot breath out her nose. It was alarmingly passionate and Simon instinctively jerked his hips away.

Morrigan separated from his lips and shook her head at him, the smile on her lips faint but inextinguishable. She smacked *his* butt with both hands, keeping him there.

Morrigan yanked his waist against hers and let out a mock gasp. "I *knew* it." She covered her mouth with one hand. "I had my suspicions, of course, but now I have been delivered grim certainty. You brutish, villainous, fiend!" She lay a limp wrist against her forehead. "You have a-"

Simon kissed her and she stopped talking.

Her limp hand quickly moved from her head to combing through his hair. With it she held him close, his forehead to hers, as she parted to catch her breath. A stillness blanketed them, and they stayed together in that embrace, the only outward force being their chests rising with breath.

The alarmingly near scrape of soles against concrete snapped them apart like they were teenagers and it were the rattle of a door-knob to their room.

The sharpness of motion startled a round, rosey-cheeked midwestern woman who laid a hand over her heart and flinched back against her husband. Clearly their stillness in the dark had concealed them, as much as their passion had blinded them to the approaching pair.

In a flash, the woman saw their embarrassment and a warm smile lit her face. She had a hairdo that reached her shoulders, and her body continued that curve, turning her into a ball of smiles and rosey cheeks. "You folks have yourselves a magical evening now, y'hear?"

The way she said it made Simon smile back warmly, despite his embarrassment.

Her husband gave him an approving nod and a wink that jostled his jowels. He was a stiff man, standing taller than his wife by half again with a salt and pepper mustache and silver scruff a shade brighter than his sun-burnt cheeks.

They looked at the two of them with such coy approval and Simon found it flattering. The strangers clearly had more confidence in Simon's powers of seduction than he did. It was a humorous notion, to Simon, that he could take a girl back to his hotel room and do anything more forward than offer them pajamas and sleep on the floor.

"Thank you." Simon managed, as the pair shuffled off, her legs stepping twice for every step of the slow swinging stride of his.

The woman slipped a persistent arm beneath her husbands. She wrapped her arms around his and leaned against him, chittering something bubbly up at him that made the man stand even taller.

They'd looked at them like a cute young couple and somehow now Simon felt like perhaps they were.

Chapter 36

Precipice

Morrigan was generous with her vowels, extending them nearly into song with her sweeping whines.

"And it *is* a good job. That makes it *worse.* If it was some shitty job I could just fuck off and hang out with *you* all day tomorrow."

"I mean... it's not like I'll really be doing anything that interesting..."

Again Morrigan expelled a titanic breath of air in a sigh. "Yeah but *now* we're like a...."

The two of them turned from the path to meet wide eyed stares. Both of them wholly unready to tackle the end of that sentence.

The two of them mumbled and stumbled through reciting: "A non-platonic, relevantly male and female, pair of buddies who go on dates," in a kind of drunken unison.

They shared a weak smile and a short laugh, and Morrigan continued on ahead lifting her chin into the wind.

Again it had been Simon who suggested the walk, following their monorail ride, and again Morrigan was the one who needed it. Her manic foot tapping on the monorail was translated now into long, slow strides.

"It's weird." He began softly, intruding on the silence.

She stopped, looking back, quick enough to swing her hair over her shoulder. "Sorry?"

"Oh, I just said it's weird. I- I'm not anxious. It feels so... *certain*. You and me, I mean. Normally I'd be on my toes, waiting for every silence to be followed with bad news. But now..." He shrugged, having no words strong enough to explain.

Her eyes twinkled, as warm as a kiss. "I'm really glad."

She looked like she wanted to say more, but her words couldn't reach her feelings. Simon gestured onwards with a nod, and began walking again. He could be more than patient for her to collect her thoughts.

In a pleasant silence they enjoyed the night together. Soon their walk had carried them some distance from the hotel. They found themselves at a dock which had a ferry tethered to it. Simon found the sound of lapping water, paired with the gentle deep knocking of hull against dock, to be incredibly relaxing. It was evident however, by the pace he had to keep behind her, that Morrigan's anxiety was unyielding.

"I definitely recognized more than a few people I used to work with, over on the haunted mansion, at the monorail station. And, you know, I don't like *know* if there's some rule against dating guests but..."

The dock was blocked off by a chained gate which was wider than where the dock connected to the path, likely to avoid people simply stepping around or hopping across a short gap. Morrigan casually slipped out of her ratty converse and swung herself around the end of the gate without explanation. She stuck her small feet, clad in mismatched neon green Invader Zim and purple Maleficent half-socks, between the bars of the fence. Morrigan easily found purchase there and scaled sideways with no more effort than balancing on a curb.

"I'm sorry to complain atcha. I don't mean to make it seem like it's like a problem or whatever. I mean *you*. I don't want you to feel like you're a burden. I'm such a bitch man. I'm sorry. You're great."

Simon had to reach a hand through the bars to grab hold of her hood to keep her from leaving him behind the gate.

She turned, her face looking tired enough to make the smile she squeezed out of it look dishonest.

"Hey thank you. Um but are we gonna uhhh."

"Oh right, my bad." Simon's hand slipped from her sweatshirt as she scaled her way back around the fence. "Forgot you weren't a bad kid like me."

Simon held out a hand to help her as she made her way back around but she completed the journey on intuition informed by experience and didn't think to take it until she didn't need it.

"How does someone as anxious as you get to be so casual about trespassing?" He asked, as she kicked her feet back into her shoes, grinding down the heels as she wriggled her foot in.

She looked at him, eyebrows pressed together. "How does someone as anxious as *you* say all that crazy shit. One second you're the biggest bitch on the planet and then, all of a sudden, you're like saying some *crazy* shit about my freckles."

Simon floundered for a moment, unsure of whether he'd insulted her, overstepped a boundary, or if he should feel insulted himself. "What- What did I say?"

"I don't *remember.*" Morrigan exclaimed, as if somehow the words themselves were irrelevant to what had been said.

He watched her wander off down the path, wondering after her meaning.

He'd been confident when he said it, *that* he remembered, but what words and in what order he didn't know. They were all one indecipherable soup of words and emotions, churning in his head. The more he tried to discern specifics, the further away from the truth of it he felt. She was right.

Morrigan glanced back at him, over her shoulder, and he jogged a step to catch up. They walked a while in silence as he assembled a sentence that could explain. Each quiet second built a pressure in Simon but, the moment he let them, the words left him as casually as a sigh.

"I guess..." Simon stopped. Morrigan was slow to, wandering some steps beyond. "I guess I just started believing you." The words took a whole breath to say and they anchored Morrigan to the spot. "Not the whole part about me being attractive, of course. I just mean that I believed- *believe* that you think I am."

She rolled her eyes so hard he could see it behind her.

"No I mean- well... First: thank you, by the way. That was really sweet of you. It made me feel just... really *okay* about being me. And I guess more importantly it made me feel like I could tell you how I felt about... *you,* and not be worried it would come off as too much or something."

"Like when you slapped chocolate all over your shirt so I

wouldn't feel like a slob?"

"Something like that... yeah..."

The night wind swept their conversation away for a moment and when the whirring in his ears had stilled Simon asked.

"Hey Morrigan? You're really awesome..."

"But."

"What?"

"I'm really awesome *but.*" She shrugged hard and her hands came slapping into her sides as she started walking again. Simon's eyes followed those hands, and squinted at what she seemed to be directing his attention to.

Butt? I didn't say anything about her butt. I think it's fine. I don't know why she thinks it's flat. Isn't it better to be smaller than fat? People always say-

"No it's alright man. Had a really great time tonight."

Wait, isn't that good?

"I get it. Home is a thousand miles away, and I'm..."

Is that a song?

"New york's got a lot of pretty girls. Bunch of Swedish models and..." Her thoughts were eaten up by a swelling stone in her throat. Simon fumbled for words to pull her ashore, as she knuckled her forehead and stomped a foot in a flash of frustration. "Look I didn't mean to ruin... I'm sorry. This is still really great. I just... I'm like a kid who doesn't wanna go home at the end of vacation. I'm-"

Simon gasped in a breath, her meaning suddenly dawning on him, then it exploded just as sharply out of him as desperate honesty.

"Morrigan, I'm not *going home*. I'm a *homeless person*. I have no home, not in New York, not anywhere. I have no credit either. I fucked my credit to death. I didn't move out. I just skipped out on rent and any other bill sent there. I even let my subway pass go to collections. I live out of that hotel room. Now will you shut up?"

I'm trying to ask you out, you idiot.

Tension dropped out of her stiff posture and she looked back at him with a pleading expression and a soft laugh at her own expense. When Simon caught up and wrapped her in a hug, she slumped against him, exhausted.

"God damn it." She shuddered against his chest. "It sounds so stupid now, but I bet it'll be back. I hold my breath after every compliment, waiting for the easy let down, braced for bad news to come. I'm sorry. I'm fucking tonight up. I'm fine, I'm fine."

"Until the next time it creeps up on you. I wish I could just tear that garbage right out of the back of your head."

She glanced up at him and recoiled from the eye-contact, blinking and drawing away. Her face was stung with embarrassment, but Simon didn't let her go far. She was tethered by the hands he held and bounced slowly back against him like a boat tied to a dock.

She shifted and shrugged, trying to physically shed the conversation from herself. "No I'm good. Really."

"Morrigan, you *can't* mess anything up. This won't break. Whatever *this* is, just doesn't break."

Her fidgeting became lethargic and her eyes settled back on him.

"I'm always gonna be your non-platonic, relevantly male, buddy whom you take on dates."

She flashed a bright smile and he was the victim of another mock assault, pounding gentle fists against his chest. It concluded with her arms wrapped tightly about him, reaching up to his shoulderblades where his shirt was clutched in the small fists of a girl.

"You're always worrying about it, and you just can't see how silly it is. I'm too much of a loser, you know? I've never broken up with *anyone.* You could *really* treat me like shit and-" His words were abbreviated by a stone forming in his throat.

Morrigan slipped her arms from his back and slid them quickly up his chest to hold him by the face. Gentle fingers gripped him just tightly enough that he couldn't look away without exerting an unpleasant force upon the girl. She blinked tears onto her cheeks and a weak smile quivered at him. "You know that's not *good,*" she told him through a throat tight with emotion.

He pulled her back against his chest, to dry her cheeks, and nodded forcefully, not trusting his throat.

There was a sniffle against his chest, followed by a mewling whimper and Simon reached around behind her head, combing his fingers through her hair and pulling her in tighter. She rose against him, laying her chin on his collarbone. A whining whisper cast itself up to his ear. "You know you have to be really good to me, because I'm the same way. I'm stuck with you Simon Magnusson."

He gave her a quick squeeze and eased her apart to look at her. Morrigan had already stifled her unwieldy emotions and her eyes met his steadily.

"Hey," he began again with an upward nod. "Would you really want to go out with a guy like me?"

She rolled her eyes at him, and gave Simon a playful shove with enough force to break from his embrace. "You think I could do better?" Her vexation spread from her eyebrow and she cocked her whole head to the side. "Dude if you went to a party with me on your arm, they'd assume I had a great personality." She shook her head with a chuckle and walked on ahead a few steps.

Simon blinked, watching her. *She's imagined us going places together as a couple?* he thought, catching up, his posture suddenly far straighter.

"They'd say shit like '*oh wow, that's so cool*' if I told them where I work, and they'd say it with wide eyes and they'd nod slowly. They would be so nauseatingly polite, but they'd be thinking it. They'd all be smiling and nice and complimentary but they'd all think it."

Simon gave her a cheeky kick to the butt and she skipped a step or two beyond his reach. "I'm serious. You'd really want me to introduce you as my *girlfriend*? to be seen holding my hand?"

"Of *course* I would." She groaned softly.

"Then lets do it. No more non-platonic, relevantly female, buddy I take on dates. Be my girlfriend."

Her grinning face was full of snarky remarks and deflections but she resigned herself to a simple sincere: "Okay."

They stared at each other for a long moment, before wind cast her bangs in front of her face. She turned into the breeze and he fell into step behind her. A length of walk sounded pleasant to him. It'd give him time to process their new status.

For all the heat of the couple, the wind blew on oblivious. It cooled and lapped against their ears. It made Morrigan's hair look beautiful; an inky banner lashing about behind her. That midnight wind carried a chill too, and Simon's button-down armored him poorly against it.

With a flash of mad bravery Simon pranced up behind his formerly 'non-platonic, relevantly female, friend' –now *girlfriend*–

and grabbed her, swinging her about in a hug. She squealed a tiny noise that made his hands swim about her with passion, hazarding even brief contact with her chest.

"Sorry, I was cold and hugging you is..."

"You scared me dumbass." She clenched her hand around his belt to make sure he wouldn't get discouraged and escape. "I'm trying to be cute and you're making me squeal like an annoying piglet."

"That was the cutest sound I've ever heard." He said with urgency on a breath too short to fit a whole sentence. "It wasn't annoying. I love those noises you make, Morrigan. They're so god damn cute."

She made another sound he hadn't heard before. The sound of giggles through teeth and pursed lips, as she bounced up onto the balls of her feet for a kiss. Then, believing him, she made another. The sound of a relaxed vocal sigh buzzed into his lips and chest.

She parted from his lips for another breath when she'd spent that one, and shined bright eyes in his. "Sorry to cut you off. Go on about the sounds and stuff?"

Chapter 37

Boiling Ice

Morrigan had always been told that the noises she made were distracting and weird and *annoying*. She'd been told to "shut up." Eye rolls and groans had bludgeoned her to silence even alone.

Now Simon told her the opposite. He told her how much he loved the sound of her voice, talking, laughing or making exaltations of ecstasy, with long stumbling sentences with words that tripped upon the next. It was beautiful and sweet, and none of it was poetry.

Morrigan was pleasantly overwhelmed. She would have recoiled and let the tension in her throat turn to tears while she blubbered some appropriate expression of gratitude, but he held her against him. Instead of retreat from him, she fell against Simon like gravity. Her full weight knocked him off balance, nearly toppling him over, but he threw his weight forward into the embrace. He regripped her almost forcefully, invigoratingly so, and Morrigan let out a tiny squeak hot enough to mist in the chill of the night air.

Welcomed or not, the sound marked an intensity she wasn't ready for. She jerked forward, parting from contact with him. She was overwhelmed and embarrassed but, though she struggled to muster words to explain herself, Simon didn't seem to need any. He blew out a sharp breath and swore softly with a sentiment so familiar it made her huff a laugh.

Simon put his hands on her shoulders and massaged her with an intimacy that was far more moderate, and controlled. She turned sharply, breaking his grip and planted her palms on his chest. Her hands served as a barrier, but a gentle one. "Fuck, man," she swore, still breathless. She took his hands, hovering uncertainly over her, and placed them back on her shoulders.

"You'd really want to be seen holding my hand?"

She punched him in the chest, playfully but sportingly hard. "Of course, you idiot. Now, would you get your fuck eyes off of me for a god damn second? I'm trying to calm down and you're all... looking at me and shit."

Simon's face was lit with a smile and he pinched her shoulders, massaging them anew. She didn't conceal how it felt, allowing soft unrestrained vocalizations to leave her. Using her breathing as a map he navigated his hands where she needed them, kneading tension from her muscles. Slowly he shifted, respectfully, from her shoulders to her back. his hand migrated gently down the curve of her spine, and then back up. His fingertips kneaded timidly under her shoulderblades and Morrigan arched her back, leaning into Simon's hands.

He slid gentle fingertips up her back to her neck and then combed through her hair and massaged her scalp. Morrigan's eyes fluttered shut. She made herself malleable in his hands, moving her head easily with any force he exerted, but the easier she let his hands manipulate her, the more restrained Simon's massage became. He was adorably sensitive to man-handling her. "It feels good." She reassured, once his touch became so delicate it bordered on ethereal. "Just not used to scalp massages."

*Could **get** used to them though.*

Her eyes came open and she watched him with a smile eclipsed by her lip nibbling. He was thoroughly distracted from their conversation, caught up in enjoying putting certain expressions on her face.

"Hey, you'd really introduce a girl like me to your parents?"

"Mhmm"

"You know I *could* dress more like... normal too, if that'd help; y'know, no eyeliner, no band-shirts..."

"*Ohhh*... is *that* why your eyes are so..."

Satisfied with herself, she watched her boyfriend with eyes that were very *something*.

As casually as a sigh he lowered his lips to hers and they began kissing. His forwardness surprised her, but his lips felt soft on hers and his hands honest. He didn't escalate the intensity, and she knew he should have with any other girl. But something about his timid lips, that could be pulled apart from without protest or frustration, set her blood on fire.

Morrigan vaulted higher on Simon, yanking herself up by his shoulders and wrapping her legs around him tightly. She hugged his neck and thrust her chest towards his face, basking in the heat of his blush. She began to slip and the hand that had been afraid to rest it's full weight on her shoulder now gripped her thigh to support her –an experienced umpire might have even called out some minor butt touching– and the first words out of his mouth weren't an apology or explanation.

"Is this real? Am I going to wake up tomorrow, and hear you

explain you got carried away? Are we really boyfriend and girlfriend?"

A stone in her throat halted her words but Morrigan nodded so fervently her hair was dislodged and eclipsed one eye messily. She almost took an arm from around his neck to fix it but his face told her it was cute and so she reached out for him instead. She played with his hair, stroked a thumb across his cheek and sighed wistfully, looking boldly down at her new *boyfriend*.

Rain announced itself first as a distant tapping but it soon arrived as cold droplets on Morrigan's bare arms, naked to the night air. The storm moved fast and their time was slow. The cold rain ran down their faces, soothing cheeks that stung with blush. Their bodies, heated by laboring hearts, steamed in the cool water. Soon Morrigan's hair was stuck to her cheek and she melted down Simon's chest to stand with him. The rain was loud and so they smiled rather than speak.

The first shiver shook off the eye contact and the pair looked out into a downpour. It was so torrential it obscured the hotel like fog. She watched dispassionately, absent any urgency to act. She only understood why when Simon spoke.

"We should get out of the rain."

We

That meant only one place; one place that '*we*' should go.

"I left my car in the Epcot lot..." Morrigan's voice cracked to project over the rain.

"I- I know." Simon's face was pale like the sun through a cloud and she couldn't help but giggle at it. She could see the tension of words struggling to be spoken through the rising tendons at the base of his neck.

In an attempt to conceal her own nervousness she raised her

hand to cup over her mouth, but it was trembling, and Simon noticed with a smile. Morrigan got two words into her blushing southern belle routine before Simon scooped her up and swung her around like a princess. She squealed an involuntary squeak and clung to him. Nestled against his chest, she could feel it heaving with soft laughter.

The two of them only got a dozen or so feet like this before she wanted to be put down. Being horizontal in the rain was no way to stay dry and, though it would be impossible to get more *wet,* they were both already shivering like they'd fallen through a frozen lake. Every drop was glacially cold, and her clothes were rendered as useless as bare flesh by saturation. She could feel her core temperature dropping as a chill filled her chest. Simon's slow, burdened pace evoked a temptation to sprint to shelter. Of course, she couldn't just ask to be set down. Simon's arms were already shaking from having lifted her up before and she refused to let him think that he was anything less than her Hercules.

Salvation came shortly, in the form of a stupid idea. Through chattering teeth she excitedly urged Simon to take a detour to the hot-tub. It would be blessedly warm and, for once, unoccupied. The moment she was set down Morrigan rushed to the temperature control.

"Wait! your phone?"

"Waterproof," he hissed between shivers, taking the steps in.

"Same," she chattered, turning as she slapped the dial, maxing out the heat.

"Besides, can't really get any more wet from being submerged."

The rain roared against the surface of the water so loud they'd need to yell to be heard and, being caught between the rain and the upwards splash of it hitting the surface, they needed to squint. Worse, the change in temperature stung their skin harshly.

"Fuck. It's like grabbing an ice-cube, but like... *all over.*"

"Hot-cold therapy. You can pay to do this at the spa. It's good for you."

Shivering converted easily to laughter.

"Alright: abort. This was retarded."

"Yep."

With that, they abandoned the hot-tub and bolted for his room. Simon led the way, pulling her along by the hand. The hot water protected them for a half dozen paces before they were freezing again. They cut through the garden and her core temperature had dropped so far the dirt felt warm through the soles of her feet.

Chapter 38

White as Snow

Morrigan's fair skin had gone from Snow-White-like to corpse-like. He'd have warmed her with his own body heat, if he had any, but he was so cold he could feel a chill on the inside of his chest. She was smaller and he imagined that same chill in *her* with dread. The mania that had sent giggles through their shivering was extinguished. Her teeth chattered almost lazily and she swayed when his hand left her shoulder.

Simon prised his card from a waterlogged wallet and opened the door only to be met with a great gust of disappointment. Simon had maxed out his AC. Florida's weather was normally hot and sunny, not a frozen monsoon.

Morrigan entered by rolling around the doorframe, loosing a long string of profanity, broken only by laughter and violent shivering.

"Lemme just shut this off." He breathed with an airy shudder.

The cold had stolen all swiftness and coordination from his hand, and his fingers obeyed his will with an almost oblivious lethargy as he popped open the air conditioning panel. Too numb for dexterity, he balled a fist and knuckled the off button. The controls were flush with the screen and had suffered hotel-wear-and-tear so only after he pressed so hard his hand shook with effort did it surrender a beep. When the noisy machine *did* stop, he heard Morrigan's voice call his name.

"Woah!" He felt small hands clap over his shoulders and noticed the floor was slanted. Then he noticed *he* was slanted. "Jesus fuck, Simon." He blinked, being forcibly stood up straight and found himself turned and walked towards the bathroom. "You look like a god damn drowned corpse."

Her concern hit his ear sweeter for all the shivering that disrupted it.

Morrigan slapped at the heated floor controls as effectively as he'd handled the air conditioner and Simon reached for a towel on the heated rack. His numb fingers lacked the coordination to properly tie a towel around Morrigan's hair, so he lingered there, burying his hands in the warmth.

The shower started and Simon looked over to see a fully clothed Morrigan inside, on one foot, tugging off a waterlogged shoe.

"Come on. Get in here and warm up." She chattered. "We can worry about being dry once we're not gonna die of fucking hypothermia."

He watched her shoe come tumbling out of the shower and found himself rooted by hesitation, in the face of the daunting momentum that first article represented.

"Come *on* dude. What's a girl gotta do to get her boyfriend to join her in the shower?"

Her voice cracked high with a note of insecurity and Simon rushed to join her. She moved aside with a hop, demonstrating a religious-like faith in her balance. He caught the teetering girl by the shoulders and she let out a short nervous laugh.

With a 'thanks' on her lips her expression melted with a sigh. "*Damn* your hands feel good. Is this what body heat feels like to a vampire?"

He gave her a short shoulder massage before her eyes came open and she dragged him into the shower with her. The large shower felt so small with her in it. There was plenty of room to stand without touching her, but he didn't dare.

She took hold of his bicep to steady herself as she took off her other shoe and looked up at him sharply. "God the rest of you is fucking *freezing*. That's what you get for being a skinny little twink."

She reached under his arm to turn up the temperature on the panel behind him. Her chest came up against his and before she could tease him about his reflexive tensing, he wrapped her in a hug.

The hot water came down like the burn of an ice-cube on bare skin. Simon let the scalding water hit his back and run off onto her, tamer. She sheltered her arms beneath his shirt, but only when the numbness began to fade did the intimacy strike him.

"You make a pretty good heater, Simon Magnusson."

"Thanks, but now that I can feel my toes it feels pretty weird to have my shoes on in the shower."

"You think the room has warmed up at all?" She asked, steadying him as he pried his waterlogged shoes off.

"Well, there isn't really heat. We're the only heaters this room has."

Morrigan groaned skyward, arching her back far enough to let her hair hang free behind her. "This is so retarded. Literally the only heat in the room is the shower." She straightened, catching her hair before it could swing forward and pinned it behind her ear. "I guess there's the bed though."

"Yeah, just gotta get out of these wet clothes and dry off." He absent-mindedly thumbed open the top button. "I guess I'll go..."

Morrigan's hand was still on his shoulder, steadying him to remove shoes that were already off, and it didn't feel like she was about to let go. He followed her laser-focused eyes to that first undone button.

Am I? Are we?

Wordlessly, he undid another, wishing all the while he knew what a man seductively stripping looked like. Her attention felt like a needle being driven into his sternum. He *knew* he was repulsive and if she kept looking she would notice. His chest was too scrawny, his ribs were too there, and his nipples were either too small or too big but definitely wrong.

Something made her glance up at his face and her face was stricken with horror. "Oh my god I'm so sorry! You look *so* uncomfortable. I'm sorry. This is weird. You can stop."

"No! It's fine! It's just that guys aren't really sexy like that. I can't like *strip* for you. I can only take off my clothes. I'm sorry I just felt silly. I can keep going it you want. I'll do whatever. I don't care."

She gave him a smack to the cheek. It was gentle, but no less shocking. "Would you cut that shit out? Simon, you're 'fuck my boyfriend hot'. You're such a pretty boy, girls have to worry about you turning their fucking boyfriends gay and stealing them. You're fucking prettier than me. If you didn't have such nice thick eyebrows and that strong nose and your *chin,* that god **damn** *chin,* then you could put on a friggin dress you're so pretty."

To Simon's ears, nothing she said was complimentary, but she spoke with near breathless hunger. He couldn't help but believe her attraction on an empathic level.

"You know what you sound like when you're beating up on your looks? You don't sound modest. You sound dumb. You sound like a dumb person. Like someone who's like *okay* can be modest, but *you* can't. It's obnoxious. Actually it's mean. Like you're calling ugly people literal cave dwelling trolls, unspeakable abominations."

Simon shook his head with alarm at the accusation but Morrigan bulldozed to her next point before he could defend himself.

"Secondly? You're my boyfriend now, right?"

He hesitated and it took no less than a second for her face to sink.

"Yes! I'm your boyfriend." On her, his hands belonged. He was touching her, comforting her, and it was staggeringly normal. "Holy shit, I *am*. You're... You're really my girlfriend."

She huffed a laugh out her nose but kept her lips pursed where a smile twitched as she nodded affirmation.

"Jesus, how the hell did *that* happen?"

"It wasn't your brazen confidence and ruthless persistence. You can be real sure of *that*." She stuck her tongue out but she still held his eyes with a hungry look.

His lips parted in protest and her finger landed there, gingerly.

"Shut up. Lemme finish," she demanded softly, as her finger slipped down off his lips, and traced his jawline over to his neck. "Now you're my boyfriend, and I can't have anyone talking shit about my boyfriend. I'll have to fight you if you don't watch your mouth." She held him by his collar, tugging at him, and Simon drifted naturally towards her.

Wide eyes fluttered at his pliability, and her demeanor sweetened immediately. Her expression softened so deeply her lips parted gently. She rose on her tip-toes, against him, thrusting her chest up as she drifted into his lips with a shudder. She trembled in a way that made him want to press her safely against his chest, and she squeaked a ragged breath in through her nose.

She broke from the kiss with a jolt. Still so close her breath puffed hot against his neck, she whispered "Wait." but her hands disagreed, raking down his back, tugging at his hair. With a jerk she stopped herself and pushed Simon's face away from hers with a wide hand.

"Alright listen, you boyband fuck," she panted, composing herself. "You have to be good. I said I didn't want to do anything."

Simon's eyebrows, which he now knew to be quite nice, came together and he cocked his head. "*Right,* but..."

"Shut up. Shut your whore mouth." She turned to pace and while the shower *was* big she took one big heated step, reached the wall, and then had to turn 180 and take another single step before she'd met another wall and decided to stop pacing. "Listen I'll do anything, and like I said before I just... I don't know... I just don't want to. I feel like it'll be bad if we-"

"Morrigan that's totally fine."

"I'm sorry."

Absent-mindedly she began to fiddle with the close of his shirt.

"You know, right now, you sound like the inside of my head." He stepped towards her and held her firmly by the shoulders. "It's a mess in there Morrigan. You should calm down."

"People get stabbed for telling crazy people to calm down,

you know."

"Please don't."

Her hands sprung from his shirt with alarm. "S-sorry, I got-"

"N-no stab me. I meant don't stab me."

"Oh! Okay."

"Morrigan, you-" he choked back a laugh. "You don't sound very convincing."

She rolled her eyes at her own rigidity. "I promise I won't stab you to death." Morrigan plucked at Simon's shirt, peeling it from his stomach. "Alright himbo, you gonna strip for me or what?"

"Himbo?"

"'Man' plus 'bimbo'."

"You mean 'him'?"

"Shut up mimbo."

He just shook his head and smiled as he began unbuttoning his shirt again.

"Actually, can I?"

He nodded and she reached delicately for his shirt only to recoil before making contact. "I'm sorry. I shouldn't. You're uncomfortable. I'm just a little excited and stressed and... well crazy I guess.

He took her hands, and placed them where they wanted to be.

"I'll let it go this time but, if you don't stop talking about my girlfriend like that, I'll have to uhhh... fuck you up."

Morrigan grinned too wide for the laughter to escape, except out her nose. Her head bowed forward but, with a ginger press of his thumb, Simon lifted her chin so he could see her smile better. She hid it behind pursed lips but he sighed a compliment unspoken and it came out again.

Her hands went on methodically, working down the rest of his shirt. When the last button came away Morrigan slid the shirt down off his shoulders, using enough force to peel the saturated material away. Despite her prior speech, making such bold declarations about his attractiveness, her gaze felt like knives as it raked across his chest. He wanted her to stop looking. He was so sure she'd figure out that he was ugly and politely tell him to cover himself up. He was so certain of this and yet she was so pleasantly carried away by it. She looked at his body like she saw something else there, like she followed a treasure map drawn in the iridescence of oil.

Then she jerked her attention to his face, and he couldn't mask his expression nearly enough.

"Sorry! I'm friggin torturing you." She pulled his shirt back over his shoulders and pulled the sides together, before tugging him toward her with both ends of his collar. "I'll get you to believe me one of these days."

"No *I'm* sorry. It's really fine. Do whatever."

She put a finger to his lips and winked, before prancing out of the shower in sopping wet Invader Zim and Maleficent half-socks. She half reached for the light-switch, but her fingers curled and her arm furled back against her chest. "I'll let you hide in the dark *this* time, but..." She looked back, over her shoulder, biting her lip. Morrigan looked sharply back to the fogged over mirror ahead of her then threw her gaze back over her shoulder to lock eyes with him.

Her eyes issued a silent demand that he not look away and then she took her shirt off like only a girl could. She crossed her wrists at the hem, and cocked her hip one way then the other as she peeled that saturated black band-shirt off her back. She posed like that, stretching forearms wrapped in a dripping black shirt to the ceiling. Her torso was bare, save for the stark burgundy of a soaked bra. That dull red was the brightest color in Simon's world for a few seconds. It was lace, fancy, and most importantly: wrapped around Morrigan, a special girl who wanted him to see it.

His blush burned so hot the water started to feel cool against his cheek.

She angled slightly towards him and stretched, sucking in her stomach to accentuate her supple ribs. Just as he saw her bra lift a millimeter up from her chest, she flung her shirt towards him. Her aim was awful, slapping wetly against the glass wall of the shower far to his right, and the tension in Simon escaped with a laugh.

"Shut *up*," she whined backhanding the lightswitch, leaving only the light pouring in through the ajar door to illuminate her. She began to pull the door shut and paused, staring at the light on her arm.

Simon stepped from the shower shrugging his shirt off and she held out a hand. "Wait. First..."

He watched her take a towel, and tap the door, letting it swing open further until his face was lit. She held the towel against her chest with an arm tucked in close, and reached back to unhook her bra. Morrigan shrugged and let it slip from her shoulders, exposing her bare back to him. She swallowed and a lock of wet hair tapped against the nape of her neck, running coursing a drop of water onto her back. It raced along the inside of a shoulderblade, all the way down beneath the gleam of her silver studded belt.

"I've gotta learn how to look at you with eyes like that, Simon. You'd never be scared to take your clothes off, then."

She pulled the door shut, yanking the light from him, leaving just a sliver to streak across her. Leaning her cheek into the beam,

Morrigan winked, then stepped backwards towards him. She vanished completely, leaving only the clink of her pyramid-stud belt unbuckling behind.

Chapter 39

Drying off

Clad only in darkness, Simon turned to the towel rack beside the shower, and no sooner had he done so did he hear Morrigan's unseen wet feet padding towards him. He felt first her fingertips, probing in the dark. He froze as they glided lightly up his stomach to his chest and lept blindly to find his forearm. Morrigan found his hand and pulled the towel from his grip gently. Rather than use it to dry herself off, she began to slowly stroke it along his skin, drying *him* instead. Her technique was awkward and stiff, but tender and carried no lustful urgency. Those delicate hands didn't inflict any looming ambiguity of expectation on Simon. Morrigan's touch exuded simple raw affection.

She explored his chest with the light grazing of scouting fingertips, and then thoroughly with a towel between them. For his hair she lay the towel over his shoulders and lifted halves up with both hands to massage his head.

"Grab me a towel?"

It was wonderfully jarring. Her voice was soft and relaxed but it was *her* voice. She didn't put on some sexy voice, she just spoke like any of this was normal. It hit his ears like a promise that it would be.

"Have you ever..."

She shook her head vigorously enough to slap his chest with a few dripping locks of hair. "Nah... I mean this is super weird, I know... I just really wanted to do this all of a sudden and I kinda figured you wouldn't stop me or get mad. Is it bothering you? I don't mean to blue ball you or anything."

"No I- I like it."

She ran the towel slowly across his chest. "I wouldn't mind this being a normal thing."

He ran a hand along an arm around him and found a shoulder, then a neck that rested against his touch, and finally hair; cold saturated hair plastered to her cheek that his fingers gingerly traced to the ends. He disturbed droplets forming on the tips of her hair and cold water streaked down his wrist. He combed his fingers through, working his way gently through without pulling. Then he lay the towel over her shoulders like she'd done, but pulled it over her like a hood. He worked his thumbs over her temples, massaging in small semi-circles, before ringing around behind her ears. Encouraged by the kinds of noises that could make a man get carried away, he interlaced his fingers and pressed up along the nape of her neck.

It felt like the most natural thing in the world that she drift forward against him, but when several points of anatomy connected they both jolted apart, nervously laughing in the dark.

Simon adjusted his towel to lay over Morrigan like a cloak, and swept his hands beneath her hair, laying it over top to dry.

"Probably a good idea," he explained. "My eyes are starting

to adjust."

Clumsily Morrigan began to tie her towel around Simon, unwittingly high up him, nearly to his chest.

"Morrigan you don't need to cover my boobs."

"Shut *up*."

She mapped him out with a groping hand and adjusted her towel placement.

"And here I thought *I* was the prude."

"Look at this guy. Gets a girlfriend and now he's all mouthy, huh?"

She dropped the towel down low enough that it was hung on his anatomy like a coat peg.

"Okay," she affirmed, as though he'd held it there with his hand and proceeded to pull it taught around his waist with a sharp tug.

Simon hissed so fiercely he startled a vocal gasp out of her. her hands sprung back from him and he recoiled, tearing the towel away."*Morrigan* why!? It doesn't *go* left."

Chapter 40

Caladbolg

"You *sure* you don't wanna just curl up in a pile of towels right *here*? The floor is **heated** *dude*."

"We can warm the bed up just as well."

She pulled her towel cloak tighter and let out a closed mouth whine.

"I can already kind of see in here already."

"That's 'cuz you've got those bright blue eyes. You have better nightvision than me. It's an adaptation to see better in your dark viking forests."

"No, you're thinking of green eyes. They're like night vision goggles. So are you decent?"

She ran her hand along her upper back, again, doing one last scan for any looming deep tissue zit ready to ruin her sex appeal.

"Y-yeah. My towel is tinkerbell-short, but yeah I'm decent."

The door came open and blaring light flooded in, revealing Simon in the towel she'd tied about his waist. He barely glanced at her, still too respectful to stare. She wanted to demand he really look at her, that he gawk and ogle, but it was so bright. Beneath a light that could illuminate stretch marks and weird veins she didn't feel brave enough. Morrigan passed him and burrowed beneath the covers.

"You know you're such a pussy, right?" She pushed past a stone forming in her throat. "You coulda gotten away with taking a look. I wouldn't've hated you."

Simon rolled his eyes so hard he nearly toppled over. "Morrigan, you're so nervous it's almost like... *insulting.* I'd rather wait until you're excited, then push when you're vulnerable."

She groaned, with her throat tight with emotion. "I bet you let way better girls than me get away by being so..."

"Unaggressive?" He offered with a sigh, sitting at the edge of the bed. "Such a pussy?"

"Hey, *hey,* I like it, you know. I really like it a lot. I don't know if I'll ever stop making fun of you for it though..."

"Good. I think if you stopped cursing or teasing me, I might not recognize you."

"I don't curse *that* much."

Shit, do I?

Simon shrugged and set about feeling for her legs through the covers. She watched his progress passively. When he found her thigh he put his hands together, crossing his thumbs and pressing through the sheets with the heels of his palms. He moved slowly up her thigh, kneading her tense muscles like dough. After their day together her legs ached with the dull burn of muscle soreness, and his hands felt incredible.

Worried that any word might blow out his forwardness like a candle, she shut her eyes and let her weight sink back against the pillows. After a minute or so, she cracked an eye to peek at him and saw him watching her face as a meter.

"Cute," she said finally, incidentally scaring his hands away. "You look so *content*."

"Oh! uh..." He sprung to his feet stiffly. "Lemme grab us some clothes to sleep in."

"It felt *good*." she called, watching him escape.

"Good. That's good. I'm glad."

"Hey... why don't you get me the room's bathrobe? Might be easier without the covers in the way."

Her words hit him like she wanted them to. Simon nodded a whole bunch and she bit her lip with a grin.

looking at his back she found herself mildly irritated at the back-acneless state of it. "You're lucky, you know. You've got perfect skin."

Simon stopped and looked at her with a cocked eyebrow. "That's a little serial killery, but... thank you?"

"Oh shut up. I mean you've got like no pimples or dryness or anything. It's a compliment you dumb fu- dumb... person."

Simon shrugged and his towel, dropped an inch. She thought for a moment that Simon was horrible at tying towels, before realizing that *she* had been the one who tied his towel on. Her awful knot was two, maybe one more shrug away from popping open.

I can't tell him. Out of the question. It'd be rude, as if I don't want to see him naked. I can't insult him like that. He's so sensitive.

"I mean doesn't that stuff all go away with puberty?"

Morrigan's attention was jerked from his waist. She could feel her eyebrow twitching involuntarily. "Simon you... I don't know if I've ever wanted to smack you before, but god *damn* that's just the..."

At the closet door Simon turned to surrender. "*Sorry,* but it's not like *you* have any achne."

Immediately, Morrigan reached to feel her back. She blinked. *I'll have to thank my fairy godmother, I guess.*

"Huh... well... thanks."

Simon pulled on a shirt from his suitcase. It was a wrinkled Maelstrom shirt that'd been stuffed into a ball more than once. It was disappointing, but Morrigan chewed her lip in silence. She didn't know if she had much of a right to complain.

Then Simon crouched down and began to fiddle with some boxers to pull on beneath his towel and she whistled sharply like a referee. Simon straightened sharply, and again her periphery caught his towel slipping lower.

"You got this sick shirt and you're gonna make your girlfriend wear the room robe?"

"What? Oh! No this is just some shirt I wear to bed."

"Gimme."

"Oh you don't want this. I don't even know when the last time I had it cleaned was."

"Good. it'll smell like you."

Morrigan grinned at the way her words inflated the man. He pulled the shirt off, tugging it over his head by the collar. He balled the thing up to throw, and jerked his head to toss back his damp blonde hair that'd fallen over his forehead. The motion was violent enough to finish it. The knot Morrigan had tied in Simon's towel failed. Half a second was plenty of time to look away, but she didn't.

"*Morrigan!*"

She jerked her attention away, slapping a hand over her face. "I *know*, I'm sorry. I shouldn't have looked. It's not fair. You were so respectful and-"

"It's *fine*. You're just staring at it, horrified, like it's some kind of monster."

"*No!*" She shifted in bed, sitting up and pinning the sheets above her breasts as she did. "No, it looks very friendly, in fact. I like it a lot. It's handsome. Really."

His balled-up shirt hit her blindfolded face, which she then lifted like a veil to see her prince's sword safely sheathed behind some boxers.

"Oh come on. You can't blame me for being a little surprised. You don't exactly carry yourself like you're packing some shit like that."

Simon blinked, his crippling embarrassment suspended by confusion.

"Listen, I completely trust you Simon. You're a gentle guy. I was just a little startled."

Simon shook his head with a disgruntled sigh and flung boxers in her direction. "Can you stop?"

Oh sweet innocent baby. No one's ever told him.

She dove momentarily under the covers to put on his shirt and boxers, without flashing him, then scrambled out of bed, wearing his shirt like a dress.

"Here, look at my forearm," she demanded, padding over to him. "Compare it to you."

He looked at his own forearm. "What? Girls have smaller-"

"Not compared to your *forearm*!"

Simon recoiled with a blink. "It's not..."

"No, but it's *close*. Right?"

She watched Simon recoil into himself, overwhelmed by processing this new information. Some conflux of emotions battled over his face, and a harsh blush won out. "I- I never really thought about... I guess as a guy you always assume... the uh... opposite."

Watching 'act_casual.exe' crash before her eyes Morrigan leapt to a new topic, as quick as she could.

"Hey, how do I look in your shirt?" she asked, plucking it away from her chest with both hands to flatten out the design.

As soon as he looked, she let the pinched corners of the shirt slip from between her fingers. The fabric was flung back against her chest. Taxed by contemplations and tired from the intense emotions of the day, Simon's mind didn't recognize her baiting out a blush. His eyes didn't roll. They swept down her, glinting like sea glass as they flitted over her. Morrigan was clad in her boyfriend's clothes, being looked at with the kind of eyes she wanted to be seen by, so she stopped and twirled for him. The big shirt swished like a skirt, so she curtsied too, springing back up with a suddenness to cheat a jiggle and win another glance at her chest from him.

He sighed wistfully and a wave of guilt crashed over her.

"Simon, you know I wouldn't stop you... Wouldn't hate you either..."

He shook his head. "It's a first date thing, right? You want to be able to brag about this story to people and you don't want... asterisks on your..."

"Fairytale," She completed with a wince.

"You say it like it's dumb, but it's not. If this is a fairytale then that makes me..." He shrugged.

She stepped into him, and he had to wrap his arms around her to keep his feet. She lay her cheek fllat against a warm, bare chest. "My prince."

His hands slipped beneath her shirt, and they were so warm even her heart took a moment to realize they belong on her skin. He pressed the heels of his palms on either side of her spine and swept them up along the inside of her shoulderblades to her shoulders. Her body couldn't deny him like her mind could, and she let out a sound against his breast with hot breath. Morrigan's shirt slipped up past her navel in the front and higher in the back. The remnants of the airconditioning raised goosebumps she knew he could feel.

Just as it had begun, suddenly the moment was over. Simon plucked her shirt back down and leaned away to get a look at her face. "I promise I won't get carried away, but I'd really like to give you a little massage before bed."

Her head bobbed on its own. "Yeah... I think I'd like that too." She turned and grabbed the back of her collar to pull her shirt up, slipping just the back over her head, holding it in front of her breasts, and flopped onto the bed. She was quick to look back at him and drink in his expression. The soft fabric slid so easily over her skin. She'd had to catch herself from pulling it off entirely. It was strange, almost dreamlike, to go so close to nudity without the cacophony of alarms in her head.

Despite the intensity, Simon was still shackled by trepidation. He sat lightly at the edge of the bed, as if his weight pressing the mattress down might disturb her. His hands were clumsier than they'd been through the sheets too. She thought for a moment it might be easier if they pulled the covers over her, but then she thought of how easy and exciting it was to lift the back of her shirt over her head. She wanted to share that with him. She wanted him to feel that excitement and freedom in touching her.

"Hey, can you do my legs first?" She asked in the smallest voice she could find.

"Mhm, sure, yeah."

He began again, this time his hands were wider, pressed harder, and explored further. It felt good so she told him with a breath that energized his hands further. But, like the tide, his confidence waned, and she needed to coax it back with tiny stretches and sounds. Each time she provoked boldness the wave crashed deeper inland and took longer to recede.

Despite her own exhaustion and the relaxing hands of her new boyfriend, cultivating this confidence in him made her heart beat quick enough to keep her awake. In one way there was something thrilling about being acted upon, and in another way it was intoxicating to have so much control. Every sound she made caused him to tweak how he handled her. She was a guitar teaching him to tune her.

After a while, Simon would ask if what he was doing was okay, or if she was enjoying herself and every time Morrigan would take great pleasure in putting all the honey she could into her "*Mhm.*"

Eventually Morrigan fixed her shirt and flipped over for the fronts of her thighs. Then she saw the tiredness in his eyes and pulled on his hands to sit up towards him. "Aw *dude*, you look so *sleepy.*"

"*Dude,*" he parroted. "Yo *dude,* wanna go on a romantic date dude?"

She sat up with a laughter sore belly to slap playfully at him.

"Oh shush. I'll figure out a pet name for you. Promise. I'll go buy myself an old norse dictionary and pick out something cute."

Simon's exhausted brain was struggling to switch from teasing to bashful and she kissed him in the meantime.

"Maybe I'll call you... Jormungandr."

"Hmm?"

She gave him a playful shove. "Go get the lights. Let's get to bed."

While he walked, she flopped back onto the bed and watched her new boyfriend. She was afforded a scandalously detailed view.

Simon you really gotta behave, if we're gonna wait, because I couldn't deny you anything right now.

He was naked, save for his boxers, and even those fit the skinny man tightly in the back. He wasn't muscular by any means, but his low bodyfat percentage made him look like one of DaVinci's anatomy drawings, every muscle outlined, though not sharply defined by exercise. If he decided to start working out, he'd soon become more like an Italian statue than a sketch and she knew the man was very malleable to her requests.

It feels wrong to even think about asking, but maybe it'd be a bonding thing with his dad?

Putting that thought away for later, She climbed under the sheets. Her legs slid against the cool summer sheets and a minor cold spasm coursed through her.

The lights went out with the loudest snap of a lightswitch she'd ever heard.

His footsteps against the carpet were quieter than her own breathing but she could still feel the soft thump through the bed.

Simon got into bed on the far side, like the husband in an old sitcom. Morrigan squeezed her eyes shut. She knew she just had to ask, but she didn't want to have to. She wanted Simon to want to hold her so badly he'd forget himself.

A minute ground by, in deathly silence, and Morrigan suggested: *maybe he's just too tired.*

Her clenched eyelids relaxed and, just as she began to drift off to sleep, she felt herself dragged to the middle of the bed. His hands were gentle but insistent, and they wrapped around her without permission.

"I don't want to hog the middle. I know you said something about... where uh..."

She turned and held him back, forcing a hand beneath to wrap around him and even laying a leg over. She squeezed him fiercely and let go suddenly, rolling to face away from him. She didn't need to ask for anything. Simon's arms followed her, wrapping around in front, and though they were hesitant to press against her front, Morrigan held them against her chest, with a less surgical placement than he might have employed.

"Is this comfortable?" Morrigan asked softly.

He affirmed above a whisper in a tone that vibrated the bare chest pressed to her back.

"Good, because I'd love to wake up like this every day."

Simon was quiet for a while, his sleepiness no doubt

lethergizing him. "That sounds nice."

"Promise you won't get tired of... *this*?"

Of me?

"Hard to... sleep without... being tired."

"Shut *up*."

He clutched her laughing chest tighter, pressing her snugly against him. His lips were near enough to her ear that she could feel a sigh graze it.

They whispered to each other like that for a long time. When they would wake the next day they wouldn't remember much of what was said in that near-sleep twilight. All she would recall vividly was that he called her a princess, *his* in fact.

Chapter 41

A trapped arm

Simon awoke to the dull, painful urging of his bladder. With his eyes still closed, his brain revved itself up to consciousness, while his body remained still, unwilling to move. As he became aware of Morrigan nuzzled against him, his mind seconded that decision.

Of course his bladder was relentless in making appeals, crushing his abdomen outwards with a blunt pressure, and Simon had no choice but to concede. To remove himself from her presence was not easy, however. The two of them were entangled in a mess of warm limbs. Cradled in his arms, she slept so peacefully it flattered him. Dreaming, she mumbled small notes into the pillow they shared, and it was so wonderfully sweet a song. He dreaded waking her, disrupting this embrace that was too wonderful not to be fragile.

He had to make a stealthy extraction. Simon lifted his left arm from Morrigan with delicacy appropriate for handling a pressure-mine. He even withdrew the limb slowly to limit the friction against the blanket over them. Then he made his attempt to slide free his right arm from under her, and he realized he couldn't feel his arm. Simon barely stiffled panic and let himself think for a moment.

It's just asleep.

An amputation scene, from a civil war movie he'd seen once, flashed through his mind. The surgeon wrapped a tourniquet around a soldier's arm to reduce blood-flow while he took out a great big rusty saw.

Simon lay flat and began to inch away from her on the bed, dragging his limp limb behind him. He moved surgically, careful not to drag the sheet with him and disturb Morrigan. To this end, when he reached the edge of the bed, he melted slowly to the floor. Once clear of the covers, he sprung energetically to his feet. First Simon peered through the darkness for signs of Morrigan waking and then turned to his arm, which flopped alarmingly limp by his side. Simon was in the process of shaking the thing like a prop chicken when he heard Morrigan call his name softly, still hushed by sleep.

"Oh I'm sorry to wake you. I'll be right back. Just gotta use the bathroom."

All she said was "Okay," but it tightened his chest.

Oh no, did I let her wake up alone? She sounded so earnest about spooning. I hope I didn't open up a scar about that.

Simon had to clench his jaw to keep from hissing with the pain that flooded his arm. The blood rushing back felt like battery acid.

He rushed to the bathroom, fingers twitching with each heartbeat. The fear of his arm falling off faded with the pins and needles sensation that butchered his nerves and his bladder's urgency rose again to the forefront. He relieved himself, aiming a fire-hose with his left hand. With bleary eyes and a dark bathroom, he verified his aim by sound alone. somehow he found himself peeing for what seemed like a supernaturally long duration. When he was finally drained, he shivered with the loss of heat from within him.

Blood did return to his arm and, with it, feeling did too. Restored, he made his way back to Morrigan who, Simon could see with his newly acquired nightvision, was staring at the ceiling. She had one arm above her head, tucked beneath the pillow they'd ended up sharing, and the other hand resting on the warm spot he'd vacated.

The covers were pulled down a bit, and he could see her in a wrinkled Maelstrom shirt, *his* shirt in fact. It was an old shirt he'd had since he was fourteen, and there this girl was laying in his bed wearing it.

That's really my girlfriend. She's wearing my ratty Maelstrom shirt, because it's mine, and she doesn't care that it's falling apart.

He was sure that the fourteen year old Simon, who bought it, would agree that no one could ever have looked better in it. Fitted for a much scrawnier frame, the wrinkled shirt clung to her chest immodestly tight creating a breathtaking outline. On her back gravity flattened and spread her chest out, pressing soft flesh against a split seam beneath one sleeve where the stitching had opened up. The skin there, that gleamed pearlescent like the moon, matched her face.

Noticing him, the stoic, contemplative expression she bore at the ceiling softened and her lips pouted in question. "Hey," she called, her voice above a whisper but her tone softer than a sigh.

"Hey," he returned, with a long wistful breath, as he returned to her side.

"Sorry, I stole your shirt," she whispered, scooting over for him as he joined her in bed.

"You're allowed," he whispered back across the pillow. "My

girlfriend, is allowed to steal my clothes."

She giggled at the emphasis, and curled onto her side to face him.

"I hope you're not uncomfortable sleeping without a shirt. I know you've got silly body issues. I was just... excited."

"What're you just laying awake contemplating your every possible mistake?"

"*Maybe* guilty."

"Didn't I tell you? You can't mess this up."

It was shockingly easy to touch her now. Their contact in the shower, while intimate, was so far from normal it felt like it happened in a dream world of no consequence. Simon slid a hand over her back and neither of them were concerned about her shirt shifting an inch or two up with his hand. He felt where a bra-strap might have been in the day and flashed a smile at the thought that he was the only one who got to see her like this. He treasured this Morrigan who wore his clothes and shared a bed with him. She smiled across a pillow at him with disheveled clothes and let him play with her hair in disarray.

She squirmed closer on the bed and his arms wrapped around her like it was the most natural response he could make. She smiled and he could see plainly that he was acting with a confidence that was a surprise to her, albeit a pleasant one.

Drowsiness returned to them quickly. Her eyes shut and her smile relaxed. He felt the tension leave Morrigan again and, as it did, her full weight rested on his right arm. He felt the arm throb a faint reminder of what happened the last time she slept on his arm. They needed a better position.

Simon rolled onto his back and tugged her gently along with him. She roused for a moment and snuggled against him, nestling her cheek against his trap. The flattery of her half conscious affection stunned him. Though soon he felt her head pinching off blood beneath his shoulder and began to consider moving her again. Before he could, however, she moved herself.

Morrigan straddled him for a moment, rolling her shoulders in a little stretch that shifted her shirt, before sliding off to the other side. She rested her cheek on his chest, over his heart, this time and left a leg across his.

Instinctively, Simon grasped her firmly and she reciprocated, squeezing him even tighter for a second before releasing him. "*Morrigan.*" He whispered to her, voice tight with emotion. "I don't know If I mentioned this yet, but I *really* like you."

His words seemed to ignite something in her. She was on top of Simon again, without warning, and forced her hands underneath him to hug him tightly. She began to sob and Simon tried to sit up, concerned, but he was thwarted by feeble abdominal muscles and the weight of a girl. "I really like you too." She sniffled into his bare chest, wetting him with tears.

"There's no 'but' coming. I swear! I'm just happy and-"

"I know, I know, I *know*..." She whined nasally as she reared her head back, trying to will her tears to recede.

Simon sat up, taking her with him. She ended up in an awkward straddle and Simon set about wordlessly wiping away her tears. She averted her eyes and used the shirt she wore to dry the tears she'd gotten on his chest.

"Sorry I'm crazy." She mumbled.

Simon wasn't very quick to invent a response and Morrigan began to push him back down onto his back. There wasn't much to be said really, or at least not that a tired brain could conjure.

Morrigan tilted forward and flopped on top of him. He'd

known her breasts were soft, but he learned then that her chin was very hard. Oblivious she slid her warm cheek over his chest and returned her ear to his heart. Seeing her eyes close he let his head rest on the pillow. She pulled her legs in from either side of him and brought them between his with a stretch that squeezed them together. She slid her fingers between his back and the bed and got her arms around him, to give him a squeeze like he was a great pillow.

"Simon?" He could feel the word buzz from her chest to his as she spoke. "Are you okay? Your heart's beating so fast."

Gently he guided the head, lifting from his chest, back against him. "Yeah I'm great. *This* is great."

"Can you sleep like this? Do you want me to get off of you?"

He returned such a certain "No." that he felt a smile against his chest as she heard it.

"I'm glad." She sighed. "I hope you don't get sick of sleeping like this. I'd really miss it."

As the wave of emotion rushed in, Simon groaned to get out ahead of it. "Ugh, if I start crying because that's the sweetest thing anyone's ever said to me are you gonna call me gay again?"

He could hear her grinning, a playful giddiness rising in her. "Mhm."

"You know *you* were crying a minute ago."

"Yeah, but I'm a *girl*. We have emotions. Only *gay* guys have emotions."

Simon reached down and smacked her butt through borrowed boxers. She jolted with surprise and it was *his* turn to let out a mischievous giggle.

"An unsolicited butt-touch? From *Simon*?" She inquired, resting her chin on his sternum. "This interest of yours in *butts* makes me rather suspicious."

Her teasing sparked a mote of mischief in him. Simon slapped both hands over her butt, grabbing hold firmly, and slid her face up to his. She let out a gasp, exaggerated like a Victorian woman aghast at a lack of etiquette, but there was real surprise there.

"We shouldn't." she said so gently it sounded like a question.

He nodded. "Got carried away."

"It's not your fault," Morrigan sighed, lifting herself off of him, her shirt hanging down against his bare chest.

Simon rolled his eyes, hearing an obvious jab coming in her barely restrained glibness.

"I'm wearing men's underwear, after all."

He looked down from the ceiling with a cocked eyebrow and his attention slipped from her glib expression to what hung freely inside the stretched out collar of that old Maelstrom shirt she wore. He averted his eyes but caught them in hers as he did.

"Such a *fag*." she teased, with extra long vowels, only broken by a bubbly giggle that bounced her gently on his chest. "You know you *are* my boyfriend now. You're allowed- no *required* to look, but if you *do*: it's only polite to spare a compliment."

She stretched like a cat on him, raising her butt and mushing her chest against his.

"Uh... They make hugs better?"

"I'll take it." She grunted, collapsing on top of him. She squeezed him in a hug energized by a newfound pride.

"Next I'll have to extort a butt compliment out of you. That'll be harder since my ass is sadly- nay *mournfully* flat."

"Mournful," he parroted, bouncing the girl with laughter. "I think I could get used to this. Falling asleep with a soft girl against a belly sore from laughing at your dumb jokes."

She mewed a sound disrupted by the vocal fry static that came from exhaustion. Simon blinked and time traveled forward at least a minute.

"I think *I* could get used to sleeping on a heated pillow that flatters me." She shot back, her words slurring.

Oh, I never rebuked her butt comment. I have to...

Simon blinked again and jerked awake interminable seconds later.

"You okay?" Asked the girl listening to his heart.

"Y-yeah, I just... You're being dumb and you don't like your butt and... I'm too tired to compliment it without being... uh... crude? but I don't wanna... not say... something."

"Shhh... Just sleep."

His limbs felt warm and heavy, but Simon jerked his hand into animation and slid it down her back to feebly pinch her butt. Cleverness dulled but he tore himself from dream a second longer to add simply: "Modest."

She huffed a laugh but the word was enough for her cheek to warm his chest.

Chapter 42

A good morning

Simon woke to the shower starting. Laying there motionless he could still feel the shadow of her weight on his chest and the warmth she'd left behind. He recollected a memory, buried half in dream, of her rising from him, shirt hanging down, sweeping across his bare chest as she moved to plant a furtive kiss on his cheek. She'd whispered something about being "sweaty and gross."

The shower was loud, and Simon wondered if the bathroom door was open. He wondered too if that was an invitation. He shook his head. The intimacy of the night before felt like a long time ago. He wasn't sure how much was them getting carried away, and how much they would get to keep. His eyes shut while mulling it over and he nodded off once more.

When he awoke again, it was to an icy touch brought by the tips of wet locks of hair grazing his chest. Heavy eyelids lifted to a girl still wearing his shirt, with its very stretched out collar, resting her chest gingerly on his as she brought her lips near enough to whisper. "It's early, really early, and we were up late. You don't have to get up, *but* I have work later so..." She began to trace her finger over his collarbone. "I was hoping you'd have breakfast with your girlfriend."

He was too groggy to articulate how giddy her request made him, so he settled for a "Sure," and a smile.

She lunged forward for a quick kiss and as she crawled backwards off the bed, he noted how good a stretched out collar could look.

"Glad to see you're kicking that habit of looking away like my tits are the ark of the covenant."

Simon groaned, with a face full of blood, and rolled out of bed. He'd been uncertain whether they'd woken up as close as they'd been when they'd gone to sleep, but seeing a pretty girl padding barefoot across his hotel room wearing nothing but one of his shirts had a way of slapping doubt of that kind out of one's head.

"I'm stealing more of your clothes. Hope that's okay." She called as he rounded the corner into the bathroom.

"Yeah, of- of course. "

Simon turned on the sink and blew out a shaky breath as he waited for it to get hot. He'd awoken to an overwhelming reality. He tried to collect himself, but thoughts wouldn't coalesce into words. Vivid memories of the night before rushed through his mind.

The chill of her shiny silver studded belt against his fingertips. The warmth of her lower back just above it, beneath her shirt. The feeling of stroking a hand across a back unbroken by a bra-strap beneath one of *his* shirts. The warm puff of whispers shared in earnest. The searing heat of secret freckles lit so sharply by blush they looked like lava.

Simon splashed water on his face and kneaded the oil from

342

the bridge of his nose.

With his eyes squeezed shut he could feel her presence like one feels the tide after a day swimming in the ocean. He could remember the pull of the invisible tether that bound them together while they walked. He could feel the force of her attention, and the striking brown eyes that bore it. Her smiling face was sharp in his mind, along with the chest she insisted he look at.

He splashed more water and groped for a washcloth. A shower seemed too time expensive. He wet the washcloth beneath the now scalding water and rubbed his face clean before likewise washing his armpits. He cleaned like a surgeon disinfecting, terrified of smelling gross to his new... He nodded.

Girlfriend.

Simon looked up at himself in the mirror and had his view eclipsed by a fogged surface. He raised a hand to wipe it clean and froze.

Something was written in the condensation on the mirror, by a small feminine finger, in loopy girl handwriting. A heart with "M+S" inside. It was silly and juvenile but Morrigan had left it there knowing it would put a tiny smile on his face; a sweet little landmine.

When Simon got out of the bathroom, Morrigan wasn't in the room. He wondered briefly if she'd left but that sour melancholy passed, once he was a few steps afield of the bathroom fan.

She was singing to herself just outside the door. He hadn't heard her sing before but he knew her voice. He'd heard the high chiming of her giggle and the low moaning that accompanied her stretches. That was enough to be sure the muffled singing on the other side of the door was hers. she swooped and ascended vocal ranges effortlessly with a mindless grace, like a lazy bird dipping it's wing to an ocean's wind.

Simon opened the door, muffled by a gust of wind, and thieved a small concert from her. The sound stirred in his chest like her dancing had done and envy grazed him. For a moment he longed for the ability to so effortlessly add color to the world.

He opened his mouth to announce himself, but he paused, struck again by how she looked in his clothes. She still wore his T-shirt. It was black so it suited her, but she modified it further to make it her own. The length she'd shortened with a knot tied at her hip, and the loose collar she'd dragged down over her shoulder, showcasing a single strap of her bra, now a darker red with its dampness. She wore his pants too, with her own black leather belt, studded with silvery pyramid studs that gleamed in the harsh daylight. His pants looked uncomfortably tight on her, a fact he was sure she'd tease him for. They were blue –not black– and it was daylight, giving her figure none of it's usual stealth. He understood now why she'd called herself a lollipop. Her legs were unusually scrawny and her butt had none of the volume her chest did. He took a long moment to examine the butt she'd been so critical of. He couldn't hate it, like she did. He'd never given butts much thought, but the fact that this butt was hers and that she didn't like it galvanized his opinion on butts. Smaller the better, and her's was the best. It didn't feel vulgar to tell her so either. He imagined her reaction with excitement, not dread. He'd take advantage of her self consciousness to pay her back a blush.

The words hovered on his lips, but he changed his mind. He'd save it. Instead he wished the most authentic good morning he'd ever wished, to the girl he shared it with.

She twirled with a start. Her hair, wet from his shower, was chaos about her as she did. She blinked at him, pinning her hair behind her ear.

They squinted at each other in the bright glare of morning and, before Simon could fumble out a compliment on her singing, she gestured with her head towards the stairs. "Breakfast?"

Chapter 43

Breakfast

Morrigan's new boyfriend ordered Mickey waffles to match her. It was cute, cuter than could be vented with a giggle and a sound like a fizzing soda came out instead. Simon reacted with an appropriately high eyebrow. She smacked at him playfully and nearly gouged out his eyes when attempting to mush his eyebrow down with her thumb. He didn't get mad, however. Instead of slapping her hand away he pulled it over his shoulder, confiscating it with a hug. Everyone who had to walk around them smiled as they excused themselves.

She squeezed her good natured boyfriend and let him go before embarrassing him too badly. They slinked off to the side to wait for their food and hands met easily. It was a casual thing, as natural as resting an elbow on an armrest.

While they waited, they were hushed by calm morning contemplations. Morrigan's mind wandered from speculation on how often the hotel she parked at would check cars for parking passes to how long she had until she had to be at work. They'd been up late, but still managed to get out of the room before eight. She had more than enough time for a power-bar and energy drink in the car, but she had no idea how long sitting down for breakfast took. She was hoping for ten minutes. Once she was at work the air conditioning could keep her awake, like a corpse preserved in a freezer.

A pleasant thought warmed the back of her mind and, reaching for it, she remembered Simon's company while she worked. Not being able to bring him felt like the first day back at school from summer vacation. Looking at the man made her want to call in sick more than anything, but she knew it would look bad. She probably wasn't the first person to know they were dating.

Still, she couldn't help but worry that they were in some honeymoon phase that would soon end. She didn't want to waste some of it by being at work. Morrigan found herself wondering if he'd ever stop blushing when she teased him.

I should get it in while I can. Once he looks over I'll throw a wink at him and stretch. Then I can say some cute shit like "hey my eyes are up here." Oh! I could do the opposite, reverse it. Oooh! I could be all sexy and ask him when he wants to take his shirt back."

When he eventually did look, it wasn't sexy or playful. Anticipation had made her wink forceful, reminiscent of slapping a buzzer in a game show. Simon wasn't seduced, but he laughed, at least. She slapped a hand over her eyes and leaned against him, without any further theatrics. A sympathetic arm held her there

After a breath spent groaning, she dragged his ear close. "Sorry, I was trying to be sexy because you're cute when you blush." Several emotions mixed in Simon's expression, and at least one made him blush, after all. Before he could vocalize anything, their number was called and She pranced off to pick up her tray.

They sat together by the window. The bright gray from a cloudy morning sky normally lit everything like a florescent light in a hospital, washing everything out, but Simon alone was lit like a movie star.

"Thanks for having breakfast with me," Simon said to his waffle. "You really made getting up this morning easy."

Morrigan smiled at her own waffle, prodding it with her fork.

"Hey, uh... Morrigan?"

She looked up, dread suddenly crushing her. Her head felt tingly and light, like she was going to faint.

Is he breaking up with me? bludgeoned the voice from her throat.

"You know... last night? We said some stuff, and uh..."

"Are you seeing someone else?"

The way he looked at her made her feel like the dumbest person. And the way he shook his head made her feel like a bad person. She covered her face and flagellated herself with apologies for being neurotic, and distrustful, and generally crazy, but Simon peeled her hands away from her face. When she met his gaze Simon was more sympathetic than offended.

"*Morrigan*, we can't *both* be this neurotic. I was going to ask something similar. So I'm just as guilty. I was going to ask if you really meant what you said about wanting to date me."

She smiled weakly but his words deserved a more profound response. For the first time it seemed like someone really understood the chaos in her head.

She squeezed his hands. "*Simon*, you're supposed to be the rock. I can't have my rock being crazy like me."

"Hey if not, we'll both go so bald, and at least we won't have to shave our armpits anymore."

"Oh shit you *do* shave your armpits don't you?"

Simon blinked, stung. "I dunno... It gets all... *itchy*."

"I guess I *did* notice that. I just didn't think about it until you said it outloud. It's very..."

They finished the sentence simultaneously, Morrigan with "*Simon*." and Simon with a word he seemed to feel she considered a synonym: "Gay?"

She tried to protest, to insist there was nothing wrong with being a femine man, but her arguments were disrupted by giggles and the sky-high eyebrow he hit her with did nothing but fuel them. Simon looked doubtful, but he didn't look offended at least. He had a touch of self satisfaction on his face, a kind of confidence. It was a good look for him.

Morrigan and Simon ended up looking at each other for a while after Morrigan stopped talking. Simon didn't shift under her gaze like she was boiling him alive with her eyes. He sighed after a while, eyes dipping to the cheeks he'd seen her secret freckles on last night, and remarked that it would be a long day. After so much had happened yesterday, it felt daunting to wade through an empty day. He spoke slowly and freely as the thoughts coalesced. Though Simon struggled to compact raw emotion into words, it was all poetry in Morrigan's ears.

He sighed, "God I'd kill for a fucking snow day."

Morrigan scrambled for her phone like the president was calling. "It rained!"

Simon blinked and began eating his waffle, his entrancement evidently broken by her crazy.

She lay her smartphone down onto the table like it was a winning poker hand. She turned the screen around so Simon could read 'flooding in your area'. "I always get off from work when there's flooding since my complex gets so flooded out. One time my boss complained and... here lemme..."

Morrigan scooped her phone up and fiddled with it until she found the video she was looking for. She turned the phone around and watched Simon's expression as she cranked the volume up. Morrigan was talking in the clip and she cringed at the sound of her voice recorded on a phone. It sounded mannish.

"Hey Sharon, sorry I can't make it in today," she apologized in the clip, panning over a housing complex that resembled a Venetian street.

Simon looked from the phone. "Is that the view from your front door? It's like Atlantis. How do you-"

She ushered him back to the phone just in time to see her hurl a small branch towards her half submerged car. Morrigan watched Simon's expression turn to horror as an alligator's jaws lurch from the murky depths to snap the stick in half with a great thrashing of water.

"She never complained again." Morrigan declared proudly.

He stifled a laugh to ask, "*Morrigan*, is that an *alligator*?"

"You make it sound like a dinosaur. *Relax*."

"I actually think it *is* a dinosaur, Morrigan."

"Shush. Focus on what's important, cutie. We get to spend the day together."

Morrigan searched her mind for all the places they could go, but she found herself snagged on the first one on the list. From the eyes across the table she knew he was too.

"I don't think anyone in downtown disney knows me," she suggested disingenuously. "Could go for a walk there... Got the lego pinewood derby thing."

"I'm curious about this Disney Quest you mentioned." He offered, participating in this dance.

The two of them went on pontificating about the many places that they could go first, when they both knew there was only one place they could go. The list went on, ever growing, absent that key destination but their eyes didn't keep a secret from each other.

As her list wound down Morrigan hung a heavy "or..." at the end of her sentence. He heard it.
There was a palpable lingering of soft lips parted. Her chest moved her shoulders as she breathed.

The end of that list existed, manifested between them by eyes alone.

Chapter 44

The only destination

It existed between them for barely a moment before her hyperventilating extinguished it. His hands, that had just so passionately slid up beneath her shirt, retreated. She let her weight fall backwards against his chest, pinning him against the door. A cheap alternative to telling him to stay with words, for a girl on an air budget.

He hugged her with his arms safely below her breasts, too safely. She could feel him hunched against her, to avoid his forearms grazing against their underside. Her breathing sounded so asthmatic, she felt like a squeaky toy.

She could stop her hyperventilating. She'd done it before. Every time she was about to get up on stage she'd start gasping just like she was in Simon's arms, and every time she'd stop it in an instant. But her method was to scream and headbutt a wall. It would not have been very romantic or sane.

Just when her frustrations reached a fever pitch, Simon's delicate touch enveloped her shoulders. He crushed the tension from her with a firm pinching grip that worked her muscles without pause to consult her on whether it felt good. His thumbs drove beneath her shoulderblades, up to her traps, then he swept up either side with the heels of his palms. Ahead of those firm palms his fingers combed into her hair and he fluttered her eyes shut with a scalp massage.

The moment's not gone. Just paused. She thought, pinching her lips together and trying to breathe through her nose.

Her clutched hand relaxed, its burden forgotten, and the paper gift-bag slipped from her numb fingers. It hit the ground and bounced onto it's side. The box of condoms she'd gotten from the concierge slid halfway out of the bag. They were both looking at it. If she'd managed to slow her breathing at all, then it sped back up to its manic pace.

Simon's lips separated as his hands slipped from her hair to rest light fingertips on her shoulders. It would be something sweet he said. He'd relieve her of obligation and she knew she might even passively agree, like a coward. She fell back harder against him and he stumbled back a few inches into the door with a thunk of the deadbolt hitting the frame.

Too low. He's taller.

She took one breath, a deep one that leaked slowly but inevitably from her nose with a wavery exhale, and rose up on her tippy toes against his chest.

His massage began again with one strong pinch, kneading her shoulders again towards her neck.

She lowered herself back down, sliding tight against him, nearly taking buttons off his shirt. She squeezed him beneath the belt with her butt and dropped down onto her heels, swiping him like a credit card.

His hands froze. She couldn't see his face. Only two fingers intruded over her collar onto bare skin.

Just keep going! Ignore my crazy gasping! She screamed it in her head, but even her thoughts felt feeble and breathless.

Simon began his massage again, kneading her shoulders, and working his way to sweep up her neck. He moved his thumbs in alternating circles, into the nape of her neck, that made her head loll forward at the mercy of an intoxicating sensation. In a show of unprecedented boldness Simon moved her head, pulling it back towards his chest. Then he ran his fingernails gently up the sides of her neck, all the way to her temples before rubbing back down in slow zig-zags back over her neck. When he reached the base of her neck those fingers dipped beneath her shirt and her hands curled into fists, clutching the hem of his shirt and his belt. He crossed the border, below her collarbone, and ran a line across the muscle there but went no further.

I'm gonna call that a question.

Simon's hand retreated back to her shoulder and Morrigan rushed to cross her arms. Just as Simon's pinkies escaped the inside of her shirt, she grabbed her sleeves with opposite hands and tugged them like she was flapping an origami crane. This widened her collar so that every one of his fingers slipped back beneath her shirt. Then she let go and her collar snapped back, overlapping his hand. She could feel his chest, against her back, draw in with a sharp breath.

Let's call that an answer.

She rolled her shoulders up, and his fingers drummed down below her collarbone again. His fingers felt cool against her softness, and she knew he could feel the blush in her chest.

Morrigan lolled her head back against his right shoulder. If he withdrew his hand now, he'd hit her head with his shoulder as he did.

This is the death grip Simon. You cannot escape.

She let him linger there, not wanting to push the timid man too far beyond his comfort zone. Her breathing had calmed significantly from his massaging, but by now her throat felt too raw for a sexy whisper of encouragement. Remembering how good his hands had felt in her hair she reached back for him, inadvertently lifting her chest towards his fingers. She was so close she could hear him swallow.

His nervousness made it all feel pure, somehow, and she wanted to share the feeling. It was beyond her to explain, even if she had breath to spend, so she touched her blushing cheek to his chin. Then she rose higher, sliding it up against his cheek.

Simon's fingers curled slightly. It was faint, but she was sure they had. With patience they slid back flat over the beginning of the slope, caressing gently, but forging no further. It wasn't enough. She wanted to feel like a succubus from a Cradle Of Filth music video. After cultivating his confidence like the tide, she wanted a tidal wave of pure welcomed lust.

The gasping rose again in her, and she could have cried with frustration. Like Morrigan had done when her band played, she converted all the nervousness into furious determination. She couldn't muster a single word so she decided to explain her feeling to Simon without them.

She reached back and grabbed a fistful of his perfect hair and dragged his head down to her as she turned up towards him, rising to the tips of her toes. Her lips grazed the underside of his chin, scraping against the lightest hint of stubble missed there. Her gasping broke out again, spilling hot breath against his jugular as she craned her neck back further to the side of his neck. There she defied her nerves, rejecting their erroneous demand for air, and gave Simon the dirtiest sucking kiss she could.

If I'm going to pass out, and miss this chance, then I want proof I was here. So god and everyone can look at his neck and know.

Over the pounding of her heart she heard him make a sound a man might be ashamed to make, and she went into a vampiric fervor. She would let there be no confusion as to what she wanted from him.

Finally his hands grabbed her, and with one final gasp her breath stilled. The marionettes of her nerves cut all at once. She fell from her tip-toes and Simon clutched her tight against him as she slid down to her heels. Stunned, her eyelids fluttered. His wave had crashed over her, extinguishing that frantic fire that brought her to his neck.

Slowly, he again began his massage. Just as she had the night before, Morrigan became a guitar teaching him to tune her. She raised her chin almost timidly, held by his confident hands, and Morrigan replied honestly. She leaned her lips against the edge of his ear and let herself breathe how his hands made her breathe. Morrigan let him experiment and learn how to play her by ear.

Then her fret hand fell limp from his hair, and Morrigan too asked a question.

Chapter 45

Acceptance

It was only when she wrapped her legs around him that he finally believed her. Legs were such clumsy things. They were far more honest than arms that way. Arms were dexterous, having far more practice in applying measured force. Morrigan's arms embraced him warmly and tightly, but her legs were frantic clung to him with the frenzy of a drowner. It made him notice her eyes, affixed as tightly to him, transfixed to his expressions. Morrigan drank in his emotion, her big brown eyes darting over him with a quickness.

He'd never been with someone so excited to be with him, who swelled with such pride at her effect on him, or who exerted themselves to the point of being out of breath in pursuit of that effect.

It filled his breast with a fantastic emotion that he could only express by reciprocation. He hadn't really known what it was like to be accepted so completely, to be connected with such intense empathy, and he thought she ought to know this feeling too.

And so, the two of them sweated out the minibar together, lost track of their clothes and stopped worrying about the thickness of the walls.

Chapter 46

Resurfacing hungry

A day spent in bed can pass terribly quickly.

When they finally took a shower that didn't excite any secondary agenda, it was time for dinner, not lunch.

It was the best workout either of them had ever had and a hot shower could only dampen the burn so much. Morrigan wanted to believe it was because they'd exhausted the hotel of its *really* hot water. They were proud of themselves as though they were great athletes, and gave each other lengthy complimentary feedback on their performances, absent the decency of timidness. Their utter exhaustion cured them of that, for the present, but Simon had no doubt it would return. Their bodies had stopped being sexual things, and become instead like statues carved of alabaster marble, worthy of observation and admiration, as they toweled off. Despite their total expenditure, they still spoke with the excitement one has walking out of a great movie at a theater.

This was only to be halted abruptly, when they left the bathroom and were greeted by a smog of stench that the shower's steam had held at bay. The sheets were soaked with their sweat. They'd been inoculated by exposure but it was still intense enough to pity the maid. Simon left a sizable tip for a maid that wouldn't come until the following day, as they'd already rejected her services earlier. They needed more towels, soap, conditioner, shampoo, sheets and even pillows. The room was as expended as they were.

By the time Simon had dressed, she was waiting for him at the door, looking strange in clothes. He knew he watched her with what she called 'first date eyes' but it didn't dissuade him.

"I'd call you handsome, but I think it'll get stale if I keep throwing compliments at you."

Her voice was hoarse and her words sweet, both on account of him, so his smile spilled laughter.

She hid her grin by wrenching the door open with both hands, groaning with her sore muscles.

As they left together, he felt this proud giddiness. The day they'd wasted away in private had made the ground solid beneath his feet, and he walked like it. When he grabbed her hand his heart noticed, but he wasn't nervous.

"Well I don't want *my* compliments to get stale either. I'll have to look up some Gaelic words. I'll need pretty, and cute and..."

Morrigan yanked him over and flopped her shoulder against him like a salmon. "*Such* a little show-off. Don't wear yourself out."

She bounced up onto the balls of her feet and gave him a kiss –probably meant for his cheek– that landed half on his jaw.

"Dammit you're so tall all of a sudden."

He laughed, giving her a squeeze. "I'm the same height I've been."

"No, now you're standing up super straight." She leaned out to catch his eye. "It's a good look."

"I guess I'm feeling more confident."

She nodded sagely. "Mmm, noticed that. Just recently."

"Yeah, something must've happened."

She gave him a playful shove, but didn't give up his hand, and quickly pulled him back against her. "How tall are you anyway?"

"Oh, I'm like six foot? Just about."

"Really?"

"Yeah I know. It doesn't seem like it, right? It's always been weird being tall. You'd expect there to be some kind of confidence to come along with it."

"Yeah you're really more of a 5' 12"."

Again she made him laugh, and the muscle burn from his abs rippled out as far as his pecs and the fronts of his thighs.

"Hey what do you say we get dinner at that Italian place on the boardwalk behind epcot? You said you liked the Italian food in new york, right?"

"Yeah... but I don't know... I don't think there's a high enough concentration of Italians here to really compete. Besides, you chose *last* time. I pick that Irish place in Downtown Disney. You were all excited to go there and I like seeing your smile more than food. Besides, I'm so hungry anything would taste good."

In lieu of words he received a squeeze in his hand. They walked in a comfortable silence for a length before Morrigan swayed into him playfully.

"Hey, think we should get some emergency candy rations so we don't starve to death on the way to the restaurant? In the name of survival."

"Hunger is the best spice."

Chapter 47

Unbreakable

The bus made a turn and the inertia spilled into its two passengers. The head, resting gently on Simon's shoulder, slipped off and he missed that physical contact immediately.

Simon didn't hesitate to reach after her. She slid into his lap so easily it was like gravity agreed that's where Morrigan belonged. She was far from deadweight in his arms; an eager participant and careful not to rest her full weight on anything precious. She sat sideways, seated on one thigh, with her legs stretched over him and the next two seats.

She didn't make an excited squeal, like she had the first time he picked her up, though he could feel it was still a pleasant surprise. There was a crisp energy in how she nestled into him. It was as if she'd imagined herself there.

Simon felt like another person. The liberty to move Morrigan so casually felt bizarrely natural. It *did* make sense. Not long ago he'd taken similar liberties with her. The girl in his lap wearing the cute black hoodie had previously been the girl in his room wearing nothing but a smile. It had been a very excited smile.

Simon blushed and Morrigan nuzzled his chest in response to his hammering heart.

It was all still so strange to him. He'd dated **Sarah** for over three years and while, of course, they'd had sex on several occasions during that time, he never felt *free* with her. He'd always felt like there was something that could break, as if a mistake or poor performance would be carved in stone and every time she looked at him and sighed it would be a heavier sigh because it would be weighed down by a mediocre orgasm.

Morrigan was so different that he felt inexperienced. She was warm and encouraging and just seemed happy to be with him. Collapsing onto a pillow with her to hold hands, catching their breath, was a feeling that trumped any physical one.

She talked to him then, on that bus, just like she had naked and sweaty in bed. The same casual tone that she'd complimented him with, she now told him about how she was glad he wanted to go to this Irish place, because the complimentary bread on the table was something called soda bread. It was like intimacy was as normal as dinner plans.

It had *never* been normal with **Sarah**. When she put an arm around him for a picture it felt strange. She only ever did it for group photos. Couple photos were to be taken with her posturing to accentuate her hourglass figure and he was to lay his right hand on her lower back wrapping his fingers around the smallest point of her torso; touching, if it was easier. The girl had been vocally against *public* signs of affection, but private ones were still token things.

"Oh I'm sorry Morrigan, I zoned out. What were you saying?"

"At least you're honest." She gave him a peck on the jaw. "Something got your head in a fog? What's up?"

"Oh..." He hesitated before he lied. "Nothing."

His face must have been too honest because she laughed. "I swear I really care."

He shook his head but she was patient and gently relentless in her interrogation, quietly waiting for him to speak.

You know better than to actually talk about it. No one's ever asked 'what's up?' and is asking to become a therapist.

He swallowed. "You know what Morrigan? You get to be the one person in the whole world, who cares about me and is not burdened by my shitty thoughts."

"Man, when we first met, you know what I was thinking about? I was wondering if I could call any of my friends and be worth their time. See, I called my mom to vent about my breakup; called her twice. The second time, she said it was '*too much emotional labor*' for her. It wasn't a fair trade, I guess. I didn't add enough value to her life to be worth listening to. My other friends all live out of town, 'cept for the whore angling on my ex, and I got to wondering whether I added enough value to their lives to be worth keeping in touch with. I know they'd say I was, but maybe they're just not as practical as my mom. After all Mars traded me for my ex, so I couldn't be worth all that much. Maybe I was very literally worthless. Dark stupid thoughts, just like those." She tapped on his temple. "Then this fucking cutie comes around the corner; a stranger with a higher calibur of character. This dude helps me believe that Mars and my ex were worthless trash and that I'm not. Guy tells me he *wants* to hear about my problems, that it'll make him feel better. I wanna be that for you, 'cause I think you were on to something. Dude, I'm fucking crazy. If I listen to *your* shitty thoughts, then I get to pretend, at least for a little while, that I have my shit together."

A weak smile crossed his face and his eyelids fluttered as he looked down. "I... I guess it's just that being happy has dredged up all these old memories. They all just make me feel like a moron for being in my last relationship for more than a day. We've been together less than twenty-four hours and I feel so much happier, which is really-"

He stopped instinctively, worried he'd overshared, but when he looked into Morrigan's face she was sympathetic and patient, waiting for him to get all of his thoughts out.

"Being happy, being *this* happy really just makes me anxious. It's like I found like way too much money on the ground. Like not a dollar or a twenty but like enough money that it's gotta belong to someone scary that's gonna blow my head off for it. Like if you had something wrong with you, it might be less terrifying. If you had like a split personality and the other Morrigan beat the shit out of me, then I'd at least feel like I could do better if this all comes crashing down."

"*Simon.*"

His eye contact derailed from her and he went on, forcefully. "Breakups aren't the same for girls. Girls are pretty. Your loneliness ends as soon as you want it to."

She turned him back to face her, with a hand so eager it came to his cheek as a smack. He knew instantly it wasn't intentional, because Morrigan looked as remorseful as if she'd just killed him. With higher spirits he'd have laughed, but with a mind muddled with black thoughts, he just managed to raise a quivering eyebrow as he felt the sting slowly dissolve into heat on his cheek.

After a drunken chorus between the two of them, made of apologies and reassurances that he was fine, she went on. "Simon, listen, I forgot what I was going to say, but it was going to be something clever about how I was really bad at seducing *you*."

"Ah... okay."

"And also that's real fucking dumb Simon. You know what I'll do if we... stop being a thing? I'll be fucking *sad*. I can't just *replace* you. Sure I could find some loser to go out with, but what the fuck does that get me? Are my bros gonna high five me? No, I'd just be a slut. Dude, you're this sweet, handsome, Prince who cares about me. *That's* what I want. I want *you.* I'm right there with you out on that ledge. I'm so happy that it's terrifying. I'm so scared of this ending that I feel like if I say the words '*break up*' it'll happen like they're magic words for a really shitty spell."

Knowing exactly that strange taboo too well, Simon mushed the girl against him.

"I'm not going to be going after any fucking creeps from work if you don't work out." She said into his shirt. "I'll be fucking buying out Wallmart's entire inventory of Reese's Pieces ice cream, Mountain Dew, Fanta and Fun-Dip. That's my recipe for root-beer floats.

She jerked apart from his chest to catch his expression and started giggling at his perplexed disgust.

"Does that taste... *good?*"

Morrigan crept up to his ear and answered only in the form of a grotesque slurping noise.

They laughed hard together and that dread in his chest melted away for the moment. When he recovered he asked about the Fun-Dip, to which she also responded with slurping noises. It fueled the fire and when the laughter finally subsided she pushed herself off of his lap, still laying her legs across him and took a hand with her into her lap with both hands. "For what it's worth, I felt twice as anxious about this whole thing yesterday, and doubled again the day before. I'm betting we'll both feel half as anxious tomorrow. I mean, every time I freak out I feel like a moron immediately afterwards, and now I know why. You sound like a fucking idiot *while* you're freaking out. I guess I did too."

Her tone was glib but she squeezed his hand, as if to say she wasn't going to let him sneak away with weighty thoughts if she could help it.

When he spoke again, it was easier. He vented the thoughts like he was exhaling them, not coughing them out desperately. "It's just that while my brain remembers the many, many moments of that relationship that I felt miserable and alone, neglected, and trapped, my heart just remembers one moment. That feeling of the floor opening up under me and being completely powerless to influence anything. There are whole albums of songs written by men trying to get women back, and for every album there's a matching one made by a woman happy to be rid of him. I just can't imagine an argument I could make that I'm worth keeping. There're just so many other guys to choose from. They've got better personalities, without these leaks that cause floods of awful thoughts like these. They're better looking and you can, without a doubt, find one that is less of a girly bitch than me."

"Simon, I don't know if you noticed but something happened this morning that might –if interpreted by someone astoudingly clever– be used to conclude that I am *in fact* atracted to girly bitches."

Simon forgot any further insecurities, like lines for a school play. Morrigan pinched his ear gently between her thumb and forefinger, feeling the heat of his blush.

"Thanks for sharing your shitty thoughts with me, Simon. You can always tell me anything if it'll feel better to get it out of you."

"Thank you." He breathed, stunned by the realization that he hadn't managed to ruin everything. He'd spat out every self sabotaging thought that his head had conjured up and she hadn't balked at a single red flag.

He dragged his hands over his face, kneading his fingers at the sides of his nose and temples. When he removed his hands, she was looking out the window. Twilight was cast over her face and while one eye was hidden by her hair, the other beamed. It didn't beam at him but the world rushing by. She was brimming with optimism, like he should have been. Now that his concerns had left him, he couldn't even remember them. All that was left was the shame at being anything but ecstatic about his new relationship.

"Hey, sorry I'm such a mess."

She shook her head and looked at him. "No, being happy *is* scary. I was stressed too. I'm glad you said something. Makes me feel less bad for being crazy too. You know to wake me up if you're feeling bad late at night, right? I won't be able to sleep if I know my boyfriend is alone feeling all..."

A bright reflection off something chrome flashed from behind Simon and Morrigan's eye squinted nearly shut like she'd tasted something sour. Taking a hand to his cheek she tilted his head to block the light. Morrigan blinked her eyes open cocking her head to match his and he smiled.

God she's cute.

"I don't know if I mentioned this before, but I really like you, Morrigan."

She smiled like a girl does when a cute boy tells her that he likes her. Her eyes made sure he knew that *he* was that cute boy. Her shoulders rose, her chest puffed up and she stroked her thumb gently over the left side of his neck where he knew she'd left a very prominent hickie.

"Too bad you don't have hair long enough to hide yours..." Morrigan mused, nibbling her lip. "Mind if I steal your phone for a second?"

At the 'S' in "Sure", Morrigan's hand slipped past Simon's into his own pocket. The sensation of her small fingers fishing for it was strange. Those goofy antics put a smile on his face and, before it'd gone, Morrigan leaned forward, nuzzled her head against his at a demure angle, and nudged his face towards hers as she snapped a selfie of them with his phone. In a claw grip she clacked the black painted nail of her forefinger down and stole another one, to capture the stunned expression that followed.

"If anyone asks you where you got that hickie, now you can show them."

She shifted to get a better position, shook down some hair onto her cheek, then swept some back before shaking down more, and then angled her face down from the camera while keeping her eyes locked on the lense. It was the same kind of manufactured selfie-cuteness he was all too familiar with, but this wasn't made for the approval of strangers. It was for him.

"Send me that one. My hickie is top-secret but, if someone *does* ask, I wanna be able to show *you* off too."

Morrigan took another with her hair swept away from her neck and her collar tugged down, showing off the small mark *he'd* left like a new tattoo. Then she slipped the phone back into his pocket, admiring the expression she'd put on his face, without any attempt at concealing her self satisfaction.

Before Simon could articulate a thanks that didn't embarrass him, the brakes of the bus began to squeak and her attention snapped to their stop, rapidly approaching out the window. She swung her slender legs from his lap and sprung to her feet, as the bus came to a halt. Morrigan twirled as she backpedaled two bouncing steps down the aisle. She looked back at him with a posture full of confidence. Her shoulders were high, her back straight, abandoning her usual hunch to make her chest more modest. Then she spun back forward, swinging hair still damp from a shower they'd shared.

It was a compelling invitation to follow, and Simon did so close behind.

The flare of the setting sun lit the chrome bits of a skyline blurred in Simon's periphery. Everything was in soft focus but her. When she stopped short, he could stop in time but only so soon that he could hug her rather than trample her. Her hands laid over his with a swiftness, like only the mastermind of that embrace could. She mewed a sound he only heard through his chest. Her hands slipped into his pockets and he leaned over her to plant a kiss on her cheek. She tilted her head to receive it and rose up on the balls of her feet to catch his lips with her own as he pulled away.

It was a light thing and, before it was even so long as a moment, she twirled around him, forced her arm under his, and wrapped herself tight onto his arm like they were on a date in the 20s. "Take me to dinner," she declared in a voice no less feminine than birdsong.

With a breath of air so light it made him stand tall beside her, he did. He strode beneath a salvo of looks from the many eyes of people coursing about the bus-stop. Some eyes rolled, others narrowed, but several cast sideways at a date of their own.

She'd talked about hanging on his arm, but it hadn't excited him. He hadn't known what it was, not viscerally, like a kiss. He'd never had a chance to feel it, that tight weightlessness of lungs full of pride. He hadn't the hubris to imagine a girl that could be so excited to be on his arm, to be seen there. And then there she was, clutching his arm too tight for any doubt of that to squeeze in between.

Chapter 48

An Irish restaurant

"*Fuck* no," Morrigan laughed. "We *just* started dating. I can't have you seeing my place. It's a disaster." She leaned back, rattling the ice-cubes in her empty cup and peered down at the band below.

The pair of them had been seated upstairs, overlooking the main floor. They were the first party to be seated in the upstairs and, since they'd been seated, no other party had joined them. As a result they'd been forgotten, abandoned to sip melted ice-cubes in a drought of refills. It was not an altogether terrible fate for two hopelessly shy lovebirds.

"Oh *please*, I live in a hotel. I don't clean at all. Like I'd be in any position to judge how messy your place is."

She was taking a sip but, ahead of swallowing, she was already shaking her head. "No, no, no. My place doesn't have *enough* clutter. If it were messier, you might not notice how shitty it is. Really what I need is eye catching clutter. I should go buy colorful- no *sparkly* confetti and shovel heaps of it around my house."

"That's how you clean?"

"Yup, heaps of confetti."

"Sparkly confetti?"

"Sometimes tin-foil. But then I have to rip it up first."

Simon looked at her for a while. She watched a phantom of a smile creep onto his lips and vanish once or twice as something corny brewed in his brain. She waited for it, crunching an ice-cube to keep her smile away.

"You know there'll be something else a lot more eye-catching there..."

She tossed her napkin over his face, like she was netting a wild animal. "Shush."

God damn. This guy gets laid and he's James Bond.

"I hope you know you're not smooth." She declared haughtily, restraining a smile. "You're just cute. You're like an unfunny hot girl, that all the guys laugh at so they can get in her pants."

Simon cocked his head, his lips quivering to postpone a laugh. "So I'm... seducing you with my face so that I can seduce you with my words?"

"Oh shut *up*. You do it too. I can prove it. Check it out: you're gonna give me a cavity."

His eyebrows came together raised. "What?"

She leaned in, cupping her hand beside a carefully restrained grin. "It's because you're so sweet."

Simon grimaced and shook his head, but laughter escaped out his nose.

Morrigan pointed an accusatory finger at his chest. "*See*? That's not funny. It's *not*." Despite her denial, she laughed too. "You're just laughing because you think I'm cute."

Simon sat back with his arms crossed. "I hate to throw a stick into the cogs of your logic machine, *but* I have an alternative explanation: Maybe you're cute *and* funny."

A protest gathered in her throat, but tension slipped from her vocal cords and a groan left her as something more like a puppy whine. It felt good, if indulgent, resigning herself to just accept sweet words.

Simon looked back at her with a cool gaze, his bright blue eyes no longer too timid to stare. His expression was relaxed, and he didn't fumble to back-pedal over his compliment or sneak in some teasing to soften it.

*For such an awkward guy, he's so comfortable just... **being** with me. It's almost intimidating.*

The music down below washed into the silence between them and a pretty Irish girl, in a pretty Irish dress, hopped onto a table to perform an Irish stepdance. In the dim dining lighting, all Morrigan could make out was a tangle of springy black curls bobbing about freckly pale shoulders, and the flash of a white smile.

She looked to Simon who watched her with some interest, but not enough to make Morrigan jealous. With each stomping step of her boots on the table, Simon unintentionally blinked in a kind of soft flinching.

Poor Simon. Sweet, gentle Simon. He's so soft, dancing is too violent for him. He's the same Simon he's always been.

The band all stopped and the fiddler began a vigorous solo, skipping forward and sitting himself at the edge of the dancer's table. Simon asked again, already knowing the answer: "That's not a violin?"

She shook her head, the smile she held too serene to break with words.

Simon too let the tide of quiet rise and they sat there in pleasant company until the waitress finally showed up. She asked if they needed anything else or just their check, and they politely reminded her that they hadn't ordered yet.

Once the girl had gone rushing back to the kitchen to put in their order, Morrigan could feel the topic smolder again so she made an effort to stomp out the embers preemptively. "You don't wanna sleep over my house. Believe me. *I* don't even want to sleep there. I barely even have a bed frame. I basically sleep on a mattress on the floor. I'll just sleep over again."

"Morrigan, my room has been *defiled*. It smells like sweat and sex. We sent the maid away and she won't return until the morning."

"So will my house, and I *have* no maid."

"We've used up every towel, *and* most of the dirty laundry. Everything is... *damp*."

"I barely even wash my clothes. My dryer is a house fire waiting to happen. It sometimes just doesn't produce any heat and my clothes get all mildewy. I run the dryer with half a dozen car air-fresheners just in case."

Simon cocked his head, processing. He didn't appear to be nearly as disgusted as he should have been.

"Sometimes I just air wash them." She added.

"Air wash?"

She hesitated. It was more than he really needed to know.

Still, she'd already said too much. "Yeah you just leave clothes out and they uh... just kinda clean by themselves."

Simon flashed her a deservedly skeptical look.

"Well... they stop smelling at least."

He shook his head, eyebrow cocked.

"No like they run out of stink. It disperses. Like *off-gassing*? When stuff smells bad, it's the particles coming off of the stuff and when it runs out of uh...."

"Is that real science? That doesn't sound like real science. I feel like you don't actually know that."

In truth, she'd known it wasn't true as soon as she heard herself say it, but it was easier to change the subject.

"Why do you want to come over anyway?" she groaned. "My house is just proof that I'm a disaster, that my whole life sucks, and one huge warning sign that you shouldn't date a loser like me with a dead-end job."

Simon got up and she felt her face flash hot with blush. "Agh, *no* don't hug me. I don't deserve a hug."

Simon hugged her, of course. As he released her she relented, detaining him a moment longer, returning the embrace.

"You *know* I don't care how messy your place is, just so long as you're in it."

Morrigan was betrayed by her own smile, undermining her, but she went on. "It'll erode you like the ocean. You say you don't care, but add up like a dozen things you don't care about and you've got a problem, because you do care. You just care like .1%. Add ten more things and then like you *do* care. 110% care."

Morrigan pulled out of their embrace and caught an amused expression on his face. "You judging my math? I ought to slap the correction right out of your mouth." She gave him a soft smack to the cheek but, unlike the stomping boots of the dancer below, her touch didn't make him blink.

His reaction stunned her, causing her hand to linger there on his cheek. Simon waited patiently for her to do as she pleased with his face, not protesting or teasing. Catching herself, Morrigan blinked and snatched her hand away with a short huffed sigh.

"A-anyway, you know I've got a crawl space under my house?"

"Oh I didn't," he said, clearly missing her point.

"Well snakes live in crawl spaces."

"Oh. Well why do you have one then?"

"When it rains the crawl space floods instead of the house."

"Well it just rained so all the snakes must be dead. Problem solved."

"No. Snakes don't drown. There's like water snakes and stuff."

"Do water snakes live in Florida? I feel like I've only seen them in documentaries about the amazon rainforest."

She thought for a moment, and then shrugged. "Well do you know what eats dead snakes?"

"The crawlspace dragon?" Simon suggested with a straight face. "Everyone knows they only eat drowned snakes, water snakes, and new boyfriends. I guess we better not go to your place then."

She laughed, cursing his shitty jokes and supplementary

cuteness.

When it had subsided, Simon gave her an up-nod and asked: "So what do you want to do instead of Disney? You said you were stuck in a dead-end job."

"Did I? Oh I mean Disney isn't bad. Only job that comes with a super legit vacation." He waited for her to say more, and she floundered for more to say. "I guess 'dead-end' isn't fair either. They keep sending me emails about management training, and I've gotten raises."

"You make that sound like a bad thing."

It was, but Morrigan was saved from explaining by their waitress showing up with refills.

"So what about *you*? what do *you* want to be doing?" She squinted. "Wait what *do* you do anyway?

She could tell immediately whatever answer he was about to give was going to be a red flag, that much he couldn't hide with silence.

"Well, I used to work as a graphic designer, but I quit. I didn't tell you this?"

She shrugged. "I think you mentioned it, briefly. So you're an artist?"

"No, not in the way you're probably thinking. It's more about designing something to get someone to look at it for a while. You make it eye catching, and readable. If you do it right, it's the kind of thing no one notices. People might look at a painting and think it's pretty, but not an advertisement or a business card. I don't have the talent to make people happy that a more traditional artist does, but I guess i *can* make people money, and I guess that's important too..."

"Well that's still impressive."

It was a canned response. She'd turned her brain off and said the thing people said. When Simon rolled his eyes, she felt she'd earned that.

He shut his eyes and pinched the bridge of his nose. "Impressive if you're at a party where everyone's got their cock out on the table, talking about how fucking successful they are. Design firm, art director, visual specialist, industry expert. Let's play pretentious hipster bingo." His eyes flashed open. "Sorry."

"No, no, go get 'em." Morrigan sat up and crossed her legs, attentive. "Bitch, dude. I'm game for it."

He smiled, but didn't continue until she egged him on further, with a little kick at his knee.

"It's just like, they all act so satisfied with themselves. They were content as long as people gave them a slow nod and a 'wow'. No one was accountable to themselves. It's so irritating how some people get away with not hating themselves. I'm stuck hating myself *and* them."

Morrigan grinned, fascinated by a ranting Simon.

"None of them could relax unless they were *killing it,* but I *was* killing it and I sure couldn't relax. Sarah would introduce me and say 'graphic designer' and then I'd give them a bullshit line with 'design firm' in it. They would all say 'wow that's so cool' but really, no one fucking wants to look at advertisements, and I make them. No one that you want to know hangs a logo on their wall."

She leaned a cheek on her fist and watched him, passionate and exacerbated. She wondered if he'd ever had a chance to rave about all this before. He rushed to end each sentence like some force was about to interrupt, and cut him off from his rant. "So? What d'ya want to make? What would you be proud hanging on a wall?" she asked, tossing another log on his bonfire.

Simon was lost in his own head for a long moment, staring into a space high above her head. "I wish I could paint landscapes. I couldn't paint reality, though. Competing with photography seems stressful. It'd have to be fantastical, something that's only real in my painting. Mossy rocks, grassy hills, waterfalls, all in excess. Something so pretty it shocks the imagination. I'd want it to be so nice you'd wanna go there and I'd stick a quaint little Snow White cottage nestled into the middle of it so you could imagine living there. I could put a pointless happy thought in someone's head and make their day a little better."

A twinge of worry struck Morrigan that she might be superficial. It hadn't occurred to her to wonder about what Simon was passionate about. She wasn't sure if she'd assumed he wasn't terribly deep or just didn't care. It wasn't that she only cared about his looks, though she *was* rather fond of them. Somehow being so enraptured by how sweet and considerate he was, and being so concerned with whether he'd keep liking her, keep treating her well, felt terribly selfish.

"I'm not that kind of artist," Simon said with a sigh weighted in his chest. "But *god* would I love to make something like that. I'd be *so* proud to hang something on a wall that could make someone's chest tight, like... like they'd seen you *dance...* or heard you sing."

Self consciousness clutched her lungs with cold claws. *He's heard me sing? Did he look me up? I never told him my stage name.* Her head swirled with conspiracy.

"Man, I couldn't understand a word, but your voice just has this... like it- it just *rides* on the air. I don't mean to flatter. I know it wasn't your best performance or whatever. you were a little hoarse but *still.* I just didn't know you could sing like that."

"You looked up my bumper sticker." She sighed, like she were a noir detective lighting a cigarette. "I'm surprised you could read the font. You know it's fine, I guess, but you really should have asked me about it. The only reason that bumper sticker hasn't been scratched off is because we got such cheap ones that they fell off in a week so we had to gorilla glue them all. If I wanted you to know my stage name I would have told you."

Simon's face watched her with a distinctive lack of shame that irked her. He cocked his head with wide eyes and an open mouth *not* busy apologizing.

"Come on *dude*. You know how self conscious I am. You think I need to worry about my new boyfriend learning about me from shitty interviews I did when I was fucking sixteen?"

"*Morrigan*, I'm sorry I- Morrigan you were singing outside when I got out of the shower."

"Fuck."

Her forehead clunked into the table.

"*Stage name?*"

"Fuck," she reiterated.

She felt a chair plant itself beside her and soon her boyfriend's hands were all over her. His fingers combed up into her hair, massaging her scalp, and worked their way down along the sides of her neck. By the time he began kneading her shoulders, she became pliable and let him bend her back away from the table. He planted a soft-lipped kiss on her hot cheek and she couldn't pull away from it.

"Incubus." She grumbled.

"That's your stage name? That sounds cool."

"No! That's a male succubus. That's you. Trying to seduce answers out of me with your massaging and..."

Amused Simon kissed her cheek again, grazing his nose over her temple as he brought his lips to her ear. "Come *on,*" he whispered. "Tell *me*."

"Simon, you gotta pay attention." She pushed him to arm's length. "Did you not notice me go from zero to 'you're a psycho stalker' in one second flat?"

"Mhm. Yeah I'm just glad it wasn't *me* being crazy this time." His words were sing-songy and quick.

He was so glib, she couldn't help but give him a kick under the table. Simon played it up to an invisible referee and a reflexive "sorry" squeaked from her. As soon as she heard the word leave her mouth she rolled her eyes.

"I can never forgive you," Simon sighed dramatically, placing the back of a limp hand on his forehead.

She left him in that state as the waitress returned with their food. He straightened up, all very proper, and returned his seat to the right side of the table. Hidden behind the waitress's back, Morrigan mimed a super villain laugh that melted his embarrassment.

Chapter 49

Disney Quest

They stood on a miniature pirate ship, just big enough for a family of five. Two swivelling cannons on each side, aimed at a surrounding wall of screens rendering a great blue ocean beneath a blazing Caribbean sun, full of other pirate ships bobbing in the tide. That was, at least, on the side of the boat that Morrigan's cannon wasn't.

"Spin us. Come *on*." She whined at him, leaning back in her ultra-wide rockstar powerstance.

The cannons were shot by yanking on a fuse, but morrigan had wrapped that string around her hand until it was taught, and proceeded to strum an air-guitar fast enough to send cannonballs onto the screen in a solid beam.

Simon spun the wheel and Morrigan hosed down the pirate ships instantly, blowing them all to smithereens. 4D tech sent splinters across the deck and the airbags beneath the boat inflated to simulate the waves rocking the boat after the explosions.

"Alright come *on*. This is timed. Go! Take us to the big fortress."

"Aye, aye." Simon called back, over the clink of treasure rushing into their ship, his eyebrow twitching with amusement. "So you played guitar too?"

"You're still on that?" she groaned, sweeping a stream of cannon balls across Tortuga's ramparts. The system was meant to accommodate excited people yanking as fast as they could, so there was no programmed cooldown per shot, but the game wasn't built for Morrigan's shredding.

All the cannon ports of the fort were turned to smoking craters in the wall with one sweep and the game barked back a dozen explosion sound effects stacked on top of each other in a cacophonous, glitchy roar. Then Simon squinted, as more bright glittering treasure than the designers had ever intended to be received at once, all came soaring out of the smoke to sparkle before their 3-D glasses clad eyes.

The sky darkened for a moment and he looked over at Morrigan, privately amused. Some song was playing in her head and it made her hair thrash about gently as her head bobbed in a little 'V'. She tapped her foot with the weight of a stomp and strummed away, blasting a giant sea-serpent into green chunks the moment it rose above the waves.

"You know, you wouldn't like my kind of music."

"Probably. But I like *you,* don't I?"

She groaned at the ceiling, arching her back. "I'm not the bitch that's gonna torture you with everything I like."

"You don't get it. I don't think you can. You've never seen *you* dance. You don't know what it feels like to be a guy falling for a girl who's just..."

Breathtaking, who's got a soul that burns bright and warm. You've never met a girl who's got eyes that glow with wild passion when

*she's telling me about celtic mythology, her grandmother, old
friends, or any of a hundred other things that fly into her head on a
whim. You just don't know.*

She heard some of it in his voice and looked over her
shoulder at him, trying to catch a peek into his head.

You deserve a guy who shouldn't feel weird telling you.

"You don't know what it's like to be around you when you're
passionate about something. When the mood strikes you, it's like a
wave. I could hear every story you've told me again, if you told it
with those same bright eyes and that eagerness that made you
squeeze every word you could out of each breath. Morrigan, the way
you dance is just..."

At this point, all the pirates were dead. They were left with
just the sound of seagulls and gentle lapping waves.

"Morrigan, if you wrote a song with all the passion you have
for music, then I bet it would sound like you dancing. And, you
know, it's not like I go to the ballet every weekend but I could still
tell your dancing was beautiful. The way your pale skin caught the
moonlight and how you moved like-"

"Alright, alright! Jesus fuck man, now that you're done being
a shy little pussy you're relentless. You're gonna make me feel bad
about myself. How am I supposed to compete with that bullshit? I
can't be that thoughtful, you asshole."

Without breaking eye-contact, Simon reached into his pocket
and pulled out his phone. "Let me call you a wambulance. Your
boyfriend is being nice. Sounds like a real emergency."

Simon barely processed the shock on her face before the girl
was upon him. Open palms smacked into his chest and grabbed hold
of his shirt with a giddy vigor. She yanked him towards her and
thrust him gently away. She shook him in slow motion, reveling
obviously in his malleability. Morrigan bit her lip, bubbling with a

kind of hunger. "You're such a little *bitch*."

She'd said it whimsically but the sour chord she'd plucked in his heart still hummed. "You won't get fucking kooties from me being honest about my feelings."

"I know." Their 3D glasses clacked together as she hopped onto her toes for a kiss. "I don't mean to-"

A 4D skeleton pirate flew between them, cackling. ***"There's one last thing you need to know about treasure!"***

"Boss fight." Morrigan sighed tersely.

Simon nodded, pursing his lips in a smile, and nudged her over to her cannon.

"You've got to defeat me to keep it!"

Morrigan, again, adopted her crazy wide powerstance and strummed apart the ghost pirate ship the second it surfaced. The programming wasn't ready for the boss to lose so quickly so the animations continued even if it couldn't attack back. She turned her back on the ghost ship, propping her elbows on the gunwale, as it submerged and resurfaced. The evil captain cackled maniacally all the while.

"Hey thanks for not making me guess how you're feeling. Keep doing that and I won't have to worry about figuring out what I did wrong." Morrigan shoved off the side of the boat and took two meandering steps towards him. Once she was close enough not to have to yell over the lightning sound effects, she added: "And hey, sorry about... Just don't let me scare you off of being sweet by being a..." She shrugged and fell easily towards him.

She rested against his chest and Simon rubbed her back. Somehow even Morrigan's clothes were softer than other people's when they hugged. She spent just long enough against him for her eyes to close, then she swayed apart and turned to watch their high-score get totaled up.

"Oh hey," Morrigan leaned over on one foot to yank a cannon cord, and onto the screen it sent a firework.

Simon grabbed his own cannon and yanked away to shoot some fireworks at the highscore screen.

"If I do my strumming trick, it'll crash it and they'll have to reset it so..."

Before he could reach out towards her back the doors swung open and they were ushered out so a family of five could get on the ride. His words had time to ferment in him while they left the Pirate attraction. The emotion built to a dangerous intensity in silence.

"Morrigan?" He began, cutting her explanation of the Dinosaur Rafting ride short. "Do I have your permission to say something involving many, *many* kooties?"

She rolled her eyes. "I hereby grant you eternal permission to be a sweet dork, and share every gross feeling of affection with me, even if they make me uncomfortable because my shitty self esteem tells me I don't deserve it."

"I need to be alone with you."

"Oh."

He shook his head. "We'll end up in the hospital if we do anything like *that*. I just need to put my arms around you and hear you breathing softly in my ear. I just *need* it. I need *you*. So take me someplace, anywhere where you'll be."

The words hit her like he needed them to. Wide eyes, pink cheeks, a smile just for him.

"Alright," she sighed lightly. "Come home with me."

Chapter 50

Snuggling

Morrigan took one last look at the man waiting in her bed, dressed in her stretched out Moonspell shirt, before flicking off the lights and padding over to him.

She fell limply into welcoming arms that pulled her into bed. Simon's arms wrapped about her like warm blankets, and she curled in the embrace, holding her arms close to her chest. She squirmed to put her hands someplace that might passively convey the same pleasant sense of belonging to her boyfriend. She found his arm, and delicate fingers clung to it. He squeezed her gently with an intensity that arced a jolt of joy to her. He'd said he *needed* this, and it was good to be needed.

Simon's pants weren't as soft as his boxers, so she'd had him jettison them, leaving bare legs to mingle with hers beneath the covers. She'd already double checked her legs for prickly sprouting hairs, like she was Indiana Jones looking for a secret door, and she was sure she wanted him to feel her skin against his. Like the rest of him, his legs were soft. His skin was supple, and even his invisible blonde body hair was peach-fuzz-soft, as though he'd used conditioner. It felt nice, and her legs ended up entwined with his. The contact made his blood burn hot for a moment, and he clutched her against him with a strength that reminded her of how he'd pulled her back from that van.

She wasn't tired but laying in his arms felt like all she could bear to do. A tension that she hadn't been aware of melted away, leaving her muscles feeble in his arms. "Thank you for this. Turns out I needed it too."

As drained as they were, Morrigan nuzzled against a thumping heart. She felt it too, an energy that suspended them from sleep. An anxiety that warned against ending this day.

"Are you tired?"

"No," she breathed, barely loud enough to be a whisper. "But I want to stay like this for a while, if that's okay."

"Do you wanna talk then?"

"About?"

"Anything. Your voice is just nice."

She crawled up her boyfriend to share the pillow with him, nuzzling against his cheek.

"I haven't washed these sheets in a long time."

There was so much stillness in their embrace and they were so close that she could feel her nose nudged by his smile.

He's hopeless, she mused, sliding back on the pillow just far enough to see his face.

He stared at the ceiling with an expression of content that looked too serene to disrupt with more teasing. His calm spread to her like warmth, relaxing her, but sleep was still an untenable argument.

"Hey," he sounded, gently above a whisper. "You remember that French couple we passed? With the kid?"

"Mmm."

"That dad... I think... he's a good dad..."

He was quiet for long enough that Morrigan wondered about Simon's father, but not long enough to decide if she should ask.

"He had two lightsabers in his hand, but that little boy didn't have any siblings."

"Oh... I didn't notice. He must have got him two so he could swing one in each hand. That kid certainly had the energy for it."

"No... I think that dad got one for himself. That way his kid would have someone to duel. I think he doesn't want his son to be lonely."

I bet you'll make an okay dad one day Simon Magnusson.

"Yeah, I think you're right."

The pleasant thought pacified Simon, but Morrigan's mind remained unquieted. Simon noticed, and his hands moved over her back, gently massaging. He was going to ask what was wrong. She could feel it. But she didn't have an answer. She didn't know what *was* wrong. So when the breath came in, she swerved in front.

"I like your hands."

"Oh?"

"Well, they're yours and they're touching me and I like it. They're good hands."

Those hands took further liberties, sliding over her and enwrapping her warmly until their bodies fit together like puzzle pieces. They clung to each other, belonging undeniably in each other's arms. It was peaceful, but her head stormed on.

They lingered too long on that precipice of sleep, and there she found it. The last excuse for her disquiet mind, her anxiety's thrashing death throw.

"Are you going to move back to New York now that you're feeling better?" It was awkwardly loud to be said in an ear but emotion made vocal cords too taught for whispers.

His arms stiffened and it was like a blanket was yanked off of her.

"Morrigan..."

"We can't stay here forever Simon. Eventually we'll both have to go back to reality. You can't just go to Disney World every day and assume your friend's business will keep you rich forever. I have to go back to work and you've got a whole life in New York." He tried to talk but she couldn't stop. She had no idea how fickle her bravery might be. "I wanna know if it's safe to fall in love with you."

He lifted her off of him and held her above him. He was suddenly so strong for a man that weighed nothing against her push. His eyes looked serious before she blinked and everything was blurry through a blob of tears.

"Morrigan my life doesn't exist. I'm homeless, unless you count my hotel room. I have no earthly possessions outside of the stuff in that hotel room. I have no job. I have no friends-"

"You do!" She squirmed, taking a hand from wiping her eyes to point at him. She was too enthusiastic in her accusation and touched him directly on the eyeball. Morrigan's shoulder's slipped from his hold as he flinched and she came crashing down on top of him. She impaled herself on her boyfriend's defined chin with a sound like knocking on a door.

"Ah my god." She groaned into the hands she'd clasped over her face. "My boyfriend beats me."

"Why did you do that?" he hissed, clutching his eye.

She rolled onto her side and began prying his hand away to examine. "Because I'm a spaz. Lemme see. You have to let me poke it twice or it won't stop hurting."

As she *did* manage to coax his hand away, Simon swore. "You're gonna need some ice, sweetie."

"Sweetie? I hope you didn't settle on that. Try out some other ones."

He ignored her and scrambled out of the bed. Morrigan touched the source of the throbbing in her face and winced. Oh shit am I gonna have a shiner? Fuck. I can't go to work. They're really gonna think you beat me."

She heard the freezer drawer open and immediately sucked in a breath between her teeth.

"*Morrigan?*"

"Oh my god. Simon I..."

"Why do you have..."

"I have to bury them. I'm so sorry. I'm bad at getting shit done. Holy shit, I'm so sorry."

"You eat ice-pops from this freezer."

"Simon, I'm sorry. I'm a crazy person."

"Do you want some haunted ice for your eye?"

Her abs were still sore from earlier but she laughed anyway. She laughed even as he iced her eye, in spite of a stomach sore from earlier jubilations and carnal exertions. He shifted her head into his lap as he sat and she stared up at the ceiling. She hoped Simon wouldn't look up. There was water damage above the bed. It was only a matter of time before it began to leak on her while she slept. She made a mental note to climb up on the roof to pour some bleach into the hole and kill the mold growing inside.

"*Simon,* do you still like me?"

"Yeah."

"Even though I'm a filthy trash monster?

"Yes," he sighed. "Although I never have been known for having good taste in girlfriends."

He palmed her chest as she tried to sit up. "Oooh, Simon *the player*?"

"Let me ice this. I'd really rather your co-workers not think I beat you. And to answer your question, my skill was more in getting dumped. But yeah, if you say yes to anyone who asks, you'll get passed around plenty."

Her stomach dropped an inch. She knew she hadn't gotten to him first, but it hurt to hear anyway. "Simon, put my hand someplace appropriate to comfort you. This angle is awkward and I think you'll leave me if I gouge your eye out again."

He stopped playing with her hair, for a moment, to put her hand someplace that wasn't his eye. He seemed to be deep in thought and she started to feel dizzy anticipating the result. She wanted to steer him to safer waters.

"So Simon..."

"Mmm."

There was nothing in her head so she reached desperately for *anything* to say. "Hey I'm Irish."

"...yeah?"

"W-what... are *you*?"

Norwegian. He said Norwegian. I know that.

"Has Morrigan Melanaphy finally run out of things to talk about?"

She made a sound of protest, resembling a dinosaur off of the Animal Kingdom ride. "I'm a nervous babbler. Babble for me."

"Oh well uhhh... Speaking of heritage, I just remembered something my dad said about mine. He did this genetic test – something to do with body building– and he said that on my grandmother's side he was ummm... *Hiberno?* Norse."

Morrigan grinned. "Dude the Hiberno Norse were the descendants of Nordic settlers in *Ireland*. You're part Irish. I knew there was a reason I was so attracted to you."

She tried to sit up and kiss him, but doctor Simon palmed her chest and kept the icepack on her eye. He tried to bend down to her but, being unable to contort himself, he took her hand and kissed it like a prince. She could feel his fingers pulsing with a heavy heartbeat that she knew. She wanted to feel for the blush it brought but, again, she didn't trust her one eyed depth perception.

"My grandmother would've been a big fan of yours, you know. You treat her grand daughter well *and* you're part Irish? I know she's smiling over in Avalon. Probably high fiving all my ancestors."

She watched the blush fade gently with laughter, then nudged him gently. "So what about your mom's side?"

"Oh well my grandmother's dad —great grandfather I guess— was a lighthouse tender on a fjord and my grandfather was from northern Norway."

"Oh? *Northern* Norway? What's there?"

"Norwegians I guess, mountains too." His hand paused in it's caress. His fingers curled slightly, grazing her scalp. "Pretty ones."

Morrigan watched him, patiently

His vacant stare gained focus and his eyelids fluttered his story back to the forefront. "My grandfather. He was a painter in the mountains. No one bought his paintings really. They could see the mountains just by looking out their door. Or at least that was his excuse. So he went to a coastal town called... I actually forget. He met my grandmother there. Her father was the lighthouse keeper. They lived up on the side of the fjord, this huge cliff, with a crazy view. They had a traditional birch roofed cottage beside the light-house. You know, the kind where grass grows on top. Her mother planted flowers there, and they always lost their petals in the wind." He spoke stiffly like he was reciting a story he'd been told dozens of times. "Anyway, She bought a painting of the mountains from him. She still has it too. It was the other side of the mountains she saw from her house growing up."

"*Aw,* that's so romantic."

"I don't know. The way she tells the story the last sweet thing he did was paint them a picture of the sea off the coast from memory, when she got homesick after they moved to the US."

She found his hand and slid her fingers between his. She couldn't promise not to turn into a bitch when half a century had gone by. It'd sound too crazy. She hoped he already knew she'd work to keep their relationship from turning sour.

"So a painter, huh? That why you want to paint pretty landscapes?"

"Maybe," he sighed. "I guess I *do* relate to him a lot. He took a job as a lithographer and made a bunch of money. His job was making sure the magazine was printing the right colors for the pictures. He'd compare the sample to what was coming off the line, like a quality checker. I actually inherited tetrachromacy from him."

"Tetrachromancy? What are you a fucking sorcerer? Shit sounds like a power metal album."

"Tetra-chro-*macy*, not '*mancy*'. It's like the opposite of being colorblind. You can see more colors than normal people. It's really rare for men to have. A lot of men are some kind of colorblind actually. And it sounds more useful than it is really. Like if I mixed two colors of paint, I apparently see more colors in between the two blobs of paint than other people. Rainbows are the same way, I guess," Simon explained passively, as he lifted the ice-bag off her eye and frowned at what she hoped wasn't too noticable of a bruise. "Doesn't really help me paint better though."

She sighed and stretched, gently grinding the hair on her scalp against his thigh. As she flung her arms back down she swung one over the edge of the bed and her knuckle struck something hard. Admittedly her bed was very near the ground as she'd solved a wobbling bed-post by knocking all four off with a hammer, but her floor was carpeted.

Simon replaced the ice and she fished around beside the bed, finding his pants there. She felt around and found the hard thing, his phone. Morrigan slipped it out of his pocket without protest and looked at the thing above her. There was a new text and she opened it. He didn't have a password. She rationalized that it was only '*kind of*' prying, since he was watching her do it.

Derek, was the name. He was the business friend. His last text had been pasted from a notes app. It had a different margin than his others and there were no spelling errors. *Nobody but psychopaths and people editing their texts use apostrophes,* Morrigan reflected. Simon had gotten this text days ago and hadn't opened it.

She glanced up at him. He was avoiding looking down at her. Morrigan took a breath, thought a moment, and then did it. She hit 'call' and put the phone to her ear. Her heart pounded with adrenaline.

"Hello?" came a groggy voice, distorted by the static of an exhale.

Simon Stiffened sharply.

"What's up Derek."

"Sorry, who is this?"

"I'm Simon's new girlfriend. We've only been official for a day, so I'm already pretty overreaching. He hasn't tried to take the phone though, so I guess it's okay."

She could hear him chuckle softly through the phone.

"Listen, Simon's too much of a bitch to call, but I'm hoping I can antagonize him into snatching the phone away from me and talking to you. He really misses you but he's too much of a pussy to just call and talk to you."

"Oh yeah?" was all that could crackle out of the man's still waking up brain.

"Yeah, he feels bad that he didn't fight his ex alienating him from his friends and feels like he doesn't deserve friends, if it's that easy to make him abandon them."

The honesty struck Simon rigid but he didn't stop her or even look down at her.

"Hey tell that bitch that I told him dating that whore- sorry."

"You're not gonna offend *me* with naughty words."

"Right, uh I *told* him it was a mistake but I also told him that I'll always be around the second he needs me. Nobody can convince a guy not to fall for the wrong girl but friends are supposed to be there when it ends, to pick up the pieces."

Simon was close enough to hear. Derek's words made him swallow hard. Morrigan put a hand over the one that had gone still in her hair.

"You sound like a good friend Derek. Let's make a deal, alright?"

"Okay, what's the deal?"

"You do me a favor and keep being a good friend to my boyfriend and I'll be a good girlfriend to your friend. Sound good?"

"Fuck yeah. Let's seal the deal over drinks. I'm buying. Right now. Let's go. I haven't seen Simon in months." He grunted over the rustling of sheets.

"Sorry, we're a bit far. We're in Orlando."

"Florida? What is-"

Simon snatched the phone. His hand was clumsy and rough. His fingers held the phone like a rock. "Derek I'm sorry. The money I invested was my life savings. I invested it because I- I just wanted to get rid of it. I'm so happy it worked out for you man. But I'm sorry I never thought it would." Simon blinked, disoriented by whirling thoughts. "I was just so sick of the creeping cost of gifts. It always had to get a little more expensive or it wasn't good enough. She'd always do this equation where she compared the price of the gift to my yearly earnings, and calculate how many days of work it was worth. No raise could ever keep me ahead. It was a percentage of my time –my life– she wanted. A wedding ring is supposed to be three months pay, so how many days is valentines day? Her birthday? Our anniversary? How many days in a year do I need to work just to have a handful of good ones when she's happy? That's what I kept asking myself. Then- then, I gave her this necklace and she just didn't care and it just drowned my god damn soul. I was so used to getting a little reprieve when I got her a gift. She'd smile, and touch me and for a little while everything was *fine*. But then she didn't. It wasn't the first time, but this time I realized that constant crushing pressure would never go away and it just felt hopeless and humiliating and I... I don't know. I guess I just resented that money." Simon's eyes shut and he knuckled his forehead. "Then, after we broke up, she wouldn't take her shit and every time I tripped over another thing I bought her, I felt so stupid and used. I had to get it away from me. I was gonna go for a walk and as soon as I just took a step outside I felt so much better. So I went back inside, packed a suitcase, and snapped my key off in the lock. I told the landlord to pawn everything in there to pay the rest of the year. All those stupid fucking gifts I bought her, my end table that was –god forbid– made in america, the shoes she texted me about, asking if her new boyfriend could have them because I looked bad in them. Everything. I told the landlord to fucking burn anything he couldn't sell and spend the surplus on-"

Simon was cut short by the stone in his throat and Morrigan could hear Derek being similarly afflicted. She knew it wasn't her place to hear their conversation, but she was his girlfriend, so she sat up and hugged him. If he'd tried to get up she would have wrapped an arm around his neck instead. She couldn't let him go anywhere.

"I know I'm fucking insane, but I just wanted to stop feeling horrible and I've got these two season passes to Disney. It was supposed to be a spontaneous thing with Sarah, but she was never gonna-"

"Yeah man, I get it. You needed to make a decision, blow some money, and screw your head on straight. That's not so weird. Some people blow a few grand in vegas. You're just doing your thing. You're alright man."

Beneath the arms and hands she'd wrapped about him, she could feel tension leave every muscle.

"Yeah..." Simon sighed, almost weak with relief.

The friends talked for a while, though they didn't say much. Eventually Morrigan loosened her grip and rubbed his back instead, laying down. At some point Derek told him to let Morrigan know that she was his favorite of his girlfriends. She could hear him but Simon relayed the message dutifully anyway.

The two friends talked for a long time, long enough for Morrigan to nod off and wake up tucked tightly into bed with every light off, save for the porch. She could hear a muffled Simon still talking out there. He was happy and it made for an adequate lullaby.

Chapter 51

That bright big beautiful tomorrow

"Wake up, Babe."

Simon blinked Morrigan into existence, shaking her head with a towel wrapped around her hair. "Nah, you're not a babe."

"Mmm?"

"Listen, can you drive me to work?"

The world was blurry and his cheek was still warm from the pillow. What came into focus first was Morrigan's chest and the poorly tied towel slowly slipping from it. He was hypnotized. "Drive?"

A finger under his chin pointed his lips up towards hers and she kissed him, parting with a whisper: "After work."

"Sorry." He shook the bleariness from his head and propped himself up on his elbow. "You want me to drive? drive *your* car? You can't drive?"

"No I can drive. If you're too tired I can drive, but you should drive."

"I should?"

She kissed him again, a light peck on the lips, before tilting his head and inspecting yesterday's work on his neck. She kissed him there too.

"Yeah, can you?"

"Sure?"

"I'm gonna get dressed real quick, then we can go."

She stood and Simon watched her walk past her wardrobe and over to the dryer to retrieve clothes. The towel was dripping off of her and Simon might have killed someone for a downpour. When she had a fistful of all the ingredients she lay them on top of the machine and turned to say something that melted away into a sly smile. Morrigan reminded him with a wink: "After work." With that, Simon thumped his head back down onto the pillow and watched the ceiling instead. He threw the covers down to keep himself from falling back asleep. While she dressed, Morrigan hummed a sweet and gentle tune. It was really a wonderful sound and he wondered if she knew.

A balled-up towel thumped into his gut and he curled, sitting up. "What are you posing for your boyband photo-shoot? I said *after* work."

There was a tightness to her expression, and a rigidity to her movements. There was genuine frustration there, and no trace of mischievious teasing. A mote of giddiness bounced about his insides at the thought of being attractive to someone, being a source of temptation. "Maybe we'll have to wake up earlier in the future."

He watched her nod and the towel wrapped about her hair slipped over one eye. She wobbled her head with an 'I Dream of

Jeannie' move, discarding the towel onto the carpet before plopping down on the edge of the bed to begin brushing her hair out. "You might be on to something there."

He thought for a moment about wrapping his arms around her and dragging her back onto the bed, but such things had a way of making one late for work, so he let out a sigh that Morrigan could understand.

"Hey did I wish you a good morning? No I don't think I did. I'm sorry. Good morning..." She turned over her shoulder toward him, looking him up and down. "Good morning my *prince*."

You're a shitty liar. You're never gonna settle on something like that for my pet name. You're just trying to be cute and put this smile on my face.

Simon swung his legs out to sit beside her on the bed. "Maidn mhaith."

She gasped like a victorian woman who'd just had her bodice cut open by a dashing rogue. "*After* work!" she snapped hitting him feebly with her hair brush.

Enduring her onslaught with a grin, he pulled on his pants, glad to have taken the time to look up some Gaelic phrases.

Once Simon finished buckling his belt, Morrigan passed him her keys. He took them and cocked his head at her. "Why am I driving you again?"

"Because after you'll have to take my car to drive to the art supplies store." She explained simply as she sprung to her feet.

He'd never before felt such a distinct temptation to yank someone backwards by their belt.

"You've got to paint me pretty Nordic mountains Simon. Go get paint, brushes, and an easel and then come back here and paint me some mountains while I'm at work. Take my debit card. Supplies are on me." She twirled to face him. "I want you to paint Simon. *You* want you to paint too."

"Morrigan I don't really-"

"You'll figure it out. Just try and fail and just keep doing until it's good, until you like it." She whined so intensely it lifted her onto the balls of her feet. "Do it and I'll show you some of my music. I'm not the kind of psycho to use sex as a bargaining chip or reward, but I *do* need to blackmail you a little bit or you won't do it. So my music, that's the barter."

Simon squeezed the keys.

"You can just watch Bob Ross videos for a couple hours. Come *on* Simon. You were so fucking cute, talking about painting those mountains. You know there's an ancient Indian saying about this?"

He shook his head and set about getting his shoes on to go.

She couldn't keep herself from giggling, so Simon couldn't be surprised by the joke, but she told him anyway. "It goes: You can fish in a man's pants and he'll be happy for a day. You can teach a man to paint pretty Nordic mountains and he'll be... uh, more happy."

"Alright, you have to sing for me."

"Deal."

Simon spent longer adjusting the seat and raising her steering wheel than he did driving her to work. The drive was over long before he'd found a way to articulate what he wanted to say. No red lights were on his side.

After she'd kissed him goodbye and opened the door, but before she got out, he grabbed her hand and pulled her back to him.

"You asked last night what I was going to do, now that I've got my head screwed on, right? You asked if I was going to leave you and run on back to New York."

Her throat was too tight for words. Her eyes were wide, haunted by a stupid fear. He had to kiss her, with haste, to exorcise it.

"I want to restart my life, with only the things I care about in it. I don't know what the fuck I'm going to do, or where I'm going, but I want *you* there. I'm a fucking mess and, if you'll have me, I want to figure out a life that has you in it. I wanna take you home for thanksgiving and show you off to my family and sleep stacked on top of each other on the twin bed in the room I grew up in. I want you to critique the posters in my room. I..."

She was smiling and crying and nodding her head. In another dimension her co-workers passed the car on their way inside, staring.

"And I wanna remember what the fuck else I was gonna say."

The girl laughs, sniffles and kisses her boyfriend.

The boy kisses her back. He inhales sharply through his nose. The world smells like her.

His lips are warm against hers. She feels him press against her with a yearning. She's embraced by it. Safe.

Her cheek is wet with hot tears when he touches her. He's distracted by wiping them away and lets their lips part. With only a few inches between them, he gets to see her face. Her cheeks are red again, and he strokes a thumb across her freckles. The girl leans subtly against his hand, and closes her eyes for a brief second.

The next second they're looking into each other's eyes. The boy realizes he's still holding her hand. With a mind absent thought, he kisses the back of it like a prince. She doesn't laugh. She smiles. The girl believes it.

In that moment her brain doesn't tell her that she's 14 minutes late for work. It doesn't remind her that she hasn't known her prince for even a month. Morrigan *knows* that this man is her prince, and she's his princess.

That moment, like every other, passes. She tells him in a whisper when to pick her up. He nods and lets her delicate hand slip from his.

Simon watches her go, and he breathes a deep breath of light air that lifts him in his seat. He sighs as she turns for one last wave and knows that he's breathing above water.

Epilogue

He *did* end up painting those mountains. They didn't come out good, not objectively, but good enough to encourage him to get better. Morrigan demanded that he never edit his first painting, not realizing how many layers of failed mountains were beneath the ones she saw.

As promised, she showed him her music and sang, but not for hours. She wanted to work him up to it. She started him with atmospheric black metal, then moved to some easily digestable sub-genres: Power Metal and Goth Metal, then moved to Folk Metal and Symphonic Metal. Once they'd gotten up to Cradle of Filth, she assessed that he could handle her own band.

Morrigan showed him her singing, though it was nothing like her gentle humming. She sang with something called 'harsh vocals' at first. His shock caused her to pause the song but Simon hit play and wrestled her away from the controls so he could listen. He didn't mind it so much.

Predictably, Simon's parents loved Morrigan. After all, she spent time every week to whine at him to call home. She could have burned the house down and they'd still invite her to Christmas.

She was shocked to find out Simon had siblings he'd never

mentioned. A brother and a sister, ten and seven years older. When she heard them talk, was when she first noticed Simon's far fainter New York accent. His whole family was big. He had a longship of uncles twice as broad as Simon, with beards made of all the colors of autumn. They spoke with triple the decibels Simon did, and slapped backs as loud as a clap with every hug. Their wives all adored Morrigan and pleaded with her to eat more, using Norwegian words like they were magic spells. 'No' was taken as 'not right now, but ask again in ten minutes'.

With their ears ringing from the party, the pair spent a night sleeping and otherwise in his childhood bed. In the morning his parents tried to convince them to stay until Christmas, coupled with threats to retire down to Florida if they wouldn't.

The pair ended up being good influences on each other. Simon convinced her to go for management training and get back into making music. She convinced him to freelance graphic design, making logos for small businesses, and to keep painting.

Derek helped him with the business end, getting him clients for graphic design and selling prints of his paintings. He hired pretty college girls and rosy-cheeked old men with pipes and flat caps to sell them at crafts fairs around the country.

Morrigan didn't end up working a management role, but somehow she ended up training people for them. Everyone who worked in training was older with families and nobody wanted to have to travel, but Morrigan was young and happy for the adventure. They sent her around quite a bit for the job and she brought along her boyfriend like luggage. In a couple years she'd dragged Simon to every Disney park in the world. While she worked, he scouted for nice cafes to work on his laptop in or explored for beautiful scenery to paint.

Once Simon convinced her to go back into music, she never let it go again. Morrigan lacked the charisma to be a frontman but she ended up singing in several bands. One even brought her to Ireland for a festival and, of course, she dragged Simon along. She rented a car, blew every vacation and sick day for the year to see as much of it as they could. She showed Simon off to some distant relatives in Connacht and met her grandmother's sister for the first time. He impressed them with some Gaelic words he'd learned for her. She took him to Kells and showed him a well there, in the middle of a grove, where the grandfather she never met proposed to her grandmother.

They were everywhere for a few years but they did find time to take Derek up on those drinks. Simon had more true friends than he'd let on and Morrigan insisted he keep in touch with them all, even the girls.

Having missed his chance in Paris, Simon proposed beneath some cherry blossoms in Japan. It was the first time she'd hyperventilated since before meeting his parents for the first time. She said yes, screamed it, when she got hold of enough air. Once she'd collected herself, she refused to leave the park, demanding paintings of everything in the vicinity as ransom.

The wedding came a little over a year later. The ring Simon had proposed with was custom made in the ringerike style, a viking age art style heavily inspired by Celtic knots after the viking expansion into Ireland. As far as Simon understood it was an art style made by a combination of both of their heritages. Morrigan was so moved by the thought she insisted on everything from table cloths to napkins featuring ringerike patterns.

Simon stood tall at the altar, with the kind of affect only a girl like Morrigan could inspire. He sparked conversation –like a slender man in a masterfully tailored suit does– that the sight of Morrigan walking down the aisle spread like wildfire. Everyone gossiped about how good looking their kids would be.

Simon said his vows softly, only concerned with Morrigan hearing them. Those in the front row didn't understand all of it, but *she* did. It was enough for her to show her freckles before their kiss.

Morrigan's great aunt watched the ceremony through a livestream on

Simon's Sister's phone, with the relatives they'd visited years before. She'd had to wear headphones because it felt rude to mute her and the woman wouldn't stop talking about her sister and how proud she'd be. Then someone in Ireland started crying and Simon's sister started a domino effect all the way over in a church in Cape May.

The reception was loud and happy. Both of their extended families made the trip, and even some of the bands Morrigan played in, including her old highschool band, made of her old highschool friends. They'd all missed each other, and been too awkward to call, but vowed not to let it happen again.

The musicians behaved for most of the reception. One band played silly power metal covers, and another played Goth Metal for slow dances. However, the groom insisted that his bride play a reunion set with her old band, and they performed an exaggerated 'War' by Burzum to hide how rusty they'd all gotten.

Simon and Morrigan's dads met there. Dressed in suits, they both seemed like shaved dogs. Morrigan's dad was the kind of guy who didn't feel at home in anything but a Hawaiian shirt and Simon's dad looked off dressed in anything but a speedo.

Simon's father paid for their honeymoon. They've gone to a finished cottage beside the sea, with a sod roof, a few miles outside of the town where his grandmother grew up, so they could both see those mountains together, from both sides. She promised his Grandparents she wouldn't come back without a new painting and a Hiberno Norse grandchild for them.

Inspired by Morrigan's late grandmother, who had always made sure young Morrigan knew she was special, Simon has endeavoured to learn more about his Nordic heritage so that he can help his future children be proud of all that they're made from; so that he can teach his kid they're the at the end of a chain of people, stretching back far into prehistory, who looked like they do, fell in love, and created a life that would one day find their own personal prince or princess and continue that chain.

Morrigan's grandmother had always impressed upon her that her ancestors, stretching back in that chain, watched over her like Mulan's did. She'd always dressed her up in pretty Irish dresses and taken her to learn the pretty Irish dances her ancestors danced. She'd taught her the stories, and mythology they shared, and cooked her the food they ate. Morrigan vowed to give that to her kid, buying an armful of books to share with Simon on the plane ride; books about the Norse, the Celts, and the Hiberno Norse.

If it's a daughter Morrigan says they'll name her Sinead after her grandmother and something Nordic if it's a boy. Simon doesn't know what he should pick but he says he'll figure it out. He probably will too.

Neither of them really know what they're going to do, or where they'll even start their family. But they'll figure *that* out too. Because they know all they need to know. Morrigan and Simon Magnusson know they'll always have each other, and *together* they'll live...

Happily Ever After

Acknowledgments

Hey! For starters, lemme thank *you* for reading. It really does mean a lot.

Then I should thank everyone who read chapters and gave me helpful feedback. My friends Conor and Katie, my cousin Mark and brother Brian all read through a chapter for me. An especially sincere thanks goes to my girlfriend Trisha who's read through a library of drafts and helped me make my cover too.

A special thanks goes to Herr Dieter Stauffmann who generously allowed me the use of his fonts, to deliver a more magical happily ever after.

On a grander scale, I guess I should thank Walt Disney. His films, with their princes and princesses, served as a promise to my younger self that one day my affection would be important, valuable, and treasured by someone I could call my princess.

On an even grander scale, I do wanna thank good people for existing. Loyal and honourable people who stand by their friends and are faithful to their lovers. These sorts of people make happy endings exist, and that makes them very easy to write about.

And of course, my supportive parents who've always believed in me.

Made in the USA
Middletown, DE
17 November 2021